THE QUEEN AND
THE MONSTER

THE QUEEN AND THE MONSTER

MATTHEW CAPUTO

www.trafford.com
North America & international
toll-free: 1 888 232 4444 (USA & Canada)
fax: 812 355 4082

CONTENTS

For Tim, my everything, thank you for helping
to keep the real monsters at bay.

"Rest assured: circumstances are currently in play far beyond your ability to comprehend," Prince Alexander, royalty and self-proclaimed deity.

"I have been told by more people than I can remember that the fact I was ever born is an abomination to all they hold as good. Some go as far as to say that my continuing existence is proof that God is dead," Catryna Corpa, entertainer and wanton whore.

"Such use of power is vulgar," Linda Blair, The Exorcist, 1973.

CHAPTER ONE

The Founding of a Kingdom

According to legend, Protace spent the latter part of his life building a bridge across the Particion River to join two hordes of barbarians under a single rule.

His rule.

By the time of the bridge's completion, he was a man of many, many years, but he still ruled the Protecian Kingdom, which he formed from the barbaric people surrounding him. He made them civilized, made them skilled, and most importantly, he made them obedient to him. During his reign, in which time continued to take its toll upon him, the barbarians continued to become more civilized and began to look up to him as more than a ruler. He was their savior, and quite a few referred to him as their god. Protace did nothing to stop them from worshipping him and doing no less than falling to their knees upon seeing him. It actually brought him great joy when his leering smile shone over a crowd of dozens or even hundreds of people, all of them dropping to their knees just to show their reverence towards him. In his mind, it was a service that he was owed. After all, he rescued them from their previous state of barbarism and had shone the light of civilization and knowledge onto them. He made their lives something worth living, rather than simply a chore to pass the time until death. His gift to them would never be fully repaid.

Nearly all the kingdom's people felt this way, but as with any people, there were those who disagreed. And those who disagree make their opinions very well known. It was one of those people who loathed Protace, and the events that followed, that sets our tale into motion.

One day in a blazing hot summer, two men were walking along the mountainside that was Protecia's border. They both black capes that were studded with red and purple gemstones, and these cloaks seemed to consume their vastly different bodies. The first was very old. A gnarled walking stick was clenched in one shaking hand, clenched so hard that the bunching knuckles were a ghostly white. It was this stick that held the man on his feet as it supported his full weight while he tried to walk, hunched over. His hair was as white as fresh snow, and his face looked as though it had seen centuries of ceaseless labor and abuse. He gasped for air with every breath he took, as if the heat of afternoon sun was poisoning him with every second. When he exhaled, it sounded like he was blowing through broken glass.

At his side was another man that appeared much younger than his companion. This man stood tall, his determined eyes focused straight ahead of him. His strides were large and quick, and he was full of life and vitality. Seeing them walking along in the brightness of the sun, one could see a distinct resemblance between them. Subtle, but definitely there.

Hidden in the shadows of a recess in the closest mountain wall was a third man. He kept his eyes over his shoulder and watched as the other two approached. Air was rushing in and out of his lungs in great gasps and sweat was dripping down his face in the heat. It ran trails down his face and into his eyes, but the stings of the salty water never even made him flinch. He was focused and determined. He was also terrified of what was going to transpire in the next few moments, but he knew it was something that needed to be done.

Someone had to take action.

Finally, the two men approached the recess in the cave, and the third man leapt out like a pouncing cobra. The sword that was clenched in his sweaty and shaking hands rose into the air, and before the two men had time to see what was going on, the blade found its target.

The entire length of the sword plunged into the dark-haired man's chest, just below the sternum. It reached far out of the man's back, its tip quivering in the glistening sun. The man hunched forward on the blade, for the first time not standing with perfect posture, and for a moment looking almost as though he was mimicking the older man holding the walking stick at his side. The sword twisted in his chest, scraping the hilt against the layers of adorned garments. The dying man pushed his walking partner to the ground with one hand in a desperate act to save him, to give him a few extra moments to get away, and the assassin reached towards his belt and drew a dagger from the folds of his shirt. This smaller blade was raised with just as much speed and accuracy as he wielded the sword, and he plunged it into his victim's neck. After issuing one quick cut, the assassin removed both blades simultaneously, leaving his victim to fall in a lifeless heap.

While blood was beginning to pool around the dead man's body, the white-haired man began to crawl backwards away from this scene. His life was spared for the moment, and he was going to use that time to get away. When he saw the assassin's eyes lock on his own, he pushed himself onto the walking stick and, using well-practiced motions, found his way back to his feet. Within a second, the assassin was charging at the old man, lifting the sword into the air again. In movement quicker than he would have thought possible of himself in the past thirty years, the old man raised his heavy walking stick as the sword sliced through the sky towards him. The walking stick batted away the sword, leaving the assassin's weight off balance and forcing him to stagger backwards a step. With the walking stick still held into the air, the old man pointed its head at the sword-wielding man and let out an ear-splitting scream.

The noise filled the hot afternoon air and echoed off the mountain wall in a way that only seemed to amplify it to the point of madness. With a contorted face, the assassin dropped both the sword and the dagger, and he held his blood-streaked hands to his ears to shut out that noise. It seemed as if his whole body was about to explode. Then, almost that exact thing happened. Flames began to creep their way through his skin like the tiny tentacles of a sea monster. He was engulfed. His body began to burn quickly and soon was reduced to nothing more than a charred remnant of humanity. Fire was still glowing along his body as the old man stopped screaming and brought the walking stick back down to the ground. With this motion, the charred sculpture that was once the assassin's body scattered in a cloud of ash. There was no more left to him but the two bloody weapons on the dirt and the dead monarch just next to them.

With the danger eliminated, the old man turned to the stabbed corpse between him and the side of the mountain. The man used his last breath to push him out the way of danger. He fell to his knees and began to cry onto the body. While the old man wept, peasants began to gather around to see what had happened. Each of their faces was a portrait of shock, fear and despair. Their eyes bulged in horror as each began to cry. They watched as the old man cried over the dead body that had years ago founded the Protecian Kingdom and had ruled it since that day. They watched as the heir to the throne cried over the deceased body of his father. Protace was dead.

It took such an assassin to finally end the elderly Protace's life and for his son, Soranace, to succeed him. By this point, Soranace was also an old man, however, unlike his father, he looked every one of his eight-six years. Soranace only ruled the kingdom for a little more than five years before dying in a cave-in while surveying the holdings of the kingdom, work that no one felt he was strong enough to do unaccompanied. When Soranace died, his five children, three sons and two daughters, all took their turns as a ruler of Protecia, and the bloodline remained for the next three hundred years. Only those that possessed Protace's blood, or their spouses if the situation called for it, were able to rule the kingdom. A committee of elders was established to settle any disputes over the bloodline and a carefully written pedigree chart was created and housed within the palace that had been built under the rule of Soranace's eldest daughter. With all of these precautions in place, there was never any great difficulty with the rule of kingdom being passed from king to queen, between spouses and to their children for centuries. The difficulties did not begin until times that were much more recent.

According to the records kept by the elders, there had been no less than two hundred heirs to the throne throughout the kingdom's history, all carefully documented by precedence. This ensured that one of Protace's direct descendants would always be available to rule the kingdom and inherit the throne if something were to happen to the current ruler. However, as with all well-established systems, several generations of misfortune played their part to create chaos. A mass assassination under the rule of King Jonathan invoked a riot that killed nearly half of the living heirs to the throne as well as over one thousand of the civilians of the kingdom. Shortly following that, as if a black cloud had descended upon Protecia, a plague broke out which wiped out the enormous kingdom's people and royalty, leaving only one branch of the royal family still alive. One last thriving limb from a rotten and dying tree. Those few decades were whispered about as the Dark Years for Protecia, and no one could help wondering if their god, the long-dead Protace, was angry at them and trying to finally end what he had begun. His bloodline had almost completely gone dry.

The widowed Queen Patricia and her two sons, Frederick and Alexander, were all that remained. During his mother's rule, Frederick married a peasant, as was custom for the royalty to do, named Wilhelmina. They remained happily married while Prince Alexander did not marry, earning him the nickname of the Royal Bachelor. When Queen Patricia died of old age, Frederick became the King of Protecia and Wilhelmina his queen.

King Frederick's rule was one of peace and prosperity for the kingdom. Nearly all the citizens in good health would fill the palace courtyard to hear all of his public addresses and throw bouquets of roses at his feet as he walked in front of the monumental stone sculptures of Protace and Soranace that appeared to look out over the new ruler and his subjects beyond him. While the elderly representations, with some artistic license in place, of the kingdom's first rulers looked on, King Frederick would speak of the matters of kingdom, and all would listen with great anticipation and excitement.

After a few years, however, all the members of the royal family and several visiting diplomats from a nearby kingdom developed an illness no one had ever seen before. Many people began saying how it was reminiscent of the plague from years ago, but not quite the same. In a few days' time, while the others recovered, King Frederick did not. He died as a result of this illness, quietly in his sleep with Wilhelmina beside him, leaving her the throne.

There were no rules against a former peasant ruling the people since Wilhelmina was already made a queen by marriage to Frederick. However, she was childless when Frederick died, and if she were to remarry, children produced from that marriage would be without the blood of Protace or any ties to his bloodline. They would be permitted to live their lives as princes or princesses without the possibility of ever rising to the title of king or queen. That meant that after Wilhelmina, Prince Alexander, the Royal Bachelor, would be the only one in line for the throne. It seemed as though Protace's kingdom was not to last another fifty years. Soon, however, things seemed to change for the better. It was as if an angel had shone a bright light onto the kingdom after these years of blackness.

It took a month after the death of Frederick for Queen Wilhelmina to bring herself to leave her mansion-like personal quarters. In that time, she only called for one visitor: Chenrile, the royal physician. Upon leaving her quarters and walking into the darkness of the royal family's private corridor within the palace, she summoned a servant to spread word that she was going to address the public the following afternoon in the palace courtyard.

In this public address, she was greeted with the same reception that her late husband always received, complete with roses raining down upon her and the eager, adoring faces of her subjects. Some of the older women in the kingdom knew what she was going to say as soon as they saw her walk out of the darkness of the palace and into the gleaming light of the courtyard. They would later say that she emanated a glow brighter than the sun could ever hope to on that day. In her first address to the public as their queen ruler, Wilhelmina announced that she was pregnant with the late King Frederick's child. That child, being of Protace's blood, would succeed her after her death and continue to lead the kingdom from these troubling times towards a future of brightness and continuing prosperity.

All cheered at the sound of this news, as if they were cheering for a new addition to their own families. In the middle of all this cheering and joy, there was Prince Alexander. A smile did surface on his face, but one look at his deep, green eyes showed the conflict within him. He was happy for his dead brother and for Wilhelmina, but at the same time, he was sorry for himself and for the Protecian Kingdom. He felt that his long sought-after prize was snatched away from him just as it was getting close, and that the future he felt he could provide the kingdom was now to be nothing more than a dream. He stood in his black cape like a cloud of misery around him. For the next eight years, that cloud of misery only darkened. It is at this point, when that cloud was at its darkest, when our story begins.

CHAPTER TWO

The Current Royal Family

"**P**rince Alexander!"

The crowd cheered at the sound of the name. It was being yelled by one of the servants standing to the far right of the stone platform, where the public addresses were delivered. Adjacent to the palace and in the shadow of the monumental sculptures of Protace and Soranace, the platform jutted from the mountainside that bordered the kingdom. What many people didn't know was that not too far from this exact location was where Protace was butchered while his elderly son looked on. Over centuries of being told and retold, the exact details of that long ago day had taken on a life of their own. A very common occurrence in Protecia.

The cheers that filled the courtyard, however, were more out of tradition than respect. Still retaining the public image of the Royal Bachelor, and now most likely a member of the ruling family that would never hold the throne, the people did not show much admiration for their prince. Since his niece's birth, he had done nothing to try to counter this image. His reputation was widely recognized. He was known for having a short and violent temper coupled with the habits of a womanizer. There were rumors of his beating his numerous female partners during sex and then obtaining their silence through threats against their wellbeing and that of their families. These were, however, simply rumors that were whispered throughout the kingdom's houses, fields, and woods. Despite this unenthusiastic response from the public, Prince Alexander went through the motions as he always did. He marched across the platform with his black cape, attached at the neck and wrists, whipping like a flag in the wind behind him. When he reached the far end of the platform, he stopped and turned to face crowd of citizens who were already looking away from him, waiting for the next name to be called.

With Alexander in his accustomed place, the servant cleared his throat and looked back at the crowd he was addressing.

"Princess Angelica!"

The daughter of Queen Wilhelmina and the late King Frederick, now at eight years old, began to march onto the platform, and the cheers from the people were in no way fake. They all but howled at her as she took her well-practiced steps across the platform towards where her uncle was waiting for her. A tiny grin curled at the corners of her lips as the cheers seemed to shake the mountains themselves. Princess Angelica was more than just the daughter of Frederick and Wilhelmina. She was the daughter of the entire kingdom. The citizens loved her as if she were their own. No more than halfway across the platform, her tiny grin broke into a full smile as she continued to walk in the bright purple gown with gold and jewels swinging down from it. She walked to her uncle's side and finally turned to face the cheering crowd. Still more than half of them were looking at her while cheering and whispering to one another with their eyes gleaming. It took a few seconds for everyone's attention to turn back to the servant that was announcing the royal family.

"The ruler of the Protecian Kingdom. Her royal highness, the Queen Wilhelmina!" This was when the real cheering began. A roar of cries and shouts came from the crowd that seemed to drown out the rest of the world as the bouquets of roses began to fly towards the platform. Under the rainstorm of red pedals, Queen Wilhelmina walked to the center of the platform standing between two gold pillars cast to represent vines, the staircase to the clouds that Protace took all those years ago, and faced the crowd. When she stopped walking, the cheers continued, and they did not stop for nearly two minutes. Wilhelmina stood still with the sun radiating off her purple and red gown that sparkled with the gold and precious stones that covered it. Once the people finally did stop cheering, the queen began to speak of the matters of the kingdom.

While Queen Wilhelmina's speech was filling the full attention span of the hundreds of people in the courtyard, the prince and princess turned and strode down a short staircase at the side of the platform and assumed their positions in the front row of the spectators to listen to their queen speak.

Alexander listened eagerly for about ten minutes before whispering to Angelica, "I have some business to attend to." With those words, he disappeared into the crowd, leaving the young girl alone.

There was nothing unusual about Prince Alexander's behavior that day. It was actually customary during the royal addresses for the prince to conduct any sort of kingdom's business. Being a member of the royal family, Alexander had a number of responsibilities within the kingdom, even though he was not the ruler. Some of these included training and heading the palace guards, a job fitting of his temperament, and also overseeing the harvesting of natural gasses from the caves that surrounded the kingdom. The latter proved to be a very beneficial undertaking, allowing for heat to be piped throughout the kingdom during the colder months, safe areas of cooking and disposal of refuse, and countless other tasks. Being a child, Angelica did not have these responsibilities yet. Mesmerized by her mother's words, she just stood and listened. Her safety was never a concern standing with the people of the kingdom. Everyone worshipped her quite openly.

Princess Angelica watched and listened while imagining that one day she would have kingdom's business to conduct during her mother's addresses, just like her uncle was doing now. As far back as she could remember, however actually only in recent years, these addresses became kingdom-wide carnivals. People came from all over the lands with their private and public business to conduct while listening to the queen speak. For hours before the address began, people would begin showing up. Jesters who dressed in elaborate costumes, which served to amuse the crowd as well as conceal the jesters' identities, would arrive to perform feats such as juggling, swallowing fire or magic. Others would show up to prepare vast feasts for anyone wishing to eat. Mostly, people came early to socialize with one another at what appeared to be the greatest town fair in the known world.

These addresses were particularly fun for Angelica. On days when her mother was scheduled to address the people, Angelica could be found roaming the courtyard for hours ahead of time. While she was there, the jesters would show up to give their performances, paying special attention to their future ruler. There were two who showed up to each public address, and these were Angelica's favorites, and they made every effort to compete with each other and the less regularly appearing jesters for the young princess's attention.

One was a short man with a green hat. This hat had large, heavily starched protrusions from it that resembled leaves. At the end of each was a tiny bell, each one making a slightly different sound. When he danced and jumped into the air, the sound of those bells made such music that one could not help but to be enwrapped by him. This man also wore a green shirt with a neck line that extended far over his face to block out everything below the eyes, which were, of course, green as well. He wore a green gown that had the purpose of hiding his legs and feet from view. There were twigs and leaves stuck to this outfit at random places, and on some days, he even arrived with an abandoned bird's nest firmly attached to his shoulder. The whole outfit was supposed to make him appear to be a tree, but his act had nothing to do with botany or the surrounding forest. He was a fire-breather. While twirling one or two lit torches in his arms, he would dance around, occasionally touching the flames to his lips. Then he would blow a stream of fire into the air above the heads of the spectators and laugh at their astonished gasps.

The other jester that usually appeared, and whom Angelica rather secretly considered to be her true favorite, was a rather tall man. He wore a costume that began with the hood and continued down to a flutter at his feet without ever stopping. There was also a mask stretched across his face covering both his nose and mouth. This entire costume was brightly colored with what appeared to be explosions of yellow, red, blue, orange, green, and white. The pattern was almost dizzying to look at, and it seemed to make the act much more believable. This jester was famed at these events as a juggler, but it was a title that hardly began to describe what he could do. Most referred to him as nothing short of a sorcerer. Angelica had seen him tossing as many as ten items into the air repeatedly four about five minutes without dropping a single one. The most astounding feats he performed usually took place around the time he really let the objects fall. He seemed to watch the crowd to make sure no one was paying too careful attention to the airborne object, and then, by some sleight of hand, he would change them into something else. Balls or stones would become bouquets of brightly colored flowers or pieces of fine jewelry, leaf-bearing branches and sticks would transform into live cats and squirrels that would be snatched out of the air quite harmlessly to scurry away, or they may even become fleets of white doves that would fly away into the afternoon sunlight. The most amazing would be when the airborne objects would simply vanish in bright flashes of light. Anyone who saw this jester perform knew that if he let his identity be known that he would be famed and known by all in the kingdom, but he kept his anonymity safely intact as if the laughter and smile from his audience were more precious than any treasure that could be purchased.

These jesters were not the only ones that caught Angelica's attention while she wandered the courtyard before her mother's addresses. The people who showed up to prepare food also took up a considerable bit of her time. Sometimes they would be roasting whole pigs with exotic fruit jammed into the opened mouths, and other days they would simply be presenting elaborate displays of vegetables. These people would charge astronomically low prices for these banquet-sized meals, and for Angelica, the food was naturally free. Those who prepared these feasts actually ran to her side insisting that she try a bite of some delicacy they had prepared, and the princess was never known to refuse.

Between dining and staring awe-struck at the jesters, Princess Angelica would socialize with the citizens of Protecia who would show up at this time. Even at eight years of age, she knew it was important to build relationships with those around her. She expected that, when she got older, she would disappear into the crowds to conduct her own business just as her uncle did now. For the time being, however, the citizens would bow their heads at her and comment on how gorgeous she looked even though she had yet to get dressed into her formal attire for the address. Mostly she just nodded, returned the compliment, and began to talk to the citizens as if she was no different from any of them.

When the time of the address drew closer, Angelica's governess, Beatrice, would show up in the crowd and escort her back into the palace to prepare for the address. Angelica would bid goodbye to all she had been speaking with as Beatrice led her out of the courtyard and into the torch-lit corridors of the palace. Once within the palace, they would talk while walking towards the queen's dressing room. By this point, Wilhelmina would almost be fully adorned in her formal gowns. She would turn from the mirror and show her radiant smile at her daughter. Then, Beatrice would begin preparing the princess for her appearance at the address. The process did not take nearly as long as with Queen Wilhelmina, since Angelica's formal attire was far less complex. There was one part of the process that Angelica insisted on fighting. Both Beatrice, and more importantly, the queen insisted it was necessary, so it was done without flaw each time. A small dagger with a blade of four inches was placed in a sheath just above Angelica's ankle. The part of the handle that protruded was entirely covered by the layers of the princess's gown, so the public would never be able to see it. Queen Wilhelmina would always tell her daughter, "This is for your own safety. Someone may wish to do you harm, and you may be forced to defend yourself." Even though she disliked having the hard piece of metal resting against her leg during these and all other formal ceremonies she was part of, she wore it anyway for no other reason than to make her mother happy.

When the queen and princess were dressed, they would walk from the dressing room, and leaning against the hallway wall would always be Alexander. He always dressed in the same manner: a full black outfit enveloped in a black cape attached by golden bands at the neck and wrists. He wore this even when he was not at a formal appearance, and Angelica felt that if she ever saw him wearing something else, it would take a lot of convincing for her to believe that it was really him. Prince Alexander would greet his sister-in-law and his niece with a bow that made his shoulder-length brown hair nearly brush against the marble floor.

Then, with his arm around Wilhelmina's waist, the three would walk through the richly adorned hallways of the palace. They would pass the painted portraits of each of the rulers of Protecia beginning with Protace himself and stretching all the way to Wilhelmina. The queen always hesitated a moment at King Frederick's portrait and whispered to it momentarily. Angelica always thought this was very strange, but then looked away towards the empty space beyond her mother's likeness. One day, her face will decorate the wall there. Right now, it was just a stone wall lined with golden relief sculptures dancing from ceiling to floor like so many of the other walls in the palace.

As their feet clicked each time they touched the marble floor, Angelica always felt as if it was the perfect accompaniment to the jester's bells that were attached to his hat. The sound of those bells got louder as the three walked through the hallways of the palace. Torches burned from elaborate sconces extending from the sides of these walls. Even those mounts had precious stones embedded in their ornate designs. Finally, the three would out into the palace's main lobby. On the domed ceiling, there was a breathtaking fresco representing Protace building his bridge across the Particion River. Clouds were drifting by him, and they almost seemed to be embracing him. The clouds seemed to know that he would be revered as a god once this task was completed. Angelica, along with everyone else who had ever passed beneath this ceiling, could not explain why the image showed Protace as appearing airborne. It was almost as if the clouds were already lifting his mortal body into its future godliness, but it seemed more than that. As she had done every other time, Princess Angelica left these thoughts in behind as she exited through the palace doors.

Once they walked outside, everyone cheered them. All but the ruler of the kingdom merely walked onto the stage for show, and then disappeared into the crowd. Back when the royal family had numbers in the hundreds, this process would take hours, but that time had long passed. Only three names needed to be called now. And after the two non-rulers had been announced, everyone's attention was focused solely on the queen, rather than the prince and princess.

This public address was no different. After Prince Alexander walked back into the depth of the crowd, Princess Angelica stood side by side with people she barely knew or didn't know at all. Usually, after twenty minutes or so, Angelica would lose interest in what her mother was saying despite all of her attempts to listen carefully. Still, out of respect and tradition, she would not leave the courtyard. Just as if she was as interested in the affairs of the kingdom as every one of its citizens, Angelica stood with a mask of attentiveness on her face.

It would appear that there was a drought and water shortage in the kingdom. Crops were dying, and without any irrigation system, there was nothing to do to save them. People would soon be dying from thirst and starvation. To remedy this problem, Queen Wilhelmina spoke of beginning the construction of a permanent irrigation system for the kingdom. Water would be channeled via underground ducts from the Particion River to several wells scattered throughout the lands that had in recent months gone dry. Wilhelmina did make an effort to point out that such construction was only in the planning phase as of yet, but she assured the people that her full attention was on turning this plan into a reality.

As the queen spoke, the carved eyes of Protace and Soranace stared at her from behind, judgmentally. Their images were a sight of comfort to all the citizens, but Angelica heard several stories about several kings and queens that felt inexpressibly uneasy about speaking in front of those sculptures. Almost as if they would be compared to the deified first rulers of the kingdom by their mere proximity. Behind those sculptures, there was a small valley before the rest of the mountain range began. Beside the statues, the great gold columns of vines stood ten feet into the sky, dwarfing the speaker that was between them. These images were the closest things to a religious icon that the kingdom had. Those skyward ladders taken by Protace and Soranace upon their deaths symbolized how their first rulers continued to look upon the Protecian people.

"There is other good news in the kingdom today, however," Wilhelmina stated proudly as she gave another of her radiant smiles to her daughter. "Prince Alexander's further excavations of the caves have yielded more benefits. Another natural gas vein has been found and tapped."

The crowd began to grumble in unison although their faces still smiled. Each of their eyes pleaded a simply question to their queen, and she knew she must answer.

"The naturally occurring gases which are being pumped from these caverns are important to our kingdom." She was hesitating. Angelica could see in her eyes that she did not know just what to say next. "For one thing, it would make the caves safer if we were able to eliminate those gases from them. With that highly flammable material embedded within the walls of the caves, a cave-in could occur at any time. Even worse, a fire may begin that can have the force to consume a large portion of the kingdom. We are currently experiencing a water shortage. At this point, a fire could more devastating than ever before."

Wilhelmina sighed deeply. Her eyes scanned the crowd from Prince Alexander. This harvesting of the natural gases had been his project since its inception, but amidst all the faces, she could not see his. He could not throw her a lifeline of any sort. "These gases are also an important resource to our kingdom."

From the middle of the crowd, someone yelled, "More important than water?" Its exact source was truly unknown, but that call was followed by a gasp from the crowd. This anger seemed to spread almost immediately. Further to the side of the crowded courtyard, another person, this time a woman, shouted, "My family is starving to death. We need water!"

Angelica was frantically looking back and forth. This was the first time she could remember such a verbal attack on her mother. Finally, Wilhelmina responded. Her words were lost under the low hum of everyone else in the courtyard. Soon, she was forced to call out.

"Please, listen to me!" Everyone silenced instantly. "The winters here are extremely cold, and until five years ago, when Prince Alexander began this task of tapping those gas veins, the number of citizens dying from conditions related to the temperature was in the hundreds. Since our harvesting of that gas, we have been able to make controlled bonfires at various locations throughout the kingdom. These fires burned hotter and longer than possible with only wood to fuel them. Since our use of that gas to heat the kingdom, no more than twenty of our citizens die every year from the cold." Wilhelmina paused a moment. There were no more cries from the crowd. She was able to reach them. "I know it is hard to see into the future when we are suffering now, but if we all pull together, we will be able to conquer this drought, along with any other obstacles that oppose us in the future." No one had a response to those words. Wilhelmina sighed deeply again and closed her eyes for a few seconds.

The rest of the address was over in a few minutes. During that time, Queen Wilhelmina seemed as calm and under control as she always did. Angelica, however, felt afraid to move or even breathe too deeply. There was almost a physical pressure of eyes boring into her back. While her body shook nervously, Angelica watched her mother finish the last few statements of her public address. She saw how relaxed Wilhelmina was, even after that shouting contest. Trying to use that as her model, Angelica took a deep breath to see if she could bring herself to that level of inner peace. She seemed unable to, and just as she was going to give up hope, Wilhelmina announced that she had no further business to announce. People began to slowly clear out of the courtyard. The jesters began to perform again, and others began to serve food again. Everything was back to normal.

Wilhelmina climbed down from the stone platform onto the trampled grass of the courtyard. No sooner did both her feet touch the ground than Angelica ran over to her with outstretched arms. The young girl wrapped her arms around her mother's waist with tears streaming down her face.

"It looks like there were some different opinions out there today, doesn't it?" Wilhelmina was nearly at the point of laughing off the whole incident, but when she saw her daughter's face, she knew that the topic could not be dismissed this easily. Angelica was reaching an age where she could understand what she was seeing in the kingdom. This needed to be discussed.

"Angelica, look at me."

The young princess tilted her head upwards so that her eyes met her mother's.

"Things like that happen. It is no big deal at all. You're going to be a ruler of this kingdom one day, and you will have to accept that not everyone is going to back you all the time. That is just not the way the world works. Do you understand?"

Angelica nodded, but the grip she had around her mother's waist didn't loosen in the slightest.

While Wilhelmina was stroking her daughter's back and feeling the smooth silk of the gown rubbing against her hand, Alexander approached.

"You knew they weren't going to love you unconditionally forever, didn't you?" he said through a twisted smile.

The queen nearly jumped, but when she saw that it was Prince Alexander, she let out a long breath of relief.

"Thank you for sticking up for my little project back there. For a minute, I thought you might abandon it entirely just to keep everyone on your side."

A smirk grew across Alexander's face, and Wilhelmina soon developed one to match it. There was an unspoken tension between them that lately had been tightening. One look at either of their eyes showed that when the tension finally exploded, whether it would be in an hour or a decade, it was going to be bad.

CHAPTER THREE

The Royal Family's Evening

In a few moments' time, Angelica had calmed down as quickly as most children her age, and the three of them began to walk back towards the palace. Upon entering the lavishly decorated hallways, and brightly-lit rooms, they all began to feel at ease. These gold and bejeweled corridors were the only home the three had known for years, two of them for their whole lives, and being home always made things feel a little better. It only took a few minutes for them to take the familiar stroll to their dining room. Beyond the heavy wooden door, a long wooden table with gold detailing stretched for nearly the length of the room. There were some days when twenty-five people would easily surround this table, but today's meal was more private. Torches protruding from the walls provided light for the room with additional light from the three candelabras on the table, and a chandelier with eight additional candles hanging from the ceiling. As the three entered the room, a door on the opposite wall opened, and the cook passed through it emerging from the kitchen. He quickly closed the door behind him so the royal family would see the food-preparation area, and with that done, began to scurry towards the table. He was an old man with pure white hair and tired face that occasionally gave off the appearance being a little lost or confused. Still, despite his age and declining mental facilities, he was an amazing cook.

The old man set a steaming dish on the table. On it, there was a large portion of pork. While the queen, the princess, and the prince began to seat themselves at their accustomed chairs around the table, the cook began to cut pieces away from the meat. Each serving was carefully lowered onto a dish that was then placed in front of a member of the royal family. First Wilhelmina, then Angelica, and last Alexander, as everything was done for them. There were no dignitaries from other kingdoms or honored civilians from Protecia joining them on this day. With so few in attendance, the cook was able to quickly serve the meal and disappear back into the kitchen.

He did reappear moments later with a large brass bowl in his hands. Carefully, he labored his was towards the table, obviously struggling under the bowl's weight. It contained the wine for the meal. The bowl sparkled in the candlelight as the cook placed it upon the table. He then bowed and left the room.

Wilhelmina was the first to dip her glass into the bowl. When it was filled, Angelica took a small portion for herself. Her place setting always had a large glass of water beside it, but she was always permitted a taste of wine with her dinner to make her feel more a part of the meal. Finally, Alexander, being the farthest from inheriting the throne and therefore of the least importance, filled his own glass. Once they all had their food and drink before them, the meal began.

After only a few minutes of eating, Wilhelmina looked at Alexander. He knew what she was going to say, but he did not interrupt her.

"I am worried about the water shortage. We really need more people to work on that irrigation system I spoke of."

Alexander nodded. He knew what was coming next.

"Your tapping of the gas veins in the caves is a slow process, and it's using a lot of the kingdom's resources," said Wilhelmina. "I am thinking about slowing it down for a while. Have some of those workers help with the irrigation system instead. It is the more important venture at this time."

Once again, Alexander only nodded.

"You know I was lying up there. When I was talking to the people. Telling them how important your collection of natural gases has been. In the past few years, the sicknesses have gone away. That was the reason for the dramatic drop in the number of deaths each winter. That more so than the use of the gas-lit bonfires around kingdom."

Alexander waited a few seconds. He saw that aside from Wilhelmina, her daughter was also staring in his direction. Before Wilhelmina even began to speak, he knew what his comeback was going to be, but he wanted to sound like he was considering her opinion carefully.

"If for no other reason, the exploration of those caves is of great strategic importance, said Alexander. "A war with a neighboring kingdom is not impossible despite how much they now appreciate our existence. One wrong word to which they take offense would result in war. We are left open to be invaded and conquered. Not only will the stockpiled gas serve as valuable for use in weaponry, but the caves, if they are made safe, would be of great help in fortifying the palace. Even if it looks like there is no escape for us, those caves would serve as a hiding place for us so that we will not be killed by invading enemies." Alexander sighed, but the queen's critical eyes didn't waver. "Need I go on?"

Before Wilhelmina has a chance to answer, another voice rang out.

"Is anyone in here?"

Alexander turned to the doorway they had walked through not half an hour ago. This man, a little bit older than Alexander, began to walk into the room. His clothes were a shade of white that almost sent shivers down all their spines. With his jet black hair combed away from his face, this man's skin almost blended into the clothes he wore.

"I just got back from the Nezzrin Kingdom," said the man. "They still haven't been able to find a doctor, and they were in need of medical assistance. Apparently, they had some kind of cave-in over there that injured about seventy people."

Alexander shot a look over to Wilhelmina. His eyes seemed to gleam with triumph over the argument they had just been completing. Finally, Alexander said to her, "I hope you don't mind, but I had asked Chenrile to join us if he returned in time. He has been spending the last week outside the kingdom."

Wilhelmina just nodded. Now that someone who did not belong to the family was here, it meant that the touchy subjects had to be dropped for sake of decorum.

Chenrile was the head physician for Protecia. Also, he had been a good friend of Alexander's since they were very young children. However, the demands placed on both of them by their occupations limited the amount of time they spent together. This is why Wilhelmina permitted them to dine together in the palace whenever possible. Their neighboring kingdom of Nezzrin had a physician that had died during the Years of Illness, as they had come to be called. Since the two kingdoms were still on good terms with each other, Chenrile rode his chariot over there every month to check up on the royal family of the Nezzrin Kingdom. Also, whenever an incident, such as this accident he spoke of, occurred, Chenrile would stay there for an extended period of time to make sure that everything was being taken care of properly.

When it came to the Nezzrin Kingdom, Chenrile always had a weak spot in his heart. His family was from that kingdom, and he was actually born there. It was unclear how he came to be separated from his roots and living in Protecia instead, but the rumor is that his family had died, and he, a five year old boy, wandered into the Protecian Kingdom. He knew his name but little more at that time, and immediately became a fixture in the kingdom. On several occasions, groups went to Nezzrin to see if they could locate any traces of his family. No one could ever explain what had happened to them, only that one day they could all be heard arguing inside the house, and the next day everyone had disappeared. Even the house had vanished as if it was never even there. After seeing how Alexander befriended him, he was raised by one of the palace servants and quickly climbed the rungs of society within Protecia.

Now, as the four of them gathered around table, the mood seemed to lighten as it always did when they were all around. They sat eating and talking for hours that seemed to pass almost instantly. They covered topics such as Chenrile's most recent trip to Nezzrin, the problems with the drought, and even Wilhelmina's irrigation plan. Everything that was spoken of was treated with utter happiness, and it almost seemed like they were a normal, happy family.

By the time they were finished, the sun had already set in the sky. The four of them stood and walked from the dining room together. Once they left, three more people entered the room. The first was their cook, the second was Beatrice, Angelica's governess, and the third was Cassandra, who was Alexander's personal servant and maid. The three of them sat around the table and finished what was left over from the dinner. They also spoke, but their topics included subjects less important to the kingdom than the group that had just left. However, in any civilization, rumors play an important role and needed to get their start somewhere.

Cassandra, of all of them, hardly spoke a word. She just stared across the room, absently picking at her food as if doing this was only a formality and not something that should really be enjoyed.

The other four walked from the palace and through the courtyard. By this time, the civilians had long since cleared out. They came early for the queen's address and stayed late once it was completed, but they rarely stayed this long. Now, the courtyard contained only four of the royal guards practicing their sword-fighting in pairs of two. As the royal family walked by, Alexander stopped to look at them for a moment. They seemed to be very skilled. He knew that he was partially responsible for their training, and it seemed as if there one thing missing from their strategies.

The element of surprise.

Alexander excused himself from the royal group and began to walk over to the guards. As he did so, he drew the sword that was attached to his belt. When the guards saw him approach, they stopped training and stood at attention. The one closest to Alexander turned to face the prince fully. Alexander raised his sword into the air, and the mock sword fight began.

While the three others that had been accompanying the prince as well as the other guards looked on, swords clashed throughout the air. The sound of reverberating metal sang out into the night sky with the gasps of the two men fighting. Alexander's cape flailed through the air with each movement he made. Finally, a grin spread across his face. He was preparing for a move that would almost certainly win the duel.

The guard brought his sword up into the air, and as he prepared to bring it back down, Alexander made a sweeping motion with his sword. First, he intersected the guard's sword, batting away from its current course. Then, Alexander formed a circle with his blade, bringing it down to the point where it almost scraped the ground, and back up. This motion took less than a second and the guard did not even have a chance to realize that Alexander's sword was now behind him as if they were about to embrace. Without an opportunity for the guard to react, Alexander struck him in the back of the head with the handle of his sword. The two dueling men were able to hear a loud thud, and it seemed obvious that the battle was almost completed at this point. The guard began to fall forward, and his sword began to lower in front of him. Without taking his eyes off the guard's face, Alexander raised his foot and stamped down on the guard's sword, forcing it from his hand. There was a brief sound of the metal's vibration dying as it hit the ground. In another amazingly fast battery of actions, Alexander brought his free hand towards the back of the guard's head to pull him forward. When the guard's head finally stopped moving, the tip of Alexander's sword was planted under his chin. For a second, Alexander left the sword pushing a dimple into the top of the guard's neck for him to have moment to replay what had just transpired. It seemed like a perfectly choreographed performance even though neither man had practiced that particular battle before.

For a moment, they stood there without making a sound or even taking a breath.

It was Alexander who eventually broke the silence. "Never assume your opponent is going to play by the strictest rules of sword-fighting. When the fight is real, any move is a fair move. That is the most shameless mistake to make in fighting a war."

The guard made a gesture that attempted to be a nod. With Alexander's sword still against his throat, it was difficult to move his head.

"What is your name?" Alexander asked as he lowered his weapon and returned it to the shroud on his belt.

The guard swallowed hard before answering. He seemed like he was doing a mental inventory to make sure he was not missing a nose or ear after that battle.

"My name is David. I have been serving as one of your Royal Guards for the past three years, Your Majesty."

Alexander was now the one to nod. The prince actually bent over and picked David's sword off the ground. The moonlight shone off that blade as Alexander returned the sword to David's hand.

While still catching his breath, David uttered, "Thank you, Your Majesty. For the valuable lesson as well."

"That is a critical lesson to learn," Alexander elaborated as he began to turn back towards the three he had arrived with. "Remember it well, and don't ever forget how you learned it." Then, in a louder voice so as to address all the guards present, "Continue practicing while there's still enough light for you to do so."

Alexander rejoined the group he had arrived with, and they continued to walk from the palace.

Chenrile turned to the prince and remarked through his own grin, "You never tire of showing off, do you?" At this, the four of them laughed as they continued to walk into the night. Three of those laughs were genuine. Wilhelmina's was not. Deep down, she was beginning to fear Alexander. This display was not just to show off or to train his guard. He was letting out his rage towards her on this man. She was scared that next time, it may be her that the subject of his attack. Still, she walked with him pretending that they were all a happy family.

CHAPTER FOUR

Alexander's Life

Early the next morning, Alexander paced back and forth amidst an audience of one hundred men, women and children. They were all eagerly looking at him as he walked with the sun beating down and casting his shadow against the rocky wall behind him. Some of the children giggled as his shadow wavered against the rock surface, but they were quickly silenced by their parents. Finally, he stopped and pointed to a young girl of about twelve year old standing near the center of the field.

"Recite section forty-three of the Prophecy."

A wave of shivers rippled through the entire group, and the silence was almost palpable. It was well known from the past lectures of this nature what happened if one had not memorized the sections of the Prophecy, their book of worship, which they were required to know. Section forty-three was considered one of the more important passages of the entire work.

The young girl stepped forward from the rest of the crowd and took a deep sigh to collect her thoughts. Her eyes looked directly into Alexander's, and began to speak as if she was reading the text right in front of her.

"And a single beast rose from the sea of thousands to pursue the evil one through the portal to her own world. If the beast is able to catch her, a new age of freedom will begin, and our world will rule the other one, the evil one. However, if she escapes the pursuit of the beast, she would force our world into slavery so that she may rule without opposition."

Relief spread throughout the entire group. Some sighed, but all relaxed a little bit at the sound of the girl's perfect recitation. The young girl stepped back into the crowd and blended into the background once again.

"Excellent," preened Alexander. "Those words are of the utmost importance to us. For the resolution of that event could mean our survival or the destruction of our people."

As if on cue, a loud hiss began to echo throughout the rocky wall that was behind Alexander, emanating from deep within its caverns. Everyone knew that this sound was one of the beasts the young girl had just spoken of.

"Cassandra!" Angelica ran through the palace's corridors towards the woman about a hundred feet before her. "Cassandra!"

At the sound of this second call, Alexander's personal servant stopped and turned to look at the young princess behind her. Up close, Angelica could see how thin and frail Cassandra looked. Her clothes draped around her and her skin hung from her emaciated face. In her typical pale gray grown, she clashed with the grandeur of the palace around her. Looking at her like this, Angelica almost forgot why she had called her in the first place. In a moment, she remembered and asked, "Have you seen Alexander today? I've been looking for him, and I cannot find him anywhere."

The woman reached down and ran her fingers through Angelica's hair. "I'm sorry, but I can't help you." Her words were listless and drawn out. Cassandra's dark brown eyes stared down the richly ornate corridor wall. It was almost as if she could not see Angelica standing before her anymore. "The last time I saw Prince Alexander was yesterday night after he returned with yourself, your mother, and Chenrile. He usually doesn't tell me of his affairs, so I can't tell you where you would find him. If I do see him, though, I'll be sure to let him know you're looking for him. Would that be all, Princess Angelica?"

Angelica looked up with concern. Her eyes met Cassandra's chin rather that her distant stare. "Yes, that's all. Thank you anyway."

With those words, Cassandra turned and continued on her way down the corridor as if nothing had happened. Angelica, on the other hand, began to stroll away in the other direction looking at the bejeweled sconces on the walls, and the golden relief images that covered the corridors.

While still keeping an eye open to find Alexander, Angelica strolled out of the palace. She walked throughout the grounds the courtyard and looked at the land around her. Last year at this time, the grounds were breathtaking. Flowers surrounded the palace and vines clung to the stone walls. Lush green fields stretched for miles in all directions. With the exception of the caves whose entrance was a mere stone's throw from the courtyard, everything was alive and growing.

This year was entirely different, though. There were hardly any signs of the beautifully growing plant life. All the plants were dead and dry. The fields had all turned brown, and even the vines were nothing more than dry shells of what had been there. The drought had been going on for close to two months, and without any effective irrigation system in place, there was no way to get water where it needed to be. The farmers of the kingdom were near the point of starving to death, and few things could postpone the inevitable.

As Angelica walked through the dry and barren field, she continued to look around her, noticing more of differences between this year and the previous one. Finally, she came upon one of the numerous cave entrances. The palace itself was built just next to a mountain range, and there was a small opening in that mountain range not too far from the palace and courtyard. That narrow opening, a tight squeeze for just about anyone that would try to squirm through, led into the caves. This was an area considered dangerous due to the possibility of explosion. Once such explosion caused the cave-in that killed Soranace, the second king of Protecia, and since then, the caves had not been entered.

This, of course, was until Prince Alexander's expedition of tapping the natural gas veins within those caves. Now, the entrance to the caves was overflowing with pipes. There were some that simply led outside the caves and then stopped, which were meant to carry fresh air for the workers, and others that continued for some distance into a back room of the palace. These were the pipes meant to carry the gas into storage tanks located indoors. One time, Alexander regaled the princess with the functionality of his little project, which is how she knew these particular facts. From within the caves, there was the constant drone of people yelling, and the sound of swinging picks or hammers of some sort or another. Their noises echoed throughout the kingdom as a constant reminder to all of the work being done.

Angelica walked closer to the caves, to see if she could possibly get a glimpse of what was going on, when she saw a hand reach up through the cave's mouth. Once she saw the gold band around the wrist and the black cape attached to it, Angelica knew it was her uncle. It took a minute for Alexander to pull himself out of the caves and onto the ground of the courtyard, and Angelica waited patiently as he did so. Finally, he stood and began to walk towards the palace.

After a few steps, Alexander stopped, almost as if he detected someone watching him. He turned and saw Angelica running towards him. When she neared her uncle, Angelica jumped into Alexander's outstretched arms and he began to carry her to the palace with him.

"I was looking for you this morning. It appeared that no one knew where you were." Angelica's eyes asked an infinite list of questions, and Alexander knew this would take some time.

Despite his knowledge of everything the young princess wanted to know, Alexander only answered the first of these questions.

"I had to get up early to oversee some work in the caves."

Angelica nodded at him as they neared to palace doors.

"Why were you so eager to find me?" Alexander stopped walking when he asked his question. The doors to the palace were less than ten feet away, and it seemed that Angelica's answer may determine if they would actually enter the palace or not.

"It's about last night," said Angelica.

Alexander nodded to allow Angelica to continue.

"I wanted to ask you what you and my mother were arguing about during dinner. She sometimes gets angry when I ask her about such things, so I thought I would ask you instead. Why were you yelling at each other?" Angelica's eyes bore into Alexander, and he hesitated for a few seconds. This was one question he had not expected to come up.

It took him a little while to put his feelings into words... He first put Angelica back on the ground. "I have been exploring the caves for several years, and using the gases we have been collected for several purposes, including the bonfires around the kingdom during the winter. Due to the drought, your mother is beginning to wonder if continuing this project is as important as it had been when I first started it. It was nothing more than that." Alexander smiled at his niece, but she seemed less than satisfied. Her lips remained silent, however. She wanted the explanation to continue, but she did not know what else to ask.

Finally, Alexander filled in the silence. "Why are you suddenly so interested in these matters?"

Angelica looked to the ground for a second. "This probably seems a bit childish to you, but I keep seeing you going off to conduct your business during my mother's addresses. You are overseeing projects nearly all the time. I was wondering if people were expecting me to become as involved in the matters of the kingdom as you are. This seemed like good place to start." Angelica looked up towards her uncle when she was finished, eyes betraying her shame.

A smile rose to Alexander's face, and for a moment, Angelica thought he was going to laugh at her. When the prince finally spoke, his words instantly comforted the child. "No one expects you to become involved in such business at your age, but I will give you some advice. If you search for matters to become concerned in, you will be trapped doing things you dislike. When people feel your services are in their need, they will come to you, and then you will know it is time for your true involvement in the kingdom to begin."

Angelica began to look relieved. Her eyes grew less intense, and her whole body seemed to relax a little bit.

"Is that all you had to ask?" Alexander said, inspecting his niece.

Angelica took a deep sigh, and Alexander could see the tension returning to her.

"I heard people saying that you acted alone when beginning this exploration of the caves. If you said that someone should come to you for help, why didn't that happen for you and the caves?"

With his niece staring up at him, Alexander began to speak again.

"Sometimes an event rather than a person asks for help."

These words confused Angelica. To Alexander, it appeared that she had not looked into this topic at the great lengths to which she alluded.

"Not long before you were born, an incident happened in the palace. I entered my room, and I found Cassandra lying on the floor. I ran over to her and began to shake her, but she would not respond. I was afraid she had died."

CHAPTER FIVE

The Gas Mines

Alexander knelt on the ground, momentarily paralyzed with fear, cradling the frail woman in his arms. Only a moment ago, he had entered his quarters to find Cassandra passed out on the floor, but in that time a thousand thoughts passed through his head. Sunlight was beaming in through the window, and it made Cassandra's face much paler than its already milky complexion.

"Wake up! Snap out of it!" he snarled. The words echoed through the palace as Alexander began to shake Cassandra again. She showed no signs of life. Beside the dust-covered rag stinking of what Alexander assumed was some sort of cleaning solvent, Cassandra was lying as lifeless as a corpse.

Finally, with nothing else to do, Alexander lifted Cassandra into his arms and began to carry her from his quarters. She offered no help or resistance when she was lifted. It felt no different than lifting a bag filled with sand.

A small bag.

Still, Alexander carried her from his room and into the main corridor. The smell of that solvent was dissipating, but it was still detectable. It was odd how that smell could still be lingering this far away from the cleaning rag. Dizziness was gripping him as he stumbled down the marble and gold hallway with a seemingly dead body in his arms. He did not get far from his quarters before he slowly lowered Cassandra to the ground. The corridor seemed to be spinning around him. Alexander found himself walking towards the wall of the corridor to steady himself. Out of nowhere, his legs were made of jelly and everything was a blur. His head weighed a thousand pounds. The world faded in and out of grayness like walking through a thick fog. He pressed his face against the cold, stone surface of the wall, and he felt like he could make it a little longer. Maybe just a little bit further and someone would notice him. While holding onto the wall, Alexander tried to get farther down the hallway.

"Chenrile!" The name echoed along the empty hallway. "Someone, get Chenrile over here!"

Alexander was only able to walk along the wall for about ten additional feet before the wall slipped away from under his fingertips. The air rushed by him for an eternity before he hit the cold ground of the hallway with the palms of his hands. On hands and knees, he was able to crawl for another few feet before collapsing completely on the ground.

When Alexander tilted his head up to look down the hallway, the image was murky. There was some sort of noise down past where he could see, but it was drowned out by the overwhelming ringing that filled his ears. This dull, monotonous noise filled up the entire world. It amazed him how he never noticed it before in his life. Still he looked down the hall at walls that had become dull yellow streaks and a floor that seemed to flow and ebb like a great white sea. He could not see anyone coming for him.

It took about fifteen minutes for Chenrile to reach Alexander. He was unable to hear the calls for help, but one of the other palace servants did hear those cries. It was this servant that ran to find Chenrile and explain to him that there may be a medical emergency just outside the private royal quarters. When Chenrile finally did arrive, there was one body of a frail woman, who appeared to be dead, and Alexander on the ground not too far from her, with his bright green eyes half-closed and staring blankly at the hall before him. There was a thin trail of drool coming from the corner of his mouth, and he was mumbling some inarticulate string of words over and over again. It seemed as though he was suffering from the beginning effects of whatever had caused Cassandra's collapse.

When Chenrile leaned over the prince to examine him, Alexander reached up with a shaky hand and grabbed the physician's shirt collar. With gurgled words, Alexander whispered, "The noise smells like it is killing us." His hand then went limp and slid away from Chenrile, and Alexander passed out.

About five minutes later, Alexander began to open his eyes again, and within another ten minutes, he was fully awake. He was lying in the medical room of the palace on a high examination table. Chenrile was beside him looking into his eyes, trying to determine if there were any signs of some more serious abnormality. When he found nothing out of the ordinary, Chenrile allowed Alexander to stand.

The prince climbed off the table and walked over to the one adjacent. On top of it, Cassandra lay, looking as emaciated and sickly as she ever did.

"Is she going to live?" Alexander asked the palace physician without ever turning from the near skeletal woman. Chenrile glanced at Alexander, who continued, "I found her on the floor of my quarters. There was some strong smell in the room, most likely a cleaning solution. I thought that may have something to do with what happened, so I tried to get her out of there. That was as far as I was able to get before the smell got to me as well."

Chenrile nodded and looked at Alexander. His eyes then went to the woman on the table. "We should go back over there. It would be a good idea to see what exactly happened." From just looking into Alexander's eyes, Chenrile could see that he did not want to leave Cassandra's side while she was in this condition. There were always rumors in the palace that the prince and Cassandra were in love, but ashamed of their feelings. Chenrile knew better. Chenrile had known Alexander his whole life, and he knew that he would never love a servant, but there was a certain amount kinship between them.

"She's going to be just fine, Alexander," said Chenrile.

Still, the two waited for about an hour. By this time, Cassandra was pulling herself out of unconsciousness. Now that she was in this hazy state, it seemed certain that she was going to be all right in a matter of time. She was in no more immediate danger, so Alexander now felt it was okay to leave his personal maid alone.

Chenrile and Alexander walked the corridors of the palace until they reached the doorway to Alexander's quarters. Through the hallways, which were now lighted exclusively by torch in the growing twilight, they walked, and they could detect the increasing smell as they approached Alexander's quarters. The smell was still strongest outside the door. Nothing could be seen past that door, however. There were no torches lit inside Alexander's quarters, and it was impossible to see anything in that room.

Alexander, using well-practiced motions, walked to the opposite wall of the hallway and removed one of the torches from its bejeweled sconce. With Chenrile following behind him, Alexander walked into his quarters. The stench got worse as they walked inside, and Alexander felt it was much worse that he remembered it this afternoon. Certainly not a cleaning solvent. As he walked further into the room, he noticed the feel of a draft.

The torchlight began to flicker in the rush of air. Alexander ignored this, since it was nothing out of the ordinary. As he was taking another step into the room, there was a loud pop. The fire from the torch lit up along the path of draft in the room like a long orange arm stretching to the wall. Alexander jumped back, and as he did, the fire died down to where it was before.

"Did you see that?" Alexander whispered, in a hush.

To eliminate any possibility of being burned, Alexander extended the torch out in front of him as far as his arm could reach, being sure not to actually take the extra step into the rush of air. The flame acted the same way it had moments ago. For an instant, the entire draft of air that was rushing through Alexander's quarters was alight with fire, and when Alexander withdrew the torch, the flame withdrew accordingly to only occupy the location just above its wooden handle. "What is that?" he wondered aloud.

Chenrile grabbed hold of Alexander's shoulder without saying a word, but Alexander would not turn around to see him. It appeared that this phenomenon had clung on to Alexander's full attention. Without any other option, the doctor escorted the prince out of the room, pedaling backwards. Once they were in the hallway with the door closed behind them, Chenrile began to speak.

"There seems to be a sort of flammable gas leaking into your room. Excessive inhalation of this sort of gas would appear to be toxic. That would be the cause of your collapse, and Cassandra's condition," said Chenrile.

For a minute, Alexander just stood, trying to process everything that had been said. The fire raged on the torch, inches from Alexander's face, but he hardly noticed the intense heat. His skin was pale, and there were dark blotches under his eyes.

He appeared almost ill, and in that light, he looked like a monster.

Oddly enough, when Chenrile saw the demonic appearance of his friend's face for the first time, it almost seemed to fit. Mostly, just so that image would no longer be in front of his eyes, Chenrile took the torch away from Alexander and replaced it back on the wall.

While attaching it to the sconce, Chenrile muttered, "We should consider finding a way to purge the gas from its source. Otherwise the entire palace would be in danger of burning down."

"So that is why I began to tap the caves of their natural gases." Alexander smiled at his niece, and she just nodded back at him. "As I said, sometimes a situation finds a way to ask for help." Alexander was happy with the explanation he have the young princess, but from the look on her face Angelica was less than convinced.

After a deep sigh and moment's thought, Angelica asked, "If it is that important, why were you and my mother arguing about it last night?"

"The main issues of safety are sufficiently solved for now." Alexander waited a moment to think some more about his answer. It was very likely that anything he said would be repeated for Queen Wilhelmina at some point or another, and he needed to be careful. "In doing that, we found a great deal of uses for the gases we collected, and to be quite frank, the kingdom has grown somewhat dependent on them. Still, there is also a need for water, and therefore, irrigation." Alexander looked into Angelica's eyes so deeply that the small girl began to shiver. "It's up to the ruler of the kingdom, your mother, to decide how to manage these different options. There are limited resources and people in the kingdom, so she will have to make a decision about where the kingdom's best interests lie." Angelica was able to see that he stopped speaking without entirely finishing his thought. The prince, known throughout the kingdom as the Royal Bachelor, meant to add, "One day, that would be your responsibility as well," but then thought he should just dismiss the topic instead. He had laid enough deep thought on the small girl for the afternoon.

With the sun high in the sky, the two walked their separate ways to deal with the affairs of young princesses and older princes as they typically did.

CHAPTER SIX

Another Public Address

Two weeks passed, and Angelica continued to walk the ever-increasing barren grounds around the kingdom. Alexander and the team he had assembled constantly stored the natural gases collected from the caves.

Wilhelmina would spend hours each night studying endless tables and scrolls concerning the drought and the uses of the natural gas. The ceaseless weighing of options and possibilities consumed her every moment. Projections and estimates, populations and mortalities filled Wilhelmina's nightly thoughts. During this time, Angelica hardly saw her mother, and Beatrice became, to an extent, the queen's replacement.

While Wilhelmina was reviewing the current farmers' situation and predictions for the next rainstorm, Beatrice spent the days playing with and watching over Angelica. Usually while resting her obese body on a chair, Beatrice kept the young princess entertained to the best of her ability. During the last few days of the two-week period, Beatrice felt like Angelica's true mother, and it was a feeling Beatrice herself would not trade for all the world.

After those two weeks had passed horsemen raced throughout the kingdom, crying, "Queen Wilhelmina is addressing the public tomorrow when the sun is at its highest!" All who heard this cry cheered for they knew of the queen's current obsession with providing relief to the drought victims. Those who did not hear the message from the queen's fleet of servants on horseback soon heard from the other citizens. In about an hour, everyone knew that the queen planned to speak.

The next day the courtyard was packed tight an hour before the queen was scheduled to address the public. As she was wont to do, Princess Angelica walked among the citizens in the courtyard before the address was to begin. This time, however, she was frightened. The hostilities that were shown ever so slightly towards her mother's last public address would almost undoubtedly reappear today. That much was evident on the face of each person she saw.

Still, the princess mingled, sampled the food that was being prepared, and marveled at the performances of the court jesters. Only two showed up this time. The one who dressed himself to appear like a tree, and the one in the multi-colored costume. He was juggling fiery torches, occasionally turning them into doves by actions that were nothing short of magical.

A little bit earlier than usual, Beatrice appeared at the palace door, calling Angelica back inside. Grudgingly, the young princess quickly finished the piece of roasted pheasant one of the citizens had insisted she sample, thanked the cook, and ran towards Beatrice. The relationship Beatrice had noticed growing between them over the past two weeks was also felt by Angelica, and she had no desire to disobey the nanny now.

As the two of them entered the palace, Beatrice immediately began to explain her action. "I know I usually let you stay out there longer, but today is different. These people are angry and afraid today. They may do…" Beatrice paused as she was visibly weighing options. "Something." Beatrice stopped walking, and Angelica took a few more steps before she did the same. With her eyes closed as if to block tears, Beatrice continued, "Something that won't be in their better judgment." The nanny opened her eyes and continued walking with Angelica. She added, "I'm only looking out for you, Angelica."

When they entered the queen's quarters, Angelica was surprised to find her mother was already completely dressed and ready to speak. She seemed very nervous, and Angelica noticed this instantly. Wilhelmina did not even turn to smile at her daughter. All she did was pace the room without stopping or even slowing down.

It did not seem long before their names were called, and each of them walked across the platform to the sound of cheering people. Those cheers, however, felt forced for the most part today. The queen walked to the middle of the platform between the towering gold vines and before the monumental sculptures of Protace and Soranace. While the crowd was applauding her, Angelica and Alexander walked off the platform and stood in front of the spectators.

After about a full minute of cheering, the noise began to die down on its own. Usually Wilhelmina raised her arms to silence the crowd, but today she felt no need to. She needed as much encouragement as she could get. When everyone was silenced, she began to speak.

"I know the topic on everyone's minds is the continuing drought. Last time I spoke to you, I said I was beginning to plan an irrigation system to bring the water from the Particion River to the wells throughout the kingdom. Since then, I have extensively continued the planning of this system."

Alexander bent down to his niece's ear and whispered, "I have some business to see to." The young girl nodded, and Alexander disappeared into the crowd of anxiously listening people. Trying her best to follow Alexander's advice, she just listened to her mother speaking rather than seeing how far her eyes could follow her uncle's black cape into the crowd to see where he was headed. Still, she looked for just a second and found he was already out of sight.

With a wide smile, Wilhelmina continued to speak. "I am pleased to say that I have weighed all options and variables, and I believe the conclusion I have reached will be a pleasing one for you. The construction of the irrigation system is difficult, not so much because of lacking supplies, but due to insufficient manpower." The queen paused for a moment. She looked quickly towards Angelica, and then her eyes began to scan through the crowd. She was looking for her brother-in-law, and could not find his face among the thousands of faces there. "Since, in my opinion, we have harvested enough natural gases to last well into the winter, and because of the unexpected extent of the drought, I have decided to suspend the tapping of the natural gas veins in the caves."

From deep in the middle of the crowd, Alexander turned from the person to whom he was speaking and looked directly at the queen. Even in the bright sunlight, Alexander looked at her with the same face Chenrile saw in the torch-lit hallway nine years earlier.

"What use would constant bonfires during the winter be if people didn't survive the summer or had no stored crops due to the drought," she continued. "I am pulling all of the workers out of the caves and setting them to work on the construction of an irrigation system. If all goes according to the schedule I have proposed, the entire system should be completed within the next two weeks."

The crowd cheered at this news, and with this momentum in place, the rest of the address went beyond smoothly. Minor topics were brought up, talked about briefly and then forgotten. Angelica was startled by how quickly the address was concluded after the news about the irrigation system was fully discussed.

Within a minute of the queen stating that there was no more business to discuss, Wilhelmina ran off the platform, grabbed her daughter by the arm, and rushed her into the palace. She did not stop dragging Angelica along until they were inside the queen's quarters. Once the door was closed, Wilhelmina locked it and began to undress. Angelica looked up at her mother and asked, "What's wrong? Everyone seemed happy at the end of the address." Her mother did not answer, so Angelica began to undress herself from her formal attire.

In a matter of minutes, Angelica had removed her formal gown and had dressed herself in the clothes she usually wore. Wilhelmina was slowly pulling on her clothes as well. As soon as she had removed her formal attire, Wilhelmina began to feel calmer. For this reason, when Angelica asked if she can see the eminent groundbreaking for the irrigation system, the queen saw no reason to deny her this. She may never see such a historical event again for years. With a nod of approval from her mother, Angelica unlocked the door and walked out into the hallway. The door closed behind her, and Wilhelmina looked at it with the last remnants of her previous fear. It locked from the inside, meaning that Angelica had no way of locking it when she left. Wilhelmina quickly dressed herself and began to walk towards the door. Usually she never bothered to lock it, but this time was different. She could not shake this feeling of fear. For the first time since she began her rule, she truly felt scared.

As Wilhelmina neared the door, she began to raise her hand to the lock located just above the door's handle. With her fingers only inches away from the lock, the door swung open. There was an instant where Wilhelmina was unable to see who was on the other side, but she was desperately hoping that it was Angelica returning to retrieve some forgotten item, or maybe even Beatrice for any number of reasons. Soon, reality caught up with Wilhelmina, and she was able to see Alexander on the other side of the door. His face was flushed and very angry, and even in the torchlight, it had that demonic look it held those years before when the gases were first discovered.

Without even giving the prince a chance to speak, Wilhelmina began to defend her decision.

"This is only a temporary measure, you realize. As soon as the irrigation system is built, you'll have your men back to work in the caves." The queen realized that she had been backing up ever since Alexander appeared on the other side of her door. She also knew it was not required of her to explain her will to anyone, including the prince, but still, she felt as though she had to. After all, she did not possess Protace's blood, which made her an outsider despite her crown.

While continuing to back farther into the dimly lit room, Wilhelmina continued to talk. "There is a much greater and more urgent need for water than for gas. We need to put that irrigation system in place now or there won't be many people left for the bonfires to keep warm in the winter. This is truly the best possible alternative. Any other options would be devastating for the people of the kingdom, and it is their needs I must look out for. I know that project meant a great deal to you, but you'll be able to pick it again in a few weeks. There really was no other alternative." By this point, Wilhelmina's back was pressed against the wall with the large window just to her right. The sunbeams reached into the room, but due to her position, they ignored her entirely. It was almost as if they had abandoned her in favor of Alexander.

Alexander had been matching each of Wilhelmina's steps, and now he was less than a foot away from her. His eyes were furious, and the queen felt as though their mere glance would drive her mad. The black cape swirling around his arm, Alexander raised his hand into the air. With all the rage that filled those eyes, Alexander brought his hand down and struck the queen's face with the back of his hand. She let out a shriek as the bent towards the ground. Her scream was drowned out by the sound of the heavy wooden door sliding closed behind them.

As if that was not enough, Alexander reached down and wrapped his fingers around Wilhelmina's throat. Her cries were choked off as he grabbed her neck and pulled her head off the ground so he could look into her eyes. While he did this, Wilhelmina's right hand drifted down beside her. It was reaching for the back of her thigh, but Alexander would not loosen his grip enough for her to retrieve what she was trying to find. He was actually lifting her onto her toes by her neck while feeling tendons and blood vessels quivering under his grasp.

With his hand choking off any attempt for her to scream, Alexander began whispering to her through a snarl. The words he uttered, however, spoke so loudly that there was no need for him to raise his voice. While spittle shot from his teeth, Alexander growled, "Cross me again, Wilhelmina, and I'll see to it they never find where I put your body." He held her there for a few more seconds to let those words sink in. When the look in her eyes showed she understood, Alexander let go.

After drawing in a raspy and exhausted breath, Wilhelmina cried out, "How dare you talk to me that way? I am the queen!" She yelled her words, but she seemed to be doing that only to hide her own fear. Only to make Alexander see that she was not as scared of him as he wanted her to be. To show that she was not as scared as she was really was. It was not like he could just kill her as she stood in her own quarters.

Or could he?

Instead, Alexander raised his hand again, and brought it down hard. He smacked Wilhelmina's cheek again, and she let out another shriek. Her body seemed to just fold up, and she fell to the floor like a sack of cloth. With her face already reddening, Alexander yelled back at her. "You are nothing! There is none of Protace's blood in you, and to me that makes you no more than a commoner. A commoner who threatens to contaminate the royal bloodline. You are nothing more than a peasant. An *expendable* peasant."

For an instant, Wilhelmina was truly afraid for her life. It seemed like an all too possible scenario for her brother-in-law to kill her right now, leave, and deny knowing a thing about what had happened. Wilhelmina reached down towards her thigh again, but before her fingers found the familiar piece if iron they searched for, Alexander had spun around. The black cape flailed through the air and rolled around his ankles as he began to walk towards to door out of the queen's quarters. Within a few seconds, he had slammed the door shut and left Wilhelmina lying in the shadows, terrified.

Despite Alexander being gone, Wilhelmina drew the dagger from its hiding place behind her thigh. Out of fear alone,

Wilhelmina held that dagger in front of her staring at nothing more than the closed door to her quarters. Tears began to flow down her face as she was lying on the floor. There she stayed. Crying, terrified, and holding a dagger out in front of her as if there was something to fight. For the next half-hour, Wilhelmina stayed in that position, afraid to move. For an additional two hours, she remained locked inside her quarters, terrified to leave.

The construction of the irrigation system began while Wilhelmina was huddled in the corner of her quarters. Before giving the address, she had given instructions to the workers from the caves to report to different assignments concerning the irrigation system. They finally did begin to work as soon as the courtyard was cleared of relieved and ecstatic citizens.

As the first shovel of dirt was pulled from the ground, the assembled spectators cheered. Princess Angelica cheered with them. As the queen had predicted, it was the most historical event the young girl had ever seen. Queen Wilhelmina was incorrect in thinking that it would be the biggest historical event for her daughter to witness in the coming years. In that respect, the queen was very, very mistaking.

With the Particion River as the source of the water, channels were constructed underground going to the selected wells throughout the kingdom. Careful attention was paid to avoid damaging the historical bridge that crossed the river. According to tradition, this bridge was constructed by Protace to unify the barbarians on each shore under his rule. What was once an impassable barrier between those two people was crossed, and a new age was allowed to commence. It was the beginning of their kingdom, and that was a symbol whose destruction most definitely would mean the eventual downfall of the entire way of life.

From early in the morning to late in the evening, the construction crews dug and assembled the irrigation system. The heat was relentless, but that only inspired the workers to exert themselves even more. Nearly every day, Queen Wilhelmina would walk through the area that was currently under construction to see how the progress was going. On each of these visits, the workers greeted her happily. It seemed like for the first time in months, a solution to all of their problems had arrived, and it was all due to the work of Queen Wilhelmina.

Alexander, however, was not pleased with Wilhelmina's projects. The exploration of the caves was much more than a simple scheme to bolster his popularity throughout the kingdom. So much more was riding on that project, and even though his crew was gone to work on the irrigation system, Alexander insisted on doing some of the easier work in the caves by himself. That is when more problems began.

While walking towards the caves several days after his confrontation with Wilhelmina, Alexander noticed a guard standing by its entrance. He was vaguely familiar with this man, as he was one of the guards that Alexander had personally trained. Alexander did not remember him as anyone who particularly stood out among the crowds of men whose training he had overseen, but being one to get through Alexander's training, he must be good.

As Alexander approached, this guard began to speak in a voice that was both authoritative and rather nervous.

"I cannot permit you to enter the caves, your Majesty."

Alexander stopped walking and looked at the guard almost as if his mere stance would change the man's mind.

"By the order of the queen, all persons are to be banned from entering the caves until further notice. Since there is no reason for caves to be entered, it would pose an unnecessary safety risk to allow anyone access." As if it were an afterthought, the guard added, "I apologize, your Majesty." It may have been those few words that pushed the situation to where it eventually landed.

A smile filled Alexander's face. "I know that I do not outrank the queen, but I certainly outrank you. Would you be so kind as to stand to the side so that I can pass? I know of the risks involved, and

I am willing to take them." Prince Alexander began to walk forward, but the guard did not move. He even began to raise a hand towards Alexander's advancement.

"Once again, I am sorry, but by the orders of Queen Wilhelmina, I cannot allow you to enter the caves, your Majesty. She was very specific that you were to be included in this restriction." The guard looked as though he was made of stone. He did not seem as if he was going to give in and allow the prince to pass. Still, Alexander felt he needed to try. To usurp the authority of this guard and, even more importantly, Wilhelmina, Alexander continued to advance. As he took an additional step forward, the guard added, "I have been instructed to use any methods necessary to keep all persons from entering the caves. That includes force, I am sorry to say."

At this, the grin on Alexander's face widened. He had trained all of the guards, and he had no intention of allowing one of his students to defeat him in battle. Prince Alexander began to drift forward again. As he approached the guard's outstretched hand, he pushed it to the side. Then, the guard began to respond with the force that he had warned.

While Alexander began to walk towards the cave entrance, the guard drew his sword. A burst of laughter rose from Alexander's mouth as he turned to the guard while drawing his sword as well. It appeared as though the guard had not anticipated this move. He seemed to be frozen in fear almost immediately. With one quick motion, Alexander hit the guard's wrist with his sword. There was a loud metallic clang as the guard dropped his weapon to the rocky ground beneath him. A trail of blood spilled on the gleaming blade from a gash across the guard's wrist. It was evident the fight had ended before it ever really started.

Despite the fact that the guard was now disarmed and would most likely let Alexander pass without any further opposition, the prince did not stop. Whether it was the fact that Wilhelmina was once again making a conscious effort to oppose him or if it was the fact that the guard he had trained had now turned against him, no one would ever really know. Most likely, Alexander did not even know what immediately possessed him to take such a drastic action, but he raised his sword again and pressed it under the guard's chin. It pushed into the soft flesh slightly, just enough for the guard to feel its point dimpling his flesh.

While the guard was shaking in fear, Alexander raised his other hand and used it to grasp the guard's chin. He pushed the chin down, opening the guard's mouth almost as if to examine it. As he did this, the point of the sword pushed deeper up under the guard's jaw. Alexander moved his mouth close to the guard's ear and began to whisper to him. "Sometimes it is better to stay silent rather than follow an order to the letter. Wouldn't you agree, now?" The guard made a grunt to show that he understood. If it were not for Alexander holding his mouth still, simple fear would have made the guard mute anyway.

Finally, Alexander forced the sword upwards. It sliced through the flesh of the guard's lower jaw and slid easily past his tongue and out from between his teeth. The guard tried to scream, but with the sword passing out of his mouth, it came out only as a garbled nightmare attempting to be words. With six inches of blade protruding from between his curled lips, the guard tried his best to scream. The noises he made sounded like the shrieks of some monstrous animal. "Maybe you'll keep that in mind next time," Alexander whispered just loud enough for the guard to hear him over his attempts at screaming.

As the guard was projecting a sound that was some kind of hybrid between moaning and retching, one of the kingdom's citizens ran over to see what was happening. Alexander turned towards this middle-aged woman wearing a plain, gray housecoat. She gasped at what she saw. Alexander now began to shout at her, "Quickly, go to the palace, and ask whoever is at the door to find Chenrile. He is to meet us at the prison immediately." The woman took a few steps back and hesitated. "Go now!" With this, she turned and run towards the doors to the palace.

Alexander twisted the sword protruding from the guard's mouth, and the man tried to scream again. "Come on," Alexander said in the most conversational tone one could imagine. "We're going to take a walk." Alexander led the guard away from the cave in this fashion, and the two walked until they reached the far side of the palace. A few hundred feet from that side of the palace wall, also built into the side of the mountainous ridge that marked the edge of the kingdom, was the prison.

Its barred door was made of iron while its walls were all made of stone. In the history of the kingdom, no one was known to have escaped and then live long enough to see another sunrise. Standing inside the door of the prison was an old man. He was actually no more than forty years of age, but he had a face that was worn and abused for each day of those forty years. He stared on as the prince escorted the guard towards the prison door. Even he looked shocked. He had been working in that post for most of his life and had never seen a sight like that before. One battered, scarred hand was on the iron plank that had to be moved to unlock that door from the inside.

As the prince approached the door, Chenrile came running from a side entrance to the palace. There was a look of caution in his eyes, and Alexander was pleased to see that had brought some medical supplies with him. As the palace's head physician approached, Alexander yanked the sword out of the guard's chin. This time, he was able to scream, and he did so loudly as a stream of blood sliced towards the ground. Blood began to pour from his mouth and from above his neck. As the guard fell to the ground outside the prison, Chenrile kneeled beside him.

Alexander muttered, "There was an incident by the entrance to the caves. See what you could do for him." While Chenrile began to slow the guard's bleeding, Alexander walked towards the prison door and spoke to the withering man inside. "I want this man held here until noon tomorrow for assault on a member of the royal family. To prevent him from re-injuring his mouth after the physician is done with him, he is not to be given any food or drink until he is released."

The man behind the door looked at the writhing guard on the ground and muttered, "You know I'll have to report this to the queen. She has to authorize this imprisonment." While the man spoke to Alexander, his eyes never left Chenrile and the guard.

Alexander grinned again. "I know that. Wilhelmina, your queen, is very busy now, what with all the little jobs she's thinking up for the kingdom. This man will be released from his sentence before she even knows he's been imprisoned." Alexander turned and began to walk away from the prison. As Alexander was walking past the guard, Chenrile turned away to retrieve fresh bandages from his bag of supplies. The bandages already that were already applied had soaked through and fresh rivers of blood were finding their way around them. Alexander turned and said, "Good day," to the man inside the prison. When he turned back, he kicked the guard firmly in the jaw and a fresh jet of blood shot away from him leaving the soaked bandages hanging in tatters from the wound. Then, as if nothing had happened, Alexander walked away with a spring in his step.

Chenrile placed fresh bandages on the guard's chin, instructed him to hold them in place, and then ran to catch up with Alexander. While the prison guard walked over to the guard and began to kneel beside him, Chenrile spoke in a tone that was almost conversational.

"Why did you do that? He was just doing what he was told."

Alexander did not reply, so Chenrile added, "Queen Wilhelmina is going to find out about this you know," as if that was the worst fate in the world.

This caused Alexander to stop walking. He turned to look at the physician who had been his life-long friend. "I want Wilhelmina to know exactly what I have done. It will be a good lesson to her. Now, she'll know that I mean what I say." Alexander started to walk again and Chenrile followed right behind him.

The prince was walking past the front of the palace, back to the caves where he had been not an hour ago. "She is the queen, but at the same time, she is of a peasant's bloodline. At most, she should be my equal. That peasant should not have the right to tell me what I may or may not do."

The two of them were approaching the entrance to the caves. It was now unguarded as it always had been before. There was already the very faint odor of natural gas come from the opening. A strange smell that could just be described as not quite right. With that sickly odor lingering around them, the two understood the kingdom was also not quite right.

Alexander bid good-bye to his friend, and then he fell to his knees and began to crawl through the narrow opening to the caves. Once inside, he grabbed onto an edge of rocks, and slid down the drop towards the larger area of the first caverns. Chenrile stood outside and watched as Alexander disappeared deeper and deeper into the caves. Soon, there was nothing to see but the unchanging view of rock.

With Alexander gone and his duties done, Chenrile walked away from the caves. He strolled along the courtyard before he entered the palace. Nodding at the guards who stood by the main entrance, Chenrile passed beneath the painted celling of Protace. The painted image showed Protace building the bridge across the Particion River with the clouds embracing him as if to sweep him off into the skies. He smiled up at the painting as he walked by underneath it. Chenrile did not get more than fifty feet down the first corridor before he heard his name called from behind him.

Queen Wilhelmina was standing behind Chenrile, and when the doctor turned, he saw the fear in her eyes. With a face that was masked by a smile, Wilhelmina said, "I heard there was a problem by the caves outside. Some sort of an injury that required your immediate attention. Did it turn out all right?"

The question was more of a test than anything else. The peasant that ran towards the palace told the first guard she came across what she was sent to say; that guard ran to find Chenrile, but Wilhelmina, who was only a few feet down the corridor, also heard the message.

With the guard searching the palace for Chenrile, the queen invited the peasant inside. After graciously accepting the invitation into the marvelously decorated hallways, the peasant told everything she saw to the queen. This included the entire situation surrounding Alexander's attack on the guard, and how he planned to detain the man he had injured. The peasant told the queen everything she saw, and she was then sent on her way with the thanks of her ruler and a story she would recite to her family and friends for the rest of her life.

Still, Wilhelmina asked the question of Chenrile, and she was surprised to hear the answer. "There was some sort of accident by the prison. A guard injured himself some way or another, but he should be fine now." Chenrile had a smile on his face, but the queen's eyes bore into him like hot pokers. "Accidents like that tend to happen from time to time. It's nothing to be alarmed about." The queen's eyes did not waver, and Chenrile did not have a clue what else to say.

Finally, Wilhelmina broke the silence. "Thank you. It's good to know our guard will be well soon."

Hearing these words, Chenrile turned and continued to walk away. Wilhelmina stayed perfectly still as if frozen. She did not move for a minute. Soon that minute became five minutes, and finally her knees buckled at the thought of what had just been described to her. If the wall had not been so close, she would have fallen to the marble floor right then. Wilhelmina pulled a deep breath into her lungs. So deep it was painful. When she slowly exhaled, she found the ability to move again. Chenrile was out of sight but she could still hear his footfalls walking away from her. She just stared and thought, "Why would he try to cover up Alexander's actions?"

CHAPTER SEVEN

Researching the Past

Not long after the dizziness had worn off, Queen Wilhelmina found herself far on the other side of the palace entering the royal family's private library. Handwritten and hand-bound books were shelved nearly fifty feet to the ceiling. Ladders were scattered about the shelves, and an assortment of highly polished, hand-carved chairs and tables filled the room. Light beamed in from a wall that consisted entirely of windows. Long black curtains were pulled to the sides to reveal the glass expanses. The sunlight shone into the room making even the dust particles it caught glow and dance. It seemed like something out of a fairytale.

As Wilhelmina took a few cautious steps inside, she looked from shelf to shelf. The main reading area of the library was walled on two sides with these shelves, and off to her right, was a seemingly endless row of freestanding shelves. Nearly every horizontal surface was stacked high with books. Their very sight was staggering, and Wilhelmina had no idea where to begin. There were texts about history and science, books that contained nursery rhymes for children, diaries of previous rulers, and almost every conceivable map and diagram of the kingdom.

From these endless caverns of books, a man walked out into the bright light of the main reading area. "Queen Wilhelmina! It is such a pleasure to see you here." The man ran over to the table closest to the window and pulled out one of the chairs. "Please sit down. This table has the best light of all of them." Wilhelmina sat at the indicated chair. It had been years since she had actually come down the palace's library. Usually, when she was in need of one of its thousands of books, Beatrice would bring her what she needed, but now, she wanted her work to remain as secretive as possible. It would not be wise to have Beatrice walking around the palace with this particular armload of books. Also, the queen was well aware of the servants' predilection for gossip.

As the librarian pushed the chair in for the queen, he asked, "What can I bring for you to read? Just make yourself comfortable. Anything you want, I will run and fetch for you." This man reminded Wilhelmina of her grandfather. He had died when she was still very young, but she never forgot the look of his face. Even his wrinkles seemed to radiate happiness when he smiled.

A smile found its way to Wilhelmina's own face, and it felt very good to be there. Almost as if it was activating parts of her face that had been dormant for some time. For once in a long time, she actually felt like the queen of Protecia and not just a public face for Alexander's bidding. With a deep sigh, she looked at the librarian and said, "I would like a book on the royal family's genealogy." She paused for a moment before adding, "As detailed as you can find." The librarian bowed and ran towards the shelves. Wilhelmina just sat back and relaxed. Still, there was one question on her mind. Chenrile had lied to her face so that he could protect Alexander's interests, and Wilhelmina could feel there was more than their friendship driving that action. There seemed to be some deeper reason behind it that she could not grasp.

She meant to see if there was some deeper connection between him and the royal family. It was well known in the kingdom that Chenrile was from Nezzrin, a neighboring land, and that his family mysteriously vanished one day. Chenrile supposedly just wandered by himself at the age of five until he was found in Protecia and adopted. Several times, people went to Nezzrin to try to uncover answers and were always met with resistance. Most of that kingdom's people did not want to speak of Chenrile's past and avoided the questions entirely. The ones that did speak would describe the family as troubled and quarrelsome. Chenrile, when spoken of at all, was described in terms that made him sound evil. It was nearly impossible to think of Chenrile as committing an evil act; still, there was something in the way he spoke to Wilhelmina that day that made her wonder.

For the next hour, the queen remained in the sunlight of the library's window going slowly through the books the librarian had supplied for her. The history of each person who attained the throne as well as those who were in line, but never became a king or queen was thoroughly documented. The books went on for what seemed like an eternity. There were hundreds of living heirs at any given time for centuries. Then, the time of the plague began, and the list significantly dwindled. Eventually, it was diminished to herself, Angelica, and Alexander.

There did not seem to be any mention of Chenrile in the genealogy meaning that his deeper and secretive connection to the ruling family was merely a figment of Wilhelmina's paranoid imagination. However, with that vast number of names, the queen could not be sure that she did not just miss the mention of him. She began to go back through the books a second time when she saw something. There was a date listed that looked very familiar. She knew it was a date that she had seen at some point in her studies of that afternoon. If it was familiar for the reason that she suspected, this could be the detail she was looking for.

The librarian walked by the queen and broke through the beaming light from the window. Just as he was doing this, Wilhelmina slammed the book shut and dropped it back onto the table. The tiny man jumped and gasped as if this was a desecration beyond anything he had ever seen before.

There was a blank look of fear in Wilhelmina's eyes. For a moment, all the emotion drained away from her body. "Would you please re-shelve these for me?" The librarian nodded at the queen, but his eyes had grown confused and uncertain. As she ran towards the door, Wilhelmina called out, "Thank you," and then she was gone.

Once back in her quarters, the queen was able to rest while the scenario she was forming began to play out in her mind. It did not seem likely that the events she was piecing together had ever happened or that they were even remotely plausible. Right now, it was an elaborate theory that barely fit the facts. Still, there was a possibility that Chenrile was going to turn against her. It was a risk that she did not wish to take. The physician had lied to her to defend Alexander, so Wilhelmina would have to discuss her problems with the prince directly if she were to truly understand what was going on.

Queen Wilhelmina marched outside into the heat of the early summer evening. The guards had already begun to train for the night, but they all stopped and bowed at her as she walked by. In her haste, she hardly noticed this gesture and certainly did not stop to return or acknowledge it. A battalion of guards was practicing archery using some far off, nearly dried out trees as targets. The queen simply marched passed them to the opening of the caves and waited. Alexander would eventually resurface.

The sun began to slip beneath the horizon, giving off rays of bright orange and deep red. Wilhelmina remained standing by the edge of the mountain watching the opening for some sign of the prince. There was none.

Soon, the sky grew dark, and eventually it was fully black. The queen had not looked away in all that time, and Alexander had not appeared. With a sigh, Wilhelmina assumed he must have left the caves before she had arrived, most likely while she was in the library or on her way here.

She walked back into the palace, admiring the torch-illuminated passages. She walked past representations of Protace constructing his famous bridge. The hallway with the portraits of all the kingdom's past leaders went by without Wilhelmina stopping or even slowing down. Finally, she entered the dining area, hoping against hope that Alexander would be sitting at the table waiting for her to arrive.

Only Angelica and the elderly chef occupied the dining room. As Wilhelmina walked in, she said, "It will just be the princess and I, tonight." With a sound of desperate hope, she added, "Unless you've heard something from Alexander this evening." The chef shook his head as he began to slice the roasted chicken that was on the table before them.

The queen continued to look for Alexander the rest of that evening and once again early in the morning. It was not until the morning was already well underway that she finally found him. He was walking across the courtyard from the direction of the cave opening she had waited by the previous night. Had he slept in the caves all night? By that time, there was already sweat running down his forehead in the profuse heat of that year.

When Wilhelmina finally caught up to the prince, she looked at him calmly and said, "I heard about what happened yesterday, and let me assure you of one thing. Any attempt to bring my citizens against me is going to fail. Is that clear?" Alexander smiled and said nothing. He continued to walk away from her, as if his time was too important to spend speaking to a lowly peasant who found herself married into power. The queen called after him, "I know about Chenrile!"

The prince stopped in his path. Wilhelmina wished she could see the look on his face when he had heard her say it, but the sudden halt in his departure was more than enough. He turned around to look at Wilhelmina again, black cape swirling. It looked like a cloud of evil and deceit that enveloped his every movement. At that moment, Wilhelmina was afraid that confronting him was a very big mistake. It was too late to stop now—the words could not be retrieved.

Wilhelmina saw the upper hand, clear as day. Chenrile's history was something Alexander had not wished anyone to know, and now that she was aware of it, there did not seem to be much Alexander could say to oppose her now or in the future.

"Our kingdom was based on a very simple fact," the queen began to lecture, posture straightening indignantly. "These people are supposed to be looked after and helped in every way possible. It's what Protace had in mind when he became our first king, and it's what all the rulers who followed used as a guide when making their decisions." Wilhelmina took a step closer to Alexander, and he did not back away. It seemed to him that she was hardly a threat even with her new-found knowledge. "I know that you are not in power, and that you will never sit upon the throne. Unfortunately, I also know that so long as you draw breath, these people are going to be prisoners in their homes." Her eyes locked on Alexander's, and she knew that there was little he could say to oppose her. "I am going to do everything in my power to see that that will change."

As if to laugh at her, Alexander simply turned and walked away. He continued away from the courtyard and through the main entrance to the palace, leaving Wilhelmina to stew in her own fury. After a few seconds, she began to compose herself again, and she walked back towards the palace.

As she passed through the palace doors she saw Beatrice running towards her. For such an overweight woman, Beatrice somehow managed to be very light on her feet.

"Queen Wilhelmina, I have just heard some wonderful news!" Beatrice exclaimed. Wilhelmina stopped and listened to what her servant had to say. "I just received a report from the head of construction for the irrigation system. It should be ready and operational by tomorrow at noon."

The scowl of hatred for Alexander lifted from Wilhelmina's face. A small smile actually began to touch the corners of her lips. "That's terrific news, Beatrice. Dispatch the royal horsemen. I am going to be addressing the public tomorrow at noon to tell them myself."

Beatrice turned and began to walk away immediately to inform the horsemen of the duties. Meanwhile, Wilhelmina walked to her quarters and began to prepare what she was going to say when she addressed the people the following day.

Everything finally seemed to be coming into place. The people were going to get an irrigation system running within another day. This would lead to an end of the problems caused by the drought. That meant she would have to find something else for the construction workers to begin with. Especially after recent events, Wilhelmina did not want Alexander to be given the crew to work on his gas mines. Without those men at his command, she would have hardly any say in the affairs of the kingdom. She was going to show him who was in control of Protecia, once and for all time.

CHAPTER EIGHT

Queen Wilhelmina

T he small crowd of spectators gasped as he blew a pillar of fire into the air. Smiles filled the faces of everyone surrounding the man dressed up to look like a tree. He performed the trick again to the continued amusement of the people around. The jester dressed in the multicolored outfit was just arriving. While everyone gathered around the fire-breathing tree, the other jester began to arrange the large wooden spheres he would begin juggling at any moment.

Angelica strolled towards the rear of the courtyard, looking at the two jesters performing their tricks. She was also munching on an apple that had been spiced and cooked by one of the people who had set up a stand. Gasps grew increasingly louder as the juggler began throwing as many as seven spheres into the air at once. While handling two of them, the other five remained airborne just long enough for him to shuffle the ones he was holding. It was a performance that seemed nothing short of magical. Within the front row of the people gawking at this spectacle, Angelica stood with her eyes wide.

Her eyes soon fixed on the rapidly moving hands of the performer. Those hands were also clad in gloves that exploded with white, red, blue, and yellow. As Angelica watched, the hands began to move slower and slower. She was even more shocked by this. Even though he was slowing down, it seemed as though the spheres remained in the air. Soon, they began to fall. The jester grabbed two of them and let another four fall to the ground with soft little thuds. When Angelica looked at his masked face, the jester said, "You catch that last one." Under the brightly colored mask, Angelica was certain she could see a huge grin spreading across his face. She looked up to ready herself for the descent of that last sphere as the jester took a step back for her move into position. Princess Angelica did catch what fell out of the sky, but it was not the wooden sphere that initially thrown into the air. A single red rose drifted lazily downward and into Angelica's waiting hands.

Her large smile turned into a shocked, gaping expression of awe, with her eyes locked on the flower that she just plucked out of the air, as effortless as if she were pulling it from one of the gardens that surrounded the palace in happier times, or from one of the vases that covered the dining room's grand wooden table. She was surprised how healthy this rose looked in spite of the drought. Even the flowers that were thrown at the queen when she first walked onto the stone platform to begin her public addresses had started to take on a sickly, wilted appearance. As Angelica lowered the flower to her nose and inhaled its beautiful aroma, the jester knelt beside her. In a voice so soft and calming that it was frightening, the jester whispered, "This is my gift to you. One we would be honored to call our future queen."

"Beatrice, I want you to do me a favor." Queen Wilhelmina spoke without taking her eyes off the mirror. She was fastening a bejeweled hairpiece to herself, and Beatrice approached thinking that was what she needed help with. As the servant reached one chubby hand towards Wilhelmina, the queen laughed. "No, I can manage this by myself." An instant later, the piece was attached, and the queen turned around to face Beatrice. The hairpiece sparkled radiantly in the light.

The servant stood with her hands folded in front of her as she had been taught was the proper way to stand in front of royalty.

"Yes, your Majesty. How can I be of assistance?" Her face was calm, and it almost appeared as if she was expecting the usual menial task of running to the library to fetch something or maybe to retrieve Angelica from the courtyard. She certainly did not expect what Wilhelmina was going to say next.

"I have learned some unpleasantness about Chenrile a few days ago. Something about both his past and his present. With this knowledge, I do not feel it would be advisable to have him in attendance at today's address." Wilhelmina closed her eyes and sighed deeply. Deep down inside, she could not believe she was actually saying this. "I am certain it's nothing, but I would not feel entirely comfortable if I saw him watching me speak."

Beatrice put an arm around Wilhelmina's waist and walked her to the bed. When Beatrice sat upon it, the queen took the invitation to sit beside her. Queen Wilhelmina was surprised how good it felt to be consoled by someone. It seemed like for years, she was consoling hundreds of people with no one to look after her. It was the job and responsibility of the ruler of a kingdom. A ruler who took her job to heart, at least. "Is there anything I would be able to do to help you with, my queen?" Beatrice's eyes were deep and dark. They were the eyes of a concerned person and a good friend despite what the two women's real roles in the kingdom were.

When she was asked this question, Queen Wilhelmina's stomach sank. She was ashamed of such a request, but it had to be made. "I want you to check the crowd to see if he's there. Before you bring Angelica back, just look around to see if you notice him in the courtyard." With a deep sigh, Wilhelmina looked back at Beatrice. "If he's there, tell him there was an accident by the Particion River that requires his attention. One of the irrigation system constructors was injured and is in urgent need of medical attention. That should get rid of him at least until I am done with the address." Beatrice nodded, but the queen's face was filled with fear and agony. Wilhelmina felt as if she was becoming part of conspiracy of some sort. If she, herself, had overheard anyone in the kingdom speaking as Beatrice and she were, Wilhelmina would have immediately had them questioned as to their motives. "If he's not there, I want you to stay in the courtyard. When he arrives, give him the message then."

While nodding again, Beatrice rose from the bed and began to walk towards the door. She opened the door and began to walk out when she heard the queen's voice from behind her again. "Please do not tell anyone that I asked this of you. I would not be able to bear all the questions." She placed an arm around her servant's shoulders. It felt good to embrace a friend like this. It felt right. "Thank you so much." Beatrice waited for the queen to finish speaking and only moved when she was certain that there was nothing left to be said. She then turned and left the queen's quarters to go complete her task.

The walk to the courtyard seemed to take hours instead of a few minutes. All that Beatrice could think about was the different steps in her task, and then she began to wonder what Wilhelmina had possibly discovered about Chenrile that was so important. So important and so secretly hidden that now she actually seemed afraid to come in contact with him again. It seemed almost ludicrous that after all these years, Chenrile would wish any harm on a member of the royal family, but Beatrice was not in full possession of the facts. This was something she knew very well, and she did not wish to venture an opinion on someone when she was not informed.

When she finally did reach the courtyard, Beatrice squinted in the sunlight. Today seemed to be brightest and hottest day of all. There was not a single cloud to break apart the bright blue sky and gleaming rays of sunlight. That meant that the irrigation system was not going to be completed a moment too soon. With the sun beating down on her, she began to sweat underneath the heavy gowns etiquette demanded that she wear for the queen's formal appearance. Soon, her eyes adjusted, and Beatrice began to walk out onto the courtyard.

Ahead of her, Angelica was standing nearly entranced by the actions of a jester. There were food stands setting up behind them, and off towards the platform, people were beginning to gather to get good positions to see the queen speak. Beatrice gave each face a careful look, and she did not see the physician anywhere among them. It was almost unnerving. She saw other faces she recognized as prominent figures in the kingdom and several she had never laid eyes on before. These were peasants that had not had past dealings that brought them into the eyes of the royal family. Among all of these faces, Chenrile's did not appear. Beatrice could not help wondering why Chenrile's presence would be considered such a threat with so many unknown people occupying the courtyard. Any one of them could attempt nearly anything, but Wilhelmina suspected Chenrile alone. Again, for some reason Beatrice was not privy to.

With the crowd thoroughly checked, Beatrice walked over to Angelica. The young princess was still standing and staring, enwrapped, at the jester almost as if hypnotized by his motions. Tightly clasped in her hand was the stem of a single red rose. When Beatrice tapped her on the shoulder, Angelica jumped and all but screamed. Not a word had to be said. Angelica turned around and began to walk away from the crowd and towards the side entrance to the palace.

Angelica walked slowly and seemed almost depressed as she wandered the halls of the palace. This was usually how she felt when she left the performance, but this time was much worse. She had been having such a great time. At no other occasion before had one of the jesters actually spoken to her. This time, he not only spoke, but he had her play a part in the show. Still, the happiness must end sometime, and it seemed like that time was now.

When Angelica walked into her mother's quarters, she was greeted with the usual bright smile that seemed to illuminate her soul. The young princess placed the rose upon the bed and began to dress. She was surprised to see that Beatrice had not arrived back in the quarters a few moments after she did. This was the first time Angelica was forced to dress herself in her formal gowns without any assistance. Still, she managed to do it with a smile thinking all along that this was a sign of her getting older.

Finally, Wilhelmina turned away from the display of mirrors and looked at her daughter. "You look great, Angelica." The frown on Wilhelmina's face lifted slightly as she added, "Someday, you'll grow up to be a beautiful woman." Angelica saw a small tear begin to roll down her mother's cheek. It was the same look the queen had given her daughter before leaving for a week-long visit to Nezzrin Kingdom two years earlier.

Angelica was able to sense the fear in her mother, so she reached towards the flower on the bed and lifted it. "The jester outside gave this to me." Wilhelmina smiled at the sight of the flower. It was beautiful, and the sight of it did lift her spirits if just for a moment. Still, the happiness looked like a mask to hide the fear and sadness. Angelica brought the rose to her nose again and smelled its beautiful aroma before extending it to her mother. "Now, I'm giving it to you."

The smile on Wilhelmina's face did not grow or shrink, but it changed. Angelica was able to see this change in her mother's expression as the queen reached down and took the rose from Angelica's small hand. The smile was no longer a mask. It was rooted deep in Wilhelmina's soul. The queen quickly fastened the rose to her gown on the left side of her chest. Its bright red color seemed to match the beautiful pattern of red jewels perfectly. After doing this, the queen bent down and kissed her daughter's cheek.

Angelica was pleased with the reaction she got from her mother. As with all children, when her mother was happy, so was she. There was one unsettling thought about this exchange that was hidden deep within Angelica's mind. When she handed the rose to her mother, there was a strange mixture of joy and finality. This stir of feelings seemed offensive to the princess. However, only the very tips of this thought reached the princess's conscious mind before her concentration was shattered.

There was a knock on the door, and when Wilhelmina opened it, she saw Alexander standing on the other side. As they usually did, the three of them walked from the queen's quarters, out the main entrance of the palace, and towards the platform at the front of the courtyard. Although they all went through the same procedures they always did, this time seemed different. There was a tension in their small group that could not be ignored. Angelica detected it and meant to ask either her mother or uncle sometime, but now was not the time. She would save her questions for after the address.

As the sun rose to its highest point in the sky, the usual servant yelled out, "Prince Alexander!" and the prince walked across the platform with his black cape flailing about behind him and the cries of the crowd filling his ears. "Princess Angelica!" There were more cheers from the spectators, but these livelier that the ones for Alexander. Angelica walked until she was standing beside her uncle. Finally, the servant called out, "The ruler of Protecian Kingdom, her royal highness, the Queen Wilhelmina!" The crowd cheered ecstatically as dried bouquets, the best the citizens could find in all the land, were thrown at the platform. The queen walked until she was standing in front of the stone monuments of Protace and Soranace. While she did this, the prince and princess walked from the platform and into the crowd.

It took several minutes for the crowd to get themselves under control, and Wilhelmina made no effort to stop them. This time, rather than to bolster her courage, she was letting them cheer for their own sake. She felt a celebration was in order with the news she planned to tell them today. When the people did calm down, Wilhelmina told them this good news immediately. "By the time I am finished talking with you today, the irrigation system will be completed." There was a unison roar of cheers from the crowd. Once the people were silent again, Wilhelmina continued to tell about the details of using the wells and praised the effort the construction personnel that build them.

Alexander leaned over to his niece and began to whisper to her. "I don't think you'll have to worry about the people being upset with your mother today. She could announce daily executions, and they'll still be cheering her on." The young girl nodded without taking her eyes off the gleaming smile on Wilhelmina's face. "I have some business to attend to. I'll speak to you later." Once again, Angelica nodded, and Alexander disappeared into the mob of cheering people.

While Wilhelmina spoke, Beatrice stood leaning against the exterior wall of the palace. She was watching the crowd carefully to see if Chenrile was to show up. So far, there was no sign of him. Everyone, including the jesters and those behind the food stands, was fully absorbed in Wilhelmina's words. There was nothing to worry about.

Beatrice turned her head to look at Wilhelmina. There was a wide grin on her face, and it felt very good to see it there after so long. Finally, everything was coming together for her, and there was nothing that could pull her down now. With so many people reacting that way, Beatrice saw no reason for alarm. It seemed as though no one would try to harm her regardless of what she may have suspected.

When her personal servant turned her eyes back to the crowd, she began to search through the faces again. As before, she saw several people that she recognized and several others she did not. It would appear that the physician had someplace else to be today rather than listening to Wilhelmina speak. As Beatrice began to turn her head to look back at the queen, she saw something out of the corner of her eye. She immediately looked back at what she saw to make certain. Despite the feelings of calmness, Beatrice now had to act. Chenrile was standing in the center of the crowd listening and watching Queen Wilhelmina as everyone else in the courtyard was doing.

Beatrice began to walk over towards Chenrile rehearsing what she was supposed to say as she did so. The large woman could feel her body shaking with every passing second. There were quite a few people in the way, and the courtyard was densely packed. Trying to get around one person seemed to take forever, and Chenrile just stood still as if no one had any reason to suspect him of any wrong-doing.

Wilhelmina continued talking excitedly with the peasants hanging on her every word. All eyes were staring at her, and she continuously looked back towards them. It seemed as though she was trying to make eye-contact with every one of the citizens in the courtyard on that afternoon. It was a wondrous occasion. Not one of the faces she saw that day looked angry or upset. Everyone appeared to be overflowing with glee.

As her eyes scanned the people in the crowd, they fell upon one face that stood out in particular. Chenrile was standing in the middle of the mob of people staring at the queen. He looked no more or less threatening than anyone else in the courtyard, but Wilhelmina did not trust him just the same. Not after what she learned of him. It did not matter, though. The queen could also see that Beatrice was making her way through the crowd to reach him. It would be unlikely that he could do anything in the time before Beatrice asks him to leave.

When Wilhelmina's face turned away from Chenrile, a shocked look began to fill her eyes. Her words came to a dead stop, and everyone looked on as she became unable to breathe. Whispers began to leap back and forth between people in the crowd. Then, after a second that seemed to last at least ten times as much, everyone saw what the queen had already seen. Their eyes fixed on what had their ruler hypnotized.

A single arrow was flying overhead. It arced gently and gracefully in the sky and began to plummet back towards the ground with increasing speed. Paralyzed with fear and surprise, Wilhelmina was able to only stand there and look at the descending arrow. Its golden tip gleamed in the sunshine as it danced through the air, rushing towards its target. People began to gasp as the arrow fell faster and faster.

Despite all the gasps and frightened whispers and even the sound of her own heart racing, Wilhelmina could not hear anything. All of the sound was drained out of the world at that moment. For the briefest of seconds, there was no kingdom, no citizens hanging on her word, no gas mines, no irrigation system, no drought, not even her daughter. The world was a gold-tipped arrow racing towards her. Everything else seemed to just fade into the background.

Beatrice was right next to Chenrile by this point. After pushing her way through the crowd, she finally reached the physician and was about to raise her hand to his shoulder to get his attention. Then, she heard the gasps of the people surrounding her, including Chenrile. With the exception of Beatrice the entire courtyard saw what was happening. Beatrice turned at the sound of the commotion and looked towards the queen. She was able to see the arrow just before it found its target.

The pointed tip of the arrow soared through Wilhelmina's neck just beneath her chin. Her skin and body offered it no resistance. Half of its length pushed through her flesh before it stopped. The queen tried to scream, but the only sound she could produce was a gravely, hoarse exhale. Her arms began to flail up in a reflex response, trying to find what was causing the agony that was crackling through her body. They were unable to. She looked like a blind woman trying to grope her way through the world. With her arms in midair, Wilhelmina stumbled a few steps back as if trying to escape the pain radiating through her.

No one in the courtyard knew how to react. For the most part, people simply stood still and stared in shocked silence. They could not fathom the idea of someone trying to hurt the queen, especially at a time like this where her popularity was at its height. From the front row of the crowd, a single voice rang out, shattering the silence. The terrified shriek of a frightened young girl: "Mommy!"

That one word resonated for a moment, echoing off the mountain walls. If the people could have gotten any quieter, they would have then. Wilhelmina tried to look towards her daughter, towards the sound of that cry, trying to fill her last moments of life with such a sight of beauty, but her head could not move. The arrow had become a key, once inserted into her body, every muscle locked up. When she did make this effort, blood began to seep out from around the arrow, and a small red trail escaped from her mouth as well. It could only be as a small miracle that she was still able to stand.

With everyone's attention fixed on the queen's staggering movements that accumulated to no more than a foot in any direction, trying to figure out what to do next, no one saw a second arrow being shot into the air. This one remained unnoticed by even Wilhelmina until it struck. It looked identical to the first arrow that had been shot, and whoever fired it was just as invisible. The entire courtyard was fixed on the queen so much more now than ever before that it was impossible to notice anything else.

As if fired by an expert marksman, the second arrow plunged into the base of the rose clipped to Wilhelmina's gown. Its tip tore the flower to pieces before driving itself deep into the queen's chest. Individual rose pedals gently glided to the stone platform. They looked almost like butterflies trying to fly but only able to fall. Soon, they were covered in droplets of blood. The arrow suspended a full six inches in Wilhelmina's chest while remaining in the center of the crushed rose pedals.

Now, Wilhelmina did fall to the ground. First, she slipped down to her knees. While kneeling on the platform, blood began to pump from the wound in her chest so hard that the arrow was moving back and forth with its pressure. After staying in that position for a few seconds, Queen Wilhelmina slowly leaned to her right, and soon she was lying on her side with the two arrows protruding from her. It looked as though she had slipped away to sleep after an exhausting day, but this was a sleep from which she would never wake.

From the middle of the courtyard, a frantic voice began to sound. "Angelica! Angelica!" The crowd began to part, and Alexander ran through the widening gap towards the platform. His black cape was rippling behind him making him appear as if he was an airborne creature with massive wings keeping him skyward. He rushed up to the platform and stopped just short of reaching the stone elevation. He grabbed Angelica and held her to his chest after sparing only a quick glance at the fallen queen. With Angelica in his arms, he leaned closer to the platform and looked at Wilhelmina. "You are going to be okay. Just keep breathing, and you will be okay."

As Alexander leaned there, a guard began to approach. There was a look of absolute guilt on his face as he neared the man who had trained him and dying woman he was supposed to protect. Alexander turned to face the guard with eyes that shown with sympathy but refused to shed a single tear. "Get Chenrile over here right away!" Those horrified and saddened eyes looked briefly again at Wilhelmina and towards the crowd that had become too curious. They were beginning to push against one another to see what was happening. If this were to continue, a riot may soon begin. "And get them out of here," Alexander told the guard without looking at him again.

The prince stood straight again and took a cautious step towards the mob that was massing and growing increasingly unruly in an effort to see what the prince was doing. Soon, everyone had their answer. Angelica was looking over Alexander's shoulder at them with tears flowing down her cheeks. Alexander wanted to remove her from this spectacle, and he began to push his way towards the palace. As he walked, she was yelling, "Mommy! Mommy!" in the same shrill voice that had captured her mother's attention a moment ago. It sounded like she was trying simply to catch her mother's attention yet again, but this time, there would be no reaction. In a minute, the two were out of sight and inside the palace walls. Alexander wanted to spare his niece as much of that sight as possible. It was too late for that, though. She had already seen the worst of it, but Alexander still had to do something.

Beatrice looked back towards Chenrile and saw that he was no longer standing just in front of her. In the dense crowd, she could not him at all anymore. She immediately assumed that he had already started on his way towards the platform when he saw what was happening. There was no way she could find him now, and even if she did, it would be impossible and unwise to send away the royal family's physician when the queen's life was in jeopardy.

Just as Beatrice was thinking these thoughts, Chenrile was walking onto the platform taking the same cleared path as Alexander. He knelt beside Wilhelmina. After placing a hand on her forehead, he began to lift her eyelids to see their reaction to the light. Chenrile looked up at the guard standing beside him. "There is no reaction. The eyes are not moving, and the pupils are not reacting to light." As Chenrile told this to the guard, Wilhelmina's fingers began to move ever so slightly. She formed a tight fist with her last ounce of life trying to get someone to realize that she was still alive. Trying to make someone try to save her. She was trying to scream at the people around her, but no one could hear. Her wind was gone, and her movements far too slight to be seen in that chaos and confusion.

Alexander did not stop running until he was closing the door to Angelica's quarters with the young girl locked inside. There was only one thought coursing through his mind as he informed her to lock the door as soon as it was closed. If Wilhelmina were to die on that platform, that child of only eight years old would be the new queen. She would be the sole ruler of the Protecian Kingdom.

Directly from the hallway of Angelica's room, Alexander began to march back out of the main door of the palace. Through the richly adorned gold and marble passageways, he walked with a much slower stride than before. There was no longer any need for his presence outside, be he felt he should be there. To keep the peace, if nothing more.

There was one occasion when Alexander actually stopped walking altogether for almost a minute. He was passing the portraits of all the former rulers of Protecia. All the way from Protace to Wilhelmina, the faces in paint stared at him, and he was unable to look away from the vacant space just beyond his sister-in-law's representation. No one as young as Angelica had ever ruled the kingdom. He did not know if she was up to the task. The fact that gnawed even more at Alexander's mind was that it was his responsibility as next in line to the throne to see if she could handle the job. There was an instance from the kingdom's history when the throne was robbed from its rightful heir due to his young age. Alexander feared that he may have to do the same to his own niece.

When he finally began to move again, Alexander walked directly to the courtyard without stopping. The sight was not a good one when he arrived. Chenrile was standing upright on the speaking platform while the guards paced around the keep the courtyard clear. Beatrice was sitting on the dried out grass, which was now vacant, leaning against the elevated edge of the platform. Tears were rolling down her cheeks. There was a look of frustration on her face as she held back the rest of the tears as best as she possibly could.

Wilhelmina had not moved since Alexander had left. Two arrows were still protruding from her, and they were keeping her from rolling onto her stomach and possibly off the platform. They were anchoring her in place almost as if she were a life-sized doll propped up for a presentation of some sort. Her eyes were closed, and her mouth and nose were covered with a dark red smear. Blood was no longer pumping out of her wounds. It was seeping at a slow and steadily decreasing rate. Almost identical to how the wells in the kingdom looked when they began to run dry. The remnants of a rose still clung to her chest almost as if trying to revive her.

As Alexander approached the platform using the path he usually took when he heard a servant announce him to the crowd, Chenrile ran to meet him. The physician tried to speak to him before he approached Wilhelmina. While placing an arm around Alexander's shoulders, the physician began to whisper to him. All the others heard were mumbles and slight changes in voice. The words were lost amidst a flow of monotones. During this whole time, Alexander nodded as if this is what he expected.

Several guards gathered around the body and began to carry it away from the palace to the far side of the courtyard. There were a series of crypts there that dated back to when Protace ruled. All people who had ruled the kingdom for any span of time were laid to rest in one of those tombs. As they filled up, more were built to accommodate the new rulers. The body would be prepared there, and finally sealed into a chamber within the crypt after a viewing the next day. That is how it was done with King Frederick, Wilhelmina's late husband, a distant descendent of Protace. It was only nine years ago that he was laid to rest, and soon the queen would be joining him in the next chamber.

After the body was carried away, people began to drift from the courtyard one at a time. Beatrice asked Alexander where he had placed Angelica, and after telling her, she left to talk with the young girl much like how she had consoled the now-dead queen barely an hour ago. The coronation for the new queen will be immediately following her mother's funeral, as was the tradition. Chenrile offered apologies and sympathies before he left, and finally Alexander walked away from the courtyard leaving it vacant and deserted. Aside from the sounds that still continued to echo there, it was as silent as the tomb where Wilhelmina would be laid to rest the following day.

CHAPTER NINE

The Burial and Transfer of Power

T he sun set on the day and the night drew cold and dark. Every fifth torch was lit in the hallway as customary when most were sleeping. Enough light to see but not enough to be bright. There was no movement within the palace. At least for the time being, the kingdom's spirit died alongside Queen Wilhelmina. Life had come to a stop that evening. The death of someone as beloved as Queen Wilhelmina did more than sadden the people of the kingdom. It devastated them, and the depression spread like wildfire.

Eventually, one soul began moving through the corridors of the palace. Angelica was walking through the dimly lit hallways with the words Beatrice had said to her still ringing in her ears. The young girl knew that her mother was dead, and she knew how it happened. She also was aware of what that made her. More than simply an orphan. For the moment she was still Princess Angelica, but in less than twelve hours, she would be ascended to queen of the Protecian Kingdom. Still, she was filled with the fear of what would happen now. Her mother was murdered in front of her and hundreds of other people. Now, she was to assume that role: the power, the responsibility, and the risks. These were fears that could not be sedated by someone such as Beatrice.

After walking short distance, Angelica stopped and faced the door to her left. Slowly, she approached it and began to knock.

"Alexander? Are you in there?" There was no response. "I need to talk to someone, and you are the only one I can trust with what I have to say. You are the only one who never lied to me." The young queen knocked again, and still there was no response from behind the door to Alexander's quarters. There were not even the sounds of movement, or the discrete sounds of one shifting in bed to find out what the noise was outside. No light came from beneath the door. The room appeared to be deserted.

Angelica soon found herself leaning against the wall beside the door as if it was the only thing to keep her standing. "It seems as if the responsibility I was wondering about has found me. I wish I could say it had not." Her breaths became louder and almost spastic. Tears began to form in her eyes, and despite her attempts to blink them away, they found their way to the surface. "I do not know what to do, and you are the only one that can help me." The tears began to spill past her cheeks and formed rivers along her neck. Her voice began to break up, but Angelica continued to speak. Her voice soon rose to a shout. "I have to talk to someone, and I have no one else to turn to! I am scared!"

Her last sentence hung in the air for a second, and she could almost hear people in other rooms start to stir to see what the problem was. No one was really sure how Angelica would react to the day's tragedy. Still, there was no sound of movement from the one bedroom she was interested in. Alexander's room was completely silent. With nothing else to do, Angelica took a step back from the wall and wrapped her hand around the door handle to his room. As the young girl began to push, the icy coldness of the metal handle seemed to bore its way into her hand like it was being carried by tiny termites, but still, the door did not budge. It had been locked from the inside, meaning that Alexander must be inside the room. How else could it have been locked? Angelica removed her hand and looked at the door handle. In the dim light she could see how shiny the metal was right where she had touched it, but nowhere else. To confirm this, she looked down at her hand, and saw a thick layer of dust sticking to her palm. With the confusion building inside her, she ran one finger along the top surface of the handle where she hand not yet touched and saw the same result. Angelica had to conclude that this door was not used in quite some time.

Angelica started at the dimly glowing light reflecting off the wiped areas of the door handle. Then, her eyes shifted to the layer of dust clinging to her hand. It did not make any sense. If this door had not been used in so long that the handle was actually covered in dust, then where was Alexander sleeping at night?

With it evident that Alexander was not going to console her, Angelica turned and walked back to her own quarters. She remained there, lying terrified on her bed, for hours before falling asleep. This was a deep and dreamless sleep. Angelica almost did not want to wake from it, but soon, morning came, and her coronation day was upon her.

When the young queen rose from her bed in the morning, there was an unfamiliar sound filling the air. It was echoing from all around her as though it originated from the very walls of the palace. Mixed with it were screams and cries from all around. Angelica immediately thought that the palace was being raided. In past years, long before she or even her parents were born, such an event did happen with devastating results. After a moment of panic, she started to realize that these sounds were not of terror or fear. The screams she heard were of joy.

Angelica rose from the bed and looked around her quarters. Her mind was still trying to catch up with her body and awaken from its sleep. She knew there was something that had saddened her the previous day, and it took a moment for her remember what it was. Finally, the memories came back like a flood of poison filling her veins. The sight of her mother dying only a few feet from her. The look of terror in her eyes as she tried to look upon her daughter as if to apologize for abandoning her. The sounds of the crowd that bore witness to this horror. Alexander scooping her up and bringing her to safety and then being nowhere to be found later that night. Angelica wanted to crawl back into bed and not leave for the day, but she knew she could not. Especially not with that noise surrounding her.

With a deep sigh, Angelica walked towards her window and looked outside. First, all she saw were people running through the courtyards and around the palace. They were laughing and shouting in joy. It seemed to be the happiest day in their lives. For an instant, Angelica wanted to call the guards over to arrest all of them, although she had never made such a demand on her authority before. Behavior like this so soon after her mother was slain is inexcusable, and Angelica was not going to let them get away with that. Her immediate reaction was that they were celebrating the death of the queen or possibly the new ruler accepting the throne. Then she saw the real reason for their excitement.

It was raining. The skies had opened up and rain was pouring towards the ground. Puddles were developing on the dirt and dry grass that was could not absorb it fast enough. Angelica watched as people celebrated the end of the drought by running through the downpour and splashing in the huge puddles. They danced in the rainfall with their clothes soaked through with water. It was almost as if the sight and feel of the cold water on their skin made them drunk with elation.

Angelica turned away from the window and began to dress in her simple clothes. The formal gown she had worn the day before lay crumpled in the corner of the room where she had thrown it what seemed like a hundred years ago. As she finished dressing, there was a knock on her door, and Angelica walked over to open it. Beatrice was on the other side, and like everyone else, she seemed very happy. "Did you see outside yet? It's raining!" Angelica simply nodded and walked back into her quarters holding the door open for Beatrice to follow. "The drought is over now. That is one big problem you won't have to worry about now that the kingdom is yours. Aren't you happy?" Beatrice waited a few more seconds before adding,

"People are saying that Queen Wilhelmina's first order of business in the afterlife was to end the drought. She'll always be watching over us now."

The young girl did not stop walking until she reached the window again. With the murky light illuminating her face, she turned back to Beatrice. "The irrigation system was a waste of time and resources. It wasn't needed, and my mother died for that useless project." Angelica looked back outside and continued to watch the people dancing in the rain like fools already realizing that what she said made little or no sense.

"I can assure you that the irrigation system was not a wasted endeavor. There may very easily be other problems in the future that would need such a system." Beatrice stood next to Angelica and looked out the window as well. "Your mother was killed by someone who was very angry, and that person most likely would have killed her whether or not she pursued such a project. She wasn't killed for an irrigation system. It's very possible we'll never know why someone decided to take her away from us, but you need to remember this always. The only thing your mother loved more than the Protecian Kingdom was you."

Angelica turned towards Beatrice and looked at her for some time. "We can try to find out why this happened." As a puzzled look filled Beatrice's face, Angelica walked towards a small desk along the wall of her room. Beatrice followed behind her waiting to see what she was planning on doing next. "If we try to find who killed my mother, then we will know, and we will be able to arrest them as well."

As she sat down in the chair beside Angelica, Beatrice spoke very calmly. "I don't think that would be a very good idea. There's no way to prove exactly who did that. No one saw anything happen. We were all taken by surprise. No one knew what to do. Without someone having seen part of what happened, we will have no way of proving any theory we may come up with." Beatrice stopped for a moment. With deep sigh she added, "You have to remember, you're the queen now. People are going to need you to show support for their immediate needs rather than spend every waking moment on a manhunt. If something surfaces, we can pursue that, but the people do not need a ruler that will be caught up on vengeance."

Slowly, Angelica nodded. It would not be a good idea to start her reign as queen with an in-depth investigation of her mother's assassination that could tear into the personal lives of everyone in the kingdom. Just because it was raining now did not mean that a new problem would not appear in a matter of weeks or even days. It would be these problems that would need her attention. The world grew so largely out of proportion over night that Angelica could hardly keep track of it anymore. Abandoning that search would mean one less thing to concern herself with.

The morning passed on in a similar fashion as every other morning. Angelica was nearly terrified to leave her quarters, however, but soon her ventured out to find Alexander. This time, he was in the hallway near his quarters, and did little more than reinforce what Beatrice had just told her. As the day was getting on, Angelica was called back into her quarters by Beatrice to prepare for her mother's viewing and funeral, which would be followed by her induction into the station of queen and ruler of the kingdom.

She dressed in the same gowns she wore to any public address. This time she was dressing herself, though, much like she had done the day before. Wilhelmina was not standing in front of the arrays of mirrors to make sure she looked okay this time, however. There was only a single, small mirror inside of Angelica's quarters, and she barely looked at it once.

Within an hour, Wilhelmina's body was sealed in her section of the crypt. She had been dressed in her formal gowns and her injuries were concealed masterfully. The royal family and high dignitaries were in the crypt to bid her farewell while nearly the rest of the kingdom gathered outside. Once Wilhelmina was sealed away next to Frederick, there did seem to be a sense of serenity in the kingdom. Based on the stories Angelica had heard, her parents had always been madly in love with one another and now were together again for all eternity.

Almost immediately afterwards, the red jewels, which had come to symbolize leadership in the kingdom, were draped over Angelica. In years past, one of the elders of the kingdom performed this task, but the panel of elders had been disbanded for some time now. It was Prince Alexander who placed the burdensome title of queen and ruler upon his niece, Angelica. She bowed, but did not say a word. Everyone was looking at her, and all she could think of was that one of those smiling and excited faces had killed her mother exactly one day ago. One of these people, standing out in the rain to watch Angelica become their queen was responsible for everything that had happened.

CHAPTER TEN

The Queen and Kingdom in Grief

With that public appearance completed, Angelica returned to the palace for the first time as its queen, and she did not leave the safety of its walls for weeks. This was very reminiscent of her mother's first weeks ruling the kingdom, and since power was always assumed through someone's death, the first weeks of many new reigns began the same way. Misery gripped Angelica and held her down so tightly she was barely able to move. It felt as though there was a leash around, and every passing day it got tighter and tighter. As the weeks passed, Angelica felt unable to move beyond the palace doors, then beyond the royal family's private corridor, then beyond her own quarters, which had been relocated to the ruler's quarters, and finally beyond the boundaries of her bed. Soon, she became a prisoner of what she was still referring to as her mother's bed, but slowly starting to feel as comfortable within the folds of its fur blankets as she did within her old bed down the hall.

The world appeared to be darker than it normally was. The sun seemed to shine for less and less time each day, and the bright colors that usually surrounded Angelica were starting to dull and turn to gray. People were not as kind, and there was an odd coldness in the air Angelica had no way of explaining. Indifference became her ruling force, and things that would have normally made her ecstatic with joy now only brought the faintest of nods from the new queen.

Life had become an exercise in getting to the next day for no reason other than it was the only option available.

There were days when the grief subsided ever so slightly, and Angelica would make an attempt to leave the palace. Then, the fear would take over, and she could feel the world spinning under her feet. Trees and mountains like they were swaying in a sickening dance with one another and the sun seemed to be laughing at her behind its veil of dark gray clouds. Soon, she could feel the leash tightening a little more around her neck, and her world got a little bit smaller. When people would pass in the halls of the palace, people whom she had known her entire life, or at least that's what she assumed from their voices, she would cower away. Soon, she started only to feel safe on the side of the bed closest to stone wall, and even the thought of rolling over sent chills throughout her body.

Nearly a month and a half passed before Beatrice saw Angelica again. The young queen would have been concerned about her governess's, or more accurately now, her servant's wellbeing, if it were not for the sound of her voice outside the heavy wooden door on an almost hourly basis. When they finally laid eyes on each other again, the meeting took place in the queen's quarters, and took place only at Beatrice's insistence. When the queen finally agreed to speak to her caregiver, it was not an optimistic meeting.

Beatrice walked into the queen's quarters, as she had done countless times before, but this time could feel the damp cloud of depression as she passed the threshold. This was far worse than Wilhelmina's feelings after the death of Frederick, or even Frederick's after the death of him mother, Queen Patricia. The room was in a clutter, and the young queen looked disheveled. This meeting took place after several weeks of absolute isolation, isolation at the insistence of the Queen Angelica, so there was no one entering the room to clean up after her. The instant that Beatrice walked into the room, after begging and then insisting from the other side of the door, she began to straighten up the mess while speaking. Regardless of title or authority, the woman that raised you will always win in the long run, and Beatrice knew this all too well. It was a few minutes of casual small talk, and very general tidying up before Beatrice's eyes fell upon the desk in the corner of the room.

Spread out on its surface was a drawing. Childish in nature, but still clearly identifiable. This was a diagram of the courtyard and speaking platform just outside of the palace. Even crude sketches of the sculptures of Protace and Soranace were present and labeled. There was even an arrow to indicate where the speaker would be standing during a public address, as well as where the remaining royal family stood at various points in the ceremony, numerically labeled by order of position, and where the servant who announced them would stand. There were indicators as to where different tables were set up on the day of Wilhelmina's death, labeled with what food or craft was prepared there if no vendor's name was available. Beatrice finally looked up at the queen who had taken an awkward position leaning on the side of the bed while staring out the window. "What is this? This is what you've been doing in here for the past month?" Beatrice began to walk towards Angelica who still refused to turn to look at her. Either out of shame or quite the opposite. There were past rulers who felt such a sense of pride that they would never look directly at a servant, but Beatrice hoped with every fiber of her being that Angelica would not become one of them. For the first time since she entered the room, the servant stopped cleaning. "I thought you and I had agreed that you wouldn't actively pursue your mother's assassination. Nothing can come of it. It doesn't matter how many diagrams you draw and study. Without the possibility of someone confessing, there wouldn't be any way to figure out who killed your mother."

Angelica remained silent. Her eyes were locked on the grounds outside her window looking into the pale sky. Even after the rain had subsided, everything looked dismal and bleak. There was no color in the world, and it felt as though the kingdom had died with

Wilhelmina. Finally, Angelica tore her eyes away from the window and looked at Beatrice. The sight of that servant's face filled Angelica with a feeling of warmth. For an instant, everything was okay. She almost forgot that Beatrice was here to attempt reprimanding her.

In the pale, dead light reaching into the room, Angelica walked towards the center of her quarters. She walked until she was right next to Beatrice and said, "I know you believe there is nothing I can do. Still, I could not keep going if I did not try." Angelica sat at the desk and rolled up the diagram of the courtyard. "I want to ask you one thing, and then I promise you will never hear another word from me about my mother. This is very important. I need to know, for my own safety, if my mother felt someone was not to be trusted. Did she think someone was going to try to kill her?"

"There are people already looking into this," Beatrice pleaded. "You have so many other things to be concerned with right now. I can assure you, all possible steps are being taken. All possible avenues are being explored. You have a kingdom to run and can't be taking your attentions off of that!"

For a moment, there was silence in the room. Beatrice was as scared as Angelica had been for the last month and a half. She had never spoken to any of the royal family this way, and never considered speaking to the ruling member like this.

When she replied, Angelica's voice was tiny and scared. "I cannot know for sure that everything is getting done until I am the one doing it." There was a contempt in her voice, and the young queen hating herself for speaking those words while they were still forming on her tongue. "Please, answer my question."

Beatrice walked towards the queen's bed and sat on the down mattress with a sigh. This was a question she knew would have to be answered eventually. "I don't know the exact reason why she feared him, or if she feared him at all. The day of the...the address, your mother asked me to make sure he wasn't in the courtyard. All she said was that she found out something about his past, and she said that she didn't want him there. As it ends up, it's a good thing that he was there. He was, at least, able to try saving her." Beatrice looked at Angelica who was anxiously staring back at her. Her eyes were intense as if her whole life was dependent on the next words that would have been uttered in that room. Finally, Beatrice said, "The physician, Chenrile. I did notice him there partway through the address. As I was walking over to him, the arrows started flying."

Angelica stood from her chair as if she were going to march from her room to the guard's station at that very moment and order the arrest of Chenrile. Beatrice's voice was drowned out by Angelica's fury, and finally she had to repeat what she was trying to say. Beatrice was now yelling, "It wasn't him!" Angelica stopped and turned back to look at Beatrice. Now, she spoke quietly since she already had the queen's attention. "I was watching him the whole time he was there. He's the one person I can truly say did not shoot those arrows. There was no way. My eyes were on him the entire time."

With tears in her eyes, Angelica walked towards the bed and sat beside Beatrice again. The woman began to stroke the queen's hair, and the young girl started to calm down. "If you'd like, I can do the same thing during your addresses. Make sure he's not in the courtyard if that would make you feel better. Feel safer." The tears had begun to dry on Angelica's cheeks, and no new ones were forming. "Would you like me to do that?"

"Addresses?" Angelica sat up straight and looked at Beatrice. Her eyes were filled with a mixture of anger and fear. It was as if the very mention of that word was insulting to her. "I am not going to make any addresses. I cannot bear to do that. What if that person is still there? What if he wants to kill me next? I am not going to take the risk of getting up in front of all those people to talk to them. I just cannot."

Beatrice looked at the small girl, and Angelica looked back. As mature as she always seemed, Angelica never looked more like a child than she did at that moment. It made Beatrice wonder what ever happened to her actual childhood. It was robbed from her at the moment she was born for betterment of kingdom. Beatrice supposed that was the way it always had been done, and there was no way that tradition was going to stop now.

With the pale light of the gloomy day shining in behind her, Beatrice looked like some kind of apparition. A creature that was better than a human can aspire to be, almost god-like in a way. "That is the reason that I wanted to talk to you." Angelica's eyes turned curious. The carved posts at the corners of the bed were inexplicably radiant in the dim light, and Angelica tried to reach for one to balance herself. It was almost as if she knew something was coming, and there was a great possibility it was something that she did not want to hear. "The people want you to address them. It has been a month and half since they have seen you, and they are starting to grow distant from you and your post. Soon, Alexander may have to fill the void you are leaving. If that happens, he may become king, and you will no longer be queen."

As if she was slapped in the face, Angelica jumped from the bed in a rage. Her blonde hair began to swirl around her as she began to pace the floor so fast that she was nearly jogging. "How can he do that? I am the queen." No one realized how closely her words mimicked her mother's in that moment, and no one would want to understand how she was headed down that same destructive path. "He cannot take that away from me because he does not like the way I run the kingdom." The pacing kept up for another minute, and then she stopped suddenly. "He cannot do that." As if that settled everything, Angelica took a deep breath, and prepared to move onto the next topic.

Beatrice simply stared at Angelica for a moment. The young queen's set facial expression showed that she was finished speaking and was now expecting Beatrice to start explaining some equally deniable fact. Beatrice had no intention of changing the subject, though. After a deep breath, Beatrice calmly said, "A similar incident happened in the history of the kingdom. When I began to hear rumors of the growing unease with you going around the land

and even inside the palace, I went to the library and researched it in the archives. It happened about seventy years ago, during the reign of King Jonathan. The conditions in the kingdom were quite bad, and a riot began."

CHAPTER ELEVEN

Robbed of the Throne

Screams rose up from the guards at the main entrance to the palace of years earlier. Some stayed at their posts while most ran. No matter how well trained someone is, when faced with his own mortality, no one can predict what will happen. A mob of twenty-five men on horseback was storming the palace. Any of the guards that stood their ground at the palace entrance were met with an onslaught of battleaxes, spikes maces, and swords. Blood was already spilling across the marble threshold when the first of the horsemen rode its mount right through the main entrance and into the first gold and marble corridor.

The exquisite ornamentation was slowly becoming spattered in blood as more guards and palace servants fell under the mob's weapons. The horses' hooves splashed through the accumulating puddles of blood, royal blood, Protace's blood, on the palace floors as the entire mob filed indoors. It glistened as the radiant sunlight beamed through the open palace door. From above, the fresco of Protace just idly watched on as the bodies of his descendants and their servants fell in these sacred hallways. All around there were the sounds of scampering feet, terrified screams, and the constant drone of hooves on the marble. The horsemen were making their way through the palace.

As more men on horseback followed, the leading horseman rode under the mural of Protace building his bridge. The image had seventy years of wear missing from the one that Wilhelmina and Angelica had been used to marveling at. The horseman did not notice, though. His mind was set on one thing: finding as many members of the royal family as he can.

With fury as their only guide, the horsemen spit up and rode throughout the palace swinging their weapons besides the animals they were mounted upon. The few servants who saw this spectacle and managed to get away were shouting, "Save the royal family! Warn them! They must hide!" As the servants raced down the halls yelling their plea, the horsemen ran after them to kill them swiftly.

One by one, the first members of the royal family were found hiding in closets and trying to make their way into secret passageways to safety. One by one, falling axes, maces, and swords slaughtered them. One by one, the more distant members of the royal family began to die. One by one, the horsemen were getting closer to their real target.

King Jonathan, his queen, and their children had been warned and were hiding as best as they could with such short notice. Most of the avenues of escape were already compromised by the mob that invaded the palace, but there were still a few ways to safety. If they got to them in time.

While the horsemen continued their search, the royal guards began to fill the palace from their stations throughout the kingdom. Arrows were slung into the air, but they simply bounced off the metal of the horsemen's armor. These assassins attacked the guards, but not before watching their movements. They were smart. By observing the direction that the royal guards were running towards, they were able to narrow down their search for the royal family. A palace filled with corridors and hidden passages was slowly being narrowed to only a very few options.

Riding in the new direction, the horsemen knocked the ornate sconces from the walls with their weapons. Jewels scattered onto the floor and rolled across the marble and through the puddles of blood that were streaming from every direction. The flames from the torches gave off explosions of sparks as they were trampled by the raging horses. While the fire scattered before burning out, the horses became more enraged and began to charge fast away from the flames and down the hallways.

The horseman in the lead was able to hear the screams of fear in the distance. It was almost like an aphrodisiac to him. A gleam came to his eyes as he looked down the hallway where the loudest screams had originated. They were drawing closer to the ruling part of the family. Closer to the ones they wanted to kill. In the flickering light and with the clicks of hooves on the ground, victory was nearly theirs.

Suddenly, a series of three doors opened on both sides of the hallway, and a flood of royal guards spilled in. Within seconds, they were kneeling on the bloody marble, assembling to defend their monarch. They fired arrows skillfully to the horsemen, hitting just between the helmets and body armor. As blood pulsed from their necks, the assassins began to fall to the ground, leaving their horses to run confused and aimlessly throughout the palace. Several of the guards were trampled, and others received blows from countless weapons hurled at them. Still, they stayed their ground and fought, only to be eliminated one at a time as the horsemen had done to the royalty the found so far. By the time the enraged mob reached the source of the screams, only a single assassin was left on horseback. The others were lying on the ground, dead assassin lying next to dead guard.

The lone remaining horseman rode his blood-soaked steed towards the last door in the hallway. With a scream of triumph, he kicked his mount so it would rear up and kick in the last door. The heavy wood stood no chance against the weight of the horse and rider. While its hinges tore from the walls, it swung open hard enough to split the wood. The man on horseback ducked as he rode through the shower of splinters into the candlelit room.

King Jonathan stood draped in a purple robe with white fur trim and strings of red jewels swinging from it. At his side, his queen was standing in a red gown. Tears were flowing from her face. Behind them, their two princesses and one prince stood nervously in a huddle looking through the sliver of space between their parents' bodies. Jonathan fell to his knees and looked up with his bearded face. "Please, spare us. You will be set free, and never harassed by a single guard under my command. As long as I live, you will never be harmed."

The horseman walked the animal carefully into the room another few feet, and the five people, the highest in the royal family, backed up, the king still on his knees, matching the animal's steps. As he approached the middle of the room, the splintering door swung shut again. There was a loud and resonating creak as the door closed on its twisted hinges. Another guard was hiding behind it, and now he was aiming an arrow directly at the rioter's throat.

As it ended up, the guard's fast movements were just a bit too slow. In the time it took him to aim the arrow, the assassin managed to turn his horse and charge at him. With one swing of his a battle-axe, the airborne arrow was batted to the ground and the guard's arm was severed at the shoulder. The stump that remained of the limb spurted blood across the room, covering the assassin and the royal family alike. Surprisingly, no one screamed. While the guard was reeling in shock and pain, the severed limb fell on top of the failed bow and arrow twitching momentarily before laying still.

While the horseman was watching the guard grab the ragged stump of flesh protruding from his torso, he felt a mixture of cold metal and hot blood hit his waistline. It was a strange sensation, and for a moment, he was not sure what it could mean. As the rioter turned back towards the room, he saw King Jonathan standing beside him holding a dagger in the space between the horseman's body and leg armor. Whatever moment of pain there was soon washed away by white-hot rage, and the rioter kicked the king away. Losing his stamina, the middle-aged man fell to the ground in a flail of purple cloth. The rioter made his horse rear up again and stomp down hard. The assassin could feel the brief hesitation before his mount's hoof found its way to the ground. Beneath him, the king's skull crushed and thick, red stew began to run out.

With elation, the horseman turned back to the remaining royal family, pulling the dagger from his waist as he did so. Finally, the queen screamed at the sight of her husband's death. The sound could have shattered glass. During her husband's final act of desperation, she had managed to get the children towards the window on the far side of the room, but the now her emotions got the best of her. Watching her husband trampled to death made her freeze in before getting her family to safety. While she was screaming and the children were trying to hide behind the folds of her gown, the assassin rode his horse over to the huddled royalty with the king's bloody dagger in his hand. Without even slowing the horse's stride, he slid the blade into her right eye and silenced her screaming forever. She made a sound oddly reminiscent of a winding down clock as she drifted towards the mosaic-tiled floor, her tears mixing with blood.

After the queen died, the horseman took only a moment to revel in his joy. Through their policies, King Jonathan and his wife had inadvertently destroyed his own life. The act of killing them did not feel as good as he had hoped, but there was no stopping now. The assassin made his horse rear up again and stomp down on the smallest child in the center of the huddled crowd. The young princess fell in a dead heap under the hooves of the horse just as her killer slammed the battle-axe into the skull of the older princess. Its weight alone nearly split her head in two. With only the young prince left, the horseman raised the battle-axe again. This time when it was high in the air, he saw the injured guard out of the corner of his eye. He had actually gotten to his feet and walked up to the horseman while he was occupied with the royal family. With his face and body streaked in blood, he used his remaining arm to grab the fallen arrow he had cast at the horseman. The guard was holding it like a dagger, high into the air. The horseman began to turn just in time to see the guard force the fallen arrow into his throat. From within the man's helmet, a scream was drowned out by the gurgling sound of blood. Red rivers were spilling from around the arrow as the horseman brought down the battle axe down on the guard's shoulder. With momentum and his weakened state against him, the horseman fell off the animal and tumbled on top of the dead guard.

The young prince stood and stared in awe, too frightened to move. A single tear rolled down his cheek as he took a careful step towards the fallen horsemen. This man had killed his entire family. This man had tried to kill him. As the prince walked passed him on the way to the door, he stopped, almost hypnotized by the sight of death surrounding him. A sight he had been shielded from until this day. While staring at his father's corpse, he was unable to see the fallen horseman reach up and pull the arrow from his own neck. When a new stream of blood sprayed out, the prince realized what was happening and turned to run. As soon as his back was turned, the rioter slammed the bloody arrow into the base of the prince's skull. The young prince stumbled a few more steps before falling to the ground as well.

It took the rest of that day and the entire next day to sort out the extent of what had happened. Bodies were identified and rounded up. Burial plans were made for Jonathan to be placed in the crypt while the others who did not hold a position of leadership in the kingdom would be buried in a cemetery farther away from the palace. Closets were searched for anyone that was hiding and secret passages were uncovered and searched for any last survivors.

While looking in one of these closets, an infant was found. He was screaming in a linen closet. Far back on the bottom shelf behind a stack of tablecloths, he was laying wrapped in a towel and screaming so loudly his tears nearly chocked him. When the servant found him in that closet, she could only imagine his nursemaid tucking him away in there and stacking the tablecloths in front of him to hide and muffle his screams. Also upon finding the body, the servant knew there would be great difficulty in the time ahead of him. There was a brief temptation to simply kill the infant right then and there to possibly save the kingdom from the confusion and risk of revolution that lay ahead. The servant resisted this. Judging from the bodies that had already been identified, this infant was to be king.

All of the members of the immediate royal family had been killed. In total, nearly a third of the previously living people that shared Protace's blood were dead in some room of the palace. After the pedigree of the royal family was studied, it was discovered that the eight-month-old infant was the rightful ruler of the kingdom.

The burial of the dead members of royalty took place the next day, but a new ruler was not crowned. There was a great discussion among the remaining members of the royal family and the kingdom's elders about what should be done next. At this meeting, it was decided that the infant child, named Victor, would not take the throne at this time. The next heir in line, his cousin, Elizabeth, would become a temporary queen. She was only fifteen years old herself, but it was considered much better than the infant who would otherwise rule. It was decided that Elizabeth would be the ruling queen until Victor reached an age where he would be able to successfully rule the kingdom. Then, Elizabeth would turn over the rule of Protecia to him.

Fourteen years passed, and during this whole time, Elizabeth ruled. The people appreciated her kindness and apparent caring for them. However, they also kept a careful eye on Victor, who grew up looking towards Queen Elizabeth as a role model. The prince waited anxiously for his fifteenth birthday, the age it was previously decided he would begin his rule, to arrive. It was thought that since Elizabeth was able to successfully rule the kingdom at the age of fifteen, Victor should assume his rightful role at that age as well.

This did not happen though. On the eve of his birthday, Victor met with Elizabeth, who now had two children of her own. With her oldest boy, Philip, playing beside them and her youngest daughter, Jennifer, sleeping on her shoulder, Victor stated, "I am turning fifteen tomorrow, and I believe that I am now able to rule." There was little reaction from Elizabeth aside from her patient nodding. She was waiting for this conversation for years. "Was it not decided that when I come of age, I will assume the role of king as I was meant to? All the ledgers say that is what was decided after the riots."

Elizabeth simply placed her free hand on Victor's shoulder. Jennifer cooed slightly with the shift of her mother's body. With a deep sigh, she said, "Victor, it would be better for the people and for you if I remained ruling for my life as any other ruler of the kingdom. For fifteen years, the people have been looking to me as their queen, their leader, and they would not want to turn to someone else now." Elizabeth removed her hand from Victor's shoulder and absently patted her daughter's back. Victor placed his fidgeting hand on the dining room table, where this meeting was taking place. With the chandelier burning above them, she continued, "Also, you would be hurt if your rule began now. As I said, the people are used to my rule, and they will continue to see me as their ruler even after you are named king. You will make policies, and they would come to me, a princess, to ask my opinion of them. It would almost be as though you were not even there."

There was a moment of silence that seemed to scream to Victor. He could almost hear the pleading cried of the people butchered within these very walls fifteen years ago. The people whose deaths caused this whole situation. Victor stood from his chair, and muttered, "I understand," as he began to walk from the dining room. He passed by Elizabeth's son, Philip, who was still running in circles around the table, and then all that was left in front of him was the door.

As Victor opened the door to leave, Elizabeth called from behind him, "Victor!" He stopped and turned to face the queen. "The situations I described to you are serious ones that should be considered gravely. However, they are irrelevant when the kingdom is changing rulers anyway." Victor began to walk back to the table as Elizabeth's eyes fell carefully on Philip who was still playing off in his own world. "My husband died of illness a little more than one year ago. You know that. He cannot fight to rule after me, which is why I believe I can resolve this situation with some ease." By this time, Victor was sitting beside Elizabeth at the table again. His full attention was on the words coming from her mouth. The words that would spell out his future and his destiny. "After my death, you can restore your birthright and become king. You will be next in line for the throne after me. This way, there would not be any problems with changing a leader at an unnatural time, and you will hold the throne like you were meant to." Victor agreed to this deal, and began to wait patiently once more for what he was always entitled to.

Victor thought it morbid to so anxiously wait for the queen to die. Also, he felt that he was not the first to feel this way in the kingdom's long history, but possibly he was feeling it more intensely than his predecessors. He should have been ruling already, and that made the years seem to pass much more slowly.

Another seventeen years drifted by while Elizabeth ruled. The last three of those years, she ruled in diminishing health. Queen Elizabeth had been diagnosed by the royal physician of those days, a man named Bennet, as having an abnormality of the stomach, which grew increasingly painful during her life. During the last six months of her rule, Philip would actually try to help his mother stand on the platform while delivering her public addresses. Soon, as all expected would happen, Elizabeth died in her sleep.

During those seventeen years, Victor did more than wait for the queen to die, however. He married and began a family. His wife bore him two sons and a daughter, the first of which was born only a year after he had made that arrangement with Elizabeth concerning his eventual rise to the throne. By the time Elizabeth finally died, his eldest child, a son named Carlton, had married and was expecting his own first child. As Victor looked at his ever-growing family, all he could think of was that one day they would be ruling the kingdom after him.

The evening after the death of Queen Elizabeth, Victor walked into the palace's dining room, much in the same way he had on the eve of his fifteenth birthday. He spoke to Philip for hours. During that time, he discussed everything that had led up to the situation they were currently in. The prince looked at Victor, and simply said, "I will have to review the details of this arrangement during the evening. I am certain that my mother would have kept records of everything you just mentioned. Tomorrow morning, I will contact you, and if you are correct, by midday, you will be the king."

Victor thanked Philip and walked from the dining room feeling triumphant. He would finally hold the position that he was meant to hold. It had been robbed from him thirty-two years ago, and it finally seemed that he would be made the king of Protecia by the next day as he was meant to be.

That night, everything changed. In the darkness, people who appeared to be bandits burst into the remote hallway of the palace where Victor and his family lived. Their screams for help went unanswered by the guards or the servants as each family member was bound, blindfolded, gagged, and carried from the palace. Soon, Victor, his wife, his children, and his daughter-in-law were loaded onto a wagon.

It felt like this ride lasted for hours. While the wagon bumped and rattled over varying types of terrain, Victor sat silently praying to Protace for their lives. As the trip progressed, the air grew colder and windier while the sounds of the woods got louder. Crickets and the screams of wild animals filled their ears as they rolled along in the back of the wagon, blind and scared of what was around them. There was some talking among the bandits driving them, but their exact words were drowned out by the beating of hooves on the ground and the monotonous sound the wagon rolling along.

After they had started to give up hope, the wagon stopped abruptly, and within five minutes, everyone was thrown onto the ground. Victor, being the first one pushed from the back of the wagon was able to free himself from the ropes on his arms and the blindfold covering his eyes before the wagon got far at all. In the instant before the rickety wooden structure was dragged into the darkness by horses, Victor was able to recognize it as one of the royal carriages. The all too familiar Protecian seal was carved into the back of the wagon. Those were not bandits, but the royal guards that had kidnapped them and dragged them away into the darkness.

After freeing the rest of his family from their restraints, Victor looked around. He recognized where he was but only vaguely from distant memories. It was far from anyplace he was meant to be. The royal guards carried them far into the Nezzrin Kingdom, away from Protecia. More likely than not, the guards that were stationed to protect the border separating these lands were instructed to kill them before readmitting them back into the Protecian Kingdom. Even if that was not the severity of their orders, one fact still remained. They were banished forever.

It took some time before Victor found exactly how to tell his family what had just discovered, but before they were able to piece together the events themselves, Victor explained everything he had deduced. They took the news as good as anyone could expect. Some tears were shed, and some screams of anger filled the deserted woods around them. By the time they all calmed down and began to accept their new life in the Nezzrin Kingdom, Philip was standing proud while one of the elders placed the jewels upon his body signifying his new role as the Protecian king.

By the time Beatrice finished telling her story, Angelica was trembling in fear. "Since that time, the plague began and wiped out nearly everyone except for Philip's two grandsons, Alexander and Frederick. Eventually, the plague was brought under control by Chenrile's intervention. Even so, a few years later, Frederick, your father, died from a rare form of the plague that resurfaced briefly, leaving his wife, your mother, in control.

"There is no real set of rules for taking power away from someone who should have inherited it. However, due to the small number of living heirs to the throne and that we no longer have a committee of elders to consult, there cannot be any real discussion about how it can be done. Any decision would be Alexander's and his alone to make. Most likely, if he does see you as being an unfit ruler, he could make his own address to the people. If he can convince them and the royal guards to follow him instead of you, they may remove you peacefully from power by request or even begging. Otherwise, they may react violently, and a riot may be possible." Beatrice hesitated a moment before adding, "I think you know what would happen then."

Angelica just stared as if she had been held under the spell of a hypnotist. Her eyes were fixed blankly at the wall as Beatrice spoke to her. "What can I do?" It was the first sign that she was actually paying attention to what the governess was saying. "How can I go up there and speak to them? The assassin is unknown, and according to you, there is no way to figure out his identity unless he strikes again. I am so scared that he would try to kill me next. Why wouldn't he? He killed my mother at a time when everyone was pleased with her decisions."

With the loving touch of a mother, Beatrice placed an arm around Angelica's shoulders. "You have to address the people. If you don't, situations will definitely be worse. The scenario you described is only a possibility. One I don't see as very likely." Beatrice placed a hand under Angelica's chin and turned the girl's head so that their eyes were staring deep into each other's. The fear in Angelica's eyes was almost enough to make Beatrice feel sick to her stomach. "We'll have guards patrolling the courtyard to make sure there is no other attempt at an assassination." A single tear found its way from Angelica's eyes and down her cheek. "They weren't expecting anything of that sort before. Now, the guards are ready for anything. You have to trust them."

The silence that followed sent shivers down Beatrice's spine. She just sat and waited for Angelica to speak again. After the silence stretched on for what could have been a full ten minutes, the young queen finally began to mumble some words. "I will address the people tomorrow at midday. Tell the horsemen to go and inform the kingdom." Angelica turned her back to Beatrice and stood on legs that were shaky at best. As if the weight of the world had been placed on her shoulders alone, Angelica stumbled towards her desk and sat down. With a stroke of fury, she threw her sketches of the courtyard to the ground, picked up a quill and began scribbling madly on a sheet of parchment. "You can leave now," she told her servant without even turning to face her. "I have to prepare something to say tomorrow."

Despite the queen's horrible feelings of fear and anticipation, Beatrice smiles. It meant that she would go through with being queen, and Alexander would stay away from a place on the throne. Beatrice knew that the people loved Angelica, and they would be patient with her while she learned her role. They would overlook mistakes made at her early age knowing that with time, she would get better and become a strong leader of the kingdom.

CHAPTER TWELVE

Queen Angelica's Address

With the sun again bright in the sky and beating down on the courtyard for the first time in days, people began to walk towards the platform jockeying for a good position to view Angelica's first public address. They stood shoulder to shoulder waiting for the new queen to arrive and speak to them for the first time since her mother's death. No one saw her before the address as they usually did. There was some disappointment, but what the people did not realize was the Beatrice had told her that as a queen she should be preparing rather than socializing during this time. Some of the citizens had gathered early just for the purpose of seeing her prior to her speaking engagement, but they realized that the roles had changed, for better or for worse. Anxiously, everyone talked and laughed and waited for the address to begin.

The same servant as always walked to the front corner of the platform and stood with a hand raised to his mouth. The crowd grew so silent it was almost unnerving, but he began to do his duty with confidence. "Prince Alexander!" As the prince walked onto the platform with his black cape rippling in the wind behind him, the crowd let out an unenthusiastic cheer. They were not interested in the prince. He was not the one they had arrived to see. Today he was in no different role in the kingdom as he was or will be on any other day of his life. When the people felt that they had cheered enough to please the Royal Bachelor, they stopped abruptly. With a sigh, the servant waited another second before beginning again. "The ruler of the Protecian Kingdom! Her royal highness, the Queen Angelica!"

The young queen, dressed in her formal gowns now bejeweled to signify her new title, began to walk towards the middle of the platform as countless kings and queens before her had done. She was wearing a purple gown of gold thread with jewels draping over her shoulders and arms. Her long blonde hair was held back with a richly ornate clasp that sparkled in the sunlight. As she passed the golden sculpture of vines representing Protace's ascension into the sky, the people began to throw bouquets of roses at her. Angelica gasped at the sight of these flowers falling from above. At first glance, she could have sworn they were arrows. Arrows that were meant to kill her. She jumped back much to the surprise of the guards and Beatrice, who was standing a few rows back. After a moment, she realized what was really happening, and began to walk forward again.

Once Queen Angelica was standing in the usual position of the speaker, the crowd's cheer rose to a level that made her ears hurt. With the stone eyes of Protace and Soranace staring down at her, Angelica cried, "Please! Please, let me speak!" The crowd did not silence down, but in fact they grew louder to cheer the beginning of her speech. As her eyes frantically scanned the crowd for anyone that may look suspicious, Angelica continued to scream, "Please! I am risking my life to speak to you!" She looked back and forth like frightened rabbit. "Let me speak!"

After a full five minutes of relentless cheering, the crowd slowly began to grow silent. It took another half a minute before they had grown entirely quiet. Angelica could see that Alexander had walked off the platform and was standing at the front row of the crowd as he always did. He was by himself, though. Angelica did not mind his being alone all that much, but his solitude also meant that she was standing here alone as well. Alone and with thousands of eyes staring at her and waiting for her to begin speaking. Finally, she managed to push out, "Thank you for your support, and thank you for being as patient with me as you have been over the past weeks."

Angelica spoke to the people as if it was the most natural thing that came to her. There were no pressing matters of the kingdom that needed her attention, so she spoke simply to allow the people to hear her and know she was trying to be a good queen. Maybe one day as good as her mother. Possibly, even better. Most of all, however, she wanted to show Alexander that she was mature enough to handle this responsibility. Perhaps she will need some assistance from him or even Beatrice, but it was a job she may be able to tackle after all.

With this introductory speech no more than in its fifth minute, Alexander looked up at Angelica and mouthed the words he had spoken to her at every prior public address. "I have some business to attend to." Angelica had never been able to read people's lips, but in this situation, it was a skill she did not need. The statement Alexander just told her was the same thing he had been telling her for years. It was the time for business, not only of the entire kingdom but all the individuals' private businesses as well. Angelica simply responded with a nod, and Alexander disappeared into the crowd.

The words continued to come from Angelica's mouth, and the people continued to listen intensely. Angelica could no longer even see Alexander amidst the faces anymore. He just blended in with the people around him. However, Angelica's eyes find someone else she had been looking for. The court jester with the brightly colored costume was standing in the crowd making his way towards the center. Just the sight of him pushing his way through the densely packed courtyard brought a smile to Angelica's lips and any nervousness she was feeling melted away.

As the tenth minute of her speech approached, the young queen was running out of things to say. She had already explained her fear and why it caused such a delay to her first address, why she felt she would make a good ruler, and she was even thanking the people before her and all citizens for being so patient with her during this time of transition.

With a deep sigh, Angelica's eyes began to scan the crowd. What exactly was she looking for, she did not really know, but it gave her the minute to think of some way to end the address. A way for her to finish speaking and allow everyone to leave with an optimistic view of the future that awaited them. As she looked from face to face in the crowd, she saw something that disturbed her. The jester was squirming almost as if he was wreathing in pain. For a moment, Angelica thought about calling the guards over to him to see if he was okay, but she reconsidered. She assumed it must have been some sort of animal he was concealing in his costume for the big finale of his juggling act.

Queen Angelica looked away and said, "You have been great to speak to today, and I hope I will not disappoint you in the future." Angelica let out a deep sigh and was preparing to walk off the platform when she saw something in the air. For an instant, she tried to convince herself that it was her imagination, or perhaps one last rose thrown by one of the spectators. It must be her nerves that had transformed this innocent object into the arrow she could see coming towards her. Soon, she realized that was not the case. This was a real arrow, and this was yet another assassination attempt.

The moment she had feared and planned for weeks to confront was now here, and she was scared. So scared that all the things she had planned to do in this event washed from her mind and left her standing paralyzed in the center of the platform. The world that seemed to move so slowly over the past month sped up to a dizzying frenzy. She could hear everyone's voices and everyone's heartbeat for a split second. Then, once voice rang out from the far right side of the platform and shattered that weird stillness of the crowd's monotonous speaking. "Queen Angelica, get down!" Another voice rang out, "Run! Get off the platform!" Mostly, there were just screams that stood out like pillars of light in the drone of inarticulate noise. The same mistakes were being made again.

Everyone was looking at Angelica, and not one set of eyes was looking for someone with a bow and arrow.

As if it was the only thing she could do, Angelica began to take nervous steps backwards. She was slowly overcoming the petrifying fear she was feeling. Far too scared, however, to begin running for cover, as she should be doing. She could almost hear the arrow talking to her. Tempting her to stay still and meet her destiny, head-on. All Angelica was able to do was take those backwards steps away from the path of the arrow.

Soon, one of those steps brought her to safety. Angelica placed her foot upon one of the bouquets that had been thrown at her a few minutes before. Her foot crushed the roses and flattened the thorns under the leather sole of her shoe. When she raised her other foot to take another step, she slipped on the remnants of the bouquet and fell onto the hard stone platform. The arrow sailed above her and drifted down to finally land feet from where she was lying.

Then, everything around her fell back into normal time instead of the maddening fast speed of that had just ensued. It seemed like that arrow had an instant to cut through the air towards her but that moment was filled with hours of information. Queen Angelica felt dizzy and disoriented as if she had hit her head, but she did not remember doing that or even banging her head on the platform. The carved images of Protace and Soranace were staring down at her, almost willing her to stand. All around her were the frightened sounds of the crowd growing more panicked. The noises were getting closer and more infuriated by the second. Perhaps they thought that the arrow had found its target.

After taking a deep breath, Angelica leapt to her feet and ran towards the golden tower of vines stretching up towards the sky. It was the only place that offered some kind of cover from a possible second arrow. When she stood, there seemed to be a visible wave of relief rolling its way through the crowd. Angelica was not relieved though. She may have dodged that first arrow, but she had no idea how many more were waiting to be fired.

From behind the intertwining gold vines, Angelica could see the entire crowd through the spaces in its intricate design. The mesh-like pattern left large areas of the courtyard visible to her, but there was also a great deal that was concealed. Angelica still stared, and soon she saw exactly what she was hoping to see. In the middle of the crowd, there was a man aiming another arrow at her. While all eyes in the courtyard were on the young queen, the man was pulling back on his bow and preparing to send another arrow towards the platform.

Finally, he released, and the arrow arced through the sky just like the first had done. There were more worried gasps from the crowd, but Angelica did not budge. She felt completely safe behind this cylindrical shield. Soon, the arrow hit. It passed through a hole in the outer edge of the vine structure, but it hit gold before passing through to the other side. Angelica was safe, and better yet, she got a clear view of who had fired that arrow.

For a moment, Angelica refused to believe what she was seeing. How could someone that had always treated her so kindly be trying to kill her? It did not make any sense, but at the same time, seemed perfectly simple. He had been gaining her trust all this time, so she would not suspect a thing when he finally attacked. But why do it at all? Still, she saw who it was, and she had to act now.

Quickly, Angelica stepped out from behind her barricade, pointed towards the man in the center of the crowd, and shouted, "There's the assassin! There he is! Guards, take him into custody! Take him, now!" The court jester, standing in the center of the crowd in his brightly colored costume looked around as all eyes turned from the queen and fell upon him. As he began to take slow steps back, the same steps Angelica had taken, he dropped the bow and arrow he had been preparing for a third shot towards the platform. Through the mob of people, the guards were pushing their way through to the assassin.

Finally, the jester turned and ran. He shoved everyone nearby to him away as he thrust himself towards the back of the courtyard.

With the guards trying to get closer to him, the jester burst from the back of the angry and confused crowd and ran towards the opening to the caves less than one hundred feet from the courtyard. He was halfway there before the guards managed to push their way from the mass of citizens in the courtyard. By the time the queen's guards had begun running towards the caves, the jester leapt towards the opening and slid across the dirt and sand, into the caves, and out of sight. It was if he had been planning that escape route for months.

As the confusion grew around her, Angelica ran down the platform stairs and began to chase after the guards towards the cave. She got no more than three steps into the courtyard when Beatrice grabbed her by the arm. "Come on. Let's get back to the palace." Beatrice gave a despairing look towards the caves where the assassin had disappeared. As she was speaking, the first two guards began to climb through the narrow opening and into the darkness after the jester. "I am sorry I convinced you to come out here to speak. There was no way we could have anticipated another attempt."

Beatrice began to lead the young queen away from the crowd and the confusion surrounding it. After a few steps, Angelica stopped walking. "I'm not going to run and hide." Her eyes looked deep into Beatrice's. "I am going into the caves to see who he is." Angelica turned and began to run. The sudden jerk in her motion caused Beatrice to lose her grip on the child's arm. As her fingers clenched at the air, Beatrice stood in shock. Angelica disappeared back into the crowd of people headed towards the caves.

The two guards crawled through the cave opening, and after about five feet, there was a drop. Each of the guards slowly climbed down this cliff towards the rocky ground beneath. All they could think of was that this man, this court jester, did all this while running. He did not even slow down as he dove through the opening and landed past the cliff on the ground below. The procedure that took them nearly a minute each to complete, the assassin ran through in no more than five seconds.

While looking carefully around them, the two guards began to walk into the caves. They were in a large opened space where stalactites stretched down from the ceiling for almost seven feet. The ceiling itself seemed at least twenty feet high. This was the interior of the mountain range. No one had ever been able to pass completely through the mountains in the history of the kingdom, and that made this almost like a trek into an unknown world.

Caves opened up in front of them. There were two to choose from, and neither showed signs of being recently travelled upon. They had to pick one of the paths to take. To sneak back out into the courtyard now would most likely mean a certain death for both of them once their backs were turned. Anyway, more guards were on their way at that moment. If they chose the wrong cave and the assassin tried to escape, the second team of guards would stop him instead.

The pair of guards entered the cave to the right. Immediately, the light began to drop off quickly as they moved away from the cave opening. Also, the smoothly cut rock walls of that first chamber ended as well. Here, the rocks looked untamed as if no one had ever bothered to disturb them. Fissures that were two feet wide stretched up to the ten-foot ceiling of these caves. As the guards walked by one of these giant cracks, the sound of falling rocks filled the caves, echoing against the walls in a way that almost mimicked laughter. For an instant, it seemed as though the rock walls were coming alive around them. They instantly feared a cave-in and began to search for cover. However, when they began to look, the only rock they saw falling was roughly the size of one of their fists. It swooped down between them and then disappeared into the shadows.

A confused look exchanged between them, but soon they both knew exactly what had happened. From the fissure they had just passed, the jester began to run. He was racing towards the exit to the chamber. The two guards began to run after him watching as the bright splashes of reds, yellows, and blues rippled before their eyes. As they ran, they saw the jester leave the cave they were in and run into the large open area they had just left. Almost as soon as they could see him in the backlight of the cave opening, he turned and began to move back towards them. He was not trying to escape into the courtyard. This man was trying to get to the other cave. It was as if he knew exactly where he was going within these rocky walls.

Making this sharp turn slowed the jester down significantly. His foot began to slip on some loose pebbles and grains of sand on the cave floor. With a scraping sound as he regained his footing, the jester began to lumber back towards the other cave opening. One of the guards ran into him and pushed him into the smoothly cut wall of the cavern. The jester began to squirm under the guard's grasp in a feeble attempt to escape. Once he knew that escape was impossible, both of his hands flew to his mask. The single sheet of brightly colored cloth crossed over his nose and drifted down until it overlapped the rest of the costume by a full six inches. It was this mask that shielded the jester from humiliation during his performances, and now it was shielding him from facing his crimes.

As if taking the cue from the jester's actions, the guard grabbed the bottom edge of the veil and began to pull it away from the jester's face. There was a scream of frustration and pain from the jester as the guard pulled on the mask. Soon, it began to loosen, and the jester's screams intensified. The guard knew that a scream that loud could put them at the risk of a cave-in, but he also knew he had to continue with what he was doing. Finally, the mask was torn from the jester's face and the four hands released it at once as though it were a completely useless item now ready to be discarded.

For a few moments, no one spoke. The caves continued to echo with the last remnants of the jester's scream while the veil continued to drift to the rocky ground, seeming like that sound would never fully end. Some loose pebbles scurried from their hiding places high up the cave walls and rolled down the rocky embankments at the sound of these echoes. It was almost as if they too wanted to see the jester's true identity, something he had so carefully kept hidden for years.

There was a moment of total shock as the guards saw the face behind the mask. They both began to back up a few cautious steps in surprise and fear. Neither of them knew how to act next. Both simply stood as still as stone looking into the eyes of the man who had trained them. A man they knew to have lethal skills.

Prince Alexander stood in the cave and looked at the two of his guards that had cornered him. As if only to complete the picture, he loosened the rest of the jester's costume with a few well-practiced shrugs of his shoulders. The costume fell to the ground around his ankles, and his black cape, which had been wrapped up around his arms unfurled as he did so. He just stood there in front of the sheer rock wall staring back at the two guards that were standing at attention, shoulder to shoulder.

As the guards stood in their trance, Alexander reached for the handle to the sword attached to his belt. While doing these careful and deliberately slow motions, the guards' eyes never broke their connection with his. "Prince Alexander?" one of them managed to utter as the prince drew his sword. In one continuous motion, he brought the sword up and struck the guard standing on the right in the neck. The man did not even have a chance to react. His head was lopped off in a second, and was nearly propelled to the far side of the cave by a jet of blood shooting from his severed neck. With his head falling to the ground behind him, the guard's arms reached up for a moment as if to verify what had just happened. Then, he quickly descended to the ground in a heap as if he were a freshly smothered candle. He never even had a chance to reach for his sword.

The other guard had a chance to arm himself. He raised his sword towards Alexander, who only smiled in return. In the guard's mind, he was reciting every lesson this man had taught him, and whether he knew it or not, his lips were moving carefully to the sounds of these lectures. The guard knew this was going to be the most difficult sword fight of his life, not only due to the skill of his opponent, but the simple knowledge of who the opponent actually was.

"I'm going in." Her words were so stern the guards understood it was not a request but an order. No one made an attempt to try changing her mind, and they began to help Angelica down into the caves. Among the guards was David, the guard Alexander had dueled in the courtyard back when Wilhelmina was happily ruling the kingdom. The one who had been given the lesson that enemies do not always fight fair. He was the one to help Angelica down from the tiny cliff and into the open area just beyond. As soon as she was down, David jumped down beside her, and the sight they saw was one they would never forget as long as either would live.

Alexander was standing still as if in total awe. On the ground, at his feet, there was a sword. Its owner was standing just before Alexander, his whole body shaking as if in the grips of some horrible convulsion. When the plague was rampant in the kingdom, this was a common sight just before someone died. There was a faint choking noise coming from the guard as he stood there, shaking. Alexander was holding a single arm extended towards this man, and his sword was held in that one hand. The blade was extending through the guard's neck and six inches of the tip was protruding from the back of his skull. The man's head was impaled on Alexander's sword. His body was trying to stay alive, but it was unable to complete that task.

When Alexander saw the next two guards coming into the caves with Angelica, he withdrew the sword completely from the guard's head. There were two more guards moving into the ground level of the cave. There were two more guards staring at Alexander with the same confusion as the first two. Still, they were able to see that Alexander was by no means going to surrender, and they began to charge at him with swords drawn.

Angelica stood back at watched in fear as the guards neared Alexander. As the first of the guards got close enough, he raised his sword to strike. No sooner did he do this than the prince buried his sword in the man's chest. David watched his fellow guard die, and he began to strike as the other guard fell to the ground adding to the pile of corpses in the caves.

In the caves, there were no formalities. No exchanges of glances or names like before or after their previous duel. Alexander just raised his sword, and hacked down towards David's arm. The blood-streaked blade slammed down on David's wrist, and the guard dropped his sword. Blood began to flow down from his hand as be readied himself to be killed by Alexander's next blow. Much like the attacks by the other three guards in the caves, the battle seemed to be over before it ever really started.

Alexander brought his sword to the side, readying it to slice off David's head. He was about to bring the blade towards the guard's throat when a burst of pain exploded in his arm. When Alexander looked away from his next victim, he saw his niece standing beside him. She had stabbed him in the forearm with the dagger she had always carried attached to her leg. Before Alexander had a chance to react, Queen Angelica twisted the dagger in his forearm. Blood began to seep from around the blade, and Alexander let out a shriek of pain. As he did, his sword fell to the ground.

The look in Queen Angelica's eyes was not one to be expected, even by the queen herself. It was not disgust or anger at having had to use this weapon. There was no fear in the danger of what she was doing. Even the very fact that it was her uncle she was attacking did not seem to faze her. All she knew was that she was hurting the man who had killed her mother, and this made her feel not only relieved but actually proud.

Without a weapon, Alexander knew he had little to do. He reached over with his uninjured hand and grabbed hold of Angelica's face from under her chin. With one hard push, he shoved her backwards. The dagger was yanked from his arm when he did this, tearing the wound to the point of looking like a wild animal bite. Angelica stumbled, fell backwards, and struck her head on the rock of the cave wall as she fell.

David turned to see if the young queen was all right, and when he did, Alexander grabbed his sword from the ground and ran down one of the caves. More guards were climbing down into the caves, and they began to pursue Alexander. After the guards, Chenrile climbed down, and finally a frantic Beatrice struggled her way through the narrow opening. The physician and the caregiver both ran to Angelica. She was in a haze, but she was conscious. One look at her eyes made it obvious how cloudy her head was at that moment. Before they had a chance to advise her otherwise, Angelica was to her feet, running with the guards to find Alexander somewhere in the caves.

CHAPTER THIRTEEN

The Pursuit of an Assassin

S oon, the guards realized this task was not as easy as they first thought. There were more than just deep cracks in the cave walls large enough for someone to hide in. Countless side caverns riddled the cave walls forming a twisted maze of dark and winding rock. The guards placed their ears to the rocks to listen for footsteps in the distance, but this did little to help. While travelling through the maze of stone and shadows, the guards would hack at the cave walls with their swords to mark every turn they made. This would be the only way they would be able to find their way back out if they were to capture Alexander or give up on the search. With a weight of sadness, every passing second made the latter option seem more likely.

They travelled like this for a few minutes that felt like several hours. Angelica marched directly behind the first line of guards brandishing her dagger, while the other non-soldiers stayed towards the rear of the group. Every other guard carried a torch to light the way, but they were all scared. While there did not seem to be any smell of gas in this part of the cave, there would be little warning if those flames ignited and caused a disaster. They walked down caves and looked in the fissures that lined the walls. When giving up seemed to be the only remaining answer, things began to change. Soon, they entered an area that looked different from the caves they had previously seen. The walls had been chiseled smooth, and actually looked polished. The ground was swept clean of debris and loose rock. There was a high ceiling that actually had openings carved into it to allow for daylight to enter. In this area, the torches were not needed due to the brightness of the room. A brightness that seemed to rival that of the courtyard at noon. This area appeared reminiscent of a shrine of some sort, but who would worship what kind of creature in the middle the gas mines that could explode at any moment.

As they cautiously stepped into this area, there was a strange quiet that swept over the group. Angelica began to whisper, "We will never find him in here. Alexander has walked these caves so many times and usually without a torch. He'd spend hours in here in the dark. He must know every crack in the walls by heart at this point. Someone that could do that could just disappear into the caves."

Angelica's mumblings were interrupted by a yelling from far in front of her. "Look! I found something over here!" Everyone ran towards where the yelling came from. It seemed almost as if their footsteps were desecrating some holy ground, and they felt a little awkward and scared to be taking those steps. They were treading in an unknown place that held unknown powers. Still, they had to continue. When everyone gathered around the guard that had yelled, they all looked at the same structure he saw. The guard began to speak again. "Why would they bring this down here? This makes no sense at all."

Every set of eyes that fell on it had the same questions, but nonetheless, here it was. Staring at them and almost beckoning them closer. On the ground in the center of the room was a stone fountain filled with water. It was circular with a diameter of only roughly three feet, standing about four feet high. There four equally shaped and sized bronze leaves decorating the rim of the pool, which seemed to be made of the same stone that surrounded them. The water inside looked strange. Thicker than the drinking water they were used to with rainbow streaks gliding along its surface. It was not still water, either. There was a constant lap tiny waves rippling along its surface and slapping the sides of the pool. It seemed to hold whoever was looking at it in some kind of hypnotic trance, almost beckoning them to jump in.

As Angelica turned away from the water to avoid this temptation, she looked around the shrine-like area. There was a small cavern opening in the wall just above the ground, and Angelica knelt to look inside of it. Any thought about damaging her formal gowns or losing one of the sacred jewels was the farthest from her mind. With Alexander's knowledge of the caves, the only chance of finding him would be finding him now. If they gave up the search for another day, he would surely find his way out through some other passage and never be heard from again. However, when Angelica looked into that cavern, she could see nothing but blackness. He could have been sitting there two feet deep, and she would never know.

Queen Angelica turned again and walked a little bit more, exploring and searching the area as everyone else was doing as well. Mostly, people were looking at the pool and speculating what this area was used for rather than searching for Alexander, but Angelica was more determined. She was, after all, the target of Alexander's elaborate plot. There would be plenty of time for speculations later. Now, they had to find Alexander while they still had that chance. With this in mind, Angelica walked a little further from the small cave she had just seen. Just ahead of her, with the sun shining in from the openings in the ceiling, she was able to make out what appeared to be the shape of a man.

With the sun starting to head down in the sky, the openings near the ceiling were providing much dimmer light than when they had first seen them. The torches held by the guards were located by the pool, and did little more than throw oddly dancing shadows around the room. There was little to see, but what was visible was terrifying. If this was Alexander, why was he standing there so still?

He must see them surrounding him and want to get away again. Why wait?

Not wanting to draw attention to her finding and send him fleeing again, Angelica walked towards the shape herself with the dagger in one outstretched hand. As she approached, the image became clearer and much easier to see, however still visible only in silhouette. There was definitely an arm and a hand holding onto something. Angelica did not want to walk any closer, so she lashed out with the dagger in one stabbing motion. The blade found its target, but the chest of the man was hard and the blade slid off with a metallic clink. The figure did not react at all. With the force of that blow, Angelica screamed out briefly, and this caused everyone to rush towards like a swarm of bees protecting their queen. As the guards got closer, their torches illuminated what she had mistaken for a man. It was a relief sculpture carved into the wall of the cave, similar to the ones of Protace and Soranace that loomed over the speaking platform.

With the guards and their torches closer to the sculpture, the details of the figure could be easily seen. It did not appear to be anyone they knew from the kingdom. The man was standing upright, dressed in peasant's clothing, with head turned to look over his shoulder and behind him. One hand was at his side, while the other, the one that Angelica had seen, was held up to his chest. There was a scroll of parchment in that hand. It was rolled up tight, but the sculpture was detailed enough that writing, too faint to be read but definitely there, was visible on the stone representation. Angelica looked at the carved eyes that were peering behind the man. They seemed content enough even though his posture was one of fear. The man seemed perfectly comfortable.

The guards began to walk along this wall, and their torches revealed other figures in the stone. People that were smiling and laughing, lounging on the ground or standing in glee. Amidst all of these sculptures pulling their way out of the stone, there were large empty spaces in the rock where the wall appeared perfectly flat and almost polished. It was almost as if this was a work in progress that had been abandoned prior to completion.

With all of these people carved in perfect, and horrifying, detail, the images that stood out most of all were not people. There were what appeared to be several pieces of a staff of some sort. These pieces were scattered over the ground throughout the relief with people standing around them. There was one piece, the bulk of the staff's head that looked like it had an animal carved into it. It was a reptile of some sort, but the position of that piece of the staff made it impossible to see any more than that. Some creature, definitely, but not something they had seen before.

There was another portion of the of the relief sculpture where fire was carved into the wall. It reached out and around what appeared to be spaces reserved for the limbs of a figure that was not there yet. Smooth portions of the fire and wall behind it would perfectly fit arms and legs. There were other areas were the trunk of a body would easily lie. Someone was meant to be there, and Angelica could not help thinking that that was who the shrine was in honor of. Waiting for his arrival in a throne of flames. Perhaps those flames were waiting for Prince Alexander.

The most horrifying image on the wall, however, was a very large reptile. It could have been what the image on the staff head was meant to represent. A tube-shaped body that was about 8 feet in length and almost a foot in diameter was coiled at the base and holding its head high in the middle. Its tail ended in a point with two spikes protruding from the sides making it into the head of a trident. Four legs reached out of its body, each about a foot in length and very muscular, ending in five clawed fingers. They body itself had the impression of scales covering its length and a row of spikes headed from snout to tail.

Even more horrifying than the creature's body was its head. Its jaw was huge and hung wide open with two rows of teeth filling it almost to the point of overcrowding. In the front of the mouth, there were two sets of interlocking fangs that were roughly four times the length of the other teeth. From behind its pointed snout and flared nostrils were large and bulging eyes. They looked like huge vacant marbles without any sign of pupil or cornea. Evenly spaced around the base of the skull and extending to the snout were four large spikes that almost appeared to be bony fingers that could close around the creature's entire skull, creating a caged helmet to protect it from attack. In the current pose that was carved into the stone, these spikes were spread so the creature's jaw could open widely and unobstructed.

When she looked at the stone image of this creature, Angelica gasped. Tears were fighting their way to the surface just at the sight of it, and chills crept over her body in a wave. It was such a horrible image to behold, and Angelica felt as if she could no longer look at it. While everyone else stared at the creature almost as if trying to analyze its stone likeness, Angelica turned her head and looked away. As she diverted her eyes, they fell upon something that troubled her even more than the creature itself. It was snarling at one of those empty spaces that seemed to be waiting for someone's image to fill it. What poor person would occupy this space? The queen both needed to know and was horrified to give it another thought. Angelica turned completely away from the sculpture and started to feel a little calmer in a few second's time.

As Angelica started to take a few wobbly steps on uncertain legs away from the carved wall of the cave, she began to breathe deeply and calm herself. She did not want to look back. The sight of that creature was far too horrifying for her to bear. Just the memory of that reptile-like thing, a memory that now seemed burned into her mind, was enough to make her feel nauseous. After a minute of looking away, however, Angelica remembered one disturbing fact. While they were examining the new discoveries uncovered within the cave, Alexander was most likely getting farther and farther into their depth. Farther than they could hope to pursue him.

With this in mind, Angelica turned around and prepared to tell all of them to continue the search for the prince. When she did finally turn, she saw something else, much more important than her announcement. The wall they were studying did not extend all the way up to the ceiling. It stopped about ten feet up, almost as it were simply a partition, closing off one section of the caves. Even more important, standing on top of that wall, looking down at them, was Alexander.

The black cape was drifting around his ankles as he was walking carefully along the edge of that wall. No one even noticed him standing up there. The horrible image of that monster was drawing all of their attentions. Alexander was slowly walking away from where the crowd had congregated while staying on top of that wall, well out of view. He was moving closer to the pool of water they had found barely five minutes ago.

Just as Angelica had done earlier in the day, although it seemed like much longer ago by this point, she pointed a finger at Alexander and shouted, "There he is!" For a moment, the guards looked around confused. For a moment, they did not know what she was talking about. The pursuit of Prince Alexander had drifted far from their minds with this new discovery. It only took a second for the guards to look up and see Alexander walking along the edge of wall. When the prince saw the guards had made eye contact with him, he began to run. A trail of loose pebbled tumbled down the rock wall as Alexander turned. He ran back along the wall for a ways, and then turned to get a running start. The guards were looking to see if there was a way they could begin scaling the wall after him. Soon Alexander's actions made them realize that they did not need to climb the wall. Alexander raced towards the edge of the wall and jumped. As he gracefully dove through the air, Alexander pulled his arms as close to his sides as he could, and plunged into the pool of water.

A splash reached up like an explosion. Rushing sounds of the waves filled the caves for a moment. Soon, the airborne water simply dissolved into the surrounding air rather than drenching the crowd that looked on at Alexander's amazing dive. The water just vanished. All that seemed to remain was the liquid in the pool, which had returned to its previous level, replenished by some unseen source, and showed no trace of Alexander within.

For a moment, everyone just stood in shock. No one even had a chance to try stopping Alexander, and even if they did, no one thought it possible that he could make that jump into such a narrow pool without injuring himself. It was almost as if he could fly. Everyone gathered around the pool with their weapons drawn, aside from Beatrice and Chenrile who were unarmed and stood back watching. After a minute, it seemed apparent that he was not planning to resurface.

Instantly, the onlookers began to speculate. Maybe he had injured himself and was currently drowning. If that was the case, do they save him? He was the prince, but he was also an assassin. And he did this to himself. Others thought that this pool must be some underground waterway and he was swimming to safety as they debated this topic. No answer seemed correct, but soon all debate stopped. The caves had started to shake.

Everyone felt certain that they were in the midst of a cave-in. These caves had claimed the life of Soranace years earlier, and now they may easily kill Queen Angelica as well as the others trapped with her. Soon, the shaking began to subside with nothing larger than a good-sized pebble being dislodged. The rumbling sound, however, gave way to a scraping sound like someone dragging a rock along the cave floor. While the guards began to look around for the source of this new sound, Beatrice shouted, "Here!"

It was the relief sculpture again. Something was happening to it. Small cracks began to develop on one of the smooth surfaces. The cracks only appeared right above the sculpted flames while the rest of the image was hard and unyielding rock. Soon, a thin layer of the wall crumpled apart and turned to dust. The dragging sound got louder as a sculpture of Alexander seemed to push itself into position around the sculpted flames. He was lying on his back with one arm reaching up to the sky. This arm was supported by stone fire as was his head and legs. It was a perfectly lifelike representation of the prince, and no one had any trouble recognizing him. His face, however, appeared in agony. Unlike the content expressions of all the other figures in the sculpture, Alexander was in pain. The queen's assumption was most certainly wrong. This was not a throne of flames, but this was intended for torture and death.

"I'm going after him." It was David. He was walking over towards the pool while returning his sword to his belt. No one was stopping him. It seemed like the best idea anyone had. If Prince Alexander was able to jump into that pool of water somehow become a sculpture on the wall, so could David. Alexander would not have used this peculiar room as an elaborate way to commit suicide, so the passage must be a safe one. More importantly, someone had to pursue Alexander wherever he went.

David had already begun to climb the edge of the pool when a voice, barely loud enough to be heard over everyone's heartbeats, called out from the shadows beyond him. "Don't go in there," it whispered. The voice seemed both urgent and very weak, but everyone could hear it. David stopped before a single finger touched the water, but still no one stepped out of the shadows. "If you go in there, you could die." The voice was calmer now, less urgent. As if to do no more than to obey what he had just heard, David climbed down from the edge of the pool. He waited in the deafening silence for a few seconds before the person who had spoken walked, sluggishly, into view.

Cassandra emerged from the shadows as she walked towards them from one of the deeper caves farther along the wall. With one hand groping the cave for support, she labored her way towards the group as if she was walking through the courtyard in the middle of a bright and sunny day. Her eyes looked glassy and ill. She seemed barely to be able to stand on her own shaking legs. It was the gas. Even though Alexander's intervention over the years had significantly drained the gases from the caves, there was still enough there to make someone as frail and sickly as Cassandra feel their effect.

After telling David not to climb into the pool, Cassandra acted as though her job was finished. She began to walk past the crowd towards the exit of the caves. Most likely, Alexander kept her in there during public addresses just in case someone tried to follow him afterwards. Finally, Angelica raised a hand and stopped Alexander's maid and servant from walking any further. "What is this?" Cassandra turned her head to look down at Angelica, and it seemed to shake for a moment like a baby first trying to hold up its head. Still, she was silent. After years of working under Alexander's thumb, she seemed scared to speak to anyone but him. "You said that going in there may be deadly. Why?"

Cassandra did not try to continue walking nor did she begin talking right away. For a moment, she just stood still as if weighing her options. Her dazed and nearly closed eyes began to scan the people in the caves looking at her. "If you want to know everything I do, it will take some time. Perhaps we should leave the caves to talk about this." She looked back at Angelica and added, "This place doesn't make me feel that good."

The queen looked at Cassandra and carefully studied her features. It did not take long to realize that she was suffering from being in here. For confirmation of this, Angelica looked over at Chenrile. He just nodded back at her, and that was all that needed to be done. Finally, Queen Angelica said, "I want two guards to stay in here at all times. Rotate shifts every hour so the gas does not start to get to you. If he comes back, I want him arrested." Two of guards indicated that they understood. "Everyone else, come with us."

It took only a few minutes for them to navigate their way back out of the caves. The guards in the lead kept a constant eye on the marks they had scratched into the cave walls. Soon, they were in the large opened area with the exit just ahead. Scattered on the ground were dead bodies. There were three in total. As some of guards continued to escort Cassandra and the others out, another two remained to clear up the dead bodies of their colleagues.

Before she left the caves, Angelica turned and looked at the ground. Everyone there was certain she was just trying to absorb the sight of death, but she was looking for something else. "There's something missing," she muttered in a voice barely more than a whisper. No one spoke as the young queen took a few steps closer to the dead bodies on the ground. "The jester's costume. It was on the ground over here when we came in. What happened to it?" Confused looks glanced back and forth. They all remembered the costume being there, but it was no longer on the ground of the cave chamber. It had disappeared, and no one knew where it was. "Someone must have taken it," the queen whispered, then added, "There's someone else helping the prince." As if that was the end of the discussion, the queen turned and continued to walk towards the exit of the caves. These were matters to be later discussed.

When they emerged from the cave opening, there were some shocked gasps and whispers filling the courtyard. Everyone was still there. It did not look like a single person had gone home even though the sun was setting rapidly above them. For a terrifying moment, Angelica considered that any one of them could have taken the jester's costume and quickly returned to the courtyard. Most likely, taken it as some sick souvenir. Cassandra's name was whispered among them, now. They all thought she was the assassin. Given time, they would realize that Alexander had not been heard from since the incident, and most likely more accurate information would be whispered throughout the kingdom. In these lands, rumors spread like sickness from person to person. It was only a matter of time before everyone in the kingdom knew the full details of the assassination attempt.

The party surrounding Angelica and Cassandra did not stop walking in the courtyard. They marched right past the gawking crowds and continued on to the main entrance of the palace. They walked down the gold, ornamented hallways until they reached the dining room. Once inside, the guards stood by the doors while Angelica, Cassandra, Beatrice and Chenrile sat at the chairs surrounding the table.

Before Cassandra began to speak, Chenrile whispered to Angelica, "How is your head feeling? I would like to take a look at that to make sure you are okay." The queen shook her head promptly. There were more important things to be dealt with. Just the act of shaking her head, though, made her dizzy, and she nearly fell off the chair. Chenrile continued, "I am going to be leaving for Nezzrin Kingdom early tomorrow morning. If problems due to your injury arise after I leave, I may not be able to get back in time to help you." Angelica hesitated, and Chenrile took the opportunity to continue speaking. "I could check while we are listening to her. You will not even realize I am here." Finally, Angelica nodded, and Chenrile began to examine the swelling lump on the back of her head.

"That pool you saw Prince Alexander jump into is much more than a pool of water," Cassandra began saying as she looked at everyone that was watching her. As with any room in the palace, there were several other ears listening as well ready to begin their gossiping as soon as she was done speaking. After being away from the caves even for that short time, Cassandra was already beginning to look stronger. Her voice started to take a more energetic tone as well. She knew there would be a great deal of explaining to do eventually, and she had been preparing this speech for some time. That still did not make the task at hand any easier. "It's a portal to another world. Alexander found it while mining in the gas caves. That and the wall of statues you saw."

CHAPTER FOURTEEN

Cassandra's Story

"Prince Alexander! Prince Alexander, get over here! You have to see this!" The workers had already begun to gather around the fallen rubble and stones that had freed themselves from the cave walls. The air was thick with dust, and dirt was flying through the air. With the sting of gas burning his nostrils and eyes, Prince Alexander walked over towards where everyone was yelling. When he finally made his way through the small but tightly packed crowd, he saw the exact same sight the guards and the queen would see five years later. A relief sculpture that had been carved right into the wall of the cave.

"Tell me exactly what happened. How did you find this?" Alexander spoke to the workers without looking at them at all. He was nearly hypnotized by the sight of that great lizard protruding from the wall. Still, the workers answered him. Their eyes did not meet Alexander's either while they spoke about how they were mining, and with one swing of a pick axe, an entire wall of rock gave way. When the dust cleared, this was starting at them.

After telling Alexander the story of what had happened, not elaborate but concise, another of the workers led him away from that and towards the pool of water about ten feet away. Despite all of the falling rocks and dirt, the water was perfectly clean. The water had the look of thickness and a rainbow film covering its surface just like it had when Queen Angelica saw it. One of the miners suggested it may be oil instead of water, but that did not seem right either. Whatever it was, there was not a single speck of dirt floating on that surface. Even the bronze leaves surrounding it were sparkling with a brilliant glow.

Alexander did a great deal of research concerning his find, but he never spoke of it to anyone. The mining for natural gas moved to a different cave, and no one was permitted back in that cavern except for Alexander himself. Throughout the following weeks, the group of five miners that had seen the sculpture turned up dead in various mining accidents, each more bizarre than the last. Never more than two died at a time, but before any rumors really got a chance to spread, each of the five had perished in their respective mishaps and the accidents stopped. Most people just considered it as a string of bad luck. A much smaller number thought that it was the work of Soranace's ghost, possibly having been disturbed after centuries of sleeping within this tomb of rock. Alexander let these rumors spread. Anything that took the attention off of him and real cause of his workers' misfortune was acceptable.

There was no way to be sure exactly how much time had passed since the creation of these sculptures and their discovery, but eventually, Alexander learned all he needed to know about what was found rather than when it was created. It was a great deal of information, but even worse, it was information that would damage the very foundation the kingdom was built upon. For months, Alexander was afraid to go anywhere near that pool of water. According to what he had read in the library archives, there is a chance, a very great chance, that he would die if he tried to submerge himself. Something about the liquid contained in that pool. It contained certain tiny creatures that only a very small percent, well under one percent actually, of people can survive.

However, one night, Alexander became drunk. He stumbled away from the palace, and eventually found himself wandering through the caves. At this point, he was still unable to navigate the caves in the dark, and before long, he realized that he was lost. After stumbling around in the darkness for about an hour, he tripped and his arm plunged into the water. It took him a moment to realize that he had wandered until he found his way to the pool he had feared so much. Felling more immortal than scared at this point, Alexander climbed in.

He did not leave the caves until the following morning, and one of the first things he did was to inform Cassandra of what he found. Since that time, he had not spent a single night in the Protecian Kingdom. Every evening, at some point or another, Alexander would leave the palace, and walk into the caves. Eventually, he would find his way into that pool. After a few months, he was able to walk the entire distance from the cave entrance to the watery portal without doing so much as opening his eyes.

Cassandra did not bother to clean Alexander's quarters anymore, and to her knowledge, the door to that room was not opened again. She would spend most of her days in the palace, walking through its hallways. The story he had told Cassandra was that this portal led to another world. There, he began to rule the uncivilized people just as Protace had done here. He named himself as their ruler, and soon they began to treat him as such. It was a relatively short about of time before they treated him as much more.

During this time, Cassandra was needed to make excused for him. People would want to know where Alexander disappeared to at times, and she would have to tell them of business he had to conduct. A web of lies began to grow with Cassandra as the spider. Keeping the lies in order and telling them convincingly became her job rather than tending to Alexander's quarters and clothes. It was a job that was most the most difficult one in the kingdom, and Cassandra managed to do it expertly for years.

Aside from managing Alexander's excuses, Cassandra also had to remain in the caves during all the public addresses. With so many people in the courtyard, there was always a possibility of someone wandering into the caves on a dare or out of simple curiosity or stupidity. If that was to happen, Cassandra was supposed to stop them at all a costs.

There was one time when Alexander brought someone else into the caves with him. Cassandra did not know this person's identity, but she saw a person covered in a blanket walking into the caves, and that person went through the portal with Alexander. Cassandra watched from the shadows of the caves as the man followed Alexander into the pool, meaning that he was one of the people that could survive this passage. He was one of the chosen people, a chosen few, who would be able to pass through that portal. The image of him that appeared on the wall was covered in some kind of costume that obscured his facial characteristics. Aside from those two, Alexander did not bring another person into that section of the caves.

"That is how Alexander came into contact with those sculptures." The looks that filled the room were enough to crucify the frail woman sitting at the table. "His plan was to kill all the rulers that stood before him and when he became the Protecian king, he would be able to unite the two worlds together and rule them both. He said it would make him the greatest ruler the kingdom had ever seen."

Angelica's eyes grew cold and almost violent. "You mean you knew he was planning these assassinations? You knew, and you did not say anything?" Angelica was on the verge of standing from her chair in fury and demanding the guards to arrest her. With Chenrile still examining the young queen's head injury, she decided to remain in her seat and let Cassandra finish. Chenrile's hand was planted firmly on her shoulder to restrain her if she did not come to this decision on her own.

Once the queen settled back into her chair and let out a deep breath, Chenrile whispered into her ear, "I think you will be okay.

Do not put yourself through any unneeded strain for a while."
He nodded at Beatrice. A simple gesture telling her to make sure
his instructions would be carried out. "I am going to leave now."
With that, Chenrile stood and walked away from the table. With
him out of the room, all eyes turned back to Cassandra. The frail
woman looked on the verge of falling over again, but she managed to
support herself by leaning one arm on the table and holding it to so
tight that her knuckles turned white and her arm trembled.

Finally, Cassandra said, "Prince Alexander has told me, in
confidence, quite a few things." Cassandra sighed deeply. Her
sunken eyes looked less dazed than they had before. The fresh air
was helping her feel better. She was the one that collapsed in the
palace when the gas had first begun to creep in, and it appeared
as though her time in the caves was making her weaker than ever
before. "Several months before you were born was when Prince
Alexander became actively trying to…" Cassandra paused. She was
carefully selecting her words. "Make himself the king.

"The plague had come and gone, thanks to Chenrile's
intervention in finding a cure. Actually, it could barely be considered
a cure at all. The plague would contaminate someone, but being
infected with a different illness would actually cure the person. This
cure attacks the illness while inside of one of its victims, and leaves
the person absolutely healthy. The second illness, this cure, has no
severe effects on the humans it was given to, and within a few days,
our bodies would fight it off and kill it. He said to me, 'We have
a natural resistance to it.' However, the royal family, and possible
heirs to the throne, was reduced to three before Chenrile was able to
stumble upon that combination of sickness. Frederick, Wilhelmina,
and Alexander were all that remained."

"Chenrile! Are you in here?" Alexander looked through the
doors of Chenrile's laboratory. There was no one inside. The walls

were lined with glass bottles and marble vessels. They were filled with liquid or powders of every sort. Notes covered the table in the middle of brightly-lit room. It looked like the cell of a madman, but Alexander understood that Chenrile was nothing of the sort. He was simply trying to keep abreast of the growing needs of the kingdom, and it was a difficult task to say the least.

Seeing that the laboratory was empty, Alexander walked inside. He slowly looked back and forth trying to decide where to search first. One thing Chenrile was very predictable about was keeping everything well documented. Most likely an admirable trait for a physician. Alexander carefully walked towards the table in the middle of the room. He looked through the papers slowly trying to decipher the scribblings written upon them. In every moment of his free time, Chenrile must have been running some kind of experiment or another. Soon, Alexander found what he was looking for.

Using the notes as a guide, Alexander walked around the laboratory, picking up and looking through jars as he did. On one of the many shelves, he eventually found a jar whose label explained that it contained a culture of the plague. Alexander grabbed the jar from the shelf. For a moment, he found himself marveling at how this tiny jar can kill thousands. Prince Alexander thought it was probably the most lethal substance he would ever come across.

With that jar in hand, Alexander continued walking around until he found the other jar containing its cure. It was interesting how different the containers themselves looked. According to what Chenrile had explained to him, mostly to brag, the cure made people sick for about two days before its effects wore off. Sometimes it may take as long as a week but that was very rare. This timeline seemed just about right to Alexander. A few days illness would make everything seem perfectly authentic. He uncapped the jar of thick, syrupy liquid, and winced at the smell. Ironically, the cure to the plague possessed the smell of death. Cold and damp and sick. After a deep sigh, he drank a single mouthful of the putrid, green fluid.

That night, Alexander went to sleep feeling well (it was still years before he even began to explore the caves). Just after he lay down to bed, he heard hooves running outside his window. His brother, Frederick was riding away from the palace. He was to be in Nezzrin Kingdom for two days negotiating with their people about patrolling the borderline they shared. Most likely after having made love with the queen and bidding her farewell, King Frederick was gone. Wilhelmina stayed at the palace to greet a pair of diplomats from another neighboring kingdom the next day. It was typical of how the kingdom was run, and no one thought anything of it. Meetings and discussions ruled the better part of everyone's life.

By the time Alexander awoke the next morning, he was barely able to step out of bed. His head was aching, and his throat was so sore that to eat or drink felt like gargling razors. This was how the cure affected anyone who took it. It was a trade. Everyone would suffer like this for a few days, and the plague was eliminated. Alexander's use of the cure was much different however. Anything that was capable of bringing life can also be used to take it away.

Alexander went about his own business through the entire day not letting anyone know how greatly he was suffering. Learning to anticipate the dizzy spells, the prince knew how to avoid being seen in the grips of one after about an hour of walking around. It hurt to walk or even to breathe, but he knew it would all be over soon. This illness was just supposed to last for a few days, and that would be plenty of time to accomplish what needed to be done.

It was around noon when the diplomats arrived from their homeland. A horse-drawn carriage with two drivers was pulling them in. It seemed obvious they were showing off the wealth of their kingdom, but no one was around to witness this display except for a few peasants tending their fields.

Wilhelmina and Alexander greeted the two diplomats upon their arrival at the palace. They were shown to their rooms near the royal family's private corridor. This was meant to show off the wealth of Protecia, and judging from their reactions, the diplomats seemed quite impressed. The two men stayed in their rooms for most of the day. The servants they brought with them had begun to unpack their few bags almost immediately allowing the diplomats to relax after their long journey here.

At dinnertime, servants escorted the two men to the dining room. Everyone was prepared for them by this time, and the present members of the royal family were already waiting for them. In her husband's absence, Queen Wilhelmina sat at the head of the table, and Alexander at her side. The two diplomats quietly found seats across the table from Alexander as if taking time to select a seat would be an insult to those present. This was a pair that seemed absolutely proper in all situations and each of their carefully chosen actions. No sooner was everyone seated than the chef entered the dining room with a beef dish that looked and smelled wonderful. He began to cut and serve everyone their meals as another servant placed a large brass bowl of wine in the middle of the table. Alexander looked at the bowl carefully. It would play an integral part in his plan.

As was usually the case, the most important people at the table took their wine first once everyone was served their food. Today, that meant Wilhelmina. She lowered her goblet into the brass bowl and lifted out a vessel of red wine. As she placed the goblet on the table beside her dish, Wilhelmina looked over at Alexander. It was his turn to draw from the bowl.

This was the part of the plan that was the most important, and once it was completed, there was no turning back. Alexander raised his hand to his mouth as if to conceal an inappropriate smile, which was not that far from the truth or out of character for him. He assumed when entertaining the foreign diplomats, such winces were impossible to avoid, so no one would notice. As he did this, he was actually spitting into his hand. Alexander felt the hot saliva, very hot with sickness, sticking to his index finger, and with that done, he reached for his goblet. No one was looking at him now, so there was no chance of someone catching on to what he was going to do. Alexander grabbed his goblet from the top, and as he lifted it to the bowl of wine, he scraped his index finger against the rim of the cup. The saliva was now on the outside of the goblet, and Alexander lowered it into the bowl. Without trying to look obvious, a difficult task with his pounding head, Alexander swirled the goblet as slightly as he could while drawing his wine, and the saliva mixed with the wine. The bowl of wine had become a bowl of sickness to be shared.

When Alexander placed his drinking vessel back on the table, the diplomats began to draw from the bowl. However, the wine they were now drinking was contaminated with the substance Alexander had drunk from Chenrile's laboratory the day before. They would both be as sick as he was by the morning, assuming they drank enough, but they would be immune from the plague for a few days, at least, as a result. Trade one illness for the other.

During the meal, Alexander watched the diplomats closely. He wanted to make certain that each drank from their goblets during the course of the dinner, and they both did. There was actually no concern at all about this as each refilled their goblets several times. They were now surely contaminated. The only one left was Wilhelmina, and Alexander was worried that getting her to drink another goblet-full from the bowl may be a difficult task.

As the meal was drawing to a close, Wilhelmina finished her dinner and drank the last of the wine from her goblet. She removed the napkin from her lap and placed it on the table. She had no intention of eating or drinking any more than she already had. Alexander had planned for this, and he now had to initiate his plan.

Trying not to show the pain he was feeling from his throat as he spoke, Alexander said, "Let me propose a toast. To good health and to the success of our discussions tomorrow when King Frederick arrives." Nods were exchanged around the table. The diplomats seemed eager to have a reason to drink again, and Wilhelmina felt that the toast was a good idea. Aside from just nodding, Wilhelmina also plunged her goblet back into the bowl to get enough wine for the toast. They all touched goblets, and they all drank from them. Alexander's eyes never left Wilhelmina as she did this. The wine slipped past her lips and slid delicately and easily down her throat. Alexander's sip of wine might as well have been liquid fire as it passed his enflamed throat. Still, his own discomfort was not a concern. He could actually see the exact moment Wilhelmina swallowed the contaminated wine. Her throat extended and she even nodded her head slightly as she swallowed. Alexander held a hand up to his mouth again, this time actually to hide the grin that had developed there. Everything was ready for tomorrow.

The rest of the day passed into night silently, but it seemed to take quite some time. The diplomats wished to walk through the courtyard and gardens surrounding the palace. Alexander and Wilhelmina walked with them. However, Alexander was struggling to walk through the haze that the sickness had cast over him. By tomorrow, they would all be feeling as poorly as he was. All except for King Frederick, of course. The group spent about an hour going up and down the hills and stopping to admire the flowers that were beginning to bloom from the gardens like tiny explosions of color in the nighttime darkness. While they all stood happily around and made pleasant conversation, Alexander could not wait to leave. He felt horribly, horribly ill and wanted to do no more than return to sleep.

Finally, they all returned to the palace and to their separate quarters. Sleep soon followed. The night was uneventful, but each of them awoke in various stages of sickness. They had all fallen victim to the virus Alexander had placed in the wine, just as he had planned for them to do. Each of them was contaminated with the cure to the plague. This was not something to stop the upcoming discussions of that evening, however. After travelling the distances that they had, it would be unwise to call of such negotiations due to the sudden spread of a virus.

As the sun was just passing its highest point in the sky, King Frederick rode his horse home. He walked into the palace and greeted the two diplomats warmly as well as his wife and brother. They were all quite sick, however. He noticed that several of the servants were ill as well, for they had feasted on the leftovers once the royalty's meal was over. Still, he came to the same conclusion that everyone else had done. These discussions should not be cancelled for such happenings.

Frederick was walking from the diplomats' rooms towards his own quarters when he passed Cassandra in one of the corridors. "It's good to see you back, your Majesty," she muttered without raising her eyes from the floor. She was walking quickly as if she had urgent appointments to keep. It was the fastest Frederick had ever seen her walk, but he did not think anything of it. Cassandra had a tendency to act strangely sometimes, and after a while, these behaviors were not considered out of place.

While Frederick went towards his quarters, Cassandra kept walking towards the dining room. She opened the doors and looked around. The candelabras were not lit, and the torches were dark. The table was not occupied by a single tray or dish or cup. It looked as if the room had been deserted for some time. Cassandra did not see any of the other servants in that room, so she walked in, closed the doors, and passed through the doors on the far side of the room.

Now, she was in the kitchen. The chef was moving between the stove, the sink, and the icebox. He was moving slower than usual, though. Most likely, he was feeling ill, as were many of the servants. Cassandra, however, felt fine. She did not have any wine while she ate with the rest of the palace staff. Alexander had warned her not to, and she never disobeyed Alexander. While looking along the counter, she greeted the chef with a smile, and he replied only half-heartedly. It was the most energy he could spare at that moment.

On the counter beside her, Cassandra could see stacks of dishes and rows of empty goblets. There was five of everything. That meant there was enough for the four that had dined yesterday as well as the king. They would all be discussing matters of their kingdoms during dinner this evening. The servant heard that these meetings had something to do with border disputes, but matters of the kingdom rarely interested her. Her preference was rumors of a more personal nature. Like the one she heard about the cook's assistant was sleeping with the librarians wife.

Cassandra grinned over this scandal as she walked closer to the dishes and examined them closely. They were the old dishes that had been used in the palace for hundreds of years. They were immaculate, appearing as if not a single morsel had been placed upon then in the history of the kingdom.

While giving another look towards the chef, Cassandra reached into one of the pockets of her plain, servant's dress. The chef was fully absorbed in the preparation of dinner. Most likely, Cassandra could have deliberately started a kitchen fire, and the chef would not know until the flames had burned away one of his limbs. Her plan, or more accurately, Alexander's plan for her, was much easier and quieter than that though. With the chef's back turned towards her, Cassandra removed the glass jar from her dress. This was the jar that contained the plague Alexander had stolen from Chenrile just two days ago. She unscrewed the cap and tilted it over the top dish in the stack. A single drop of the red-tinted liquid fell from the mouth of the jar and hit the top dish. One tiny drop of liquid changed the course of a kingdom for years to come.

Cassandra quickly removed that top dish and placed it beside the stack on the counter. The same procedure was done to the second dish in the stack. While the chef was bustling back and forth, Cassandra went through all five dishes, contaminating them with the plague. When the stack was finished, she recapped the jar and slid it back into her pocket. Then, to make sure everything looked the way it should, she slid the stack of dishes back to original location on the counter. Given his current condition, she doubted the cook would notice a misplaced dish, but why take the risk.

With a deep sigh, Cassandra turned and left the kitchen. She walked quickly without establishing eye-contact with anyone. It was imperative that no one see her leaving the kitchen or walking through the corridors of the palace with that jar in her possession. It was concealed, but there was the chance that its bulge would be noticed on her dress. That could be a giveaway as to what was going on. Such a slip would most likely mean death for her and possibly for Alexander as well.

Like a shamed child, Cassandra walked with her head down until she reached the door to Alexander's quarters. The door was closed but not locked. Cassandra just walked in without knocking as she was instructed to do the day before. When she entered, she saw Alexander standing by the window looking out into the courtyard. His black clothing framed by the light of the surrounding window looked like a lesion developing on otherwise porcelain skin. Cassandra closed the door behind her, a little more concerned than usual about being closed in with him, and walked towards the center of the pristine room.

"Is it done?" The words were almost whispers. For a moment, Cassandra did not know if they were intended for her to hear, but then Prince Alexander turned around and looked at her. She watched his silhouette moving against the blinding light from the window beyond him. His bright green eyes looked distant and glassy. Almost as if they were not really his. They also looked eager for an answer, and she knew not to upset him, so she nodded quickly. "Where is the bottle?" His face was drawn and creased. Its pallor made him look almost like a corpse. While breathing shallowly so as not to share his air, Cassandra handed him the partly filled bottle. She was scared of upsetting him. He certainly did not look well and she had no idea what slight action of hers would set him into a violent rage.

Alexander walked towards her, and his eyes never left hers. Those eyes made her feel both scared and sick. As he got closer to her, she looked away in fear. "You are never to speak a word of what you have done to anyone." She was trembling so much she could not form the words to reply. "You understand, yes?" Finally, she managed to nod again. Alexander placed his hand under her chin and turned her head so that they were facing each other again. Under his touch, her skin began to crawl. "You did a good job. Now, you may leave." She did so without hesitation.

The next few hours passed very slowly. As soon as Cassandra walked away, Alexander locked his door tightly. With the stolen jar of plague serum on his desk, he did not one anyone unexpected walking in. He would go and return it to Chenrile's laboratory after the sun sets. Until then, the safest place for it to be was right on Alexander's desk where he could see it. Most likely, Cassandra was furiously scrubbing her hands at this moment until they went raw and bled in a desperate attempt to wash away any traces of the plague from her skin. That action would be a luxury some people would not be getting.

Eventually, Frederick, Wilhelmina, Alexander, and the two foreign diplomats met in the dining room. They all sat at the different place settings which had been pre-arranged at this meal, and they watched as the ill chef came to serve a chicken dinner to them. Before anything was placed on his dish, Alexander studied the plate carefully. There was a slight discoloration in its center. A slight pink hue. Hardly noticeable, unless one was looking for it. This meant that, most likely, no one would even notice the stain on his or her dish. The stains were just too faint.

They began to eat as they discussed the matters of relations between their two civilizations. As they spoke, it was quite obvious that four of the five people at the table were ill. The only one who was still healthy was the king. So he tried to hold back his usually flamboyant demeanor so as not to boast to those who were unable to eat in comfort. Eventually, the meal was finished, with far less gusto than the night before. Their discussion was also at an end, and the parties went back to their individual rooms.

The diplomats were going to stay the night before heading back to tell their people of the new trade arrangements and border safety they had discussed with the rulers of Protecia. Alexander rested in his room, and he noticed he was beginning to feel better as time went on. The illness from the plague's cure was starting to wear off. Everyone else would be getting better in a day or so. Everyone except King Frederick. When he gets sick, it will be with something far worse than what everyone else had suffered. They all were only feeling the side effects of being inoculated with the plague's cure. When Frederick gets sick, it will be with the plague, and he would be the only one of the group be unable to fight it off.

In the morning, King Frederick awoke ill. No one thought this surprising, since they were all just getting over their own illnesses. They two diplomats still did not feel well enough to travel, so they decided to stay another day in the Protecian Kingdom. Alexander awoke feeling as good as new. No trace of the plague or the symptoms from its cure. Just as everyone had claimed, the illness from the plague cure was gone in two days' time. Everyone else began to feel better as the day went on as well. The only exception was, of course, King Frederick.

The next morning, Queen Wilhelmina awoke. King Frederick was lying next to her still asleep, very soundly. She was surprised to discover that she felt fine. It was such a shock that it actually took her a minute to realize how good she felt. The illness had passed, and she was perfectly healthy again.

After a deep sigh of relief, Wilhelmina reached over to her husband and shook his shoulder. "Wake up. You may feel bad now, but by tomorrow, you'll be great again. Trust me." Wilhelmina gave Frederick another brisk shake. This time he did move. He rolled towards her, and for a moment, Wilhelmina thought he was still asleep. Then she saw his eyes. They were opened halfway and their gaze just stared at her with meaningless absence. A single tear found its way from the corner of his right eye as if in his last breath, he knew what he was condemning his wife to. Wilhelmina just stared back for a second, and then she began to scream.

Chenrile arrived shortly after word had spread throughout the palace, and he was able to determine what the queen already knew. King Frederick had died. The cause of his death was simply classified as the illness they had all experienced and recovered from that morning. The physician's best explanation was that all the travelling Frederick had just done had weakened him considerably. Possibly he even had picked up some less volatile infection while in Nezzrin Kingdom and the combination was something his body could not handle. Whatever the case was, King Frederick was declared as dead due to illness. Later on that same day, to ensure his condition could not spread to others, he was placed in the crypt, and Queen Wilhelmina was declared the ruler of the Protecian Kingdom.

Much like when her daughter would eventually assume power, Wilhelmina spent a month terrified to leave her room. Since she was not a child, though, there was nothing Alexander could do to remove her from power. So, Queen Wilhelmina stayed locked in the isolation of her quarters for nearly a month. She was mourning, as was everyone else in the kingdom, over the death of King Frederick.

The people of the land were also afraid, not so much for the welfare of their queen, but for the future of their kingdom. Wilhelmina had no children, and that would mean that there were only two possibilities. One was that she could marry Prince Alexander, and bear children that would be of Protace's bloodline that would eventually rule in time. The other possibility would be to remain childless or marry someone that was not of royal descent. In either of those situations, Alexander would have power over the kingdom after Wilhelmina's death. The people of the kingdom already disliked Prince Alexander for some time. What scared them more than his temper and his cruelty was the way he was referred to as the Royal Bachelor. If he did not produce an heir, Protace's bloodline would have gone dry. He seemed to be ignorant of the people's needs and wants. In life, he seemed to exist for his own benefit alone.

During this time of solitude, the queen only had one visitor. It was Chenrile. He was summoned to the queen's quarters after she claimed to be feeling strange. She had an explanation of why she was feeling as she did, but she needed Chenrile to verify her thoughts.

When he confirmed the theory she had developed, it was if a bright light had shone through to brighten her most dismal and miserable day. She was pregnant. In a matter of months, she would be giving birth to King Frederick's child. This would allow Wilhelmina's family to stay in power rather than surrendering that control to Alexander.

Shortly after receiving this news, Wilhelmina held her first public address as queen. The citizens were anxious to hear her speak since she was greatly loved as much as her husband was. Her first address what very similar to Angelica's. She thanked the people for being so patient with her, and she declared her hopes to be able to rule them fairly and justly. The only difference was that instead of an assassination attempt, there was announcement about the future arrival of a baby.

No sooner did Wilhelmina say these words, than the people began to cheer. Their hopes had been answered. Instead of being forced into oppression under Alexander's eventual rule, a child was to be born to Queen Wilhelmina. That child would eventually grow to be the ruler of the kingdom, and Protace's blood will continue without Alexander's rule.

Prince Alexander, standing in the front row of people in the courtyard was the only one who did not cheer. A smile found its way to his lips, but he simply stood there feeling horrible. After all the work and risk he went through to kill Frederick, his own brother, it seemed as though he would still be unable to rule the kingdom. He just stood with a smile on his face and his arms folded. While Queen Wilhelmina, the ruler of the Protecian Kingdom, beamed from the speaking platform, plans for her assassination were already starting to form in Alexander's mind.

CHAPTER FIFTEEN

Soranace and the Portal

There was a moment of terrifying, dead silence. The air itself had taken on a quality of weight making it capable of choking them all. Angelica sat in her chair looking at Cassandra and trying to hold back her tears. Instead of crying, she only made a few sounds that almost were hiccups. Soon, it passed. The entire time, Cassandra just sat and stared at the young queen. The child's very life had ruined nearly ten years of Prince Alexander's planning. Cassandra sat quietly as the sunlight coming through the window continued to fade into darker and darker night. She knew that Alexander had ways of coming back from the brink of disaster, and he would be thinking of a plan already to overcome this minor snag. It was only a matter of time.

David finally walked closer to the table from the dining room door where he had been standing. With the slowness of a woman twice her age, Cassandra turned to look at him. Her eyes were deep and sunken. She looked ill, and the sight of her almost made David back away against the wall where he had been during her confession. After a moment, that feeling passed, and the guard asked, "How did that portal get there? You said Prince Alexander researched its origins, and eventually he realized how it came to be. I want to know how."

Cassandra looked at him for a moment. "Do you?" she muttered quietly. The servant knew very well that she had not done anything wrong since she was following the demands of royalty when she acted. She also knew this guard had no right to interrogate her if the queen did not want her to continue. If working under Alexander had taught her nothing else, it was how to be arrogant. As if to show this, Cassandra looked away from the guard and back towards Angelica. The look from that child was one that seemed damning. The smirk that had developed on Cassandra's face after speaking to David now faded away. She actually looked back at the guard since his eyes were the least domineering in the room.

After a second to gather her thoughts, Cassandra began to speak again. "What difference does it make how it got there? It's there, and there's nothing that can be done about it." She stopped and waited for a response. It was strange. After all that Prince Alexander had done, she had no hesitation in telling his story, but the creation of that portal was a topic she wanted to avoid. It was almost as though she felt that tale would betray someone much more powerful than the murdering prince. When no one responded to her plea, Cassandra began to speak again. "According to legend, Protace died at an age of 127 from an assassin's blade. There were rumors back then, just as there are now, and most people had heard and believed the rumor that if Protace hadn't been murdered, he would have lived forever. Some people thought he made a deal with the Creators of the world, others thought that he was simply damned from the moment he was born. Very few, however, thought he was nothing short of a god. However, his age when he died really doesn't matter. What's more important is that his son, Soranace, succeeded him. Actually, Soranace watched on as Protace was slaughtered and immediately killed the assassin." With the smirk returned to her face, Cassandra looked briefly at Queen Angelica before continuing. "By the time Protace died, Soranace was well into his eighties. The old man didn't seem like he had another forty years of life in him like his father did, so he began to act quickly. He was desperate to create some kind of legacy of his own and not be remembered as the king that ruled briefly after Protace."

Soranace spent his life until the time of his rule as a student. During that time, he had become a mathematical and scientific genius, or at least what could be considered as such in that time. He developed theories that helped to time crop seasons, to control fire by using an assortment of fuels, even how to develop new substance from ones that already existed.

Wherever he went, he carried a heavy ledger in a shoulder pack. This book contained all of the notes he had taken on things he had learned, observed or created. Most the ledgers remained housed in the palace library for the centuries after Soranace died. Still, very few of them were of great use to anyone but Soranace himself. They were simply too advanced for most people to comprehend. The majority of these books contained astronomical diagrams and pictures of worlds coming together by means of spiraling circular tunnels. Soranace claimed that the known world contained what he called "soft spots:" areas where it was possible to leave this world and find oneself in a different one. Volumes of these notes were studied for centuries, but even the most learned scientists in the kingdom were dumbfounded by the writings in those ledgers.

Later on in his life, Soranace felt he had learned all there was to know about the physical world, and he turned his attentions to the dark arts. This, combined with his vast knowledge of the sciences, made him seem almost god-like while he was alive. He would turn trees that had stood tall for years into piles of wreathing, hissing snakes. These snakes would slither away only to burrow themselves into the ground and become full-grown trees again in a matter of seconds. Rumors spread that the woods at the far corner of the kingdom were created by Soranace and one his feats similar to this. By a simply wave of his hands, or by throwing jars of powders of liquids to the ground, he would make people levitate to almost fifty feet in the air. People revered Soranace as a great person to look up to, and someone whose power will usher in a new age of innovation throughout the lands.

Innovation or not, Soranace thought his reign would be quickly forgotten. He was following the first and greatest leader these people would ever have, and there was a good chance that he would not be able to make an equal mark as his father had done in the few years he would have left to rule. Soranace waited much longer than anyone had expected before he assumed the rule of the throne. Protace had reached the age of 127 years before an assassin finally struck him down. The king died in his son's arms and left an old man to succeed him. For this reason, when Soranace obtained his rule of the kingdom, he intended to do more than annex adjoining people and tribes. He planned to spread Protecia into an area no one had ever thought possible before.

Some would say it took five years for Soranace to finally plan what would be his legacy. More accurately, he had been planning it for closer to twenty years. Far before he became king, he was thinking of a way to spread his rule far and wide, once he obtained his rule. The final touches, the parts people saw and recognized the most, took these five last years to complete, but when they were done, he was ready to initiate his plan.

His most abstract and complex ledgers came from this time, and everyone knew something extraordinary would come of his work. Exactly what it would be, no one could say for certain. For the last week before his plan would begin, Soranace remained in isolation. Servants were making constant trips back and forth to the palace's library for him. They were obtaining books on nearly every kind of science imaginable. In that one week, Soranace had written slightly more than one thousand pages of his own theories based on the texts he had read.

On the last day before his work would begin, Soranace spent the day being carted around the entire kingdom by horse and carriage. He looked at everyone living out their lives, and he saw several things that disturbed him. Neighbors fighting with one another over a morsel of bread. Mothers beating their children until they bled and drifted into unconsciousness. People talking about how things were better in the old days when Protace ruled. Conversations about how their ruler was a monster or a sorcerer of some sort. These were things that Soranace felt would endanger the very concept of what he was preparing to do. Soranace's plan, as it turned out, was to build a passageway between this world and another via the soft spots that he had theorized about. Once this conduit was complete, sending people between worlds would be a simple matter. Protecia would colonize and the rule of the kingdom would double at the very minimum.

After his tour of the kingdom, though, Soranace was having second thoughts. These people were civilized less than a single century. Before then, they were barbarians and cave men, living their short lives scavenging for food and attacking each other for a dry corner of a cave to sleep in. They were not ready for the concept Soranace would bring to them. Travelling to another world and interacting with unusual people and strange organisms would be too devastating an event for them. They would simply go mad, trying to assault and kill the other people they saw simply because they were different. In a few years' time, Soranace feared they would be barbarians again.

Soranace would still build the conduit connecting the worlds, but it would be different. Only certain people would be able to pass through it initially, and others would die if they were to try. These would not be people living in the kingdom today, though. They would be people that would not be born in the kingdom as well as the world it was to connect to for several centuries. When the time comes, they would be drawn to that portal, and they would pass through. All it would take is one person passing through this tunnel before they knew the time was right. Then, by having everyone able to travel the conduit from one world passing into the other, a new portal would open and anyone willing to travel between the worlds would be able to. A new roadway connecting these differing lands would exist and be easily travelled by all.

But only in a time when the kingdom had matured.

With his modified plan intact, Soranace set out to the caves first thing the next morning. There was a feeling of immense power emanating from that great stone structure, and he could all feel the vibrating resonance of one of the soft spots he spoke of. This would be where his portal would be built. Carrying the final ledger and some of his chemicals in his pack, he proceeded into the caves unaccompanied. This was before any restrictions were placed on the access to the caves, and they were considered perfectly safe to travel.

Soranace travelled through the rocky corridors, laboring along with his heavy walking stick, and through the large cracks in the walls around him. He continued to march; carrying his ledger and supplies such as jars of powders and liquids whose purpose was unknown to most people, into the darkness. A soft glow emanated from the tip of his walking staff, one of the numerous incantations he had perfected years earlier. He walked for nearly an hour through the murky darkness until he came to large opening in the cavern that would suit his needs. Then, the spell began.

As hours drifted by, Soranace began to yell words of a strange language into the caves and listened as his voice echoed back to him. He threw the chemicals onto the ground one by one as he continued his incantation. Plumes of smoke came up into the air as the chemicals mixed and fizzed on the rocky ground. The spell was nearing completion. He was almost done, and then his mark would be left upon the kingdom. As he shouted the last word of the spell, and cast the last bottle of power onto the ground, smoke began to hiss up from it. Sparks began to shoot up from the ground in a crackling symphony that sounded like a swarm of insects being disturbed from their sleep. Soranace took a step back and watched with glee. It was working. The spell was working.

The wall of rocks ahead of him began to move. One of the cave passageways leading off of that chamber closed in as the caves became alive. It looked like the throat of some mighty beast constricting before death. From that wall that had been a cave opening moments ago, shapes began to take form. People and animals began to claw their way out of the rocky surface before becoming frozen in time. Each of them seemed to bring a piece of life from that other world across with them. Soranace was speechless with joy. All of his work was paying off. The portal was being created.

On the ground beside him, where he had mixed the growing stew of chemicals, the rocks began to stretch upwards, reaching into the air. This formation widened out and began to form the pool of oddly thick water that somehow held a constant current. As the stone bowl completed, brass leaves began to sprout from its sides and grow towards the center of the water almost as if to guard it against accidental contact. Soon, these stopped growing, and like the sculptures, they froze in time while the murky water began to fill from the bottom of the pool. Soranace took a few steps back and watched the pool fill. It was amazing. This would be the way to get into that other world.

There was an energy radiating from this area. The caves themselves seemed to make Soranace feel as though his powers were growing faster than they ever had before. It was as if the mystical powers of that other, unexplored world were leaching towards him through the rock itself. He felt capable of anything at that moment.

As the water reached the rim of the pool, there was an explosion of sparks from the top of it. It was nothing Soranace did not expect, but what happened next shocked him. The sparks reached as far up as the ceiling of the caves where they became large balls of fire. This fire quickly grew arms and soon, the entire rocky surface of the cave ceiling was invisible past the wall of flames. The natural gases, still dormant but undiscovered as of that time, had ignited. Fire began to fill the air like some giant creature that was rising from a deep slumber. Soranace turned and ran in the direction he had come holding his softly glowing walking staff in front of him.

It did not take long before the fire began to burn inside the walls of rock. There was a loud explosion, and Soranace stopped to look behind him to see what had happened. The walls were coming down, and if he did not leave immediately, he would be crushed. As best as he could, the old man began to run. Back-tracking his steps towards the exit of the caves, he raced with the sound of falling rocks getting closer and closer from behind him.

Before he had a chance to run for even a minute, a large rock fell from the ceiling of the caves and hit him in the shoulder. Soranace stumbled and fell to the ground like the countless trees he had uprooted with his mind. Still, he tried to drag himself further towards the exit, leaving his staff behind him, but it was of no use. He was stormed with falling rocks, and soon he was buried beneath them.

No one knew what had happened until that evening. Then, finally, Soranace crawled from the entrance to the caves. He had managed to pull himself out of the rocks that had landed on top of him, and was able to get to freedom. When Soranace did crawl back from the caves to the courtyard, he was bleeding from his head, mouth and innumerable injuries covering his body. He appeared to be the victim of a brutal assault. His oldest son, Sciaus, was in the courtyard, pacing and nervous about his father when he had not returned. Sciaus ran over to his father to see what had happened, but he knew immediately that there was little that could be done. Soranace fell fully to the dirt ground as Sciaus knelt beside him. The king was lying in the moonlight with is final ledger still strapped to his back. Scaius knelt beside him and tried futilely to revive the old man, but nothing happened. Soranace was dead, and with his death, the portal within the caves went undetected for hundreds of years to come.

Since then, no one was known to enter the caves until Alexander began his exploration of them. It was he that eventually discovered the portal that Soranace had created all those hundreds of years ago. He discovered the portal right on time. It was people from his generation that were able to pass between the worlds, and eventually create a portal for all to travel. After his ill-conceived trip to the other world, he saw who was meant to pass over and who was not. According to the ledgers he had later read in the palace's library, if all the people able to travel between worlds were on one side or the other, then the portal will be opened permanently for all people to travel across in either direction whenever they wished. The worlds would be merged forever. Controlling such a passage was what Alexander wanted, and had wanted for as long as he could remember. Wanted so desperately.

CHAPTER SIXTEEN

Escape to the Other World

With a deep sigh, Cassandra folded her arms in front of small bosom. This was all she knew, and no one had to ask to be sure of it. Just one look at that face showed that she had told them all about the portal and Alexander's plans that she had ever been told. She looked strangely satisfied and at ease with herself. With this great burden of secrecy relieved from her, Cassandra actually straightened up her back and almost looked a little healthier. There was no more for her to tell, and now Cassandra was to be set free.

As she indicated, she had done nothing wrong. Alexander told her everything she had to do, and she was his servant, so she had to follow his orders without question. That was exactly what she did, and no one was able to punish her for it. Alexander and one other person that Cassandra was unable to identify were able to pass between the two worlds. At least that they knew of. Aside from that one other person, no one would be able to track Alexander to where he was hiding in that other world. It seemed as though he had executed a flawless escape.

With a grin, Cassandra stood from her chair and walked out of the dining room. All the eyes in the room were boring into her back as she opened the door to the hallway and walked out. No one followed her. They just looked at each other for a few moments, and they all waited for Angelica to tell them what to do next.

"I want to find the other person that can pass between worlds safely," Angelica whispered as she stood from her chair as well. "Alexander had an accomplice. That jester's costume did not belong to him. I have seen the two of them together. That jester must have let Alexander use to costume to avoid suspicion. The costume was taken from the caves while we were looking in there for Alexander, so his accomplice probably has it again. Now, we have to find him before he tries to get through that portal as well. That jester must have been helping Alexander this entire time. At least two guards are to be stationed by that portal and another two just inside the entrance to the caves. If he tries to get through that portal, I want him taken into custody before he gets that chance. Maybe then, he can lead us to Alexander."

Angelica walked out of the room and towards her quarters. There, she spent the rest of the night in tears. It seemed as though the last time she was in this room was years ago rather than earlier that day. That was before the public address where an attempt was made on her life. It was before she knew of Alexander's involvement in the assassination of both her parents. Most especially, it was before the knowledge of this portal to another world that had allowed Alexander to escape. He may be making his own kingdom over there, and when the two worlds eventually do become united, there would be no way to anticipate what would happen next.

Still, with all of these thoughts coursing through her mind, Angelica managed to fall asleep in her tear-soaked pillow within an hour. However, the sleep was fitful, and what little deep sleep she had was plagued by horrible nightmares. She was standing in darkness in front of a large cave. There was a faint smell of gas around her, and she was able to recognize the pool of water at her side. There was something different about the caves, though. The heavily sculpted wall of rock had changed. In place of the images of people and creatures from the other world able to travel through the portal, there was only a smooth surface. None of those sculptures was there, and Angelica assumed that it was done. All of the creatures crossed over to this side, and now there was a gateway between worlds that anyone can pass through. Angelica stood still and stared at this gateway. A barrel vault carved into the caves connecting this world and the next. The dark blue sky on the other side of the portal was enough to show the silhouette of a person in a cape or a cloak of some sort. There was a staff in this person's hand similar to the one Angelica remembered seeing in sculpted pieces on the wall. Now, it was whole again, and she could see a bright light emanating from two points on the head of the staff. The blinding, yellow light was shooting out in beams forming stars around the man and staff. It looked almost like a sun glowing for him alone.

Then, there was the laughter. It was like a deep growl that was broken apart just enough so that it almost sounded like the chortle of an obese man. Angelica knew this was not the voice of a man anymore. This was a creature. A monster of some sort. Perhaps once a man, but now an inhuman entity so gruesome that it would horrify anyone that laid eyes upon it. This creature laughed and laughed, and with each passing second of laughter, the points of light on the staff grew brighter and brighter. This went on until the light nearly blocked out everything else in the caves making it impossible for the young queen to see anything but that blinding glow. The entire tunnel filled with blinding yellow light and soon there was just a bright and glowing sphere that her eyes could not penetrate.

Angelica awoke screaming. Her vision remained blurry and almost purple after seeing the light from that staff. It took her moment to catch her breath, and soon, spastic and useless convulsions of her lungs settled into a normal breath. After quickly letting her eyes scan the room, she realized that it was, in fact, only a dream and not something to fear upon waking. Or was it. She was not positive if this was simply a precursor of events to come. If that were the case, then some creature would come between the worlds and that may be the end of Protecia. With a deep sigh, Angelica tried to dismiss what she saw, but it remained lingering in the back of her mind like so many nightmares tend to do.

A total of four guards remained in the caves during the night. They paced back and forth without incident. No one seemed to be making an attempt to enter the caves this night. The people finally began to leave the courtyard by the time the evening came, and by the time the darkness had its full grip on the world, it was finally empty. People saw Cassandra being brought out of the caves and eventually released from the palace. Soon, they would begin to piece together who was really behind the assassinations, but for the time being, they just left the courtyard and went about their own lives. For the time being.

Soon, the two by the cave entrance looked towards the opening to the courtyard. There was a single point of fire hovering just by the entrance to the caves. As they began to approach this flame so that they could identify it, the fire began to move. It seemed as if it simply hovered through the air like a comet that had lost its way from the night sky. Lazily bobbing in the night, through the sky leaving a trail of flaming fingers behind it. It soared into the cave opening, past the two guards, and up towards the ceiling of the cave entrance. By the time it reached the rocky ceiling, all the air in that entrance chamber to the caves ignited.

The two guards were incinerated instantly. Within an instant, that entire entryway to the caves was filled with a bright blue fireball as the gas ignited and burned. A second later, the fire burned out, leaving nothing but smoke and the stench of burnt flesh. The charred remains of the two guards crumbled to the ground in a cloud of dust. Then the rumbling began.

There was a sound of frantic footsteps as the two guards near the portal began to run towards the exit to see what had happened. This sound was lost in the din of rocks falling from the ceiling and stalactites giving way to crash to the ground like great spears. Through the veil of falling debris, stones, and smoke, a single figure leapt through the cave entrance and began to run. He ran without any concern towards the falling rocks. The rocks fell around him without ever coming close to touching him. He passed the entrance chamber and ran towards the cave the housed the portal. When he arrived at this cavern, he passed the two guards stationed deep within the caves. The guards froze for a second at the sight they were looking upon for the second time that day.

A man, dressed in the brightly-colored jester's costume, was running passed the falling rocks and into the relatively safer cavern. He ran right passed the two flabbergasted guards as if he did not even see them. The guards turned and began to run after the fleeing man in the jester costume. If they kept this pace, they would be unable to catch up, but they tried their best. With the two guards running behind him, the man expertly navigated the winding caves. If the guards did not know exactly where this man was headed, they would have been unable to follow. The caves were simply too dark and the settling dust and dirt obscured all vision. Still, following the scratches in the walls left by that day's earlier trek into the caves, the guards gave chase.

Soon, the man reached the opening that appeared to be a sanctuary to that portal and the sculpture that accompanied it. The brightness of the costume was turning dull with the dirt falling from the ceiling towards the ground, and it made the man almost blend in with the caves around him. He was running towards the pool of water. One of the guards leapt towards him in a last attempt to stop his escape. The man in the jester's costume was tackled by the guard, and he fell to hard ground with a dense thud. This scuffle caused the mask to loosen slightly so that his nose was exposed from the shield of anonymity.

In that instant, the guards became more interested in the face behind the mask than they were at restraining the man. With this critical flaw, the man was able to throw them off. He crawled from the pair of guards and continued on his way to the portal. Still, in this part of the cave, streams of pebbles fell from the ceiling as drips of water would do on most other days. This gravel did, however, cause the jester to lose his footing while trying to stand. Regardless, he was able to get a few steps ahead of the guards. Holding his mask in place with his hand, he ran the last remaining distance towards the pool. As he reached the edge of the stone portal, the guards were approaching him again. Acting as naturally as possible, the man turned and slashed a small dagger at the air in front of him. It was nowhere near making contact with either of the two remaining guards, but it was enough to keep them at bay. Judging from his actions, this man seemed comfortable with the blade, but not with fighting someone that was willing to fight back. He had his goal of the portal in mind, and was determined to only do what he needed to do to get that far.

Being held back by the point of the dagger, the guards were only able to watch as the man climbed up the side of the pool. His eyes never left the pair behind him. Then, with one careful step backwards, he slid into the pool of water and was gone. Within seconds, the ripples in the water began to calm to their normal intensity, and the caves began to shake again.

It only took ten minutes for the queen to summoned, already awake with nightmares, and to find herself standing at this point within the caves. Queen Angelica looked angry beyond belief; actually the angriest she had seemed at any point during the day so far. The two living guards knew that they would be the focal point of her fury. With a scowl on her face and her arms folded, she nearly spit the words, "How did he get passed all of you? How could you let him get back through that portal?" It was the first time her voice actually sounded like it belonged to a person of her title.

The two guards stood shoulder to shoulder as the one to the left answered. "He rigged an explosion in the caves. That's what killed the other two. He must have ignited the one of the gas veins in there. There was a small cave in, and he was able to use that as cover. When cornered, he began to slash as us with a dagger." No more words were spoken for a few minutes in which they all just stood smelling the odor of the gases within those caves.

Finally, with a deep sigh, Angelica walked through the caverns along the same path she had taken earlier that day. Everyone followed behind her, and they were all equally shocked by what they saw. On the wall beyond the pool, there was a new figure in stone that had pushed its way out of the rock. A man was partially lying on the ground with his torso propped up on one arm. He was looking out towards the pool of water he had used to escape. The costume was still cloaking his body and obscuring any of his distinguishable features. It swirled around his barely visible contours and exposed only the strip of his face around his eyes, the hand that was holding the dagger, and one other thing. A rose was lying in one of the folds of his costume almost like a bouquet in a wedding portrait.

Queen Angelica was almost in tears as she turned and walked away from that sculpture. Now, they were back to the beginning. Alexander had escaped to freedom. The only other person they knew of that was able to cross between the worlds has now escaped there as well. The assassin and accomplice were both gone, and there was no way to go after them. Catching them could only possibly occur if they dared to venture back to this world, which seemed unlikely.

"I want two guards right here at all times." The pair of guards walked towards the wall with the new addition of a sculpture. There was a bit of fear running through them as to what Angelica might want them to do. "If one of them tries to come back through to this world, I want you to be right here to arrest them. The accomplice may try to return so that his identity would not be suspected." Angelica turned and walked back towards the cavern leading to the courtyard. After only a few steps on the sandy ground, she turned and said, "Tomorrow, I will decide what to do next. For right now, just guard that portal."

The next few hours could have lasted for days. Angelica was lying in bed, but there was no sleep for her. She could not stop thinking of ways she could possibly find the identity of the accomplice that had managed to escape. There seemed to be no answer that would work easily. The court jesters went through great pains to keep their identity hidden from the public. This way they could entertain people and not be subject to the ridicule they would experience if their names were known. Angelica had not known of anyone to have actually found the identity of one of these jesters, and she did not think she would be the first to uncover that mystery.

Out of the dozens of ideas that passed through Angelica's mind during the course of the night, one stood out. It would be the only one that could work, and it was all because of the accomplice escaping to the other world. His absence will force his identity to be known if they were only willing to look.

CHAPTER SEVENTEEN

Searching for the Accomplice

"**D**avid, come over here!" The guard walked towards Queen Angelica who had dark purple blotches under her eyes and seemed as though she had not slept in some time. It had been two days since the masked accomplice had escaped through the portal, and since then, there was no sign of him. When David walked to his queen's side, she simply said, "I have a plan to find Alexander's accomplice. Dispatch the royal horsemen with a list of known people in the kingdom. We should have one from a few months ago when we took a census of the land's citizens. Tell the horsemen to go to every residence and to form a list of people that were not there. People who should be in their homes, but are missing without a reason. That will narrow down the people who possibly can be an accomplice." Angelica sighed deeply and closed her eyes for a second. "Please go tell them now."

Within the hour, a fleet of horsemen rode from the palace to every edge of the kingdom. In each of their saddlebags, part of the list of citizens of Protecia was packed. Most people willingly let the guards into their homes to investigate. It was, after all, in an effort to find the person who had a part in the killing of one beloved queen and the attempt at another. Checks were places next to the names of people that had been found, and dashes were placed through the names of people that had died since this list was formed. The guards saw the burial grounds where those people had been laid to rest and identified the name on the markers, but they still had to indicate that these were people not found.

There was one person who offered quite a bit of resistance towards the guards. It was one of their own. A guard that had been in the service of the royal family for nearly four years. He nearly had to be restrained as his fellow royal guards pushed their way into his home. Certain that he was hiding someone in the cellar or back room, the guards persisted. Upon completing their search, they discovered why the guard had been so reluctant. There was a small square cut into the wall near the stove. When the guards examined it more closely, they saw that it was a tiny door, and within that door, there was a green costume. It was complete with a fern-like hat and bells that were attached to each leaf. This was the other jester. His identity was now discovered.

As the guards found this room, their comrade walked away. When the guards finally returned into the room with the jester standing inside of it, the one in the lead said, "Don't worry. Your secret won't leave this room." The jester nodded, but he still never went to a single public address wearing his costume again. He was just too embarrassed to do so.

Aside from this minor setback, the horsemen and guards went through their job quickly and efficiently. It took a little bit less than a week to go through the entire list. At this time, a new list was formulated of all the citizens they were unable to find. This list contained eight names, and each name had an occupation next to it.

A full week after he was given the directive, David knocked on the door of the queen's quarters. The sound of her footsteps, slow and weak, got closer to the door, and after a minute, she opened it. Without saying a word, she turned and walked back towards the bed where she simply threw herself as if her legs were too weak to support her own weight. David walked into the room a few steps behind the queen with the list in his hand and looked around. After all he had seen in the caves, he thought that he would never lay eyes on such atrocities again. This was far worse.

Angelica was lying on the bed starting up at the ceiling. She was wearing the pajamas she had been sleeping in for days even though it was almost noon. Her hair was disheveled, and there were dark circles under her eyes, which were almost becoming accustomed to being there. A breakfast of scrambled eggs and ham was lying on the desk, untouched on its silver tray. The metal gleamed in the dull sunlight, and it seemed to be the only point of light in the room. There was dust and even cobwebs clinging to the walls. Most likely, Queen Angelica had not left the room long enough in this week for Beatrice to be able to clean. It seemed as though she were clinging to life by the barest of threads, and she was not concerned if those threads would snap under the strain.

A deep depression had gripped onto Queen Angelica so thoroughly that it seemed to be killing her. Alexander's arrows had failed in their job of extinguishing her life, but now this depression was taking over where they left off. Queen Angelica was holding onto the idea of catching her parents' killers so completely that now, with the possibility of not finding them becoming closer to a certainty more and more, all she was holding onto seemed to be slipping away.

Finally, David sighed deeply and approached the bed. Angelica turned her head slightly so that her eyes met David's. Those eyes seemed lost in a cloud. "I have a list of people we were unable to find. Those who had recently died are not included on this list. If you would like to see their names as well, I can retrieve them." David stood at attention and awaited further instructions.

Angelica did not speak a word. She simply sat up, and with great effort, stood from her bed. As she walked towards the desk, she grasped the list that was rolled in David's outstretched hand. She did not say a word or slow down at all. Her path did not deviate until she reached the desk. Upon arriving there, as if it was the most natural thing in the world, Angelica raised her arm and swept the silver tray off the edge of the desk and onto the floor. It clattered to the ground, and the dishes shattered sending bits of food, porcelain, and glass onto the floor around the now dented tray.

Without acknowledging the spilt food, Angelica sat at the desk with the list in front of her. While slowly unraveling it, she looked at the names, one at a time. All but one of the names belonged to guards. Finally, the last name on the list was "Chenrile." Angelica just looked at the list for a moment and then sighed. Now that she had obtained this information, she did not know what to do with it. As if the sight of it detested her, Angelica dropped the sheet of parchment. It rolled up again on its own as she did this. The list she had pinned all her hopes to rolled off the desk and landed on the queen's knees. Soon, it rolled onto the floor and landed in the bits of food and drink that were spoiling there.

"All of them have legitimate excuses for being absent from their residences. The guards are all on assignment patrolling the kingdom's borders. They would be extremely difficult to find since they would be sleeping in shifts in tents at random places along the kingdom's boundary lines. Chenrile, as he told you the day of the," for a moment, David hesitated, and finally continued, "the incident, he is in the Nezzrin Kingdom helping them get through an outbreak of disease. He would also be nearly impossible to find even if we were given permission to enter their kingdom." David stood still, and waited for Angelica to say that he did a good job and to be on his way.

No such words came from her mouth. When she first spread her lips, no sound issued from them at all. More likely than not, she had not spoken a word in a week, and it was difficult getting started again. Finally, a dry and strained voice whispered, "You will have to keep looking. Have the guards and horsemen patrol the boundaries of the kingdom. They are to keep patrolling until they can swear that any guard that would be on the borders has been found or is missing." Angelica looked at the spilt milk lying in the broken service pieces on the floor next to the desk. "As for Chenrile, we will just have to wait until he comes back. If he does not return in another week, I will send a message to the Nezzrin king to ask for Chenrile's whereabouts."

David turned and began to walk towards the door to carry out his new orders. Before he got even halfway there, Angelica called out, "Please get Beatrice in here to clean my quarters." The guard nodded as he left the room. As soon as he left, a smile began to form on his face. Wanting the quarters cleaned meant that she was starting on her way out of the depression. What he did not see was that Angelica began to dress in her clothes as soon as the door was shut. Within five minutes, she was walking out into the hallway for the first time in a week. It finally seemed as though they may find the assassin at last.

CHAPTER EIGHTEEN

The Staff of Protace

By that afternoon, Angelica had a new idea. While David was searching for the remaining people on his list trying to narrow down the possibilities for Alexander's accomplice, Angelica could try to see if Alexander had left any clues behind. Cassandra had said that after the prince's discovery of the portal and that he could pass through it, he had been spending every night over there. His quarters had not been used, and Angelica was able to confirm that from the time she went to knock on his door and found the handle covered in dust. Still, even though he had not been there in so long, it was possible that he had left some clue in that room as to whom his accomplice was or an indication of someone else that could pass through the portal. Angelica was determined to find this clue.

With Cassandra, Beatrice, and two guards surrounding her, Angelica walked over to Alexander's door. The handle was covered in dust again, except this time, the dusty film was slightly less dense over the area Angelica had touched it over a month ago. This time she just grabbed hold of the handle and pushed on it as hard as she could. The door did not budge. Angelica pushed again, but there was still not movement. It was impossible for him to lock the door from the outside, so it must just be stuck. Most likely it was from years of not being opened. Finally, one of the guards pushed with her. On it rusty hinges, the door swung open with enough force to slam it into the wall beyond.

There was a loud shriek as the door opened. For a moment everyone jumped back thinking that someone was in there. Possibly someone that Alexander had been holding captive for years. As the torchlight from the hallway reached into the darkness of the room, a large rat looked up at the group with black eyes. It let out another shriek as it turned and scurried into the darkness. After the rodent found its hiding place, it took a moment for the in the room to settle. There was a stench of decay and stale air coming from within the room, but from nowhere in particular. As their eyes adjusted to the dim light provided by the torches, they could see a film of mold and mildew covering the bottom third of all the walls and nearly every flat surface. Mixed in to the black spots that were growing on the walls and floors, there were tiny spots of rodent feces. The smell was horrible.

It took about five minutes for the stench to thin out enough for anyone to enter. Angelica fought back the urge to vomit, and she could see from everyone's expressions, they had a similar urge. Once the smell dissipated, they all filed in. There was a thick layer of dust on the ground, and a dense network of spider webs filled the far corner of the room. From that massive cavern of webs, thousands of newly hatched spiders were scurrying down the walls and across the ceiling. It looked like Alexander nailed a sheet of wool over the only window in the room forcing it into total darkness. It also made it impossible for someone to see in from the outside. That and the disuse of the room for so long made a perfect combination for this disgust.

Still, they all walked in to examine. There was a large sheet of parchment of the desk, but it was nearly hidden under a blanket of dust, mold, and rat droppings. Holding down the corner of the parchment was a metal cup that was half filled with a thick, nearly black stinking liquid. Squirming within this liquid were dozens of maggots. One of guards walked over to the desk, slid the parchment out from underneath the cup and tapped its edge of the desk to shake off the excessive dust and dirt. Underneath, now visible under a significantly thinner layer of dust, there was a drawing. On this sheet of parchment in Alexander's distinct and sloppy handwriting was a sketch of what appeared to be a staff. There were cracks drawn in it to show where it had been broken. It was long and labeled as being made of both metal and stone. The shaft itself had a spiraling design going up and down its entire length, and the staff's head held the representation of a monster. Judging from the reptilian body and the horns protruding from around its head as a protective measure, Angelica was able to recognize it as the staff she saw on the carved wall inside the caves right down to where it had been broken. On its head was the creature she had seen represented on that same wall. There was something unusual about the eyes of the creature in this drawing, though. They were drawn darker and that somehow made them appear to leap out of the parchment at them. The drawing was no more than a sketch, but those eyes still seemed to have some magical quality to them.

Angelica had to look away in fear and disgust for a moment. The sight behind her was just as distasteful. Molds and mildews seemed to fill the walls. On the bed, there was torn fabric and what appeared to be a nest of animals living inside. Angelica said softly, "Search the room. See if there is anything else of use in here. Especially something concerning his accomplice and that portal."

While she was looking away from the desk and that sketch, Angelica saw something else propped in the corner of the room near the bed. It was a large wooden staff that appeared to be gnarled and worn down from years of being held tightly. She walked over to this staff and looked at it while the others gathered around behind her. The wood it was fashioned from had petrified over time. There were tiny cracks covering its surface, and after a minute she remembered where she had seen it before. Beatrice confirmed what Angelica was already thinking when she whispered into her ear, "It's Soranace's walking stick. All the murals and sculptures of him show him holding it." Angelica just nodded. She could only assume that this cane was lost in the caves when Soranace was killed in the cave-in, and it was only uncovered when Alexander began the excavations years later. The fact that he left it here could only mean that he was unable to unlock its powers as Soranace was rumored to do. However, Soranace was a great sorcerer. The staff probably would be nothing more than a wooden stick in anyone else's hands.

Angelica turned away from the walking stick and left the room. The image of that lizard-like creature wrapped around the staff remained haunting her mind. Alexander knew about it as well. Judging from his room, he seemed to be obsessed with it and the secrets it held. As Angelica walked away from Alexander's quarters towards her own, she realized that she was just as trapped by its spell. There was nothing that could push the image of that creature and that staff from her mind.

That evening, Angelica walked into the palace library. A servant had told her that Beatrice and Cassandra were searching some old texts in there to see if they could some references to either the walking stick they found or the staff they saw the sketch of. The notes on the sides of that drawing as well as almost a hundred other sheets of parchment led them in the correct direction, and soon they were able to find some information about those items. Then, they asked a servant to summon the queen.

As Queen Angelica entered, the librarian ran over to greet her in a fashion almost identical to the way he greeted Wilhelmina a few months earlier. Queen Angelica nodded and spoke politely to the elderly librarian, and he brought her to the table where Beatrice and Cassandra were sitting with books scattered in a pile before them.

"I heard you came up with something." The two servants stopped looking through the books and turned to face their queen. "Please tell what those staffs were and what it means that Alexander was so fixated on them." Without breaking eye contact with the two women, Angelica lowered herself into one of the chairs surrounding the table.

Beatrice was the first who spoke, but her tone of voice was not one of happiness or optimism. "It seems that the wooden walking stick we found was exactly what we thought. Soranace's cane. He sometimes used it to perform magic. Sometimes he was able to do these things without it though. Most likely, it was just a prop for him, which is why Prince Alexander found no need in it.

"According to the notes Alexander kept, the other staff, the one in the drawing, he had found broken into pieces while mining the caves. It was about a week before the portal was discovered, and its location was in a side cavern just opposite from that portal." Beatrice stopped speaking for a moment, and Angelica used this time to reflect on what was said. She remembered seeing that side cavern when searching for Alexander.

Alexander himself was overseeing the digging in the caves on that particular day while they excavated the farthest point they had ever reached. One of the miners struck the cave wall, and a large rock just shifted out of the way. A cloud of dust plumed up from it emanating a smell of stale air and the noxious fumes of the gas. As the miner backed away and coughed, Alexander took a step closer. He was able to see the narrow opening into the wall of the cave and immediately recognized it as no naturally occurring cavern. It was mined deliberately and then sealed off with a large rock. This most likely meant that it was for the purpose of hiding something, and now Alexander was curious what that something could be. Only two weeks earlier he had uncovered Soranace's cane in those caves closer to the surface, but this was an intentional effort to hide something. Alexander was immediately intrigued.

With the worker still backing away from the stale air that was drifting up in a cloud from the narrow opening, Alexander pushed the rock the rest of the way from the tiny cave mouth. At its widest point, it was about two feet across, and Alexander felt that he could easily fit inside. Quickly looking around to see if anyone was watching him (the worker that had discovered the cave had walked to another area to breathe cleaner air), Alexander fell to his knees and climbed inside.

Still, before even moving closer to the narrow cave, he could see something in the darkness. Some sort of shape. He reached in and grabbed hold of the object just in front of him. It was so cold it felt like a series of needles being stuck into his fingers, but he did not let go. He actually held it tighter, relishing the pain and the possibility of profit from this item he was to uncover. While it felt cold, somehow there was an indescribable heat just beneath its surface. It felt almost like something waking up at the feeling of those fingers sliding across it. When he dragged it out, he nearly screamed. Alexander fell backwards and scrambled another two steps before he was able to calm himself. A second later, he was kneeling again and staring into the stone eyes of the beast that was wrapped around the head of the staff. All that was there was the staff's head, and even it was in pieces. The tail of this creature had been cracked off as was the shaft of the staff. There were other, smaller cracks covering the rest of the creature, but it seemed to be holding together.

With this piece recovered, Alexander was unable to stop. He placed down the head of the staff and began to crawl into the narrow cave on his hands and knees. With the light fading more and more as he dragged himself deeper into the cave, he found three other pieces to the staff, one at a time. Some were just lying on the ground, and others were lodged into the rock. With each piece that he recovered, Alexander placed the broken remnants together so that he could find what was still missing, and soon he had it all.

These four pieces were hoarded by Alexander in his quarters where he drew the diagram of what it would look like assembled. Then, he began to research it as best as he could while taking notes on parchments all around his quarters. He would spend nearly ten hours each day scribbling down notes to find the origin of this staff and to answer all the questions it seemed to pose. Then, however, something more important consumed his attention. Namely, the discovery of the portal, and he abandoned his research on the staff.

"As best as we could tell, that was how it happened. Alexander had the broken remnants of the staff in his possession, and he kept them for some time. Eventually, after he discovered his ability to travel between the worlds, he brought the staff across as well. Now, those broken pieces appear on the wall with the rest of the images."

Angelica just sat and stared at the two women for a moment. After listening to Beatrice's speech, there was nothing else that could be done. Finally, the young queen managed to push out the words, "What else have you found? The story you just told me was most likely from Alexander's notes in the margins of the parchment with the sketch on it. Where else did his leads take you?"

It was Cassandra who spoke now. She leaned forward in her seat looking more alive than she ever had before. With Alexander's absence, she had not been making all of those trips into the caves, and it seemed to be helping her a great deal. When she finally spoke, her voice seemed almost uncertain of its words, but she said them anyway. "Unfortunately, the information we found about that staff is quite limited, and what we did discover is terribly depressing."

Angelica did not take the opportunity to back down. As if to give her every last opportunity, Cassandra waited a few seconds before she began to speak again. "That was the staff of Protace." All the air disappeared from the room for a moment, and Cassandra waited again before continuing. She did not want to continue speaking. That much was obvious by her voice and body language, but she knew she had to. "As most people know, according to the legends, Protace built a bridge across the Particion River and united the barbarian clans under his rule, creating the kingdom of Protecia. Once these people were united, Protace was naturally accepted as the ruler by both sides, because both of these peoples swore to the fact that he had originally lived on their side of the river. It appeared as though he was living on both sides of the river his whole life. People on both sides of the river clearly remember growing up with him. Both groups also remember his son, Soranace, as living on their side, and they both remembered that staff as well.

"What isn't known to most legends is that there was some opposition to his building of that bridge. A small amount, but opposition just the same. However, all the people that openly protested against Protace and his ideas of unification would disappear without a trace. Massive searches wouldn't uncover a body or any kind of remains from those people. They were just erased from existence. It made people afraid of Protace, and his ideals soon became unquestioned. There was a small group of people that went as far as to call him a monster.

"Concerning his staff, the references are few. We were unable to find a single picture of it, aside from what you saw in Alexander's quarters. Alexander did seem able to deduce its origin. By following his notes, we were able to conclude that it was, in fact, the staff of Protace. Once again, according to legend, about twenty years after the founding of Protecia, Protace seemed that the kingdom's foundations were solid enough that he wouldn't need to use fear to rule his people as he had before. He walked into the caves with that staff, and legend maintains that he smashed it and sealed it within a small cavern deep within the caves where no one would be able to find it. He was afraid that someone else would be able to unlock its powers and use them against him. There, it was supposed to remain for all time. It did remain there for a while, but Alexander recovered it eventually. Now, it belongs to him."

Cassandra stopped talking with a wide smile on her face. After listening to that story, Angelica was barely able to move. She just sat and stared blindly at the wall in front of her. It took the calm, soothing voice of Beatrice to bring her out of her trance.

"There is more to that staff, though. Protace was known for challenging people to duels with that as his weapon against their swords or clubs, but it seems to have much more power than any normal weapon. We don't know how that staff came into existence or how it got its strength, but there were a few myths, very few, that talk of it having magical powers when handled by Protace alone. It was said that the staff of Protace could alter people's bodies, turning them into things that were more monster than human, that it could make people fly into the air as though they had wings no one could see, and even could make people disappear without a trace. It was said the Protace was able to draw his powers from this staff and that was how he lived as long as he did. This myth continues to explain how Protace was the only one who was known to control the staff's powers, and despite attempts of his child and grandchildren to summon its powers, it did no more for them than any piece of metal or stone.

"There was one exception to this, however. It was one story concerning Soranace's youngest son, Arrtenus. It was said that his attempt to use the staff went badly. That was the word Soranace wrote in his diary. Badly. However, it did say that in a few months' time, Arrtenus was able to walk and speak again, however he would go off on rants about seeing things that only he could see and how he could hear screaming in his mind constantly. Years later, when Arrtenus ruled the kingdom, his rule was brief. He killed himself by plunging a dagger through one of his eyes."

Beatrice took hold of Angelica's hand and added in a whisper, "Whatever is going on in that world, be thankful that it's not happening here. I know you want to see Alexander pay for what he did, but you cannot let your revenge be the only point of your rule as queen. Please. You are better than that, and the people deserve more than that."

Angelica nodded. She then thanked the two women for their hard work, and after a minute, she left the library. With the darkness getting still darker outside, the queen walked by torchlight towards her quarters. She made certain not to stop or slow down as she passed Alexander's room. The door was closed again, but the simple thought of what was lying inside of there made her both terrified and nauseous. When she finally reached her quarters, Angelica stormed in and locked the door behind her.

"Queen Angelica," a voice whispered behind her. With fear as her only guide, she swung around and pulled the dagger from her ankle sheaf. While holding it out in front of her, she looked around the room. No one was in there with her. "Queen Angelica, are you in there?" The voice sounded so much like Alexander's the queen did not know what to think. There was no one in the room, so the voice must have been coming from outside. Without lowering the dagger, the queen walked towards the door she had just closed and locked. Quickly, she unlocked and opened the door extending the dagger towards the widening gap between the door and the doorjamb as she opening it.

There was a moment of shock as the man in the hallway let out a gasp. It was David. He must have seen her walk into the room and followed her to the door. "Yes, what is it? I've had a very hurtful day." Without waiting for an answer, Angelica turned around and began to walk back into the room. She left the door opened, and David followed her in. There was another list in his hand, and something else. When Angelica reached her bed, she sat down facing the guard, and asked again, "What is it?"

Slowly, David took another few steps towards the bed and extended his hand towards the queen. "I have this. It's another list. The people we haven't been able to find after another search." Angelica took the list and looked at it briefly. There were two names on it. She read it aloud as David watched. "Carl, guard patrolling boundaries. Chenrile, royal physician away in Nezzrin." Once she finished, she looked back up at David seeing that there was something else in his hand. "And what is that?"

The guard handed it to Angelica seemingly unable to speak because this additional piece of parchment could solve everything. It was a small note, and as Angelica began to read it, David summarized its contents. "It's from the Nezzrin king. He is reiterating his kingdom's urgent need of a physician due to the recent outbreak of disease." Angelica finished reading the note silently and looked up to David. Finally, the guard spoke again, "He's requesting that Chenrile go there and help with the sick. Chenrile never got to the Nezzrin Kingdom. He's not at his home here, and he's not over there. Either something's happened to him, and Carl is the accomplice to Alexander, or Chenrile is now in that other world with Alexander." With a spastic, deep breath, David added, "What are we going to do now?"

Angelica did not move or speak for a long time. The thought of Chenrile, the man who had been trying to console her and examine her injuries as Cassandra told everything, may be the very person who helped Alexander kill her mother and try to kill her. It was a great shock, and Angelica refused to believe it. "I do not want anyone, including you or me, to jump to conclusions. Do not go announcing your findings to anyone, including your other guards." Angelica stood from the bed and walked over to her desk on the far side of the room. While only gliding her fingers along its polished surface, Angelica said, "I want to leave first thing tomorrow morning. Travel along the path to the Nezzrin Kingdom, and look carefully for any sign of Chenrile of his carriage. Maybe an injured person or an accident detained him. Anything could have happened that could have delayed his arrival." Angelica now turned her eyes from the desk to David and continued. "When you return, then we will have to make a more extensive search if nothing is found."

With a face that was expressionless with fear, David turned and walked from the queen's quarters, closing the door behind him. Angelica now threw herself onto the desk chair and began to think of the possibilities that may lie ahead of her. She knew that she should be going to sleep, but sleep refused to come. Finally, Angelica realized what she must do. Without taking a single item her, Angelica left her quarters and then palace itself.

CHAPTER NINETEEN

Planning to Chase Alexander

The young girl walked until she reached the bridge across the Particion River. It was the bridge that Protace supposedly built, and most likely it was the inspiration Alexander needed to build his own bridge across worlds. Angelica stood on the arcing bridge at its highest point and looked down. The vast Particion River, years ago considered an impassable boundary, raged beneath her. The currents looked strong and small waves crashed up onto the banks. It was a wide and turbulent body of water, and Angelica knew this very well. With this thought on her mind, Angelica jumped in.

For an instant, Angelica felt the cold nighttime air rushing by her. Her hair flew up around her, and her simple pajamas rippled in the rush of wind. Finally, she hit the water below and felt as though she was attacked by million biting fish. The pain of coldness stabbed into her for a few seconds, but dissipated soon as her body adjusted to the temperature, and then she clawed her way through the water back towards the surface. Water danced around her as Queen Angelica broke the surface of the water and exploded into the night air again. She took a deep breath of air and then plunged back underneath.

Angelica reached out and pulled the water towards her, and soon she found she was moving. Feeling the air in her lungs almost pushing against her ribs, Angelica continued to pull the water behind her by the handful. Without slowing her arms in the slightest, the queen slowly began to let the air out of her lungs. Finally, when there was no more air left in her body and an ache began to grow in her diaphragm, she pulled herself towards the surface again. When she came up, she quickly turned around while wading in the water and looked at the bridge she had jumped from. It was about ten feet away. Angelica just nodded in self-admiration and dove back beneath the surface of the water to see if she could swim back towards and past the bridge this time.

After nearly two hours of teaching herself to swim, Angelica returned home. When she originally dove in, she was telling herself that it was just a precaution. The portal appeared to be made of water, so she would have to know how to swim. She may have to go through that portal if Alexander was to return with the purpose of destroying her. It may be her only way out. Still, no matter how much she told herself this, Angelica knew deep down that this was not the reason. She knew that Alexander would not come back willingly, and she was willing to go get him. If that meant swimming through the portal into that other world, then that is what she must do. Since she wanted to keep these ideas to herself, this meant that she would have to teach herself to swim rather than asking for the assistance of another.

Sleep still did not come easily for the queen. After all of that exercise, she was still wide-awake when she finally placed herself down on her bed. It was in that position, entirely awake, that Angelic was lying until the sun came up the following morning. From her window, she was able to see David riding a horse away from the palace in the direction of Nezzrin Kingdom. He was off to see if there really was a reason to start blaming Chenrile for the crimes committed against the royal family.

Angelica knew she could not simply lie in bed until he returned, so she rose and began to dress. Her wet pajamas were hanging on the bedpost and were almost completely dry by the time she climbed out of bed again. She dressed in her simply day clothes and walked from her room. The palace seemed to be just as active as it always had been, but Angelica was unable to fully rise from the sleepiness that washed over her as soon as the sun rose.

It was not very long before Beatrice found Angelica and pulled the queen aside. The woman seemed almost ecstatic, but that still did not help Angelica's condition in the slightest. While another servant went along the wall extinguishing the torches for the halls to be lit with sunlight rather than firelight, Beatrice said, "I hope you don't mind the liberty I took, but after what we discovered last night, I felt something should be done." Beatrice began to reach into a small bag she was carrying with her. "I was beginning to think that if you need to protect yourself, with all that's going on now, your dagger may not be enough. You never know how long it may take a guard to get over to you and help you, so you may have to save yourself sometime. I had one of the metalworkers make this for you."

The object Beatrice pulled from the bag was a complete shock to Angelica. She had been expecting a larger dagger or something along those lines, but this was quite different. What Beatrice was holding out to her was a slingshot. It was a strip of cloth with a hardened cup on the end of it. Angelica took the slingshot and held it in her hands. "This is very nice, but why did you need a metalworker to make this for you?"

A smile developed on Beatrice's face that Angelica feel almost as excited as her caregiver was. "That's the most important part." Beatrice removed three metal discs, each of about an inch and half in diameter. Angelica lifted one of them and gasped as she did. "Be careful. They're very sharp." As Beatrice took the one disc back from Angelica, the queen looked at a bead of blood developing on her fingertip. "Are you okay?" Angelica just nodded and reached for the disc again. This time careful to hold it only from the smooth center, and she admired it closely this time.

It was beautiful. Nearly sculpted out of metal so shiny it reflected every surface of the hallway, it seemed as though it was the focal point of all the light around it. Beatrice continued to talk. "There are three of them. This way if you are attacked by someone with a bow and arrow like last time, you would be able to fight back with these." Beatrice waited a second before adding, "It's better to be prepared than not."

Angelica thanked Beatrice greatly, and she already knew that the rest of the day would be spent trying to improve her aim with the slingshot. After spending the day doing that, the night would be spent improving her swimming. She had no idea how long she would have to stay submerged if she was to travel to the other world, and she also was clueless as to how small a target she may have to hit if that situation came to that. If Angelica were needed to stand up for herself, then she would have to spend a much longer time in training than she had been.

For hours, David rode his horse along the road towards the Nezzrin Kingdom. If Chenrile was delayed, he would find him or some evidence of what had happened somewhere along this road or in the kingdom itself. Whatever the case, David had to ride until he either found something or reached the kingdom. The scenery was one that he had seen hundreds of times already, and so far there was nothing new. He was still inside of Protecia, but the boundary line was approaching quickly. Soon, he began to doubt that he would find anything.

Still, he rode on. David's horse galloped along dirt road to the Nezzrin Kingdom as that road winded through a forest. Eventually, David saw something. It was as the boundary line between the kingdoms was barely within sight in the distance. He noticed a disturbance in the bushes along the edge of the road. David slowed the horse and looked more closely. About ten feet into the surrounding woods there was carriage of some sort. With dread, David realized how horribly familiar that carriage looked.

David's horse came to a stop, and he dismounted quickly. After taking a few steps towards the woods and the wreckage, he saw the wolves. There were six of them walking over the wrecked pieces of wooden planks that were scattered around the trees. One by one, they began to turn and look at David. Without taking his eyes away from the pack of wolves, David knelt down and picked up a large rock from the ground. As if he was bringing all the fury he had been feeling in the past weeks behind that rock, he threw it with all his might against a tree at the center of the wolves. When the rock stuck the tree, the animals began to stir around. They were hungry by nature and not going to run unless they needed to. The rock startled them enough to get their attention but not enough to make them scatter. When David shouted at them, they did run back, however. Out of sight behind the dense cover of trees, the wolves retreated, but not too far. David could still hear the low growl of their presence.

With the wolves gone, David approached the carriage wreckage. There was not much left to it. Splintered pieces of wood in the shapes of both planks and wheels were lying around a heavy tree that was reaching upwards to the sky. Whoever was driving it must have lost control of the carriage or simply lost the road and crashed into this tree. There was no sign of the horses anywhere over here, and David assumed they must have escaped without being harmed, or had already been killed and eaten completely by the wolves. Either way, the horses were not David's main concern. There was some remains left of the driver, however. The wolves did not leave much, but the entire area of the crushed wagon that was near the tree was soaked red in blood. This was probably the result of the wolves more than the accident.

As David tried to get closer to the wagon, the growling got louder. He froze in mid-step and looked for the source of that noise. The wolves were all around, and they were slowly walking closer to David and the wagon. There was no time to do anything. David turned and ran from the wreckage. As he began to pick up pace, the wolves began to chase him, and he just made it to his horse in time. The animal began to gallop as soon as David was on its back, and he left the wolves and the wrecked carriage behind.

While David rode, he could hear the howling of the wolves behind him. That soon began to fade away, and David tired his best to recall what Chenrile's carriage looked like. In that wreckage with those wolves surrounding him, he did not have time to look for any specific marks of identification. Still, he could not find any other possible explanation. Chenrile must have died in a carriage accident.

To avoid the possibility of crossing paths with the wolves again, David took another trail back to the palace. This path would take him across the Particion River, but he would not arrive until nighttime. Still, it was the safest path to take. David rode with the woods behind him while the sun set behind the mountains to his far right that marked the farthest border of Protecia, and the world as he understood it. He continued to travel into the darkness, and soon he came to the bridge.

By this time, the night sky was at the darkest it would be that night. The moon kept everything well lit, and David was able to see everything around him as he slowed his horse to cross the bridge, and then he heard the splash. In a panic, he looked over and saw only the waves beneath him. After a few seconds of watching, what appeared to be a head erupted from the surface of the water. David was going to wait to see if this person needed help getting back to shore, and while looking towards this person, he was able to eventually see a face. It was Queen Angelica coming to the surface.

Before David got a chance to see that the queen was actually swimming rather than drowning, he leapt from his horse and dove in after her. Within a second, she was struggling under his arm as David wrestled her towards the land. Finally, when he placed her ashore, and she saw who it was, she stopped fighting. While Angelica was catching her breath, it was David who spoke first, "What are you doing out here, your Majesty?"

For a second, the queen only looked at him. It took her a while, but eventually she said, "You have to promise that this is in the strictest confidence." David nodded, so Queen Angelica continued. "I have been teaching myself to swim. In the event that I would have to travel to that other world, I would have to go under water, and I want to make sure that I would be able to do it."

David pulled himself out of the water now and helped the queen to her feet. "There's no reason for you to do that. If Alexander stays on that side, he wouldn't pose a problem towards us, and if he doesn't, there are guards waiting to arrest him the instant he comes through that portal. You don't have to worry about things like that."

The two of them were walking onto the bridge now where David's horse was waiting. "Yes, I do have to worry about it." They both stopped, and their eyes found each other in a glare that was absolutely terrifying. Moonlight is funny that way. "I'm thinking about going to that other world after him. That may be the only way to make sure he will not become a threat in the future." David let go of her hand for the first time since he pulled her from the river. Now that he did this, Angelica took advantage of it. She ran to the edge of the bridge and jumped in again. Then, she went under and swam. David just stood and watched for a little while. Eventually, he got back on his horse and left her there. She seemed fine, and David did not want to push the issue at that time. After all, she was the queen.

The next morning, David's knock on the door was what woke Angelica. When she let him in, he looked at her with worried eyes. "I am assuming you are not here to tell me that what I am doing is foolish and dangerous." Angelica turned her back to David and walked towards the middle of the room. "This is something I have to do, and there is no way you could stop me from doing it."

"In that case, I'll tell you about Chenrile." Angelica spun around so quickly that David thought she would fall to the ground. She stared at him, and he simply looked back, stone-faced. "I believe that he is dead. On the way to the Nezzrin Kingdom, I saw a crashed carriage with blood all over it. There were wolves surrounding it, so I wasn't able to get a very close look, but it looked like Chenrile's carriage."

Angelica looked down at the floor as tears began to flow from her eyes. "I guess that would mean Carl, the missing guard, is the accomplice to Alexander." Angelica sat on the bed and looked at David with tears spilling down her cheeks. "That makes some sense, I guess. Alexander did train the guards, so I suppose he could have had his pick of people to help him with the assassination attempts." Angelica looked back down at the floor. "That is it, you can leave now."

With that, David turned to leave. He got halfway to the door before he stopped and said, "Would you please, at least, discuss your ideas about going after Alexander with Beatrice? See what she thinks about it." David did not wait for a response. He knew that none would be given even if he did wait. Simply, he just continued on his way out the door and closed it behind him.

Alone with her tears, Angelica sat on the bed thinking about what David had said. If she was seriously going to think about chasing after Alexander, she would have to tell everyone eventually. They would find out one way or another, and they might as well hear it from her. Then she could at least make sure they knew exactly why she was doing this. They would also want to know that she was prepared for this mission.

It was afternoon when Angelica finally sat down with Beatrice to discuss her pursuit of Alexander. They had met each other after lunch in the dining room. Angelica was getting ready to speak to her servant, but she did not get the chance. When she saw her caregiver, however, it was Beatrice who spoke first. "There's a serious problem in the kingdom." Angelica was closed her mouth with the words she had prepared dying on her tongue. She thought it was best to let Beatrice finish what she was saying first. "We knew this would happen eventually. Everyone saw us chasing someone into the caves, and they saw us walking out with Cassandra. Then, they see that Cassandra was released. In the following weeks, no one has seen or heard from Alexander. It was only a matter of time before they started to suspect Alexander's involvement." With a deep sigh, Beatrice continued, "I began to hear rumors. They are piecing together everything that's happened. Riots may begin if these rumors go unanswered."

Angelica waited a second. This may be the chance she was waiting for. "Maybe, then, this is a good time to mention what I had been planning." As if in shame, Angelica looked away. "I have been teaching myself to swim. You have seen me learning how to use the slingshot. I think I will be perfectly safe if I try this." Angelica paused for a moment. It seemed too difficult to continue, but she knew she had to actually say the words she needed to.

Finally, while the queen was trying to formulate the words in her mouth, Beatrice filled in the blanks for her. "You're thinking about going after him. Chasing him back to that other world." Beatrice placed a hand underneath the queen's chin and turned the young girl's head so they could see eye to eye. "Why?" Angelica was struggling under the caregiver's grip, but she could not bring herself to order the woman to let go. Finally, she just relaxed her head in Beatrice's hand.

"This is something I have to do," she nearly spit. "I have been living in fear since I saw that monster kill my mother and now that I know who he is and who's helping him, I know that I will never be at peace again until I see him dead." Angelica realized that she had said too much. Beatrice had not known about Chenrile's death and the fact that one of the guards was assisting Alexander in these crimes. It did not matter, though. Neither did the fact that Angelica had yelled about wanting to kill out of simple revenge. Still, she did not want to fall in Beatrice's eyes. If there was one person left alive whose opinion she admired, it would be her servant.

To the young queen's relief, Beatrice did not even notice this extra information. "That is a very bad idea. You've been learning how to swim, but you have absolutely no idea how long you'll have to be underwater before you come out on the other side. Even if you can swim the distance and hold your breath long enough, you have no way of knowing if you were meant to travel across that passageway. Remember what Cassandra said. Only certain people can travel across the passage. If anyone else tries to, they will die. But let's say you get across. Alexander is the ruler there. He'll have fleets of soldiers trying to find you and kill you. You'll be dead before you even see the sun set."

Angelica sat for a moment. With the setting sun coming in through the dining room window, she thought carefully about everything Beatrice had said. These had all been arguments Angelica had planned to counteract, and that was exactly what she intended to do. "I saw Alexander before he dove into the water, and based on the guards' account of the accomplice going in as well, the two men hardly prepared. They did not stop and catch their breaths. There was no attempt to take a deep breath before diving in. The distance could not be that much if they dove in so casually.

"On the other side, Alexander would not even be expecting me to arrive," Angelica continued going to the next issue without giving Beatrice a chance to respond. "There would not be a legion of guards or soldiers waiting by the portal to kill me. I will go through and go into hiding immediately. If I go during the night, most likely I will have a few hours to hide before anyone even realizes that I am there.

"Finally, the portal itself. Will it accept me?" Angelica paused a moment, but she continued soon enough. She still did not want Beatrice to get a chance to respond. "I think it will. My mother was already well into her rule when Alexander discovered the portal. If she was meant to travel across, it would not have mattered at that point. By the time Alexander found that passage, the people had already taken a liking to their queen. To kill her then would be to risk a riot or even execution. He waited until she made a move against him, a move that would keep him out of the caves and away from the portal before he chose to eliminate her." Beatrice sat and listened. The queen was now to the point of casually talking about her mother's death. It was a great improvement, but that may have just been an act. Deep down, Beatrice feared that Angelica's strong behavior was just a façade over a much worse situation. It seemed as though she were becoming numb to her surroundings, and Beatrice was scared that she may be headed down the same road as Alexander. A road that ended in cruelty towards nearly everyone. "When I came to power, he tried to kill me immediately. He was afraid of me ruling the kingdom. Afraid of something I might do. I think it was not so much about what I could do as the queen of Protecia, but the possibility of me going to the other world and destroying what he had built there. What would happen if he was ruling, and I show up telling everyone that I was in command over him in another world? His rule there would be threatened. I believe he tried to kill me to keep that from happening."

Beatrice could not find the words the counter what the queen had said. "You'll be by yourself over there. As soon as you can, befriend someone to send back. He'll be able to get everyone from over here that's able to pass through the portal. Then you'll have some help over there." Angelica smiled to show her victory. Even though she was queen, Angelica was happy that Beatrice was now agreeing with her not because she was ordered to, but because she respected her decision. She had won her first battle, at least, in this voyage. It appeared that she managed to convince Beatrice that this was actually a good idea. Within a moment, Beatrice stomped down this thought of Angelica's. "Let me assure you, I don't like think this is a worthy plan for you. In my opinion, you'll be placing Alexander on a throne here by getting killed over there." Beatrice winced to hold back some tears. It was not successful. "Still, you're the queen, and I cannot stop you." This seemed to be the first time Angelica was actually realizing that that was the case. She was the queen, and she was beginning to act like it.

CHAPTER TWENTY

The Voyage to the Other World

With those words said, preparations began. Angelica spent the day studying the entire story that had been laid out in front of her by Cassandra and Beatrice. She studied the texts of Soranace to find out all of the peculiarities of the portal. These proved to make to be little help since Soranace died before he could experiment with the portal in any way. Still, Angelica learned everything she could that could possibly help her in the upcoming voyage to the other world. Finally, by that night, she was ready. Or at least she felt she was.

When the moon was at its highest, Angelica walked towards the caves. Behind her, there was growing crowd. It started with just her and Beatrice who was carefully carrying a lantern beside her (this was considered the safest alternative to a torch inside the caves). As they walked, Cassandra, David, and a growing mob of servants and guards began to join them. By the time they reached the caves, there were about fifteen people following Angelica into the rocky darkness.

The group marched along the same path they had taken more than a month ago when they were chasing Alexander through the caves. Several of the same faces were in this group progressing through the caves on this day. Before they knew how far this tangled web of deceit and terror truly reached. They marched over the fallen stones and sand that were left over from the costumed accomplice's race to the portal. The accomplice Angelica now knew to be the guard, Carl. This procession continued for about fifteen minutes, and soon it met the two guards who were currently stationed by the portal. They were standing at attention and eagerly waiting to see what would happen next. When Angelica approached, they looked at her with sadness and fear. They knew that this could easily be the last time they would lay eyes upon their queen.

Finally, as if it was what she had been waiting to do the entire eight years of her life, Angelica climbed up the side of the pool. With her feet firmly planted on one of the brass leaves, and with the lantern light shining in her face, Angelica looked at herself up and down quickly. Her dagger was attached to her calf where it finally started to feel natural. The leather pouch with the slingshot and metal discs contained inside of it was strapped to her waist. She was wearing her dress gown without the royal beads on it. After some consideration, she thought that would be best. If she needed to convince a person in the other world of her title in this world, that gown may be the edge she would need. It looked almost as if she was going to walk onto the platform for one of the public addresses. Everyone knew this was not the case, though. She was going to do something much worse.

With a deep sigh, Angelica's eyes passed over each one of the people that had come to see her off. Finally, without whispering a single word, she drew in a deep breath and casually stepped off the brass leaf. Without a single splash, her body dropped into the pool immediately as if it was almost drawn inside by some unimaginable force.

Angelica tried to swim but found she could not move. Something was holding her to the surface of the pool. For one terrifying moment, Angelica was certain this meant she was not destined to travel across the worlds. The invisible creatures in the pool were now going to kill her, and then Alexander would be able to rule at his leisure. Then, she realized that it was not her that the pool was rejecting. The leather pouch strapped to her waist was not meant to go across worlds, and that was holding her back like an anchor to this world. Angelica quickly reached down and untied the pouch from her waist. It quickly floated to the top of the pool, and Angelica began to swim down into the murky water.

Moving her arms out in great arcs in front of her and kicking her feet furiously, Angelica swam towards the only discernible destination. A pulsing, white light that was nearly thirty feet in front of her. It looked like a large star suspended in the water. Then, it faded down until it was little more than a single speck twinkling in the gloominess before the cycle repeated, pulsing in time with Angelica's heartbeat. It looked just like a star in the night sky, and Angelica knew that was where she should go.

As if she had been practicing these motions for years rather than days, Angelica swam towards the light quickly and easily. Her body cut through the thick, murky water that felt almost alive around her. It was almost as if a warm, greasy hand was holding her body and pushing it farther along towards the light. The instant Angelica's outstretched hand touched this shining, glowing star, everything went white. For a moment, Angelica felt lost. She was able to breathe comfortably while in this whiteness, but she felt disconnected from all existence. Was this the world she had travelled to? There was nothing around her but the glaring, blinding white. It was completely soundless and terribly cold. As she stayed here, though, she began to see dim patches, shadows of people moving around. And there was a noise beginning as well. Mostly just laughing or moaning. There was some conversation, but Angelica could not make out the words. It sounded like the garbled voices she sometimes heard in dreams. She was quite certain, however, that underneath it all, there was an intense growling or hissing. Then, all at once, the whiteness seemed to fade out completely.

Beatrice reached into the pool and pulled out the leather bag containing the slingshot she had the metalworkers make for

Angelica's use. Tears were flowing from the woman's eyes as she handled the completely dry bag. It was as if the water in the pool would not cling to that bag as she lifted it out. Beatrice touched the bag as though it was the last remains of the queen. From just behind her, David whispered, "She just wasn't meant to take that with her." He waited a moment before adding, "I'm sure she'll be fine without it." Deep down, though, he was not even sure if she died already.

To answer with words would mean to let the tears begin to flow freely, and Beatrice was trying to hold them back as long as possible. This effort twisted her face into a contortion of pain. She simply nodded in acknowledgment. For an instant that seemed to last forever, nothing happened. Beatrice began to fear that Angelica, whether or not she was meant to pass between worlds, was not able to swim the distance and drowned somewhere between worlds. Lost forever in some strange passage. Then, the rumbling began.

Everyone looked towards the wall with all of the sculptures carved into it. Their eyes frantically darted to every corner to see where Angelica's image would appear, and then a portion of the wall began to develop cracks. A space just next to the large reptilian monster began to crumble away, and soon, in a cloud of dust, the sculpture began to slide into view. Angelica's image was kneeling on the ground facing the creature with the dagger in her hand. There was a smile on her face, and her eyes looked amazingly content despite the hideous monster inches from her. The tip of the dagger was pointed slightly upwards from her extended hand. It came to rest just touching the bottom surface of the creature's mouth. As if to lighten the mood, but having the exact opposite effect, Cassandra whispered, "She's tempting the monster."

For nearly an hour, no one was able to move. They could only look at the image of their queen, suspended in time, inches from death.

The blinding white light did not clear gradually, but it vanished instantly in a flash. Angelica was shocked. It was like being shaken awake. She looked around desperately afraid for a moment, not knowing where she was or what had happened. In her mind, she always assumed she would just be swimming out of another pool of murky water on this side. Angelica had no idea there would be such an ordeal before she appeared over here.

This begged the question, where was here? Angelica looked around. There were bushes in front of her and mountains behind and to the right of her. Her dagger was clenched in her hand so tightly her knuckles hurt even though it was sheathed behind her thigh when she went into the pool. Angelica looked ahead and slightly to the right, and she saw a sharp drop-off. This was a platform just like the one in her world. Angelica tried to walk forward and soon found she was unable to. There was something holding her back against the wall.

Angelica began to slide to her right slowly, feeling a stone protrusion scraping against her chest. Whatever it was, this object was pinning her to the wall. Whatever it was, she seemed unable to free herself of it. It took a few minutes of struggling, but she reached the end of whatever that structure was and fell to the ground. When she looked back up, pure terror gripped her. She had been standing against another wall similar to the one in the caves of her world. Most likely, her body just appeared where her stone sculpture had been. This was not the only shock, though. Angelica saw the stone protrusion that was holder her down. Her eyes locked onto the stone image of Wilhelmina, her mother. The former queen's eyes were terrified and frantic, and it was her stone hand that had been holding Angelica to the wall. Protecting and shielding her from whatever was in this world.

Unable to find her legs, Angelica crawled away from the wall for about ten feet. She then stopped and looked at the relief image carefully. She saw ten people from her world looking back at her with stone eyes. These people were able to pass through the portal to this world. Soon, she would have to find someone to travel back to tell Beatrice exactly who these people were. It also seemed that the late Queen Wilhelmina was able to travel between worlds, but she never got that opportunity. Alexander saw to that.

Not too far from the wall, there was a pool, very similar to the one she had jumped into to get here. It was filled with that same murky, rainbow stained liquid with an endless current rolling through it. Everything on her side of the portal had a counterpart in this world.

Angelica looked and saw the sun was beginning to rise over the mountains. It did not matter that no one was around now. She had to hide somewhere as soon as she could. As soon as someone seems the wall, they would know by smooth stone where her image had been that she was now here, and most likely, Alexander will send people out to find her. If he had positioned himself as a man of royal authority, there would be legions of soldiers ready to follow his will. Angelica had to, at least, get off the platform to somewhere that was less noticeable. So, feeling naked and alone despite the elaborate robes she was still wearing, the queen of Protecia began to walk into this new world.

To keep her cover as best as she could, Angelica replaced the dagger on her leg, and walked towards a row of bushes that was not too far ahead of her. They were about six feet tall and bowed down to create an archway that was just about her size. Carefully, she walked through, listening to every twig rupture beneath her feet and each leaf crinkle under her weight. She continued to walk along these bushes until she reached a solid stone wall. There did not appear to be any doorways or other openings in this wall, so Angelica simply began to walk alongside it with her fingertips gliding on its rough surface.

The cold rock seemed to be reaching into her. Angelica could feel her fingertips growing cold and then even numb. Still, she would not let go of that wall. With the bushes blocking what little light there was, this was all that kept her wandering away completely. It was nearly impossible to see anything, so she had to guide herself with her fingers. If she were to discover that this was a bad idea, she would have to be able to find her way back to the portal as quickly as possible. Losing this wall may very easily mean losing her way back home.

However, no matter what Angelica wished, the wall eventually ended. She took a few steps away from it and the safety of the bushes. After quickly looking around the gloominess, she was able to see a courtyard, much like the one in her own world. This one, however, was walled off by mountains on three sides. There were ledges and caverns covering the sides of these mountains, and most likely, they were all filled with eager spectators whenever Alexander spoke to these people.

Angelica took a few steps into the courtyard, first making sure it was deserted, before she stopped. There was a horrible screaming sound from behind her, and Angelica turned quickly to see what it was. When she finally saw the source of that scream, she wished she had just run away instead of turning to look. Carved into the side of one of the mountainous walls, the mountain at the front of the courtyard, below what most likely served as a speaking platform, was a large room. It seemed to extend twenty feet into the air and went at least as much into the mountain. There were metal bars about four inches apart from one another running up and down the entire height of this enclosure, and behind them was what had terrified Angelica the most when coming here.

The reptile she had seen on the wall of the cave was now here. There were hundreds of them all piled into that carved cell. Their bodies were green, and their eyes were just as dark and featureless as the mountain they were trapped in. They piled on top of one another, slithering within the enclosure to get a better look at the person that was now here before them. All the while, they were shrieking that high pitched howl. The horns that protruded from around their necks were all closed to cover the heads of the monsters as if to protect it from whatever may be around to attack them.

This they used to their advantage, slamming their heads against the bars trying to get out, but not hurting themselves in the least. The courtyard resonated with the sound of those horns hitting the metal bars. That mixed with their shrieking howl shattered the previous calm of the morning.

Above this cell was something much worse, though. It appeared to be the main speaking platform of this courtyard. Most likely it was the only place where the speaker would stand while the crowds waited below and on the other ledges. It was as deep as the cage beneath it, and it was perfectly clear of all statuary or images of any kind. The only item that was located on this platform was the staff she had seen on the wall in her world. It was fully intact, and it looked horrifying. There was a series of hooks carved into the wall at the back of the speaking platform so that staff, Protace's staff, would be honored properly. Its dark, blind eyes, the eyes of one of those reptiles, just stared out into the brightening courtyard. From below, the staff was barely visible, but Angelica did not need such a clear view to know of the horrors this staff was capable of. That much was evident by the most cursory glance. Still, she wanted to hold it. It seemed to be calling to her. There was an energy radiating off of that staff in waves that were almost visible to Angelica. She wanted to know if she could harness those powers like Protace had done according to the texts she had seen. Maybe it was possible, but she was too scared to try. At least, she will not try right now.

Angelica turned away and began to walk from the platform. She wanted to get away from this place, but she could not return to her world yet. The only possibility was to find a village, a town where the people of this world lived. Only then would she be able to hide among them. Staying in the courtyard would ensure her being captured or killed.

As Angelica turned to run away from the platform and the snarling beasts beneath it, she saw a group of four people walking towards her. They were just dark images in the pale morning, but they did not seem to be of any harm. Two adults and two children judging from their size. Angelica did not run towards or away from them. She just waited to see what they would do when they saw her. With her hand ready to grab the dagger on her leg, she stood still with the sun rising over the family before her.

The group approached, and soon they came close enough so that Angelica could see their faces. They were all yawning and chuckling to one another. When they finally saw Angelica, the man looked over to her and said, "Good morning. How are you?" Angelica did not know how to respond. She was expecting a chase or a conflict or at the very least and argument or questioning about her origins. These people did not appear to know or care who she was. The woman simply threw a blanket on the courtyard ground and sat down upon it like a family preparing for a picnic. The children began to lie down and go back to sleep while the two adults just sat and began whispering to each other in their unusual accent.

After a few minutes, the man looked back over to Angelica. "You look very familiar to me. Do I know you from somewhere?" Angelica looked at the man closely. She knew him as well, or at least, she recognized him. This was a man carved on the wall back in her world. He was the one holding the scroll of parchment against his chest. This man was able to travel across the pathway between the worlds just as she had done, but most likely Alexander never told him anything of this ability. He was probably nothing more than a simple farmer, based on his clothes and the beaten, callused look of his hands. Finally, the man pieced it together. "You're the one from the wall. The one that woman is holding back. You came through the portal."

Angelica tried to speak, but soon she found that no words were coming out. Only able to make choking noises, Angelica began to back away from this family as if they just accused her of murder. The man and his wife looked at each other nervously, and then their eyes returned to Angelica. "The Prophecy says that you're the evil one. You're the one that will destroy everything we have here and take over his rule." It looked as if they were getting ready to stand. They were going to call for help, call for Alexander's guards to come over and arrest this evil one that had arrived in their world.

Finally, Angelica found the strength to speak. "I do not know what he had been telling you, but I am not the evil one." The two adults sitting on the blanket did not seem convinced. They continued rising to their feet to call for help. Angelica had to say something to convince them fast. "He is the one you should be afraid of." Their actions began to slow down. They were interested in what she had to say. Almost as if confirming what they had already known. Or maybe just the accent from Protecia that they were not used to hearing. "I came here because he killed my parents and tried to kill me. It seems to make sense that he would tell you that I am evil, because I want to destroy him. He was right about that. I want to end his rule here. That is the only way I know that my people and I will be safe in my own world!" They seemed happy with that answer, but still it was not enough. There was a lingering doubt on their faces, and Angelica knew she had to win them over entirely. In the short time she had been here, there was only one thing she could think of that may work.

With this as her last, and only, option, she said, "You are able to travel between the worlds, too. He did not tell you that, did he?" The man looked stunned. He just stared at Angelica for a moment with the expression of someone that had been kicked in the stomach. "If he is as kind as he claims, why did he not tell everyone who is able to pass between worlds of that ability? Why does he try to limit that ability to himself and his accomplice, his closest friend? Why?"

They sat and looked at the young girl and seemed to be thinking carefully about everything she had just told them. Finally, the man asked, "Do you know why we have come out here this early for a public address that won't start until the sun is at its highest?" Angelica did not know, but even if she did, she was not given the opportunity to answer. "He has a public address every day, and everyone is required to attend. Whoever doesn't attend is executed, and if everyone does show up, the last person to arrive is killed. They are thrown into the cage with those beasts." He nodded towards the cage with the growling and snarling lizards. "My name is Martin. This is my wife, Lenore."

Having no idea what to do next, Angelica just looked at them for a moment. She was shocked by the quick change in their attitude towards her, as well as the truth about Alexander's treatment of his subjects that she had just been told. His cruelty was well-known, but she did not think even he could be capable of this tyranny. Finally, Angelica said, "My name is Angelica. I am the queen of Protecia, the kingdom in the other world." She was not sure that was not enough, so the queen added, "I am not here to harm you or anyone else." Mentally, she added, with the exception of Alexander, but she kept that thought to herself. It would not be wise to let all of her motives be known that quickly.

Martin looked at Angelica again. "If you are who you say you are, and he sees you here, you're going to get thrown in with those monsters no matter when you arrived in the courtyard." He extended a hand and Angelica took it. "I'm going to take you to my cottage. Sometimes, they don't even bother to check inside each home when he starts speaking to find anyone who didn't show up. Usually they don't check homes at all, so you should be safe there." With a chuckle, he added, "Safer than here, anyway."

The two of them walked off and did so quickly. Martin had no intention of being the last one to arrive at the courtyard because he was helping someone he hardly knew to his cottage for shelter. They walked far from the courtyard and into a small village. There were small huts and cottages set randomly though the area. It seemed like the sketches of Protecia from years ago that Angelica had seen in the library. Small farms were being tended to, but there was a sense of urgency in the air. Everyone kept a careful eye on those around them to see when their neighbors began leaving. People wanted to work their fields as long as possible without being the last one to arrive at the public address.

Finally, Martin approached one of the modest-sized cottages. "This is mine," he whispered as he opened the door. Angelica walked in quickly so as no one would notice the gown she was wearing or that she was entering a house rather than preparing to leave like so many others were doing. Martin looked down at her carefully as if to tell if she was saying the truth. Despite the fact that he was easily twenty years older than her, she was completely comfortable with him. Her uncle, whom she had trusted with her life up until a month ago, was nearly the same age.

When they entered, Angelica gave the place a shocked look. The entire cottage was about the size of her quarters in the palace. In one corner, there was a large bed, and along the opposite wall was a table. In the middle, there was a large empty space, most likely where the children would play or the adults would converse. Light was beginning to shine through the vacant hole in the wall that was supposed to be a window. Angelica let go of Martin's hand and took a few steps into the cottage's single room.

As if she was not even there, Martin walked over to the table and knelt down beside it. He reached towards the center of the space under the table and began to sweep some loose dirt away from the floor beneath it. When he did this, Angelica began to walk over to see what was going on. He uncovered a large piece of slate that was under the table. As he grabbed the edge and pulled the rock towards himself, Angelica knelt beside him. She could see an opening beneath the slate that led down into darkness.

Martin looked at her and smiled. "If you see guards or a man wearing all different colors, just jump down there. They probably won't do a very extensive search if they come in here at all. I don't think they even know this room down here exists, so they wouldn't be checking it. There are some sheets or cloth down there as well. See if you could make something out of them to cover up that dress you're wearing. If too many people see you with that on, they'll know exactly who you are."

While Angelica just stared down into the dirt-walled room beneath her, Martin stood. He began to walk towards the door when Angelica yelled out, "Thank you, very much." Martin just nodded at her and left. From where she was crouching under the table, Angelica was able to hear him making small-talk with some of village's people before walking back to the courtyard.

CHAPTER TWENTY-ONE

The Day in the Cottage

For the next hour, Angelica sat beneath the warping wooden table listening for a knock at the door. She was ready to race down the ladder and drag the slate back in place if there was any sign of a guard coming. Nothing happened, so the queen finally stood and began to walk around the cottage. The tiny cottage was nearly devoid of any diversion or activity. These were people who found living to be, in itself, a luxury. They spent nearly half of every day waiting for their leader to make his public address, and the rest of their time was spent trying to survive on the land as best as they could.

Angelica walked to the makeshift window and began to look out into the daylight. The cottages went on for about a mile and after that there were trees. Most likely that was where civilization ended. All these people were entirely contained between a mountain and a forest. While staring into the picturesque landscape, Angelica made certain to watch and listening for anyone approaching. It would appear that any living thing had left the village to hear their king.

As she looked at the scenery, beginning to take in her surroundings, Angelica saw a small group walking in her direction. "Move it!" someone yelled, and that was followed by a loud scream of pain. Angelica took a step back and ducked behind the edge of the window. She continued to peek out, however. It took about five minutes for this group to get close enough for her to see exactly what they were doing. Ten people were both pushing and pulling a large metal cage, easily half the size of the cottage she was currently hiding in. Its construction was similar to the one in the courtyard, except it was made of bars on all sides and not cut into a mountain. Inside, there were another three of the reptiles. With every step the people took, there was a series of shrieks and cries from inside the cage. Another man who stood on top of the cage was yelling at them to move faster. Every once in a while, he would punctuate this order by hitting one of the men with a moist tree branch. It was only about an inch in diameter, but they screamed whenever the man struck them with the whip-like limb.

As they neared the cottage, the young queen continued to watch with mounting fear and curiosity. As the continued to get closer, another voice rang out. This one Angelica recognized, and it terrified her. "Another delivery? How many this time?"

Whoever spoke this was walking alongside the cottage now, and getting closer to the window. It was a voice she definitely recognized, but she could not attach a name or a face to it. The man sitting atop the cage yelled back, "We got three of 'em this time." He laughed heartily and continued yelling. "I swear, it's gettin' harder and harder to find these things. Either we're runnin' out of them, or they're getting better at hidin'."

The man on foot, the one with the familiar voice, was getting closer to the window now. To Angelica, his voice was almost as loud as if he was standing just before her. "Well, you must keep looking until we get the right one. It does not matter if we have to wipe out this entire species. There is only one of these creatures that is important to us, and until we find it, we will keep looking." Angelica was watching closely, and then the man finally stepped into her field of view.

It took all of Angelica's energy to stifle the scream that was rising to her lips. She fell back away from the window in absolute terror, and part of her was sure the man had seen her do this. It was the man in the brightly colored costume, the court jester. Now, Angelica knew him to be Carl, one of the royal guards that had sided with Alexander and betrayed two queens. This man was here, and from the way he spoke, he was in a position of authority.

Angelica backed against the wall just next to the window and slid down to the ground. There, she remained gasping for air as silently as she knew how. With terror gripping its icy fingers around her, she could hear the man talking and the constant whine of the creatures they were hauling. All those sounds were drowned out by the deafening thud of Angelica's heartbeat. They had not reacted to her, but Angelica did not want to take any chances. She laid flat on the ground and dragged herself towards the old wooden table. The voices continued to drone on behind her. With the dirt scraping against her knees, Angelica crawled over to the hole in the floor and slipped inside.

As soon as she began to go down the rickety wooden ladder, she stopped to drag the slate back into place. It was heavier than it appeared and quite cold. Once in place, it had blocked out all light. Angelica went down the ladder very slowly, and when she reached the bottom, she simply stood there. It was impossible to see anything in front of her at all. For all she knew, there was a fleet of soldiers already waiting down there for her.

She remained like this for a few moments. Soon, she realized that Martin would have not directed her down here to stay in the darkness. There must be a torch or a lantern near the bottom of the ladder. Angelica fell to her hands and knees and began to grope along the dirt floor searching for something that could be a source of light. Her hands fell upon a piece of heavy cloth. Most likely, this was what Martin had intended for her to make some clothes out of. First, she would need light before she could make anything. Angelica pulled the cloth to one side, and she realized that it did not move. It fell from above.

When the heavy sheet of cloth fell, this small room filled with light. There was a barred opening near the ceiling, and the cloth was intended to cover it so that it would not draw attention when it was not needed. Martin had said that the guards did not know that this room existed, so this was probably just a precaution to keep it that way.

Angelica looked at this opening closely. It was also covered with a much thinner, much lighter cloth. The light shone through this one easily, but it prevented people from looking in if they should not be. Even with is cautionary sheet of cloth, Angelica was able to see everything quite clearly. Within a few seconds, she found the sheets of fabric, which was actually a collection of empty grain sacks, that Martin had told her about as well as a length of thread.

Beatrice had taught her the basics of sewing. It was more of a lesson given to fill time on a particularly boring day than being something Beatrice had intended the queen to use. Now, the queen was glad that this was a skill that she had learned. She grabbed the cloth, the thread, and a nearby needle, and she began to sew.

Once a simple garment was made, Angelica found herself unable to do anything but wait. After seeing the jester outside, she was too afraid to leave the safety of this room until Martin and Lenore get home. Still, there was the possibility of guards showing up at the residence to see if anyone was missing from the address. This basement was the safest play to stay.

Angelica just waited. She did not leave that room until she was certain that a full day had passed, and that Martin and Lenore were both killed. They would never return home, and she could be lost in this world. Just about the time that Angelica was giving up, she began to hear footsteps. These were not the steps of a happy family returning home to begin their farming or hunting chores. They were serious, business-like steps. It was one or several of the guards searching the cottage.

When he had spoken to her, Martin was certain that the guards looked very briefly at the cottages they chose to search, but this particular search seemed intense. Maybe they knew she was here and hiding someplace. Angelica was able to hear the sounds of furniture being moved around. They were going to find her. That was the bed they had just dragged, and now the steps were coming across the single room and towards the table.

Angelica looked around frantically. There did no place to hide. This room consisted of a dirt floor and walls. Stacks of grain sacks were against one wall, and old farm equipment was scattered around the rest of the room. Angelica was able to hear the table being dragged out of the way. They were going to find her. There was no doubt about that now.

From above, she heard the muffled call, "Hey, look at this?" Someone had seen the slate cover. In seconds, they would be moving it out of the way to look down here. Angelica looked around again to see if there was another way out of this room. There was none, but she did see a way that she may be able to hide. Angelica grabbed the heavy cloth that had covered the thin slits that constituted a window. Looking up, she saw the hooks it had been suspended to the wall just next to the ladder. Angelica began to climb up, holding the cloth in one hand and using the other hand on the ladder. More footsteps were headed towards this side of the room, and now another voice said, "Move it over. Maybe there's something under it."

With one hand holding onto the rung of the ladder, Angelica reached over towards the first hook. There were three of them lined up one after the other. She could feel her hand slipping along the ladder rung as she reached farther towards the first hook. Finally, she was able to pin the cloth to the first hook, and began to reach farther towards the second. Her foot began to slip along its rung, and soon she could feel that she was only holding on by her toe. She got the cloth snagged on the second hook. Now, there was only one left. Her hand slipped a little bit more, and she could feel a larger splinter embedding itself in her palm. She began to whine in pain as she heard the guards begin to lift the edge of the slate. Light from the window was dimming, but a single bright beam was shooting in from the partially lifted stone. They were not looking in yet. This was just to get their hands underneath to begin sliding it. Angelica reached a little bit farther and was almost the last hook when her right foot slipped off the rung. Only holding onto the ladder with one foot and a single, bleeding hand, Angelica pushed herself a little bit more. Her left foot began to shake on that rung, but she had to keep trying. The slate began to move, and the beam of light from above widened. Angelica gave a small leap and caught the cloth on the third hook.

In her relief, she lost what little footing she had. Angelica fell from the ladder and landed on one of the full grain sacks. The sack almost gasped when she hit it, and it deflated like a pillow. Angelica did not have time to relax, though. She wrapped her arms around the sack and rolled onto her back. With the grain sack on top of her, she was no longer able to see the guards' progress with the slate, but she could hear it sliding along the dirt above her. The loose dirt made sounds like the hiss of a snake as it fell down from the slate opening.

Finally, the sliding sound stopped. Angelica held her breath in fear. She could feel her heart thumping in her chest. "It looks like some sort of room." The voices above her were talking loudly as if shocked by what they were seeing. "Storage from the looks of it. There's no one down there." For a moment, Angelica felt she was safe. The footsteps began to move away from her, but then someone yelled, "Wait a second!" All the air around Angelica turned acidic and hot. She was spotted. The footsteps were coming back towards the opening to the basement, and then the guard spoke again, "We've gotta put that slate back in place. Remember, he said to make it look like we were never here."

Once the guards left the cottage, Angelica crept out from under the sack of grain. She stood perfectly still in the darkness. If she tried, she could get a hold of the black curtain to remove it from the window, but she did not want to. Doing that would expose her to the people outside the cottage. Angelica was afraid to leave the safety of this underground room. No matter how much she wanted to climb out to see Martin and Lenore when they arrived back home, she was terrified of another check by the guards. Angelica stayed in the darkness until Martin and the others arrived home about an hour later.

"Angelica, where are you?" The voice was muffled and low, but still, she could hear it. The voice sounded familiar enough, but she was not certain. After only speaking to Martin once, she could not be sure of the sound of his voice, especially after so much had happened that day. For all she knew, this was the court jester or even Alexander himself disguising their voices to try to find her. Angelica just stood still until she saw the slate being moved out of place again. The face that looked down was Martin's, and Angelica nearly screamed in relief to see him.

Once she came up from that underground room, the family spoke with her for a long while. They asked question on topics ranged widely from Angelica's childhood to the reasons why she came here and eventually to what the trip through the portal was like. Angelica paid special attention to speaking about that last topic in great detail since she was almost certainly going to send Martin back to speak with Beatrice.

Finally, Angelica got a chance to ask her questions. "I saw some people moving a cage of those creatures earlier today. Why are they doing that?" Angelica considered adding the fact that she had seen the court jester with them, but that would lead to the fact that she was almost spotted by someone. That was a subject she most definitely wished to avoid speaking about, just for her own comfort. These people trusted her, and her curiosity almost got her caught. Thinking of what fate would unfold for this family if they were found helping her made Angelica shudder.

A careful glance was exchanged between Martin and his wife. When Martin looked back at Angelica, his face had grown as grave as if a friend had just announced a deadly illness. "On your world, there's one of those creatures on the wall, correct? The wall that goes with your side of the portal?" Angelica simply nodded. In her mind, this all began to come together, but she was terrified to put that solution into words. "Only one of those beasts is able to travel through the portal, but they have no distinguishing characteristics that we can see. Anyway, he is searching for the correct beast to send across into your world. He has some people whose job is exclusively to search the caves in the mountains as well as the forest for as many of those beasts as they could find. Every day, at the end of his public address, he has some servants take one of the beasts and force it into the pool of water. So far, each one he has tried sending over has died as soon as it was immersed. It's been estimated by some people that he's wiped out more than half of their population doing this every day."

Angelica's face looked grave. "If one of those creatures gets across to my world, no one will know how to combat it. That thing will destroy everything it comes across. With that on his side, he will have my kingdom on its knees without ever leaving the safety of his kingdom here."

Without waiting for another question to be asked, Martin continued to speak. One look at his eyes could measure the severity of his comment. "According to our Prophecy, one of the walls must be completed in order for the two worlds to be united permanently and for anyone. He's trying to complete his side of the wall so that he'll have the upper hand and become the ruler of both worlds. Once again, that is according to his Prophecy."

Lenore spoke up finally as if she had been holding this in all this time. "Some of us doubt what his Prophecy even means. He's the one that wrote it and forced each of us to memorize it verbatim. Forcing us to know that book by heart only shows that he uncertain of who would follow him." A smirk developed on Lenore's face, but it did not seem to spread into the rest of her face and her body language looked more tense than ever. "He's trying to brainwash everyone."

Finally, Angelica added, "I am going with you tomorrow to the address. I want to see him for myself. See what he is doing in this world. It is something I need to do." The other two nodded as the two children stared eagerly at the strange girl who was now in their home. To those children, Angelica looked close to their age, but she acted so much more like their parents. They could sense it would be wrong to ask her to join in their play. "Do you need any help around here? I am going to be stuck here for a while, and I do not want to be a burden on you."

It looked as if Lenore was about to rattle off some things for the foreign queen to begin tending to, but Martin spoke first. "You should try to stay out of public attention as much as possible for a while. Tomorrow, you're going to stay in the back of the crowd at the address. I don't want him to see you. It looked like he sent out nearly every guard and soldier he had in his command when he saw your image wasn't on the wall anymore. If he sees you, he'll kill you on the spot."

So with that, Angelica spent the rest of the day indoors. She helped Lenore with some things that needed to be done inside the cottage, such as sweeping and preparation of their meal. Most of the day however, Angelica spent playing little games with the children in the disinterested way a babysitter would play with a child. This was a task that Angelica quickly found to be boring and tedious. After being given the roles and responsibilities of an adult for her entire life, going back to the playtime of a child was impossible to do.

They ate a simple dinner of boiled vegetables in a soup, and they spent the rest of the evening talking to one another. Judging from the way they were carrying themselves, the four were very tired. Their days began before sunrise, trying to get out to the courtyard before anyone else. Afternoons were spent engulfed in household chores. That was the only way to ensure their continued survival.

Later on that night, all five of them crawled into the single bed. Lying side by side with each other, there was little room to spare especially with one extra person. About half an hour after the children had fallen asleep, Angelica was awoken by movement in the bed. She opened her eyes slightly. Since she was still afraid for her life whether or not she was in the safety of this house, bursting into full wakefulness would be a bad idea. Lying on the bed, she saw

Martin and Lenore standing and walking to the other side of the room. They spoke briefly, gave a glance towards the bed, and then walked out of the cottage together.

Angelica wondered what they were doing, but she did not think she was in any danger. If they were going to tell the guards about her presence here, most likely, they would have made certain that their children were nowhere around, just in case the guards grab the wrong child by mistake. Still, they left, and Angelica did not want to go back to sleep until they returned. It was difficult to tell time during the night in this cottage. In her palace, there were large hourglasses indicating the seconds and minutes that slipped by. These had always been in her quarters. There was nothing like that here. At night, there was not even the sun to use as a means of estimation. Still, she assumed it was about an hour or two before Martin and Lenore quietly walked back into the cottage. Without saying a word, the two slipped over to the bed and lied down again. Their children did not even shift in their sleep as this happened, and most likely, they did not even know that Angelica had been watching as they left. It did not matter, though. Angelica knew they had gone, but she had to push that out of her mind for now and go back to sleep. She needed her rest of tomorrow.

CHAPTER TWENTY-TWO

Alexander's Address

As soon as the sun rose the next day, Martin woke Angelica along with his wife and children. They all gathered in the opened area of the room and grabbed a few items each to take with them. Things such as blankets, some light breakfast foods, and a candle were distributed among them, and they all left for the courtyard. This time, Angelica walked with them as if she was any other citizen of this strange civilization.

This morning when they reached the courtyard, there were a few more people there ahead of them. Martin tossed the heaviest blanket on the ground towards the back of the partially enclosed field, so Angelica would stay somewhat out of view. Keeping to their well-established routine, the children lowered themselves onto the blanket, and within a minute, there were asleep with their own blankets wrapped around them. Angelica sat with Martin and Lenore while the courtyard slowly filled with people.

As they sat and watched half sleeping men and women stumble their way into the courtyard, the sun continued to rise over the mountains. The immense shadows cast by these great cliffs began to recede and shorten. A pale and almost cruel-looking light began to fill the courtyard. This was the light of first morning, the morning of a day that would contain at least one death. Cold and bitter, the light bathed everyone's face as if to inspect them for any weakness. Some days the morning brings an explosion of colors and the potential for anything. Other mornings were like this. Washed out colors and a sterile feeling of lifelessness.

After a few moments of watching the sun and the people, Angelica mentioned, "I told you previously that your image is on the wall of my world." Her words were directed towards Martin, but both he and his wife listened intensely. "There's a favor I need to ask of you. Today, I will write a list of people in my world that are able to pass through the portal. If you bring that list across the portal to a woman on the other side, named Beatrice, she will assemble these people and send them back with you." Angelica stopped for a moment and watched as Martin began to debate the issue in his mind. "I will need some people over here to help me, and know that group will be loyal to be me."

"Help you do what?" Lenore asked and Angelica froze with fear. In the one day she was here, she had suspected that these people disliked Alexander and his method of ruling. However, she was never certain of this thought and truly had no idea how they would react to something like this. Lenore had a persistent look in her eyes. She wanted an answer to her question.

Angelica began to open her mouth to speak. The words would not come, though. It was a difficult question to answer, especially since she had no real plan. Finally, Angelica was saved by the words of another. "Martin, how are you doing today?"

There was a man standing behind Angelica who had begun speaking to the small group. Martin spoke back very naturally, introducing Angelica as a servant the family had recently acquired. To this, the man finally responded, "Can we speak without your new servant listening in?" The man's eyes fell on Angelica, and she was too ashamed to return the look. Her eyes fell to the ground, and they simply stayed there.

No one was saying anything. The man did not repeat his request. Martin did not say anything to send away or keep Angelica here. This was a silence that would do no more than draw attention to Angelica.

Finally, she decided that she would break it. Speaking in a way that she had heard the servants around her palace speak, she said, "I'll go back to the cottage and make sure everything's okay there. There's time before everyone else gets here, right?" There were nods from everyone there, so Angelica stood from the blanket and walked away.

Keeping her hooded cloth outfit covering her mostly from head to foot, she began to make her way back to the village. Still, she kept her eyes to the ground to keep from anyone possibly recognizing her from the image the used to be on the wall. As it ended up, this was what caused her identity to be known. Angelica walked with her eyes studying only the beaten and grass-free path, and finally, she hit something. There was a pair of sandal-clad feet on the dirt in front of her. When she saw the colors on the bottom of a gown near the ground, she knew that she had stumbled into a great deal of trouble.

Angelica had just walked into the legs of the court jester. Most likely this man had been searching for her for about a day now, and he had just stumbled upon her. This was one of her royal guards, a man named Carl, who had helped in the attempt at her life. She did not know what to do as this man said to her, "Watch where you're going." As if that was all, Angelica nodded and walked to the side. She began to sigh in relief as if she had gotten off the hook. Then, a hand clenched down on her arm, and she was forced back to where she had just been. "I do not recognize you from around here." One hand clad in multicolored cloth grabbed the edge of Angelica's hood and lifted it from her head.

The instant that Angelica's face was plunged into the rising sunlight, she looked up at the jester, knowing that she was to be arrested and most likely killed by the end of the day. There was a shocked look in the eyes of the man staring at her. That was all that Angelica could see since the costume concealed the rest of him. All she needed was a second to get a head start running from him, and she had an idea what would create it. "I know who you are too, Carl."

At this, the jester did not react in shock or even surprise. He just laughed. In his fit of laughter, his hand only tightened around

Angelica's arm. There was no moment of shock that she had anticipated. It actually seemed as though she had played into his hand like a fly snared in a spider web. As his laughter subsided, the jester began to speak. "Carl. He came to me asking for help. Some injury in the field. I killed him and rigged the carriage to crash into a tree. The wolves must have taken care of the rest. It is too bad you will never get an opportunity to tell anyone of your new, little discovery. It is a true pity."

Angelica felt frozen with fear. For a moment, she was only able to stare at those eyes, and then their familiarity came rushing towards her like a released floodgate. It was as if those eyes filled the world. Angelica was on the verge of screaming when all of her emotions began sending crackling shockwaves through her body. Instead of screaming, she spoke a single name. "Chenrile," she whispered as if it was the only action she was capable of and each letter of it hurt her as it passed her tongue. That name was all that filled her mind, and it was all she was able to act on. He had been so close to her the entire time. After the assassination attempt, he checked her for injuries, nearly insisted on making sure that was not injured. Despite this act, he had been trying to kill her all along.

Even though Chenrile was still holding onto her, Angelica tried to run. She turned to the right and began to take a few steps, but his hand kept her from getting any further. It did not loosen under the strain, but tightened instead. Angelica's feet slipped from the ground, and she fell to the dirt path beneath her. When she fell, however, Chenrile's hand did release her arm. It was as though that was the one move he did not anticipate. Angelica dug her fingers into the dirt and began to drag herself away from this madman. Still, she did not get far at all. Before she dragged herself more than two feet, her hand hit a rock rather than dirt and she lost traction. There was nothing for her to dig her fingers into, and she had to reposition her hand away from the rock to keep moving. This slight loss in momentum allowed a strong hand to grasp her ankle. Angelica stopped trying to crawl, knowing it would be wasted effort. Instead, she reached for the rock again and pulled it from the ground. It was heavy and almost too large in her hand, but she was able to manage it. Most likely, by this time, Chenrile would be bending down to get a grip of her arm again. This is when Angelica had to strike.

As fast and hard as she could manage, Angelica swung her arm into the air as she turned to face the sky. The rock swiped through the still coldness of the early morning and struck Chenrile on the side of the head. He let out an angered scream and fell to the ground beside her. Angelica immediately stood and spared one look back at the physician dressed as a jester. The costume was already changing color by the right temple. Red was leaching into the other colors and conquering them. Chenrile's eyes were half opened, but he was dazed. Dazed enough for Angelica to make a fast getaway.

She ran from him as fast as she could, and Chenrile made no attempt to chase. As if completely confused, Angelica ran towards the center of the town. Very few people even spared her a glance as she darted by. They were far too concerned about finishing as much farm work as they could before they had to leave for the public address. Once she reached the center of the small village, Angelica stopped. She took a deep breath, replaced the hood on her head and walked very calmly back towards the courtyard making certain not to take the same path by which she came. Chenrile, most likely just regaining his balance, did not see her making her way back towards the assembly in the courtyard, and she did so quite easily.

By the time Angelica reached the courtyard again, the sun was nearly full in the sky. The mountains no longer cast their shadow over the courtyard to flood it with a chill. That meant it must be near to another five hours before the address would begin. Martin had finished speaking with his neighbor. Now, he was sitting with his wife and children on the blanket they had laid down when they arrived. When Angelica came back, the first thing Martin said was, "That was Bryan. He's a neighbor and a very good friend of ours." Angelica nodded and sat beside them with her head tilted down.

"I'm sorry you had to go like that, but we can't have any suspicion. Or at least as little as possible."

Angelica finally looked up. There was still so much fear running through her body that she could not find any words to speak. Her arms and legs were quivering in fear, and it almost appeared as if she was having a fit of some sort. She just sat and watched the courtyard fill with people. There must have been at least a hundred here already, and their group was sitting almost at the center of the others that were arriving. With this many people around them, Angelica found it unlikely that Chenrile would be able to spot her again. She simply blended in with the crowd.

Despite the veil the crowd supplied, she sat still and silently. Occasionally, her eyes slanted upwards to look at Martin and his wife. The children were now fully awake as well, and they were busily playing games with one another. For a moment, they wanted Angelica to join in, but she would not. She could not. The thought of simply moving made her terrified. She just sat perfectly still as the sun rose higher above them. Finally, it was at its highest point in the sky.

The courtyard was filled with people. Packed shoulder to shoulder and back to back, the citizens of this strange civilization filled the courtyard. On the cliffs above, there were mobs of people waiting and watching every action below them. The addresses in Protecia never seemed as crowded, but also those people had an option to attend. Their lives did not depend on it.

Everyone rose at the sight of two men walking through the courtyard. The people parted down the center as they walked through. Alexander with his black cape flailing behind him walked first, and Chenrile marched just behind him in his multi-colored costume. There was someone else as well. A young woman of about fifteen years of age. Chenrile was dragging her along by her arm, and she was fighting and screaming every step of the way. It was the exact manner he had begun to escort Angelica back to Alexander. As the girl tried to anchor herself to the ground with her leather-soled shoes, Chenrile continued to drag her, and the crowd began to sigh in relief. They were happy that they were not the one chosen to be sacrificed that day.

As the pair walked towards the platform, Angelica looked throughout the crowd. There could not have been more than three hundred people here. They would not even last a single year if they executed one every day. There were people most likely hiding in their homes or in the forest, but still, the civilization would be exhausted of it citizens very quickly. Then, Angelica realized what had happened. She had been introduced as a newly acquired servant. Most likely, these people would travel outside the realm of their village to find people to make into servants. They would then grow up and have children of their own. Possibly, they would shed the bonds of servitude and become members of the civilization on their own. Perhaps they would even search and find servants for themselves as well. This would allow the population to grow constantly, and that would allow for this sick ritual to continue.

Alexander walked to the side of the platform and quickly ascended a ladder carved into its surface. As he walked across the platform towards the center, everyone cheered for him. Those cheers were not like the strained ones when he walked across in Protecia. They were real cries of happiness at seeing him. Angelica found herself both disgusted and amazed at this fact.

Finally, Chenrile climbed the ladder dragging the young woman behind him. With the assistance of some nearby guards, she was forced up the ladder and onto the platform as well. Those guards then climbed up and began to hold the girl still so that Chenrile could continue his other business.

Alexander spoke for only a few minutes, and everyone listened intensely. His voice did not travel far back that well, but Angelica could make out a few words of what he was saying. Something about the evil one being here, and that all should spend their days searching for her. Her assault on Chenrile was even mentioned, but Angelica was barely able to hear the exact words of it. She thought it would be interesting to listen to how Alexander distorted the events of that morning, but she was not able to hear. Finally, the speaking was over.

On a cue from Alexander, Chenrile walked towards the center of the platform. He knelt on the ground and seemed to disengaging a series of locks. Finally, he lifted a large door on the floor of the platform. The beasts began to growl and snarl again as the girl that was being held still on the platform began to shriek in fear. The guards were used to this sound, and they did not even hear it anymore. At least not when they were awake. The guards carried the girl towards the opening in the platform. She was fighting them to release her, but their hold would not falter. Finally, they reached the opening in the stone floor. The girl was squirming in their arms, and after a few moments of fighting, one of the guards had to stomp down on her leg so that she would stop fighting. For a brief moment, the crowd could see where her leg had broken under the guard's sandal. Once this was done, it was as simple a task as letting go.

The girl let out another scream as she plummeted down into the cage of the beasts. For an instant, the spectators were able to see her through the bars, and then she vanished into a sea of green scales. Her screams soon stopped and blood began to spray out from between the bars of the cage. Any tearing sounds of her flesh ripping were drowned out by the howls of the beasts and the cheers of the spectators in the front that were getting doused in the girl's blood. The girl whose only crime was being the last one to arrive at Alexander's address.

As everyone was watching this spectacle, Martin leaned over to Angelica and began to whisper, "Those really are spectacular creatures. People usually don't know it to look at them, but they're really very smart. The barred front of that cage had to be specially designed and redesigned several times because they kept finding out how ways to open it. I believe now there's some kind of lock on the top of the bars that could be unlocked from the platform. They can't figure out how to undo that one. At least not yet.

"Also, they are impossible to kill. They can breathe in air or under water. Those horns coming from their necks usually fold around their heads to block any attack. They're very fast and very strong." Martin smiled and then looked back at the beasts, which were now beginning to settle down again. Finally, they grew still, and when they did, Angelica could not see a single trace of the girl that had been thrown in. Not so much as a bone or a drop of blood.

Chenrile was still standing by the opening to the cage and was just looking down. The guards gathered around the opening as well, and they were even joined by two others. Chenrile removed the sword from his belt and pointed it into the hole. He slowly rotated the sword just as one might bait a lion. Everyone in the crowd watched excitedly, but Angelica just looked at him with confusion. Finally, she saw exactly why he was doing this.

One of the beasts leapt up from the mound of beasts in the cage. It was jumping towards the sword as if it was another sacrifice. Chenrile quickly withdrew the weapon and backed away. As the beast jumped for the hole, two of the guards reached in and grabbed it. They were each holding onto those strange protruding teeth from the creature's neck and began to pull the beast from the cage. When half of its eight foot body had emerged from the hole, the other two guards grabbed hold in between its front and back legs. All four began to carry the beast away swaying towards and from one another as the reptile fought freedom from all those hands. As soon as it cleared the hole, Chenrile slammed the door shut, locked it, and stood to wait.

For a while, nothing happened. Alexander and Chenrile just stood on the platform staring out into the crowd and talking amongst themselves. The guards disappeared with the beast and everything grew quiet for a while. After about five minutes, the four guards reappeared on the platform carrying the dead body of the beast they had just carried away. Its reptilian body was hanging limp in their arms, and its flawless black eyes remained bugging and wide. When the guards carried it to the center of the stage,

Alexander walked towards the front of the platform again. He began to call, "This creature is not the one destined to go to the other world and save us from their ruler. Their ruler is now here, and until she is returned to her own world, it is up to us and not these creatures to find and kill her."

Silently, Alexander stood at the front edge of the platform and stared out into the people. Chenrile walked towards the back wall and removed the staff from its hooks there. It looked menacing as Chenrile carried the staff with the stone reptile coiled around its head. Under its massive weight, Chenrile was struggling to carry it across the platform towards Alexander. His work as a physician did not demand much physical exertion, and he never made an effort to get stronger. Still, he carried the staff of Protace over towards their ruler.

Everyone in the crowd waited breathlessly and soundlessly. They all watched as Alexander slowly reached over and wrapped his fingers around the staff. His every movement seemed to hypnotize them. As soon as the staff was passed between the two people, Chenrile backed away and watched as Alexander became gripped by a seizure of some sort. His eyes and mouth clamped shut so tightly all the features on his face began to fuse into one smooth orb. While his right hand held the staff perfectly vertical next to him, the left hand was clenched in a fist. Alexander began to moan as if in pain, but no one reacted. None of the people on the platform with him or those watching from the crowd made a motion to help their leader. He was shrieking as loud as the woman that was just slaughtered by the beasts, but no one reacted in any way. There was not even the sound of the people breathing as Alexander quaked on the platform.

"Angelica," Martin whispered from next to her, but she was too entranced to listen. "Angelica, there's something I forgot to tell you about these addresses. I feel you should know before you see it happen." Angelica could not hear him, though. She just stood and stared as the staff came to life. The eyes lit up and beams of yellow light shot away from them. This nearly blinding illumination burst from every direction of those eyes creating two exploding stars atop the platform. The light that shot away from those eyes went on for miles and miles, illuminating the platform carved into the mountain. Even in the perfect, flawless sun, that light brightened everything to point of losing all the contrast in the world and bathing every surface in a dull glow. It consumed Alexander's convulsing body and blurred away everything taking place on that platform.

Soon, the light faded away, and the staff grew dark again. "That staff; it changes him." Martin was practically pleading with Angelica to listen, but there was no way for her to hear. "It transforms him into something else!" Those words cut through the trance that had gripped Angelica, and her attention shifted to Martin without her eyes deviating from the platform in the slightest. The memories of her nightmare staring into the cave with some creature laughing back at her all came rushing to her mind, but she could not look away. Even though she wanted to with every inch of her body, she could not possible look away from her uncle. He stopped convulsing and just stood, perfectly still, as if out of breath.

Finally, his hand nearly burst out of the fist so that all the fingers were splayed far apart from each other. On the end of each was a black claw about an inch and half in length. The five of the curved, black talons nearly glistened in the daylight, but that was nothing compared to what would happen next. Alexander still had his eyes and mouth shut. His head was facing the ground bobbing slightly on a weak neck. Slowly, at first, he began to raise his head. It went halfway up, and then he stopped. A second later, his eyes and mouth were opened, and he was turning his face to fully look at the crowd and let them look at him. His eyes were entirely black as if they were made of volcanic glass. Even from this distance, Angelica could swear she saw her face reflected in those eyes. In his opened mouth, fangs were extended from the bottom and top jaw. There were eight fangs in all, and they were all about two inches with a string of saliva glistening from them in the sunlight. His tongue was turned and pointed back into the mouth making it appear to be nothing more than a lump of pink flesh. As he tilted his partially altered and mutated face towards the crowd and the sky above, he began to scream. It was the same high-pitched howl that the beasts would shout at the sight of someone entering the courtyard. At the sound of Alexander's cry, all of the beasts began to shriek as well. Added to that, the cheers of the people in the courtyard rose up making a roar that was probably heard for ten miles around.

Angelica was the only one not screaming. She just stared at all of the people cheering at this monster that was before them. They were celebrating the arrival of a monster that had just executed one of their own for being the last one to arrive at the courtyard. Not even arriving late, but just arriving last. This was the monster that proceeded to kill an animal hoping that it would be able to travel to another world to wipe out his enemies. This was the monster that had killed Wilhelmina, Frederick, and countless others who stood in its way. This was the monster everyone was cheering.

As if she had just been kicked in the stomach, Angelica doubled over. She looked at the ground and tried to catch her breath even though it hurt to draw in air. Tears were flowing from her eyes and dripping down her nose in stinging beads of fire before eventually falling to the ground. After thirty seconds of forcing air in through her choked windpipe, Angelica was able to stand upright again. The cheering had not faltered in the slightest while she was bent over. If anything, it gained more power.

Martin leaned over to her again. "Are you okay? I know it's a real shock the first time you see him do that. I remember when I saw him change the first time. I was afraid of my own shadow for a week." Angelica just looked at Martin. His face said no more than if he had just told her that once he had a bad dream when he was kid. He spoke so calmly about events anyone in her world would consider horrific. Still, the shocked look on her face did not fade at all. "Angelica, are you okay? Just relax. And breathe."

Finally, she was able to draw in a deep enough breath to speak a few words. "I just never thought that Alexander could change into a monster. I knew he always acted like a monster, but to really become one." With a deep sigh, she added, "I grew up with him. It is more of a shock than what you received." Angelica felt a little bit better after having spoken about it, but she noticed a confused look on Martin's face.

"Did you say Alexander?" Angelica looked up at Martin preparing herself for another blow, but not knowing if she would be able to handle it. Lately, that has been all she receiving. One bad blow after another. "His name isn't Alexander. I thought you knew that." She remembered that in the two days she had been here, the subject of the prince seemed to disgust everyone to the point where they would not even refer to him by name. She never thought anything of it. Actually, it was comforting for Angelica not to say his name out loud. Martin looked at her as if she was an invalid or a very bad liar. For a moment, Angelica did not know how to respond, and she just stood there staring back at him. "His name is Protace, and the one wearing all the colors is Soranace." Angelica felt that feeling of shortness of breath returning, but it was worse this time. Her stomach began to burn, and she could feel its acidity trying to get back up. The world began fade in and out for a moment as if everything in it was vibrating. All she could think of were those two names. They were names that were worshipped on her world, and here they represent a monster and his henchman. It was the biggest and most revolting insult she had ever received. Just by using the names of people so revered made Angelica hate them even more, but right now shock was more powerful than hate or disgust. Colors began to swim into one another, and all Angelica could hear was her own breathing. The rush of wind in and out of her body drowned out all the screaming and cheering. It was the only sound in the world. Soon, the queen found herself falling towards the ground with confused and concerned faces looking at her.

CHAPTER TWENTY-THREE

The Face of the Monster

Slowly, Angelica opened her eyes to find herself lying on the bed back at the cottage. It appeared to be the middle of the day. The cottage's single room was filled with light mostly likely from the sunshine beaming in through that single opening in the wall. Without standing or even sitting up in bed, Angelica turned her head to look out that window. When her eyes finally did find the outside, what she saw frightened her. Outside the cottage, it was dark. So dark that it must have been the middle of the night. The stars and moon were clearly visible in the sky, but why was it so bright in the cottage?

Angelica sat up in the bed and looked around. There was no sign of Martin, Lenore, or the children. She was alone in the cottage, or so it seemed for the time being. Maybe they were all hiding in the underground room, but why would they be doing that? Angelica looked around the room again, and then she saw the figure sitting on the opposite side of the bed to her. It was facing the other way and draped in a cape. There was a single item that identified him immediately. A staff in his hand that was also pointed away from her and towards the wall.

Just as Angelica saw this man sitting on the bed, he began to move. He was turning towards her, and Angelica knew it must be Alexander. No matter what he was calling himself now, she knew exactly who and what he was. Alexander turned to face her, and the staff turned with him. As it came around, she could see the brightly glowing, yellow eyes staring at her. They were making the room as bright as it was. Those eyes were as bright as the sun when it was in the sky. As Alexander's altered, monster-like face turned towards her, he began to howl as he had done at the address.

"NO!" Angelica sprung from the bed screaming and batting her arms at anything coming near her. "No! No!" Someone was grabbing her, but she could not see who it was. If she stopped fighting, she would certainly be killed. Her arms kept slamming down in front of her, and she could feel eyes boring into her from all around. As her arms fought, another pair from in front of her was trying to fight back.

A voice was piercing through Angelica's screams as if having practiced on numerous tantrums throughout the years. "Calm down." Finally, Angelica stopped beating her arms just for long enough to see who was in front of her. It was Martin. When she finally made eye contact with him, she fell forward into his arms and wrapped hers around him. "It was just a nightmare, Angelica. You're safe now." It took a moment for Angelica to calm down entirely, but soon enough, she was back to normal.

She was lying on the bed in the cottage, but unlike in her dream, there were other people here. Everyone who was supposed to be here was, and the room was not as bright as she had dreamt. From the window, she could see the dim but beautiful light of a sunset gleaming in. Everything was the way it should be, at least the way things in this world usually were.

When Angelica had a moment to take a few deep breaths, Martin began to speak to her as if nothing had happened. "You fainted at the address. Are you okay?" Angelica nodded obediently. She was terrified to make eye contact with any of the four people in the room with her most likely in embarrassment for fainting then for screaming when she woke up. "It seemed like his name scared you more than anything else. I can't say that's how it was when I first saw him. That face was what gave me nightmares."

Finally, Angelica looked up. Martin was there watching her with careful and caring eyes. Lenore was standing behind him, far behind him, and her eyes were filled with distrust. The children were playing on the floor as if they did not realize Angelica had even woken up. "His face does not scare me. I know what exists behind it, and that is much worse than anything he can show you." Martin just nodded as if he knew this was a wound that should not be reopened. "The name is what scared me the most, you were right about that. In my world, the world Alexander, or Protace as you call him, came from, our legends say that our civilization was founded by a single man named Protace. He united uncivilized people under his rule, and he ruled for a great while. After he died, his son, Soranace, succeeded him on the throne." Angelica sighed deeply and then continued. "You can only imagine my disgust when I find that these two killers changed their names from Alexander and Chenrile to Protace and Soranace. It is as if they are trying to make themselves into gods." Angelica did not share the information they had recently obtained about how the original Protace, the one from her history, may not have been as benevolent as they originally thought.

No one said anything for some time. They just continued doing what they had been. It was not a story that was easily recovered from. Finally, it was Lenore who broke the silence. "Our meal is almost ready." There was a series of nods from around the room, and everyone began to gather around the table to eat. Within five minutes, bowls of soup were being placed before them all.

As they ate, Martin spoke. "The one thing I am glad about is that our kids wouldn't go through the event you just did." He nodded towards Angelica as he continued, "You see, everyone who grew up around here is used to seeing that. They'd seen it from the time they were very young, and it comes to be natural to them. Aside from the people that were already here when Protace and Soranace showed up, there's always the servants brought in from outside that react the same way you did. It's a shock, I guess." Angelica did not know what to think about this. The idea of that spectacle being considered a commonplace event was not something she would have wanted for her children when she would have them, but she kept that idea to herself as well.

That was the extent of the conversation that night. Angelica was still scared from what she had seen that day to begin composing the list of names for Martin to bring across to Beatrice. That would have to wait for another day, and until then, she would have to go through life as she did this day. Running from people determined to kill her, staring into the face of a demon, and telling people about how her world was so much better than this. She just hoped that by tomorrow, she would have won their trust enough so that Martin would agree to travel to her world with the list of names. Names and one very important question concerning Chenrile and his ties to those with Protace's blood.

Above all, the rulers of Protecia had to be of Protace's bloodline or have married into it and succeeded a dead spouse. If Alexander is truly considering Chenrile to be his successor, as it would suggest by the names they had chosen, it would seem necessary for Chenrile to have Protace's blood. That was the question Angelica felt she must ask. To truly know what they were dealing with, they would have to know Chenrile's real involvement in this distorted kingdom.

Still, that was a question to be put off until tomorrow. Right now, Angelica was concerned with sleep, as were the others. Although she had been sleeping for hours during the afternoon, she still was amazingly exhausted. They all crowded into the bed and fell asleep as they did the night before. Angelica's sleep was very light, though. The thought that they would all leave during the night for her to be attacked by Alexander was constantly recurring in her mind. That was why she awoke instantly when Martin and Lenore rose from the bed.

It was the exact same exchange as the night before. They walked towards the area in the middle of the cottage where they spoke for a moment. Then, they began to move towards the door. This is when tonight began to differ, though. Lenore stopped about halfway to the door and looked back towards the room. The two of them spoke for a moment more, and then they walked over to Angelica to wake her.

Despite how nervous she was when Martin began to shake her, Angelica managed to look as if she was being startled from a deep sleep. With her eyes appearing to look groggy, she stared up at Martin and Lenore, who whispered to her, "Get out of bed quietly. We have somewhere we want to bring you." Their faces looked sincere, but Angelica was afraid to get out of the bed. She had no idea what they might be planning to do to her once she followed them out the door to wherever they go during the night.

Still, there were little alternatives, so Angelica rose quietly from the bed. She was careful not to wake the two other children that were sleeping beside her. As she set her feet to the cold ground below, a chill raced up Angelica's spine. No matter how warm the daytime is here, the middle of the night got very cold. With the two adults guiding, she walked towards the door but stopped before through. "Where are we going?" she whispered to them.

As if it was a terribly difficult question to answer, Martin and Lenore looked at each other hesitantly. Sparing another look towards the bed, Martin answered, "We'll tell you outside. Come on." It was hard to make out their faces in the dark, but Angelica could almost feel the concerned look etched on Martin's face as well as the glare of indifference Lenore casually wore. With no alternative, Angelica followed the two out of the cottage door and beneath the starlight outside.

"Since you finally saw Protace's real face today, we felt it may be the best time for you to see something else as well." Angelica smiled at Martin's honesty and consistency. No sooner were they out the door than he began to explain exactly where they were going. "I have no reason to doubt what you said about who you really are and what Protace had done to you. There is a small, but growing, group of us. We're trying to oppose him, and I think that your presence there would be a great help to everyone involved."

Angelica was at a loss for words. She just nodded as Martin spoke and occasionally made a few grunts to show she understood. They walked past the boundaries of the cottage and towards the mountain range that stretched across the edge of their civilization. In the darkness, Angelica could see a few more silhouettes walking towards the same destination as they. These were probably the other members of this group Martin had mentioned.

As they walked, Martin continued to speak to Angelica. "We have to meet in secret so that Protace and his guards don't find out. If they do, we'll all be as good as dead." After a few more steps, he continued his story. "It only took a few times of watching the people you've come to know and love being torn apart by those monsters before some of us formed this group. We are trying to plan a way to remove him and Soranace from power. He did do a great job of giving us a civilization, but his methods are unbearable. You see how we spend half of every day waiting for his address because we know whoever arrives last is going to be killed. What kind of life is that?" Once again, Angelica found herself unable to answer, but Martin did not wait long. He knew what her reaction would be, so there was no need to watch for it. "We want to find a way to live in a civilization while being free of that monster."

Martin did not say another word. Lenore did not speak since they had left the cottage. Still, Angelica tried to speak and realized she could not. So they continued to go the rest of the way to the mountain without uttering a single word to one another. When they reached the mountain, Martin crouched on the ground and crawled into a small cave that was barely visible from five feet away. Within an instant, he vanished into the wall of rock.

Angelica lowered herself to her knees and began to crawl towards the rocky formation before her. There was nothing to see before her but a deep, dark shadow. With one hand extended, Angelica crawled a little bit closer. Groping at the shadow as if she were blind, she soon was able to find an opening in the side of the mountain. It was much smaller than she had expected, and it was nearly impossible to see considering the way the shadow fell upon it. Still, she had to enter through it, so that was just what she did.

Once inside the cave, she saw it was much different than the one in her world. There was no wide opening as soon as she entered. Instead, the cave continued on just as narrow as that opening. Martin was stretched out just a few feet in front of her, and she continued to follow him as he dragged himself along the ground of the cave. Angelica followed close behind him without saying a word. She was able to hear Lenore entering the cave behind her, but the space was too constricted for her to even turn her head to look. With no ability to look at Lenore, Angelica kept her attention focused on Martin and continued following him deeper into the cave.

Finally, Martin stopped and said, "There's a little bit of a drop here. Be careful." Too nervous for words, Angelica muttered an inarticulate response and watched as Martin slowly lowered himself in front of her. She was able to see him turn around once he had climbed down. He was looking into the cave at eye-level now. That new part of the cave was high enough for him to stand in. With her eyes firmly fixed on his, Angelica crawled the rest of the way towards the drop where he helped her climb down.

At this point, she was able to look around and see the cave around her. It was illuminated by a soft glow coming from a nearby cavern, but the light was still very low. The cave itself felt unbearably humid, and there was actually a coating of water over every surface in here. It was almost as if a hot, wet hand was squeezing Angelica constantly. Still, despite the drop, the space was indeed very cramped and Angelica felt the need to leave. Staying here was not a good idea. Especially with Alexander's guards and those reptile beasts roaming around outside. Still, Martin's nearly shadow-ridden eyes insisted that they continue.

While Lenore was climbing down from the smaller cave into the larger, Martin took Angelica by the arm. He led her towards the source of the dim light, and she followed willingly. This was not the place to argue. They walked down a short cavern towards a fork in the cave. The path to the right led to the dim light source, and the path to the left was only leading to dense blackness. Angelica began to move towards the light, but Martin extended his arm in front of her. He whispered, "That's a trap in case we're discovered by the guards." After saying that, he led Angelica towards the light while keeping her arm held tightly. They approached a widening in the cave that was nearly drowned out by the light when Martin stopped walking. With that brightness, it was difficult to see much of anything, which was why this trap worked so well. Angelica leaned forward to get a better look, and she was able to see the trap. If she had not been looking for it, she would have simply gone into it like any intruder was intended to.

A drop of about fifty feet was just beyond the opening. It ended in a bed of stalagmites that reached upward with jagged points. On the other side of the drop was a small ledge. It was on that ledge that a single torch was burning. The light supplied by this torch would be enough to drive any ambitious guard to his death. The people of this group were not willing or able to take any chances.

After seeing this trap, Martin led Angelica away from this path and towards the left fork in the cave. Here, they met up with Lenore, and the three of them walked about ten feet down a totally dark cavern. Finally, they reached the end. The cave just stopped. Angelica was certain that this would be where these two launched their own trap. They had isolated Angelica in this darkness. Instead, Martin just knelt down and reached for a handle that could not be seen in the darkness. It took a second to grope for the stone protrusion, but soon he found it and began to pull. There was the dragging sound of stone against stone, and soon an opening revealed itself, and more light began to spill through.

With the stone moved out of the way, there was an opening that was also well lit. Martin crawled through immediately, and Angelica followed right behind him. Just after her, Lenore dragged herself through. She stopped for a moment in the doorway to drag the stone back in place behind her. Now, with the rest of the caverns blocked off, they walked deeper into the cave. There was a circle of people sitting on the floor in this area. Just behind this circle, a path bent to the right, most likely leading to the ledge on the other side of the drop. This would be where they would place the torch to lure any of Alexander's guards away from their meeting. The people in the circle all began to turn their heads and look at Angelica. She was a stranger, but the only thing that kept them from reacting violently was the fact that she was escorted by these two people they trusted. She was now part of this group as well.

CHAPTER TWENTY-FOUR

The Group Meeting

M artin finally stepped forward and spoke to the group sitting on the stony ground. He had been the focal point of every set of eyes in the room for a moment that could have lasted an eternity. There was no need for anyone to ask him the question they had on their minds. It was obvious what they were thinking. "This is Angelica. She's Protace's niece from the other world. Yesterday morning, she came here across the portal to this world with the intent of destroying both Protace and Soranace." There was a moment of whispers being passed among the people sitting on the ground. Martin continued to speak of the story Angelica had told him. How her mother was assassinated and how an attempt was made on her life. He even told them about the Protace and Soranace Angelica knew from her world's legends. How they were the founders of their civilization, and how these imposters were simply trying to take credit for their work in this world.

When Martin stopped speaking, the members of the group mumbled amongst themselves for a few minutes. Angelica could feel sweat dripping down her face. What if they felt her story was a lie? They may end up throwing her into that drop off to die below. While her terror was at its fullest, one of the people in the group called out to her, "Our Prophecy says that you're an evil person. That the reason you're here to destroy our way of life and bring us into the slavery of your rule. How do we know you're not the same or even worse than Protace? You're his blood. You may be just as bad as him." Angelica looked at the dimly lit faces of the people sitting before her. She had no idea which of them had asked the question of her, but she was certain they all wanted the answer. For years, they had been told to fear her and to turn her in or kill her outright if they should find her in this world. Now, they are asked to believe that she is going to help them. Angelica knew she had to say something to convince them of her intentions, but the words did not come easily.

After taking a few nervous steps forward, just as Martin had done before addressing the group, Angelica began to speak. "There is no real proof I can offer you to support my intentions. All I can say is that I came here to eliminate the threat of Alexander, or Protace as you call him. He fled here after attempting to kill me, and I know that my kingdom would not be safe until I know he has been destroyed. The Prophecy you spoke of is one that he created and forced all of you to memorize. It is filled not only with the visions he claimed to have over the years but also with the lies he wants you to believe so that you would help him. He routinely kills one of you each day. The only way to keep your civilization intact is to abduct servants and foreigners from its boundaries to sacrifice them instead. There is not much I can say to win your support, but there is one thought I can offer in my favor. Who do you have nightmares of? Someone like me, or that creature he becomes when he is holding his staff? Do you want a monster like that to be not only your ruler, but the one to keep you enslaved as well?"

It felt as if she had just delivered another of her public addresses, probably the most important address she would deliver in her life. This time, however, it had more purpose than to win the support of the people that were forced to follow her. It was her kingdom, this other kingdom, and her own life that were all on the line now. If this group decided that the story she told was a fallacy, then everything she had worked for would be destroyed in a matter of moments.

Angelica's eyes darted around to the faces of the people in the cave. They were all nodding as they began to mumble to each other again. Angelica could feel the sweat rolling from her forehead and down the sides of her face. Fear was running through her veins as she listened to the dull wordless drone of these people talking and deciding, for all purposes, whether she should live or die. Finally, after an eternity, they stopped. All of the eyes fell upon her again, and a single voice rose up from them. "We're pleased and grateful to have you as one of us."

A sigh of relief filled Angelica, and she nearly fell to the ground. Lenore reached out and caught her from behind. This gave Angelica a chance to regain her feet, and she walked towards Martin who, in turn, led her to the rest of the group. He began introduce each of the eight other members. There was Bryan, whom she had been introduced to before the public address that day, as well as his wife. The three other men were Patrick, William, and Michael, all of whom also came with their wives. As Angelica looked at these people she noticed something. With the exception of Lenore, they were all able to travel across the worlds. All of their images were on the wall in Protecia. With the addition of Angelica, their group now had eleven members. Small compared to the armies Alexander would have at his disposal, but large enough to make a profound impact if they organized properly.

The three of them joined the circle the rest of the group was sitting in, and they began to speak. Ideas about how to obtain more members while avoiding suspicion were brought up. The family of the girl that was killed by the beasts in the cage that afternoon was a likely possibility. It was Patrick that mentioned her name. Isabelle. That was the name of the girl that had been torn to pieces while the crowds cheered. Her family seemed as likely a possibility as anyone else did. Right now, they would be most distrustful and angry of the monster they knew as Protace.

Other things that were discussed included more drastic measures. The thought of a public assassination attempt or a simple attack on Soranace as a message to Protace were both brought up. This is when Angelica said, "In the other world, there are about five people I could gather that would be able to come across to help us. Some are soldiers while others are only farmers, but that would increase our numbers by nearly a third. If we are going to launch an attack like that, our numbers should be as large as possible."

It was agreed among the members of this group that this should be done before launching any serious attacks on their two rulers. "I can write up a list of names tonight, and one of you could take it across to the other world. You are all able to travel that portal, so we would be able to fight Protace no matter where he tries to hide." Angelica felt compelled to mention that Lenore could not travel as the others could, but she thought it would be better to tell her later in private rather than in this public forum. Such a thing would not be a detail she would want the whole group to hear. Angelica also could not deny that she felt it a good omen of their success that this group of people fighting secretly against Alexander could travel between worlds as she could. It was agreed. Martin said he would go across to the other world as soon as Angelica wrote up the list.

It appeared, to Angelica at least, that this group was good-intentioned, but needed leadership. They had no idea how to proceed with their lofty plans until she arrived to take the reins. Now that she did, there would be nothing to stop this group, combined with the people from her world, from accomplishing what she had travelled there to do. They were going to dismantle Alexander's rule and secure safety for this world as well as her own.

The meeting went on. Other topics were discussed, but none offered as much enthusiasm as they ones they had just completed. Partway through the discussion, Lenore actually rose to her feet and left. She moved the stone out of the way and quietly exited the cave. As she was pushing the large rock back into place, Angelica could not help but notice that no one else had stopped talking. It was quite normal for some members to leave partway through the meeting.

Angelica quickly assumed she must be running back home to check on the children, and she would be returning again shortly.

As it turned out, Lenore did return eventually. It was some time later, and the meeting had progressed as if she had not even left. No one even stopped talking when the sound of the rock being moved filled the cave again. Lenore stepped through the opening and took a few strides into the room. This did draw all of their attention, however. She did not stop to put the rock back in place, and what she did after that alerted everyone to exactly what she had in mind. Lenore reached into one baggy sleeve of the simple cloth robe she was wearing and removed a six inch dagger from it. Then, as if it was the most normal action in the world, she just stepped to the side of the opening into the meeting area.

Heralded by a series of gasps, a parade of Alexander's soldiers began to march through the opening each with their sword drawn. They walked right past Lenore and towards the people sitting in the circle. Everyone rose at once. Angelica looked around frantically as twenty guards filled the cramped area and began swinging their swords. She grabbed the dagger that was attached to her calf as the other group members retrieved either swords or daggers of their own. Angelica knew she had to get out of there as soon as she can, but the swarm of soldiers that had just arrived blocked the exit to the cave. There was only one other possibility.

She ran away from the guards towards the ledge where the torch was, behind where the group was meeting. There was the drop and then the right fork of the cave beyond it. Angelica did not know these caves very well, but she thought there might be some chance of a way to get out from this side. A rope to swing across, or a path that could only be seen when standing over here, or anything that would get her out of this. When Angelica did get past the torch and towards the drop, she saw no more than she had from the other side. A drop to her death that she would never be able to jump over and the caves beyond that. A cave that might as well have been a thousand miles away.

As Angelica was looking down the drop she thought she was beginning to see another cave underneath her side of the ledge, but she could not look very long. There were footsteps coming from behind her. Angelica turned and saw a soldier standing before her with his sword raised in the air. Using the dagger against this trained soldier would most certainly mean her death, so she ran to the wall of the cave as he hacked down with his sword. She was able to see the fury in his eyes as well as his premature feelings of triumph. He already thought he was going to kill the little girl that the Prophecy referred to as the Evil One, and that he would be revered as greatest soldier in their kingdom until the day he died.

Angelica, however, had no intention of letting this happen. As the guard was raising his sword from the ground again, Angelica ran towards him holding the dagger out in front of her. She raced forward aiming at the side of his chest, but as soon as she got close to him, he reached out and shoved her back to the ground. Angelica spilled to the rocky surface of the cave floor, and the dagger fell from her hand. As she was beginning to regain her footing, Angelica could see the soldier coming at her again. She ran towards the closest thing that could be used as a weapon. The torch.

With the soldier right behind her, Angelica grabbed the torch from its stand and swung around holding it away from her. Its weight was so great she could barely hold onto it, but she managed to hit the soldier on the side of his face with the fiery end of the torch. The guard screamed as the fire ignited his hair and the collar of his uniform. His sword fell to the ground, and his hands reached up to try smothering the flames. It was no use though. The fire was spreading over his body too quickly.

Angelica dropped the torch to the ground and ran to the soldier to help him. She wanted desperately to save him from the pain that she had caused, but she was unable to. At the sight of Angelica coming towards him, the soldier, disoriented and nearly blind by this point, tried to get away. Angelica screamed for him to stop, but he was unable to hear anything over his own screams. He turned and ran from her. In her own fear and sadness, she looked away as he ran over the ledge and fell to his death below.

There was no time to grieve over what she had done. Angelica grabbed her dagger off the ground and began to make her way back to the main room. On the way, she could hear the screams of the soldiers and the group members. They were fighting for their lives, and there was nothing she could do to help aside from trying to save herself. Angelica ran back to the main room and scanned the scene with her eyes. The soldiers were still fighting the rebels with their swords although a number of people missing. Not enough to account for the two dead women and one man on the ground as well as the slain soldiers. Several of the group's members seemed to have found their way out into the caves.

As Angelica watched the last two men, William and Bryan, fighting off the last six guards, she was attacked from the side. Lenore ran into her with her dagger raised. There was a shrill whine of a scream coming from her as she raised her large dagger to stab down at Angelica. The young queen had no room to run, so she simply raised her own dagger into the musky air and plunged at Lenore's tricep. The woman screamed in pain, but her dagger still found its way down and sliced a cut along Angelica's arm.

In shock and pain, Angelica backed away from Lenore towards the far wall. As she did, Bryan grabbed her by the arm and shoved her towards a wall on the far left of the room. His weight was like battering ram pushing her to the side. She did not know if he was pushing her to safety or sacrificing her to the soldiers to save himself. After all she had seen that day, she did not know what people were capable of anymore. There was a large crack in the cave wall, but still too small for him to fit through. It was large enough for the young queen, however. He practically threw Angelica into this crack and whispered, "Take the path as far it goes. Take the right at the first fork and left at every fork in the path after that. It'll lead you out of the caves. Make your way to the village and hide. We'll look for you tomorrow."

Angelica started on her way into the crack when she turned back. "Where is Martin? Is he still alive?" Her eyes were scanning the bodies on the ground. She could not see him, but there was the possibility of his body falling somewhere she cannot see like that soldier had. The soldier she had killed, Angelica corrected herself. She just looked at Bryan pleading with him for an answer.

"Just go!" A soldier ran towards them, and Bryan plunged the full length of his sword through the man's chest. What hurt Angelica so much to do, Bryan did with such ease that it seemed to be second nature to him. "Just get out of here! Now!" With this, Angelica turned and began to crawl along the narrow passageway according to the directions Bryan had given her. There was no light, and she was only able to navigate her path by keeping one hand gliding along both walls at all time. This was the only way she knew when the forks in the cave's path had arrived and when to take them.

Back in the meeting room, William killed the last guard that was there, and the two remaining men stood there for a moment looking at Lenore. She was holding one hand over the stab wound in her arm that Angelica had carved there. They just looked at her for a while, looking at her cold and emotionless face, before Bryan eventually said, "How could you do this? How could you betray all of us like this?"

Lenore did not say a word. She just stood there and listened to more footsteps coming through the caves. Finally, Soranace ducked through the opening from the darkness with his sword drawn and a smile in his eyes. Next, Protace walked through the opening with his black cape furling around him. Protace gave a single look to Lenore before he also drew his sword and walked deeper into that meeting room.

In that instant, William and Bryan exchanged a frightened look to one another. There was little they could do to fight off both Protace and Soranace who always appeared to be expert sword fighters. Still, they had little choice. Aside from possibly finding a way to escape, there was nothing to do but fight.

Soranace was the first to charge the two men. Bryan stepped forward and fought back. The sound of metallic clangs filled the cave as the two began to fight. William kept his eyes carefully fixed on Protace who, right now, did not move at all. Their civilization's leader was watching as Soranace fought Bryan, and as Bryan slowly tried to bring the fight into the small passage by the drop. After every blow with their swords, Bryan took a step in the direction, and soon they were out of sight from the others.

As he entered this area, Bryan saw the evidence of Angelica's squirmish there. Bryan was growing tired. He had been fighting this flood of soldiers for almost fifteen minutes, and he did not think he had much effort left in him to fight any longer. Still, he knew how he had to leave the caves. He also knew there was an escape route getting very close.

Soranace sliced across the air with his sword, and Bryan ducked out of the way. He was able to hear the rush of air as the sword sailed across the caves above him. Bryan fell to the stone ground to avoid the onslaught of sword swings, and in doing so, dropped his own sword. While on the ground, Bryan grabbed hold of the torch's handle much like Angelica had done. He lifted the torch and swung it at Soranace. The man in the brightly colored costume jumped back in fear. The thought of being burned terrified him. With this slight advantage, Bryan crawled a few more feet towards the drop. Soranace was beginning to come towards him again, so Bryan threw the torch at him with a hurl that consumed the last bit of his strength. With the roar of the torch fire filling the caves, Soranace swung his sword at the torch to bat it away. This was more effort than he had anticipated. The force of that torch pushed Soranace back a several steps and almost made him fall to the ground. This gave Bryan the few seconds he needed.

With Soranace trying to regain his balance, Bryan crawled the rest of the way towards the drop. When he reached the edge, he could not help looking down at the burning corpse of the guard at the bottom. It was barely visible from up here, and there was no time to waste watching it continue to burn. Bryan turned around and got to his knees. He then lowered himself off the ledge so he was hanging down into the drop. Then, he bent his legs out in front of him, and did not hit rock but drifted into an opening in the wall. His toes were able to touch the ground of this cave, and he used them to pull himself farther into the tunnel. Finally, he let go of the edge, and fell not fifty feet but only five feet to ground of the cave below.

As Bryan was regaining his footing on the ground, he looked up and saw Soranace standing on the ledge and staring down at him. He saw the passageway, and it was only a matter of time before he came chasing after Bryan. Into the darkness, Bryan ran. The cavern was large enough for him to be standing fully as he navigated the forks and side caverns in the cave. Soon, he had vanished into the darkness.

Soranace landed in this other cave an instant later. He quickly ran in the direction of the footsteps he heard, but he did not go far. After about twenty feet, he stopped. He had no idea where Bryan could have gone. These caves stretched for miles in all directions, and if he was to take a single wrong turn, he may never find his way out. Soranace returned to the edge of the drop and waited for Protace to come to help him out.

The instant that Soranace and Bryan had moved into the other chamber of the caves where the torch was burning, Protace attacked. William began to fight back, but his moves were matched and nearly doubled by the swings of Protace's sword. Trying to maneuver similarly to how Bryan had done, William attempted to move with each swing of his sword deeper into the meeting area. There was another passage that would bring him out of the mountain about a mile from the village, and the entrance to this cavern was about thirty feet back from where they were now.

Protace continued to swing his sword gracefully through the air as William fought back with fumbling arcs trying to make his way towards the passageway out of the caves. One heavy strike of Protace's sword, however, had pinned him against the cave wall. He was pushing his sword against Protace's but he would not budge. Protace was pushing with all of his strength and weight against William, leaving him nowhere to run. There was another opening in the cave wall just a few feet from him. It only led to a dead end, but it would give him a minute to regain his bearings at least. William tried to take a step to his right while not yielding under the force of Protace's sword.

Before he was able to complete this single step, however, William felt a pain in his back. It felt like liquid fire sliding into his body and stabbing directly into his soul. He slightly turned his head and saw Lenore standing beside him with her dagger extended. The pain was tingling through William's body, and he felt the swords drifting closer to him. He could not combat both of them at once. The pain was too great. Protace's sword sliced down and hit William's shoulder. Blood began to find its way to the surface while Protace lifted his sword again. He plunged the full length of the blade under William's sternum. Choking noises echoed off the walls of the caves, and soon William fell silent. His sword slipped from his hand and fell to the ground. Then, his body did the same.

Protace and Lenore both walked away from the body and through the other dead bodies that were covering the floor of the cave. As they walked, Lenore was carefully scanning the ground for Martin. Before she had a chance to complete the search, Protace said, "Your husband got away. Through one of the openings in the cave. He had probably found his way out of the mountain by this point." Lenore just nodded as the two continued to walk towards where Soranace was waiting for them.

Angelica continued to crawl through the tight cave. From even here, she was able to hear the screams of the soldiers fighting her group's members behind her. Through these screams, she could hear any footfalls coming after her. Aside from those agonized echoes, the small cavern she was in was absolutely silent. Angelica continued dragging herself along the rock, feeling the rawness of her skin. Even with the rough cloth in between her and the stone, she was sore from the journey.

Soon, she saw a faint light ahead of her, and she began to move quicker. The thought of being free of this cave was an overwhelming one, and she wanted to be out now. Not just to be away from the echoing screams that reverberated off the rock walls, but to be out in the open air when she could breathe freely. Her body was sore and her throat hurt from the dirt and she had been breathing in. Aside from that, simple fear and exhaustion were too much for her to contend with. Her faster speed was not all that much faster than she had been travelling due to the rocks grabbing hold of her body and simply due to fatigue. It took her about five minutes to go the remaining fifteen feet to the dim light ahead.

Finally, she stuck her head out of the mountain's side. She seemed to be high up. From where she was, nothing looking familiar, and for a moment, she even debated just turning around and taking the tunnel back to the meeting room. Still, she realized she would not know her way through the caves from that direction either. When she arrived, she had been following Martin through the darkness without much understanding of where she was travelling. Now, that she was outside of the caves, or at least her head was, and she should be able to get down and find her way back to the village from here. With a quick look around though, she realized it would not be that simple. There were guards everywhere.

Angelica knew she had little choice concerning where to go now, so she squeezed her arms through the opening and began to feel around for something to grab hold of. She did find a small protrusion just above the hole. Her cold and bleeding hands grabbed onto this rock, and Angelica began to pull herself out of the hole and onto the side of the mountain. When these passages were discovered by the group members, they made certain that there were places to grab hold of and areas to climb from. These escape routes seemed perfect in nearly every aspect.

This surface of the mountain was almost entirely smooth. There was hardly anything to hold onto. Still, Angelica could not turn back now. She was lying against the side of the mountain holding on with weakening hands to a rock jutting from the surface. She had to do something quickly or she would fall. There was a narrow ledge a few feet beneath her. With her toes and fingers resting against the mountain surface, she let go of the rock. Her hands and feet were enough to slow her fall to the ledge below. This part of the mountain was not that steep, so she slid to the ledge, holding her breath in absolute fear, with her hands and toes rubbing against the rock. Soon, her toes touched the ledge, and she released a sigh of relief.

Angelica looked around. This ledge was very narrow, but it was something to stand on at least. At about three inches wide, Angelica found that the ledge could only hold her toes, but it was enough for her to slowly creep to her right where it gradually widened. While breathing as shallowly as she knew how and with sweat dripping from her forehead, Angelica crept to her right where the ledge widened to about four feet in width. It took a few minutes, but soon, she got there.

The cold night air was biting into her, making her shiver. There was hardly any wind, but the mountain side resonated with icy vibes. She knew she could not stop now, though. Doing that would certainly mean her death. Her only chance was to make it to safety before she was spotted. With her arms wrapped around her torso for warmth, Angelica turned and looked around to see where she was. Mountains were surrounding nearly the entire area, but there was one thing that was easily visible even in the dark that made her know exactly where she was. Carved into one of these mountains was a large cage with iron bars extending down the front. Angelica never realized until now how much higher this platform was that the one on her world. Easily thirty feet in height, either so Alexander can look down on his subjects easily or just to make room for that huge dwelling of beasts. Inside, dozens of lizard-like creatures were squirming and rolling over one another. They were absolutely silent even with the guards filling the courtyard, but it did not matter. This was all Angelica needed to see to know exactly where she was and how to get back to the village.

Still, if she were to just run right now, the guards would almost certainly catch her before she even got out of the courtyard. Just like Chenrile had done to escape from the Protecian Kingdom through the caves, Angelica needed a distraction. She knew exactly what it could be as well.

In the absolute silence, Angelica walked to the end of the ledge she was on. There was a ladder carved into the mountain at this point for people to climb up and down during the public addresses. This would be how she escapes, but first she needed to distract the guards' attention. There was a stone beside her one the ledge. It was no larger than Angelica's hand, but that was good enough. With the stone clenched tightly in her raw and bleeding fingers, Angelica turned towards the cage filled with the beasts. All the strength she had left in her went into her arm, and she hurled that stone at the cage as hard as she possibly could.

The stone rolled through the air, first arcing up and then beginning to fall down just as the arrows fired at her and her mother had done. It did manage to stay airborne just long enough to hit a bar of the cage just near the ground. This was all that was needed, though. The sound of the rock hitting the metal made all the guards turn to look. Even more importantly, it made all of the beasts begin to growl and howl in surprise. The guards began yelling at each other, but the hissing of the beasts drowned their voices out almost completely.

With this amount of noise filling the courtyard, Angelica raced down the ladder and began to run towards the village. Still, even in all of this noise, the sound of her running was noticed by some of the guards. She got almost half a minute head start before the guards were able to get the attentions of one another and begin running after her. Angelica was running for her life, and she was able to get to the village without being caught.

Tired, out of breath, and in pain, Angelica found her way to the center of the village with the guards running behind her, but she needed a place to hide. She knew Lenore was working for Protace, but that cottage still seemed like the best possibility. It was the only place Angelica knew of with a secret room to hide in. From the center of the village, Angelica ran towards the back of Martin's cottage. To go to the front door would mean walking right across the guards' path as they ran after her. The large window on the back wall of the cottage was the best way to get in undetected at this point.

As the frantic footsteps of the guards got closer, Angelica hoisted herself up onto the windowsill and fell in on the other side. There, she waited for a few seconds, curled up on the floor against the wall with the freezing cold surrounding her and the sounds of marching guards outside. They did not see where she went. Their steps just continued on right past the window. Angelica considered this to be a good sign. Even if they do begin to search the cottages later on, she would have an opportunity to hide by then.

Despite the soreness consuming her body from crawling through the cave, Angelica began to drag herself across the room to the table. The cottage was completely deserted, without a sign of the children or any kind of struggle. Her body screamed in agony as she placed her hands forward and pulled herself along the ground a few more feet. She was too scared that someone outside may see her if she stood. Finally, she reached the table and dragged the slate out of its place beneath. With the care of an elderly woman lowering herself into a chair, Angelica began to place her legs in the hole and lower herself in.

Her feet found the ladder, and she began to step down onto the first rung. Then, she moved a little bit farther into the hole and began to step onto the second rung, but her foot could not find it. Angelica lowered herself down a little bit more, but the rung was not there. She turned to look down the hole, but it was just blackness. Her body was twisted around trying to hold onto the ground with her hands and keep her one foot on the first rung. It was not a strong grip at all, and she did not know how much longer she could hold it. When she tried to turn back towards the ladder, she slipped. Angelica's other foot slid off the rung and she fell into the hole. As her hands glided through the opening, they managed to grab hold of the single rung that was there. Angelica's body was jarred to stop sending a wave of fresh pain through her body, and she felt the strain filling her shoulders immediately. A tiny gasp escaped from her mouth, and her body began to relax. She knew, however, that there was more to do. Without the slate being put back in place, there was no purpose in hiding down here. Anyone would be able to easily spot the opening to the underground room.

Angelica pulled herself up on the single rung and wrapped one arm around it, moving the strain of her weight from her shoulder to her elbow. There was a moment of relief as a new part of her body received the pressure letting the already sore parts rest, but this feeling only lasted a few seconds, and Angelica began to moan in pain. Still, she was higher up than before, and she would be able to reach out for a hold of the slate. Angelica let go of the rung with one hand and began to reach up putting her weight entirely on the opposite elbow. She reached up out of the hole and began to grope for the slate. After only a second, her fingers found it resting just beside the hole. Angelica grabbed it and dragged it back over the opening. From her position, Angelica was not able to make it completely cover the opening into this room, but it was good enough. A single bar of dim moonlight cut its way into the darkness of the underground room. This small space left opened would not be noticed by a casual glance.

Now, Angelica was in nearly complete darkness hanging on to the only rung of a ladder. There was no point in trying to stay like that. She knew very well that it might be hours before someone looks in here for her. So, without any alternative, Angelica lowered herself as much as possible. Her hands were wrapped around the single rung, and she was almost able to feel the sacks of grain beneath her toes. The knuckles of her hands were screaming in agony, and soon they would give on their own if she did not let go. Angelica then exhaled fully to relax herself and released the rung.

The fall seemed to last about ten seconds even though Angelica was sure it could not have been more than one. She did not hit the soft grain sacks like she had hoped, but instead she landed on a rigid wooden structure beneath her. It was the ladder. Someone had cut it just below the first rung and left the rest to drop to the ground. Angelica was in pain from landing there, but she was also relieved. At least for the time being, she was safe. There were no guards chasing after her or mountains that needed to be scaled. She was able to lie in the darkness on the floor of this underground room. A single bar of dim light was her only link to the outside world, and for now, that seemed perfect.

Angelica remained there, lying with her back against the wooden ladder for nearly an hour. Despite her attempts, she was unable to fall asleep. The thought of anyone who moved the slate being able to see her was terrifying, but her body did not want to budge. Once the hour had passed, Angelica decided she had to move. After all of the effort she went through to get away from the guards, it would an unfortunate turn of events if she was to be captured by a searching guard now.

In the same way she had done the day she arrived, Angelica rolled to her side in the twilight and pulled one of the bags on grain on top of her. With her arms wrapped around this large and heavy sack, Angelica just lied on the cold ground trying to calm herself after what had happened. This time, it did not take long for her to fall deeply asleep on the dirt floor of this underground room.

CHAPTER TWENTY-FIVE

Lenore's Confession

The noise that eventually forced Angelica back to being fully awake was the sound of footsteps above her. They sounded the same as when the guards went looking for her on the day she arrived. These, however, were much fewer in number, possibly a single person. The foot falls walked towards the center of the cottage and hesitated for a moment before moving towards the table.

Within a minute, the slate was moved out of the way and light was fully beaming down into the room. Angelica pressed her face deeper into the sack of grain. The sack must have covered her entire body because the person that was looking down did not say a word. For a little while, at least. After a few seconds, he began to call out in a muffled voice, "Angelica, are you down there?" The young girl's initial reaction was to pull the sack closer to her body, but then she relaxed and waited for the voice again. "Angelica?"

It was Martin's voice. He was alive, and now he was looking for her. Probably, he came to the same solution that she had done. This was the only place she really knew of in the village to hide in. Angelica began to move out from under the sack, but then she froze. Lenore had turned on her, and there was a possibility that Martin may do the same. A horrible fear filled Angelica for a few seconds, but then she realized that it was not Lenore she was seeing, but it was Martin. Lenore had betrayed him just like she had everyone else. Also, Martin and rest of the group members were images on the wall and could travel between worlds. Lenore's image was not there. That may mean nothing, but it was a difference she felt was very significant. Angelica quickly called out, "I am here," just loud enough to be heard by Martin and no one else that may be listening.

After that, Angelica crawled out from under the sack of grain, and Martin looked at her as if disgusted. That chill of fear ran through her again at the sight of Martin's reaction. Most likely, she was bruised and cut and looking nothing like the queen that had been introduced to him two days ago. Still, he watched as she came under the opening and called up, "Someone cut the ladder." Martin nodded without saying a word. He simply walked away from the opening and returned a second later with a large rope.

It took five minutes for Angelica to make her way out of the room, but once this was done, she was filled with an unbelievable sense of relief. For nearly the entire night, Angelica had either been fighting for her life or wondering if anyone would find her down here. Now, all of that was over. Angelica wrapped her arms around Martin as if they had not seen each other in years. It was one of the greatest feelings Angelica had experienced since before her mother was killed.

Martin walked away from Angelica quickly as if he was offended by having been hugged by her. Without sparing a second, he walked over to the bed, and snatched a sheet of parchment from the top of the one blanket. While he did this, Angelica looked out the window, careful not to get too close. It seemed to be early morning. The sun was just coming up, and most likely people would begin making their way to the courtyard any time now.

"They're gone," Martin whimpered as he walked away from the bed with the paper in his hand. There was writing on one side of it, and Angelica could only assume that it was Lenore's hand that had scrawled those words. Martin lifted the paper before his eyes and began to read from it. "I'm sorry I had to do that, but it was something beyond my control. I have taken the children as well.

They are out of harm's way now, being protected by Protace's guards as am I. For now, I am going to tell them that you were killed in a cave-in along with Angelica so that they won't ask for you or try to look for you. I am sorry I had to form such an alliance with Protace, but there was no alternative. It began three years ago, actually."

Lenore was walking into the cottage with the sun beating down on her shoulders and her arms full of crops from the garden. She had been outside gathering up some vegetables for only a few moments, but as things worked out, that was long enough to bring trouble. Martin had been gone since the end of that day's public address trying to hunt down something so they could have meat with their dinner. Now, it seemed the least important of their problems.

The cottage was empty. Lenore had left both of children in the room playing on the floor when she walked outside, and now neither one of them was here anymore. Lying on the floor in a pile of the children's toys was a rolled up sheet of parchment. The scroll was tied with a strand of hair and sealed with a smudge of blood. In a moment of nauseating clarity, Lenore recognized that hair as belonging to her oldest son. It was the length of his hair and the same light brown color. She could only assume that the blood belonged to one of her children as well.

It was a moment she had feared from the time she had met Martin. Some days, the fear waned enough that she could let the children wander from her sight for a few moments at a time, but most days, it was a debilitating panic. Lenore's life was never one of luxury or even peace of mind, and now, it felt like she had been made to live in unending suffering.

Lenore wasted no time tearing open the letter to find a very simple note inside. Fighting back the acidic feeling of her stomach turning and her mouth filling with a hot, sick saliva, Lenore read the words, "If you do not wish any additional harm to befall your children, meet me in my palace immediately." No signature was provided, but none was needed. There were instructions about how to enter and navigate the caves in the mountain near the speaking platform. This would be the location of Protace's palace. A palace built within the mountain. A palace that he kept hidden from the people.

Without taking time to second-guess herself, Lenore followed these instructions and ran back to courtyard they had left less than an hour ago, passed the cage of snarling beasts, and through the spattering of blood from that day's sacrifice. She entered the nearly invisible cave opening and proceeded down elaborately decorated corridors towards the first room that she saw.

Inside that room, Protace and Soranace were both standing with Lenore's two children among them. Protace's sword was drawn, and the point of the blade was pressed against her one-year-old's chest. The baby was neither crying nor fighting. He just stayed perfectly still on the stone ground while their civilization's leader held him an inch from death. The older soon, now three years old, was being held still by Soranace. He did not seem to be in any danger, but Lenore knew that could change within a fraction of a second. She did notice, however, tears were flowing steadily from his eyes, and there was a tiny trail of dried blood crusting under his nose.

Lenore's attempts to remain calm failed in matter of seconds. Lenore began to shriek and cry. Protace took the sword off of the infant's chest and walked over to her. With an arm placed around her shoulders, Protace brought Lenore towards a bench in the corner of the room and had her sit down. Calmly as possible, she muttered for him to please not hurt her children. The words came out as blubbery whines and nothing more.

In a voice that was conversational and calm as ever, Protace responded, "I have no intention of harming you or your children any more than you force me to." He began to smile, showing his sickening white teeth, not the teeth of a monster, but certainly not the teeth of a peasant. "If you help me, that is. Do you intend to help me or to hurt me?" Lenore did not answer. Her sobs weakened in intensity like a river bed that had begun to dry out. She began to draw in slow breaths to force calmness upon her. Protace continued, "It has come to my attention that you and your husband have recently become involved with a group of individuals. A group whose sole purpose is my opposition, possibly even the removal of me from power. Do not deny this for I know it to be true. To deny it would just be insulting your intelligence and mine. To deny it would be endangering our budding friendship and thereby endangering the lives of your children." Protace waited a few more seconds, and during that time, Lenore's crying stopped entirely. The river had finally dried up. A new kind of fear had taken over. She was losing her ability to bargain for her children's lives. "I need for you to continued attending the meetings of this group. Keep track of what is done and who its members are. After the meetings, you are to find some way of contacting either Soranace or me. Is that understood?"

Lenore nodded quickly. Her eyes remained dancing between her two children. One lying soundlessly on the floor and the other looking like he wanted to start fighting against Soranace's clenched hands. While she listened to his additional instructions, she knew that a day would come where everyone that had ever trusted her would be betrayed, but that was the cost she will have to pay. That would be the cost for her and her children to remain alive in this civilization, and she felt that it was a reasonable fee.

Lenore nodded a feeble nod of the head, and immediately, Protace slapped her across the face. She fell to the stone ground with her cheek tingling. Her head hit the rocky surface, and the world began to cloud over. She looked over to the side of the room to see her children, but they were not there. Neither was Soranace. They must have been led away. The world was cloudy and gray at that moment, but Lenore could feel her clothes being torn from her. Or maybe she was removing them by herself. The black clouds filling her mind began to block out any rational thought. Protace was on top of her and soon he was inside of her. Through her spinning head, she was not quite sure if this was something she was dreaming or not, but despite her confusion, some part of her kept thinking, "I am becoming a queen." When he stopped, he walked out of the room without saying another word, and Lenore lay on the ground for some time. She was not sure how long, but once the room stopped moving and she felt like she was able to stand without the swimming feeling in her head overcoming her, she did so and left the room.

Her children were sitting in the corridor outside this room. Her older son was holding her baby girl in his arms while sitting against the cold stone. None of them spoke. Lenore simply took the infant in her arms and the older boy stood to follow her out of the cave, through the courtyard and back to the cottage, where they arrived only a few minutes before Martin arrived back from his hunt, empty-handed.

So for years, Lenore continued attending the daily meetings of the group who opposed Protace's rule, and after each of those meetings, she reported to Protace exactly what was said and who had said it. It came to be her usual routine, and she was almost terrified that it may accidentally slip out in normal conversation. On some of these meetings, Protace beat and raped her, leaving her come up with some excuse about why she was developing bruises, usually an accident in navigating the caves back from the meetings or slipping and falling at home. Still, she managed to stay absolutely silent to her husband and friends about what she was doing. The only one she spoke to about this arrangement was Protace himself.

After about two years of reporting information like this, Lenore came to realize something she had been trying to avoid or justify for what seemed like an eternity. She was falling in love with Protace. Not just his power or his title, but, in some twisted way, how he treated her. When she came to report this information, she almost felt like she was royalty for those few minutes every day. Protace would speak to her like an equal, and on occasion, he would actually bring her some tea or bread depending on when she arrived to make her report. It was a feeling of appreciation that she felt her other life, her honest life, was lacking. That feeling made it all the easier to continue betraying her husband and his group.

Once she admitted this sad truth to herself, Lenore took action on their next meeting. After making her report to Protace, he turned and nodded to the door for her to leave. She did not. Instead, she reached under his cape and her fingers found their way to his belt. She began to unfasten his pants when he pulled away. Protace turned to her with a look of fury in his eyes that she had never seen before on the face of any man. Before she could find the words to apologize, his hands were around her throat, and she could feel the blood building up in her face. Her nose began to bleed as his hands grew tighter around her. Lenore was certain that he was going to kill her that day, but somehow she did not care. She could not care. They were together. Protace spun her around, pushed her face into the stone wall, breaking her nose and her eye socket. He raped her more violently that day than he ever had before or since. With each thrust her head was forced into the stone wall, once hard enough to make her black out. When she came to, she was lying on the ground, and Protace was still thrusting himself inside her body.

Lenore did not make it back to the cottage that night. When Protace was finished with her, she was unable to stand from the palace floor. Blood was pooling around her, and her head was cloudier than the first time he raped her. She had no idea how long she was lying there or how many times he had raped her while she was drifting in an out of consciousness. Finally, Protace called for two of his guards to take her to the courtyard and leave her there. "Get that out of my palace," were the exact words he used as he wiped her blood off his body and dressed himself. They did just that, but once in the courtyard, they raped her as well. Lenore had the image of a master throwing table scraps to a dog in her mind while the moonlight shone down on her attack and eventually gave way to dawn light. Lenore just lied on the dirt and let them finish what they were going to do whether or not she fought back. One of them actually spat on her as they walked away, leaving her in the pale, cruel light of a cold morning.

Not long had passed before Martin found her. He had been frantically looking around for hours. They usually took different routes back from the meetings so as not to draw attention, so they arrived to the cottage at different times. When Lenore did not return within a few hours, Martin began to search and found her by morning. Lenore told him that she was attacked and raped. What she did not tell him was who or why. This stayed her secret until she wrote him a note a lifetime later after betraying him in yet another, more serious, way.

When the announcement of Angelica's arrival in this world was made, Lenore knew she had to tell Protace immediately. This was the sole reason he insisted on invading the caves on this particular evening after three years of being a passive observer and only monitoring their plans. The chance to kill Angelica was worth the exposure of what he had been scheming for so long. Protace left Lenore with the instructions of making certain that Angelica was in attendance at that meeting on that particular night. With that in mind, Lenore convinced, or nearly forced, Martin to bring Angelica with them. He had thought that it was a bad idea to expose her to anything of that sort until they knew her better, but eventually Lenore talked him into bringing the young queen along.

During the meeting, Lenore sat impatiently. After enough time had passed so that it would not seem suspicious, she left. First, she ran back to the cottage. A guard was waiting outside the door for her, and walked him inside. As she walked over to the bed, Lenore gestured the guard towards the slate beneath the table. He found the room and cut the ladder while Lenore was carefully waking the children. He thought that a fall like that would kill or severely incapacitate Angelica, so if she retreated here, she was as good as dead. With this done, Lenore began walking everyone towards the door, making certain to leave the note on the bed as soon as the children were out of it, and away from the cottage. The children were left with a guard in Protace's palace, and from there, a group of soldiers followed Lenore back to the caves.

"I believe you know what happened after that. I am sorry I had to do this to you, but as you can see, my choices were limited. However, I sincerely hope that you manage to escape the caves before you received any injuries. If I made any attempt to warn you, it would be at the cost of our children's lives. I hope you understand and forgive me for what I have done." Martin lowered the parchment from his face and looked at Angelica for a moment. In those brief moments, however, he hated the young girl. She was the reason all this had happened. That feeling lasted only for a few seconds, but it was enough to make Martin afraid of what he may do in the future. How he may take his revenge out on the young girl. He forced himself to remember that Angelica was no more at fault that he was. They were all innocent in this. Finally, Martin said, "We have to go. They'll probably be looking here shortly."

Angelica grabbed the parchment away from Martin as they walked out of the cottage. "Do you think you will still want to travel to the other world? We do need more people to help us, especially after this." Martin just nodded without even looking at Angelica. They continued to walk away from the cottage and back towards the mountains.

"Tomorrow night, I'll go." He continued to walk with his eyes straight ahead. The look on his face seemed to be one of shock and disbelief. It was a look that was frozen there. Most likely it was the same look Angelica had been wearing when she realized that her uncle was the assassin in her own world. It was a shock that needed to be overcome. Martin finally spoke again. His words were nearly whispers in the warming, morning air. "Until then, we have to find everyone that got through last night. I know Michael and his wife got out through one of the passages just before I did. The rest I cannot speak for."

Angelica debated for a few seconds about whether or not to speak. While considering this, she tucked the parchment with Lenore's note under the clothes she sewed the day before. It was not certain her words would be appreciated or even acknowledged if she spoke them now, but it was worth a try, "I saw Patrick was dead. So was William's wife. When I left, William and Bryan were the only two that were still in the caves fighting." Angelica continued walking beside Martin. He did not react to her words at all. It was almost as if she were speaking to herself rather than to him.

CHAPTER TWENTY-SIX

The Alternate Meeting Place

W hen Martin spoke again, he sounded more relieved. There was still a great deal of distance to go before he would sound anything like he did a day ago, but it was a slight improvement. And a well appreciated one, at that. "There's another place. A different cave in the mountains that the soldiers should not be able to penetrate. The gear they carry would make it impossible. We all agreed to meet there if something like this happened, but I don't know if anyone will be there. We never expected one of us to turn on the group."

They continued to walk until they reached yet another small opening in the mountainside. It was similar to the one they had traveled yesterday although in a different part of the mountain. A narrow, dark, endless passage stretched out before them. Angelica followed behind Martin as she did the day before. They began to crawl, single file, through the cramped cave towards the group's alternate meeting place. Martin did not speak for another ten minutes, then he simply whispered, "We have to cross a stream up ahead. You'll have to go underwater, about ten feet down, and there will be another opening to a different cave. Go into that cave and crawl quickly down it. Usually the cave is filled with water for about five feet and then begins to dry from drainage through the rocks. Do you understand?" Angelica called out an affirmative response, and she watched Martin spill off the passage they were on. Up ahead, she heard the faint sound of a splash.

Angelica crawled up the rest of the way until she could see the stream rolling by beneath her. She took a deep breath much like she did before going through the passage between worlds. With her arms spreading out in front of her, Angelica pulled herself deeper into the water. She was barely able to see Martin's kicking just a few feet ahead, but it was enough to follow. As she went deeper, she could feel a huge hand squeezing into a fist around her body. It was the pressure. This force was almost luring her to complacency where she would happily give up. This feeling kept getting stronger and harder to resist as she went deeper. The water felt slimy and somehow thicker than normal water. Angelica kept going despite the feeling that her lungs wanted to rupture to end the ache that existed within them. Soon, she saw Martin's feet disappear into an opening, and she followed him right in.

Angelica slapped her hands onto the edge of the cave opening and pulled herself in. Martin was right; the cave appeared to be entirely flooded. For an instant, Angelica felt the unbelievable urge to inhale, as if the cavern itself was coaxing her to take a breath, but had to stifle that feeling. Her chest ached, but she continued to pull herself forward as quickly as she could. This cavern bent its way upward, and Angelica followed it as the water slowly thinned out. Eventually, she burst through the surface of the water into a different cave. She took a deep breath as soon as she was out of the water, and her lungs screamed in pain from stretching so widely again.

Martin was ahead of her waiting for her to catch her breath. "Are you okay?" She did not respond, but he could see that was going to be fine in another minute two. A little out of breath was all. "Protace's soldiers wouldn't ever be able to travel through that water like we did. There's no real waterway around village for them to practice swimming, and their gear will weight them down too much to effectively maneuver. Also, they would not appreciate this, up ahead." Martin moved forward a little bit more, and Angelica crawled to meet him. There was a narrow crack in the floor of this cavern. Angelica peered into it and gasped at the sight that was waiting there. About twenty feet below them, there was a nest of the beasts. The five reptilian monsters, some juvenile and some adult judging from their size, that crawled around beneath them did not seem to notice Angelica staring down at them. "The beasts don't know how to climb a rock wall. They're smart, but I guess they never needed to learn how to do that. I can guarantee you, if there was a reason to climb a rock wall, they would figure it out right away. The soldiers would probably make a big ordeal trying to attack and capture them," Martin stopped for a second to take another breath. The swim may have worn him out a bit as well. "But if you just ignore them, they'll leave you alone."

After a quick nod, the two of them started on their way again. It really did not matter to Angelica how much Martin insisted that the beasts would not harm her. She saw what they did to that girl yesterday, and did not want that to happen to her. These acted so much differently than the ones in cage though. They were calm where the caged ones always seemed hostile and violent. Angelica could assume it was her uncle's influence on them. Abducting them by force, dragging them from their home, and keeping them imprisoned to eat only what was thrown at them.

As they crawled, Martin assured her that they were almost to the meeting place. They crawled for a few more feet, and then he said, "The path ends here. There is another right beneath it. Don't worry about the beasts, it's nowhere near them. They're much lower than this path. This one is right beneath. You'll have to hold on and lower yourself down." She watched as Martin did what he just instructed. His hands firmly gripped the edge of the floor he was standing on, and then he lowered himself through a tight opening and soon disappeared. A moment later, his two hands slid from the ledge they were grasping and disappeared with the rest of him.

Angelica went after him and tried the same thing. The passageway between the two layered floors was very tight. If she was any larger, Angelica feared she may have to scrape her skin raw doing this. Still, she managed to get down to this other path, and she quickly followed Martin only another ten feet to an opening towards the right, where Angelica noticed a familiar glow. They walked in, and Angelica saw part of the group she had been introduced to during the night pacing the floor and waiting for them. There were no elaborate light tricks as in their usual meeting place. Just finding this location seemed enough of a test to prove one belonged to the group. Angelica could also understand why this was not their primary meeting place. It took so much time and effort to get here that it was impractical for daily use, however, it could have saved several of their lives. It was a tough call, and Angelica was thankful that it was not hers to make.

As they entered, Bryan walked over to greet them. He began talking immediately with sadness that was cloaked in anger. "Patrick is dead; William and his wife are both dead." He looked towards the ground for a moment, and then quickly added, "It's good to see the two of you got out alive." His eyes returned to meet Martin's and there was a brief hug between them. Even though she was too new to the group to receive such a greeting, she felt welcomed just the same.

The members of their group that had survived the attack were already here. It was time for damage control, now. They had to decide what should be done to eliminate the ruling powers. It was obvious the coexisting was impossible, and now Protace and Soranace had Lenore on their side. They would never be able to leave the caves in daylight again, since their identities were all known. They probably were not even safe in this alternate meeting place. Legions of soldiers may be waiting for them around every turn or behind every tree. The only way they would ever be safe again, as well as secure a safe future for their children, was to assassinate both Protace and Soranace. Martin was reluctant to add that his wife, Lenore, must be killed as well. She admitted, in her letter, to being in love with Protace, so she would most likely fight to the death blindly to keep his cause alive. The three of them had to be removed in order for them truly succeed in their mission.

Angelica was the one to once again bring up the idea of people from her world coming through to help. Martin's stone image on the wall was holding a parchment scroll in one hand, and she could only guess that that was what it meant. He was meant to be the one to make that trip. It would nearly double their current membership, and that would provide a great deal of help for them. Even if the people she brought over were inactive in the actual fighting, just their number would enough to show the rulers of this world that they had significant opposition.

So it was decided that Martin would go across to the other world that night and bring back as many people as he could. Angelica held up the letter than Lenore had written. It was nearly soaked through and the writing had bled off to the point where one side only contained a dark smudge rather than words. This did not matter, though. Parchment was scarce in that village and this provided a surface for her to write the names Martin needed. Now, she left it near the torch to dry.

They spent nearly the rest of the day in that cave. No one really spoke to one another, and it was even more seldom for people to look at each other. There was a cloth bag containing bread and some vegetables in the cave. One of the group members must have brought it here earlier. It was hardly soggy by this point. Also, several jugs of water were here, and once again, Angelica thought about that stream, and wondered if it was water from that stream that they had all just swam through. Her life of royalty did not leave her prepared for such things. Still, it was enough for them survive on for the day.

After a while that seemed like an eternity, one of the group members said, "I could feel it getting colder. The sun must be setting around now." With that, all of the members rose to their feet and began to walk back the way back the way they had come. Bryan carried a torch ahead of the group and walked carefully and quietly. There was a bit of uneasiness among all of them when passing over the crack with the beasts nesting below, but they all did it without hesitation.

While they walked, Angelica began to fold the sheet of parchment. I seemed like the best way for sheet to stay as dry as possible when crossing the stream would be right against her skin. She had her simple cloth gown made from the grain sack, and her royal gown beneath. Placing the paper against her skin would allow it to get as little water on it as possible.

Soon, they reached the water in the cave, and one by one, they dove in. Angelica felt that it was much harder to swim up the ten feet of water and jump to the ledge above to arrive to the meeting place than it was doing those reverse directions to leave. Her skin did not feel too wet after climbing out of the water, so she felt the paper must be mostly dry as well. There was no time to waste retrieving it from under the two layers of gowns, though. Now, in the dark, the torch had extinguished in the water, they began to crawl the rest of the way until they finally climbed out of the mountain. Angelica looked around quickly for any opposition, and then simply began to follow everyone else. They were all headed in one direction, towards the courtyard and the portal beyond it.

CHAPTER TWENTY-SEVEN

Martin's Voyage to Protecia

By the time they reached the portal opening, the parchment Angelica had carried was nearly dry again. Bryan re-ignited the torch from one that was burning at the edge of the village. These lights were kept going all night, as in the Protecian Kingdom, to allow people to see their way in the darkness. In this world, they also served the purpose of eliminating one excuse as to why people cannot get the courtyard on time for a public address. It was helpful to them, however, so they were able to light the path they walked.

Angelica knelt beside the wall with the sculptures of all the people who were able to travel from her world to this one. None of them was carrying a quill or had ink though. Such luxuries were not available to these people. Reluctantly, Angelica realized that there was only one thing they could do. At her request, Martin pricked Angelica's finger with the tip of his sword. Blood began to seep out forming a small bead on her fingertip, and for one horrible moment, Angelica stared at her blood. Her royal blood that had created so many hardships. Pushing this thought away, Angelica used a nearby twig on the ground to write the list with her own blood.

The writing was sloppy under these conditions, but Angelica managed to make the list of names so Beatrice could read it on the other side. On the top of list was David's name. The guard that had helped her so often before she came over here ended up being able to travel across the worlds as well. There were four other names beneath his. One guard, and three farmers. All of them, however, were able-bodied and would be willing to help her.

Angelica extended the list to Martin, but she took it back quickly. Her minor injury was hardly bleeding anymore, but she managed to write at the bottom of the list, "Chenrile is the jester. Any blood relation to Alexander?" With this added, Angelica sighed deeply, and handed the parchment to Martin, who quickly handed to Bryan to hold while he prepared.

As Martin walked towards the portal, Bryan held the torch over the paper so the blood would dry as much as possible before Martin had to take it across. While Martin was standing apprehensively by the stone pool with its brass leaves surrounding the rim, Angelica told him everything that would happen as he travelled the portal. With apprehension filling him, Martin found that he was only able to nod.

After a minute of drying the parchment, Bryan handed it to Martin. There was nothing left to do now. Martin had to dive and go across to the other world. He tucked the paper into the waist string of his pants. Then, without any further hesitation, Martin climbed onto the edge of the pool. He took a deep breath, closed his eyes, and slid into the water.

Beatrice and Cassandra were waiting in the caves. While Cassandra sat calmly on the stone ground as if she were lasing at a picnic, Beatrice paced the floor nervously. As always, two guards were on duty watching the portal, and they just stood by without saying a word. Aside from the few lanterns that been brought into the caves, these caverns were entirely dark.

Since Angelica went through the portal to that other world, Beatrice spent nearly every waking hour in that shrine-like room. Cassandra came and left, but she tried to stay as much as she could.

The guards as well as Beatrice were not certain if Cassandra's actions were out of loyalty to their queen or to Alexander, but they tolerated her being there just the same.

Finally, the cave was filled with a blinding white light. One of the statues on the wall had begun to glow, but the sudden intensity of this light made it impossible to see which one. The guards immediately drew their swords and stepped forward. Making sure they were between the wall with its glowing image and the two servants, they waited with their swords pointed towards what appeared to be the center of the brightness.

Soon, the glowing subsided and eventually disappeared. Martin was standing against the wall just where his image has been. The parchment was no longer folded in his waist string, but it was now rolled in his hand and held close to his chest. Panicked, he looked around for a moment and then froze when he say the guards staring at him.

"I do not mean any of you harm," he mumbled as firmly as he could. His eyes then drifted from the guards to Beatrice, who was now standing rigidly behind them. "I have a list for you. It's from Angelica. These are people that are able to travel through the portal to my world." For an instant, the look on Martin's face seemed to be one of immense pride. He had just gone through the portal as he had wished to do for years. It was difficult to say if his jittery behavior was from fear over where he had appeared or giddiness at having travelled the portal. Then, reality came back to him. "Angelica is fine. She is with a group of good people. People that can be trusted."

Finally, Beatrice walked past the guards and towards Martin. She reached out and took the rolled up parchment from him. "What is your name?" Beatrice hardly seemed interested in the list she was now holding. Martin's name seemed to be all that was important to her now.

Martin introduced himself, and Beatrice took his hand. She walked him out of the caves with Cassandra following close behind them. As they walked, the two servants introduced themselves to Martin, but there was a great sense of urgency. They needed to find the people Angelica had requested and get them to go to the other world to help her. Martin began to tell them about the group of people opposing Protace and both Beatrice and Cassandra stopped walking in their tracks.

It was the same shock that Angelica had hearing that name, so Martin began to speak immediately to explain what he had said. "I believe you know him as Alexander. Angelica was quite shocked to hear that he referred to himself by that name, as well. She said that was the name of your civilization's founder, yes?" Beatrice nodded and continued to walk. This seemed to place a new urgency on everything that was going on, but still, there was another time to worry about that.

Quite naturally, Beatrice and Cassandra walked Martin into the palace so they could go through the list. As soon as they entered, Cassandra broke away from them and said, "I'll go get David." When she walked away, Beatrice continued on her way to the palace dining room, which had become a sort of unofficial meeting room since Angelica assumed the throne, but she noticed that Martin was not following too closely behind her. His eyes were continuously wandering up the walls and to the elaborate murals and ornamentation surrounding him. Beatrice slowed down to let him look at these things. She suspected that he had lived a very simple life and had never seen such things before.

It did take them nearly twenty minutes to make the trip from the palace's main entrance to the dining room, and when they did arrive, Cassandra and David were already there waiting for them. Introductions were made between all of them while Martin slowly lowered himself into one of the chairs. His eyes were still wandering from the walls to the chandelier suspended from the ceiling. He was absolutely overwhelmed.

While he was taking in all of this, Beatrice handed the parchment to David. He unrolled it quickly and read through it immediately. "I'm on this list. It looks like I'll be able to go help Queen Angelica." He stood from the table and tore the parchment in two. The top and larger piece David took and held in his hand, and he gave the smaller piece, the one with only the question about Chenrile and Alexander to Beatrice. As he walked towards the door, he muttered, "I'll start looking for these people. See what you can find in the library to answer her question."

Beatrice looked at the piece of parchment David had left behind. With shocked eyes, she read the question over and over again. Those few words dredged up horrible memories that were long forgotten but were right under the surface all along. Without saying a word, Beatrice passed the paper to Cassandra who reacted in a similar way. Finally, Beatrice mumbled to Martin, "Come with us. There's a lot of work for us to do."

The three of them walked from the dining room to the palace library. As they walked, Cassandra and Martin were speaking of the queen's welfare in the other world. Beatrice was unable to hear a word that was said. Her mind was focused on something said to her months ago. One the day of her assassination, Wilhelmina told Beatrice that she was afraid to see Chenrile that day. Somehow the late queen managed to figure out that Chenrile was part of the plot against her, but she never suspected that Alexander would be the one to actually strike. Now, with this new question in mind, it seemed as though they were forced to find the same truths that Wilhelmina had.

As they entered the library, Beatrice thought, "Wilhelmina found whatever she found using only her hunches, intuition, and this library. These shelves hold everything they would need to possibly connect Chenrile to the royal family." As they walked to a table by the large window, the sun began to peek over the horizon. A pale light filled the sky and the library alike. Finally, the small group sat around one of the tables amidst books that reached towards the sky.

Beatrice began speaking to Martin immediately. "In your world, Soranace is the second in command. Understandably, if something were to happen to Protace, Soranace will begin to rule." Martin just nodded, so Beatrice continued. "In our world, he goes by the name Chenrile, and used to be our royal physician. To our knowledge, he had no royal blood in him, meaning that he would never hold a ruling position in this kingdom." Once again, Martin nodded. He was beginning to piece together what Beatrice was trying to explain, but he kept silent nonetheless. At least on an unofficial level, Beatrice seemed in charge of this small band on this world, and Martin did not want to seem as though he was offending her. "I don't think Alexander, or Protace as you call him, would want to end the bloodline we've kept for hundreds of years. It was something he was very adamant about, actually. This is why we're here. We have to verify whether or not Chenrile does have royal blood in him. Knowing exactly what his plans are may help us to fight him. There's a possibility that we may be able to predict his moves which will give us the upper hand in fighting him."

With that, Beatrice stopped talking. There was a soft tap of approaching footsteps, and when everyone looked to see where they were coming from, they saw the old librarian approaching. "I thought I heard someone in here. Isn't this a bit early to be looking through these old books?" The old man rubbed his eyes as he approached, but he came towards them just the same. As always, there was a broad smile on his wrinkled face and a slight skip in his walk, despite how tired he looked. "What can I help you find today?"

Beatrice simply asked for the books about the royal genealogy. It was difficult to know where to begin looking though. There were literally hundreds of branches of Protace's descendants, all of whom had died off except for Alexander and Angelica. Still, there had to be some sort of inconsistency that would make way for the possibility of illegitimate birth. The royal family went through great pains to keep records of such affairs, but there could be a royal heir that was birthed secretly, maybe to begin a coup or maybe just the result of indiscretion. That would impossible to trace. Since Beatrice is almost certain that Wilhelmina had found the connection they were looking for, they had a fighting chance.

The librarian returned after ten minutes with a stack of large texts, some dating back three hundred years and some very recent. He brought one additional text, which did not include any royalty, but the birth records of the palace servants and help. Anyone who was brought to the palace in servitude had to verify a family history of one generation back. This policy, begun by the elders centuries ago, was in reaction to King Tobias marrying his servant. From that time on, it seemed a good idea to record some abbreviated family history of the palace servants. Beatrice immediately took this text and turned to the entries for the royal physicians. There were several past physicians, but at the bottom of the list was Chenrile. Accompanying his name was the year he was born and the same information for both parents. It also contained the year the parents died, both when Chenrile would have been five years old. Beatrice passed this book to Cassandra and she passed over to Martin. When they all had a chance to look at these dates, they began to look through the other books to see if any of these dates matched.

Before opening the first book, Martin reiterated what he had just read, as if to ask for clarification, "Chenrile's parent's both died when he was five?" Martin had a saddened look on his face as his thoughts went back to his children, now being raised by Protace and being told that he was dead. "What happened?"

Cassandra, being the most prominent follower of gossip at the table, was happy to answer. "No one knows for sure. Chenrile was found wandering around this kingdom when he was five. He couldn't say what happened or much of anything else. Some of the guards along with Queen Patricia, herself brought him to Nezzrin Kingdom to see if anyone recognized him. They more or less said that they didn't want him back. Not only did his parents die, but their entire home just disappeared. They said it was like magic. One minute, they could hear everyone in that house arguing like they did most every night, and by morning, the house was gone, Chenrile was gone, and his parents were gone. Chenrile was the only one that ever resurfaced. And he reappeared here, in Protecia, about a six day walk from where went missing with no supplies, water, food, nothing. The people thought that somehow Chenrile had something to do with it, but probably that was just because he was the only one that lived. They said his whole life he did weird things. A lot of people said he was evil. Queen Patricia wanted to hear no part of that, so we took him in here. Nothing weird about him ever turned up. Until this."

They turned back to the books, Beatrice and Cassandra acting as though nothing had happened, but Martin was horror-struck. He was not used to the way that rumors escalate to the ludicrous so quickly when people are not fighting for their lives on a daily basis. Beatrice finally added to Cassandra's story, "It's a rumor. Consider it mumblings in the hallways. No one really puts that much weight in it. People exaggerate things all the time." Beatrice gave Cassandra a harsh look when she said this. "I am sure a few stories have already started to make their way around the palace concerning you." The two women grinned at this. Martin only looked back down at the massive text before him.

With the books in front of them, there was a lot of work to be completed. Since the years they had to compare to were fairly recent, they began with the more recent texts. It took hours to go through the endless pages of family trees and heirs to the throne. Their eyes were burning, and their head's aches, but each of them felt they must continue. By finding the information they needed, they may very easily unlock the key to defeating Chenrile, and that would help them destroy Alexander as well. This work in the dusty sun-bathed library may very well help towards saving the kingdom.

After about two and a half hours, Beatrice was halfway through the next to most recent text. There was a branch of the royal family tree for Victor and his family. These branches eventually all ended with the word, "Exiled," and a year. Victor was the only heir to the throne that was overlooked because of his extreme young age, under a year old, at the time he should have been made king. Beatrice began to weep as she recalled the details of the story she told Angelica so recently. As Victor got older, he tried to get his rightful title back, and Philip, who was ruling at that time, ordered that Victor and all of his descendants be exiled from Protecia.

Beatrice slid the heavy text towards the middle of the table, and said, "I think I found something." While the other two began to lean over the family tree the book was opened to, Beatrice grabbed the text with Chenrile's information. "Look at the tree for Victor's son, Carlton." They all looked, but saw nothing of consequence. The book showered that Carlton was married and had no children at the time of their exile. Beatrice immediately elaborated. "Carlton didn't have any children, but his wife was pregnant when they were exiled. It doesn't say anything about the child because it hadn't been born when they were banished from the kingdom." Beatrice stopped talking and waited for a reaction from the other two. When no one spoke, Beatrice finally continued with frustration in her voice. "Look at the years." Beatrice took a deep breath. "Chenrile's father was born the same year Carlton's son would have been born."

The three of them began to flip through pages to see if another inconsistency could be found, but there were none. They did not expect to find any either. It was too strange a coincidence for it to be just by chance. Now, they knew Chenrile's story. He should have been in line to the throne before Frederick. That could be why he came here when he was a boy, and why he befriended Alexander. Somehow he understood that was where he belonged. It could very easily be the reason for him being in a position to regain the throne of the kingdom. With Alexander's victory over both worlds, Chenrile would find himself in the role he was supposed to have as a birthright.

With a deep sigh, Beatrice stood from her chair. She looked around quickly and saw the librarian was nowhere in sight. Most likely, he was off having his breakfast since it was still quite early in the morning. Rather than just leaving the books on the table for him when he returned, Beatrice said, "Let's get these together and bring them back to the shelves." The two others nodded, and they began to stack the texts of royal genealogy. One thing that was always true in their palace was that they servants united together to help one another. There was no sense in leaving the books for the librarian to take back when they were capable of such a chore.

Beatrice picked up a stack of books, as did the two other people. They all began to walk towards the shelves when Beatrice's foot hit a nearby chair. She let out a small yelp of pain, and she lifted her foot as reflex. The top book slid from the stack she was holding. It fell from her arms and landed on its spine. As the book fell to one side, the cover opened, and one of the first pages was revealed. It took all of Beatrice's strength to keep from dropping the other books when she saw the image on that page.

Looking back at them was a small sketch on the first page of the dropped book. It was Alexander's face staring back towards them. The way he looked just before he escaped into the other world. There was a sketch of him right there, on the front page of the genealogy book, where the founders of the civilization were supposed to be. Alexander's image was on this page, and that thought nearly repulsed everyone. However, the writing beneath it made that feeling much worse. "Protace, age 30," was written in a fancy script beneath that illustration. Protace's name and Alexander's face. It seemed to confirm what Martin said was happening in his world.

Beatrice was frozen in fear as she stared down at that book. Both Martin and Cassandra lowered the books they were carrying and ran behind Beatrice. She was beginning to fall under the weight of the other texts in her arms. As her stability became uncertain, Martin placed his hands on her shoulders, and Cassandra began to lift the books from her. Soon, Beatrice was not carrying anything, and Martin was helping her to a nearby chair.

For a moment, they were worried that Beatrice may die right before their eyes. She was gasping, but her breaths sounded strained and almost inhuman. Her entire body was shaking as if she was having a seizure. A film of sweat of covering her forehead, and a single drop began its way down the side of her nose, across her plump cheek, and towards her chin. It looked like she was holding onto the last threads of life.

As Beatrice was beginning to breathe more slowly and calming again, the librarian raced in. "Are you okay?" He stumbled forward to see if she was recovering. For the first time, there was no smile stretched across the librarian's lips. "I thought I heard someone fall down. Are you hurt?" The librarian began to look at Beatrice's face, and after one glance, it did appear that she had fallen. It looked as if she had taken quite a bad fall, actually.

Cassandra quickly began to explain what had happened, but before she got more than two words out, Beatrice overrode her. "That picture," she mumbled while extending one shaky and trembling finger. "Is there an original somewhere?" Beatrice was forcing the air in and out of her lungs with so much energy the librarian thought she was going to pass out soon. Still she managed to hold onto consciousness. "I need to see it." Her words were quiet and strained, but still very audible.

Slowly, as if considering such a strange request, the librarian walked over to the book on the floor. He knelt to pick it up, and when he saw the sketching, he actually laughed a little. "Certainly looks a bit like Alexander, doesn't it?" With a smirk on his face, the librarian placed the book on the table. "I believe we have an original someone in here. I'll have to look. No one's ever asked for it before."

The fact this was an atypical request was evident by the amount of time it took for the librarian to come back. Nearly an hour had passed before he walked out from a back room nearly covered in dust with a scroll in his hands. "I believe this is what you're looking for." Beatrice had not moved an inch that entire time. Martin and Cassandra had been replacing the genealogy books on the shelves, but now everyone was back at the table in the middle of the room.

They all looked on anxiously as the librarian placed the scroll in the middle of the table and unrolled it up and downward. This representation was in color, and it was much more detailed than the sketch in that book. Cassandra was now the one to look in disbelief since she had not gotten a look at the picture before. No one spoke for some time. This color representation pictured Protace, younger than any other representation, prior to his construction of the bridge across the Particion River. His bright green eyes were peering down to his right, but they still seemed as hypnotic as if he was there looking at the four of them. Clenched against his chest was the staff. It was intact, and the eyes of the creature on its head were painted to be almost glowing in some way.

After staring at that face and the rest of the picture, they all looked at the sheet of parchment attached to the bottom. It looked much more recent, and the writing seemed to be the neat and tight penmanship of a past librarian. "This rare representation of Protace shows him at an age of thirty years, long before he began construction on the bridge that famed him into being a deity. The artist is unknown, but the representation was originally found near the shores of the Particion River. In Protace's hand is his staff, which had since become a symbol of his supreme power."

For a while longer, no one was able to speak. Soon, Beatrice said, "Alexander must have seen this. It's all the same bloodline. It is possible for them to look similar, but this is too much to be a coincidence. They're identical." After taking a few very deep breaths, Beatrice began to speak again. "He must have seen this, and now he thinks that he's Protace. He is trying to unite two different people by creating a bridge between worlds. But he is not Protace's second coming. He can't be." With these words, Beatrice broke into tears, and no one tried to calm her down. None of the legends ever predicted Protace's return to the kingdom he had founded, but some people believed that when times were at their hardest, their founder may appear to help them. This frightening resemblance may mean nothing, but some may consider it to mean just that.

Beatrice feared there would be no way to unite people against Alexander if they saw this. The painting was too clear a resemblance of Alexander's roots to be beneficial to any resistance against him. If the people were to see such an illustration, they would see Alexander as being nearly a deity already. Through her tears, Beatrice muttered, "I have to take this out of here. I don't want anyone to look at it."

It took a moment for the librarian to reluctantly agree. He seemed upset to let an important piece of the kingdom's history go into the hands of a simple servant, but he understood her rationale. Alexander was a killer, and there was nothing to stop him from killing again. If the only way to keep him from committing another assassination would be to hide a remnant of this past, then not doing so would make all of them as guilty as he.

Beatrice left the library with the rolled up scroll in her hands. With that filling her mind, she did not even see the group of people that David had assembled to go back to the other world. Each of them was eager and willing to help the queen no matter where it would lead them. However, with Beatrice in the state she was in, Cassandra thanked David for his work and suggested that they wait until that evening to speak to Beatrice again.

CHAPTER TWENTY-EIGHT

The Angelic Army

Just as the sun was beginning to set, Beatrice left her quarters. The scroll was no longer in her hands, nor did she wish it to be anywhere near her. With the sunset filling the palace with a soft golden glow, Beatrice began to nearly drag herself towards the dining room. It was dinnertime, so Cassandra was probably bringing Martin in there to eat.

When Beatrice arrived, she saw that everyone she had walked by in the hallway that day was in the dining room. Guards and farmers were eating with the royal servants as well as their guest from the other world. Beatrice sat at one of the empty chairs. She felt unable to put food in her plate, so she just sat and listened to the conversation in the room. Eventually, she turned to Martin and whispered, "I want you to send Angelica back here as soon as you get there. What I saw in the library today." A visible wave of chills washed over her when this thought reentered her mind. "I need to tell her about it, and I need to do it in person."

Martin quickly agreed. "You know that she's safe with us, don't you?" Without giving Beatrice a chance to reply, Martin continued, "Our group will protect her with all of our lives. She is the most important piece of our cause. A born leader." This time Beatrice managed a nod, but she kept silent. Deep down, beyond all the senseless fear and worry, she did know how these people would protect their queen. There were still doubts, however. They may be willing to protect her with all their ability and even their lives, but that may not be enough. Not with the power that Alexander had begun to possess. "We'll take good care of her," Martin added, and Beatrice thanked him for doing so.

While everyone else ate, Beatrice sat and looked silently at the people around her. These were to be the ones who would most possibly save not only their world but another as well. It was beyond their station in life, simple people who bowed down to the royalty around them, to be the ones bringing in a new age of peace. There was also fear. Fear that they may fail in this great mission and that would almost certainly mean doom for not only Angelica but all of Protecia as well. Beatrice tried to hold her faith in Soranace and the spell he cast three hundred years ago. These people were selected as the group that would bring the worlds together. They may be exactly the people needed for the task.

It was dark by the time the group of five people as well as Martin, Beatrice, Cassandra, and two other guards all marched into the caves carrying lanterns with them. They all marched as if they were an army ready to fight for their people's freedom and ready to die for their cause if it came to that. Through the tunnels and caverns, Beatrice led as she had done so many times in the past few days. Those who followed behind her were anxious and excited about what may happen to them on the other side. Ideas of grand battles and saving the world filled each of their minds along with the endless ache of fear that would never to leave them alone.

When they reached the wall with all of the sculptures on it and the small stone pool, Martin stepped forward. Since he was the only one of the group that had gone through before, it was decided that he would go first. With much less fear than the time he had previously gone through the portal, he climbed onto the edge of the pool and took a deep breath. Everyone else watched as he stepped into the water and vanished from sight.

About a minute later, the rumbling began. There was that familiar feeling that the cave was going to tear itself apart, but just like all the other times, the rock walls held true. Not even a pebble tumbled from the ceiling above. Soon, however, the sculpted wall began to crumble apart in one section. Accompanied by the sound of dragging stones, an image of Martin pushed its way out into the opening. He was still standing there with the parchment clenched to his chest even though he no longer had it with him. There he was. Just a stone sculpture once more.

One at a time, everyone who was meant to travel across the portal did so. They climbed onto the pool edge and stepped in quite simply, just as Martin had. The rumbling became almost constant as five more sculptures pushed their way to the surface of the wall. Their images were all content and happy with wide smiles and content eyes. It was almost as if they were enjoying a picnic in the sunshine. All but the image of Alexander who was lying on his back in a field of flames trying to pull himself out. Beatrice thought it quite fitting.

When the rumbling finally did stop and the cave began to still itself, Beatrice and Cassandra were able to take a good look at the wall as it was now. The sight was beautiful. There was a figure in the middle that was missing, but every other space was taken. It looked like the image from the mural of the palace ceiling where Protace brought happiness and peace to the barbarian hordes untied under his rule. This reminded Beatrice of everything they had learned about Protace. With all the knowledge they had just recently acquired about their founder, she had to wonder about whom he really was versus whom history had made him.

The number of people appearing to simply fall out of the carved mountain wall was astounding to Angelica. She had arrived with the remaining group members just as the darkness was setting in. Her clothes were still wet from the swim through the water to get from the new hiding place, but she barely noticed. It was such a relief to see people she knew well. People she could trust and people she knew would help her.

For a while, they just introduced each other under the moonlight. This did not take very long, however. There were no long speeches like the one Martin gave before introducing Angelica to his group. At this point, they all were very grateful to have someone, anyone else willing to help them. The introductions were completed quickly, and it was eventually Martin that brought about their end. There were more important things to discuss.

The smile on Angelica's face faded to nothing within seconds when Martin began to speak to her. "Beatrice found some information, and she wants you to go back so she could tell you herself." Angelica looked calmly ahead as if she had been given the hardest blow of her life and did not want anyone else to know what she was feeling. Any sign of frailty would make it even more difficult for these people to follow her rule. "It's a matter of some importance, and she feels only she could tell it to you."

Angelica walked over to the pool and looked into it again. She saw her reflection wavering in the rainbow streaked, not quite watery, liquid, and she knew she had to go back. On the wall, there was only her mother's image now. The former queen was alone with that terrified look on her face holding out one a hand to protect her daughter that was no longer there. With some fear and relief mixing as they coursed through her, Angelica began to climb up the wall of the pool. She quickly turned to everyone there and quietly whispered, "I'll be back tomorrow. There may be some guards trying to kill me as soon as I come through. Please do what you can to help me get back." There were some mumbled of agreement. Angelica removed the simple cloth she had been wearing over her bright red and purple gown of the queen and handed it to Martin. With that in his hand, Angelica dove into the pool and easily slipped below the surface to swim towards the bright pulsing light ahead of her.

Only about fifteen minutes after the rumbling stopped in the caves, a bright light began to glow from the wall. Beatrice was able to see it was coming from Angelica's sculpture before it got too strong and blocked out everything. As if they had not seen each other in years, Beatrice ran towards the light and waited for Angelica to come through. Finally, she did, and the light faded to nothing.

Angelica was kneeling in the position her sculpture had been in. Her eyes were starting into that of the stone beast, and her dagger was in her hand. In revulsion, Angelica fell to the ground and let out a loud gasp. Before she could stop herself, she had backed away from the carving of the beast with a scowl twisted across her face. When she stopped the awkward, backwards crawling, she yelled out, "That was where I was? With that thing?" She was on the ground still taking another slow stride backwards away from that sculpture. She kept backing up until she was leaning against Beatrice's legs.

After only these few days, Beatrice was overjoyed to see Angelica. She was barely able to find the words to show how much she missed the young girl, but soon she remembered the reason for calling her back. She looked at the queen, and realized how much she had matured in such a short time. She may have left this world with the title, but she truly did return as the queen. "There's something I have to show you." Beatrice felt the words die in the air, and Angelica looked up at her as if she knew it was all bad news.

As they walked towards the palace, neither of them said a word. Beatrice was trying to avoid telling Angelica whatever had to be said for as long as she could. Still, while they walked, Angelica looked around. It seemed like such a long time since she had been there, even though it had only been a few days. She noticed something else as well. The black pouch that contained Angelica's sling shot and the three sharp metal discs to use with it was now attached to Beatrice's belt. Most likely she did not need that item for her own protection, so she was holding it like that as a reminder of Angelica. Just a little token of her queen while she was away. More likely than not, she would gladly return them as soon as the young girl returned to the kingdom permanently.

A few minutes later, they were both in Beatrice's small quarters looking at the unrolled scroll of Protace at a younger age. Angelica did not become faint as Beatrice had done. By now, she had seen far too much for that sort of reaction. The queen simply looked at the painting for a few moments and then began to cry. As she moaned in both pain and misery, she backed away from the bed where the painting lay and walked towards the window. The tears rolled down her cheeks, glistening in the soft moonlight, as she looked out into the darkness. "I cannot believe it. Do you have any idea what this means?"

Beatrice just wrapped an arm around Angelica to calm her. For the first time, she truly noticed all of the injuries Angelica had sustained in those few days. Despite all that, the queen was eager to continue fighting. Beatrice, with sorrow in her voice, whispered, "All the royalty is from the same family. It's just a coincidence from that relation. There is nothing more to it than that. They look the same, but it means nothing else." Beatrice was looking into Angelica's eyes, and she could see the young girl wanting to believe this. It was not happening, though. No matter how much she wanted to believe what Beatrice was saying, these were too many coincidences coming together at once.

"I just came from another world where someone named Protace made barbarians into a civilized people under his rule. Now we find out that he is identical to the Protace that founded our civilization the same way." Angelica looked down to the bed they were sitting on and began to cry harder than before. "What if that portal is not to another world, but to another time? Alexander may be the founder of our civilization. He went back in time to set the foundations of Protecia knowing that in three hundred he would be born and have to go do it all again." Angelica was frozen in fear. She stared out the window into the blackness of the sky and just watched. The stars twinkled above her, and for the first time in months, she nearly felt her mother's warm eyes looking down upon her.

Beatrice did not know how to respond. There had to be some flaw to Angelica's theory, if nothing more, just because Alexander was no one who would try to establish a civilization. "Alexander isn't Protace. It's just not the case." Beatrice was about to tell Angelica of her reasoning when something else occurred to her. "In our histories, Soranace is the son of Protace. Chenrile isn't Alexander's son. The ages don't work out right. That can't be what is happening."

"That does not matter," Angelica whispered. "I saw Alexander become a monster, and the texts speak about Protace's staff turning people into monsters." Beatrice only nodded, and Angelica continued. "The book said the staff does not work for anyone. Only Protace. Now, it is working for Alexander. Alexander is part of Protace's bloodline, and so am I. Does that mean that I am a monster as well?"

Beatrice looked at those desperately concerned eyes and wondered how to answer that. "Protace and Alexander may look the same, and they may have other similar characteristics we can't see. They are not the same person, no matter how you think about it." That answered the first question. Now for the more serious of the two. "Most likely it's those invisible characteristics that allow the staff to work for Alexander. It may turn him into a monster, but deep down, he always was a monster. You're not a monster, Angelica. You're the farthest thing from that."

This seemed to offer the hope that Angelica so desperately needed. She turned and looked at Beatrice again. "Did you find anything about Chenrile?" It did not seem as important as it did a moment ago, but this was still a single fact that may help her in the future. "Does he have any relation to the royal family?"

Before answering, Beatrice took a deep sigh. This news was not anywhere near as traumatic as what she had just shone Angelica. It was actually something she had expected to find out. "Chenrile is a distant cousin of Alexander." Angelica did not react at all. She just stood in the torchlight and stared blankly at Beatrice. The tears were drying on her face, and her eyes seemed to be calming quite a bit even though there was reddening around them. "Do you remember the story I told you about how Prince Victor was banished in favor of Philip?" Angelica nodded. It was this story that finally forced her to deliver her first public address. "Victor's son, Carlton, was married to a pregnant wife when they were all banished from the kingdom. That child was Chenrile's father." Beatrice paused for a moment and then continued. "He should have been in line to the throne before you, your mother, or even your father. Now, he is most likely trying to get the title that was robbed from him." Beatrice paused again before finishing. "It could make him a very difficult enemy to conquer."

Angelica nodded. For almost two hours, she just sat on the bed in Beatrice's quarters going over everything in her mind. There was so much more that had to be considered now. Chenrile had more motives than his friendship with Alexander. There was the fact that they were related, and that he was robbed of the throne. This made a great difference, but it still did not explain why they took the names of Protecia's first two kings.

Finally, Angelica mumbled, "Alexander must have seen that picture. When he was going through Soranace's old texts. Looking for any information about that portal he could find. Alexander must have stumbled upon that painting, and who knows what his reaction was." Angelica looked up at Beatrice with pleading eyes. Now, she needed more help and support than ever before. "He probably thinks he is some kind of re-born Protace. After finding out that he could travel between worlds, he was most likely certain of the fact. There is no way of knowing how long ago Chenrile had told Alexander about his royal blood, but at some time, he did. After that, Chenrile's image on the wall made Alexander think of him as a second in command. They must have assumed those names to further their importance. Both worlds would look up to them with that sort of identity."

Beatrice looked at Angelica cautiously for a few seconds. "And his uniting these two worlds would be like Protace's building the bridge over the Particion River." Beatrice smiled as if they did more than make a guess about Alexander's motives. She seemed to feel as if they had already defeated him.

It was Angelica's words that brought them back to reality. "You said the books spoke of Protace's staff as coming alive and being powerful when it was held by Protace himself." Angelica was nearly trembling with fear as she spoke. Behind her, the sun was coming up with a pale white glow that was nearly blinding if one was to look directly at it. "When Alexander holds the staff, he turns into a monster of some sort. I think he takes on some traits of the beast on the staff's head." She took a deep breath and added, "He becomes a monster."

When Angelica spoke, Beatrice began to think about exactly what was being said. The young queen had already explained to the servant about Alexander's reaction to the staff, but this time, she heard something else as well. Alexander did not just look like a monster when he held the staff, he actually turned into one. Deep down, he was a monster all along. It was that creature that the other world looked up to as their leader. To them, Protace was a demon of some sort, and Beatrice began to wonder if the Protace they had known from history was a monster himself as well.

"Protace, wake up!" Alexander, or Protace in that world, rolled over in his bed. Lenore was lying next to him, but she did not react at all to the noise. When Protace opened his eyes, he saw Soranace standing in the arched doorway of his bedroom. Large wooden posts stretched up from each of the bed's corners making it as majestic as his bed back in Protecia. Light had begun to shine through the high window on the wall past the bed, and it made Soranace sweat under its heat. The look in Protace's eyes showed he did not want to be disturbed. "There's something I have to show you. It's very important." Protace's look remained unchanged, so Soranace added, "This may be the break we are looking for."

Within ten minutes, Protace was out of bed, dressed, and following Soranace to the wall and the portal. He walked slowly as if his mind was still partially asleep, but when he got closer to the wall, he became fully awake instantly. The sight was an amazing one. The wall was entirely smooth except for Wilhelmina and Angelica. Those two remained frozen in an eternal moment of fear. To Protace, it was truly a sight of beauty.

"They are all over her now," Soranace marveled. "One of the guards noticed this early in the morning, and he told me right away. Everyone able to travel across the portal is here, except for those two." He extended his finger towards the representations on the wall. "Do you think that means she is trying to unite the worlds now? Trying to complete her side of the wall?" Even though the multi-colored mask draped across his nose, Soranace's smile was evident.

Protace did not smile, however. His happiness was contained, but he was glad for a different reason than his distant cousin. "She would not try to unite these worlds until she was certain that I had been removed from power permanently. What she is doing is building an army of people that would help her on this world. Then, they would try to kill me, and only after succeeding, they would begin to attempt forming a permanent passageway between the worlds." Soranace began to frown, but Protace still seemed optimistic. "The situation is not without hope, though. If she is over there and plans to assassinate me over here, she is going to have to pass through that portal again. The young queen will be completely vulnerable to attack when she comes through. Between the moment of disorientation and the fact that her mother is holding her to the wall, we would be able to kill her at the instant she comes back here."

Soranace nodded. After a moment, he added, "That group she is forming will try to stop us. If they do hold her up as their leader, then they would die to save her life."

"Then they shall," Protace whispered. With a swirl of his cape, he began to walk away from the portal and back towards his palace that was carved deep in the mountain. "Have all but four of the guards standing by for when she comes back. I do not want us to be defeated by a group of farmers with a couple of mediocre guards, understand?" Protace did not wait for a response. He simply walked away towards his palace.

In Protecia, the rest of the day was spent without such thoughts being spoken aloud again. All ideas of Alexander and Chenrile, Protace and Soranace, were dismissed. Angelica spent the day walking through her kingdom as she did the last time before leaving for the other world. The thought went through her mind that she should give a public address but decided against it. What would she possibly tell them? That two people they had come to trust were actually assassins? That she was trying to kill them with a group of people in another world she had just discovered? They would not believe her. Even more than that, they would not consider her to be fit as a queen after saying something like that. She always had to impress them as being mature beyond her years, and telling such a story, no matter how true it was, would accomplish quite the opposite.

If she were to maintain a strong relationship with her people, Angelica would have to stay quiet about her actions until this was entirely resolved. After then, she would decide what needed to be told and what she would keep between her closest companions and advisors. There was still more information that she intended to tell no one else. Facts such as these would be kept locked up inside her, and then she would be certain that no one else would think her unsuited to her role. These thoughts included the feelings of rage she felt towards Alexander, and the fact that wanted nothing more than to bury her dagger into his chest. What would the people think of her if she were say such a thing to them?

After deciding against giving the public address, Angelica spent the day walking, or more accurately, strolling through the kingdom. It was something she had taken for granted as the princess. In the other world, her being seen outdoors in the middle of the day would almost certainly mean her death. She would have never thought how good it would feel to just walk in the sun for a while. Everything was in full bloom now that the drought was over. The sun was high above them, and the sky was a brightest of blue. It was the most beautiful day Angelica could ever remember, but of course, it had to come to an end.

It did not seem like very long at all, but the sun eventually drifted behind the mountains. The light it gave off grew orange and eventually red. When the sky began to grow dark, Angelica knew she would have to go back soon. Judging from the depressed look on Beatrice's face, her servant knew this as well. Angelica ate dinner before leaving, and the chef was more than eager to make the best dish he knew how. Roasted lamb was served and eaten, and soon, Angelica knew it was time for her to leave for the other world again.

There was something different about this trip, however. She was scared. Angelica was finding reasons to postpone her voyage for a few minutes here and there. Petty excuses that had no real foundation, and, of course, no opposition from Beatrice or Cassandra. Angelica was worried about going through the portal this time, and she was not quite sure as to why. She passed through without difficulty before, but this time just seemed to be different for so many reasons.

Aside from Beatrice and Cassandra, no one accompanied Angelica through the caves towards the portal. The three of them walked in silence through the dimly lit corridors illuminated by Beatrice's lantern. It seemed as if deep down, they all knew of the permanence of this trip. Last time, it was mostly just to investigate, but this time, the voyage was to act. They were going to destroy Alexander once and for all, and that was a very risky task to undertake. The tension held their tongues like clamps making it impossible for any of them to speak.

When they finally reached the pool and the wall of relief sculptures, a moment of sadness gripped them all. A single tear squeezed its way from the corner of Beatrice's right eye as Angelica climbed onto the edge of the small pool. She looked over at the wall and saw it in its almost completed beauty. There was an empty space where she was supposed to be and another in the middle, most likely where Wilhelmina was meant to stand. Angelica breathed deeply, turned back to Beatrice, and said, "Good bye." With that, she stepped into the pool and slid easily beneath the surface of the water.

CHAPTER TWENTY-NINE

The Return

As she had done the other times, Angelica began to swim towards the bright pulsing light ahead of her. She could not help thinking how much it looked like a star, and it made her feel as if she was flying towards the sky. The light filled the water for an instant, and then dimmed to single pinpoint. After a moment like this, it burst into complete, nearly blinding brilliance. Angelica continued to swim towards that light and as she got closer, the flashes came faster and faster like the heartbeat of someone that was excited. Or scared. It almost was having the stellar equivalent of a spasm, and to Angelica, this was frightening. Soon, she was able to reach the light, and, as before, she was soon in a world of complete whiteness. This lasted for only a few seconds before she appeared in the other world with Wilhelmina's stone hand holding her against the wall.

A smile formed on Angelica's face when she arrived back here, but it faded almost immediately. There was no one around. The entire group that was supposed to be there to help her was missing. Angelica began to slide out from beneath the stone hand when she saw the soldiers running towards her from all around. They were a good distance away, probably to avoid detection, but they were approaching quickly. Running in the center of the line were Alexander and Chenrile, Protace and Soranace.

Angelica froze with fear immediately. The sight of all these soldiers racing towards her was too much to handle. The stone fingers of her mother were nothing compared to firm hand of terror holding her paralyzed against the wall. With that amount of fear, she did not even have the energy to scream for help or run for safety. Angelica stood and stared blankly as the swarm of soldiers got closer. Then, she felt the jerk to her side and went falling out from behind her mother's stone hand and towards the ground.

Within a second, Angelica was being escorted away from the portal at a run. She looked to her side and saw David holding her arm. The sound of the soldiers was getting quieter as they darted behind the high bushes and into another cave. This was a wide cave opening which soon led them out into the courtyard. It was a shortcut most likely charted by the group of rebels and unknown to the soldiers. This helped them get the lead they needed to keep from being caught. From there, the two of them ran until they reached the village. Angelica took one quick look behind them and saw only a single person still keeping pursuit. All of the guards had been lost, but Soranace was still running after them. It seemed as though he had a speed and agility that was somehow beyond a normal man's.

Angelica seemed oblivious to what was going on. Her entire body was at the whim of David, and she just was along for the ride. Before she had even gotten a chance to fully gain her bearings after materializing in this world, the chase was on, and she could barely keep track of anything that was happening around her.

David managed to gasp, "Hold on," as he made a sharp turn around the corner of one of the cottages in the village. Then, he immediately dove to the ground with Angelica beside him. As the young girl caught her breath, she looked up and saw all the other group members waiting here. The faint glow from a distant torch was enough to make out their faces but little more.

A second later, Soranace came sprinting around the corner, and immediately he was attacked. From the ground, Angelica was now able to see that each of the group was holding either small tree branch or a large rock. They began to swing these at Soranace. There was no time to draw a sword or even retreat at this point. As if it was saving his life, he began to repel the attacks with nothing more than his arms and bare hands. This did little but delay each blow by a fraction of a second. Still, he seemed to be using this slight but constant gain of time to his advantage. He was backing away from the attack.

Angelica looked on as the man who had entertained her by turning torches to doves and juggling spheres to roses was under attack. The group of men seemed eager to kill him because of everything Angelica had told them and all that they had witnessed themselves. Soranace continued batting away the branches and stones having little success, but then something changed in his eyes. It was a look of deceit and surprise in the making.

One of the villagers lifted a tree branch into the air and began to lower it towards Soranace's head. With a gleam in his eyes, the man in the colorful cloak threw an arm towards the branch. It appeared to be another attempt to defend himself, but Angelica knew differently. She could see in those eyes that there was something much worse underway.

When Soranace made contact with the branch, there was a loud cracking noise. It did not should like the breaking of a bone as much as the splintering of wood. For a moment, everyone was silent, but then the scream of an animal rose up in the village. The villager that had swung the branch at Soranace was now holding a live rat rather than a tree limb. The branch had exploded in a burst of splinters revealing a large rat underneath. It screamed and squirmed in the villager's hand until in horror, it was dropped to the ground.

As the rodent landed on ground and scurried away, more people swung their makeshift weapons towards Soranace. Even though they were bewildered, they had no idea what else to do. A stone, almost too large to be held in a single hand, slashed down through the sky. At the slight touch of Soranace's fingers, the stone crumbled to a cloud of dust, and a dove took to flight from where it was. The more the villagers fought, the more creatures stormed away from the sight of the battle. Birds, snakes, rats, and any other order of creature were birthed from the weapons that Soranace deflected. The villagers were quickly running out of their makeshift armaments, and Soranace was not tiring in the least. He simply stood his ground performing his feats just as he had done before each of Wilhelmina's addresses.

Finally, one of the guards from Protecia navigated a log through the trap of Soranace's hands and managed to hit him. A single swing of the branch hit Soranace in the face just beside his left eye. Only the edge of the branch struck him, and it left a large scrape going down his face. Also, it tore the mask away from him. Now, there was nothing to hide Chenrile's face, and those group members who were from the Protecian Kingdom began to gasp. With his identity revealed, Soranace stopped fighting. It appeared that all of his strength, as well as his sorcery, vanished with his anonymity. He just turned and ran.

There was a moment of anxiety that seemed to stretch out for an eternity. Everyone in the mob looked back and forth at one another, and finally all eyes focused on Angelica. Martin handed her the simple cloth gown, and she slipped into it quickly. Instantly, she was no longer a queen but a young girl trying to survive. With a deep sigh, Angelica followed the rest of the group members back into their alternate meeting place. Along the way, they made a few stops to gather water and food for their stay in the caves.

After twenty minutes of travelling and navigating obstacles, they were all sitting in a circle inside the caves. A torch was soon lit by knocking two stones together, and then they had nothing to do but wait and plan. It was Martin who finally spoke. "There's only so long before we are all captured and killed one by one or all at once. Protace must have every guard in his power searching for us, and we can't stay hidden in this cave forever. We have to begin action now."

There was a mumble of agreement before Angelica began to speak. "If we do this, we are going to have to do it all the way.

Protace and Soranace have to be killed at the same time or as close to it as possible." Reluctantly, Angelica turned her eyes to Martin and added, "If Lenore is as close to them as it seems, we will have to at least find some way of restraining her." It did not seem proper to demand that Martin kill his own wife. She was not an essential part of Protace's organization, so her death may not even be necessary.

Despite this, Martin just nodded and said, "We'll have to kill her as well." He closed his eyes and tilted his head to the ground. "She betrayed us once, and nothing is going to stop her from doing it again. If this is going to succeed, all of them need to be killed." As he finished speaking, Martin looked up at the others and saw solemn faces staring back. It had been said, now the particulars had to be planned out.

Angelica spoke first, falling into the role of the group's leader almost automatically. She was a natural queen despite all that had happened to her. "I want to be the one to kill Alexander. Protace, I mean." Almost immediately, a look of concern and fear filled the faces of everyone in the caves. Angelica knew where this was going, and she felt she must start convincing them of her case before anyone even had a chance to speak against her. "He's hurt me more than anyone else here. I have every right to be the one that kills him. After he's made me live in fear for months, I want to be the one to put an end to that fear by putting an end to him."

The faces of worried rejection did not fade in the slightest. David quickly said, "You're the queen of Protecia. Because of that fact alone, we can't risk your life. Alexander isn't going to go without a fight, and even if we do manage to get an element of surprise, it's not going to be easy. If anything is to happen to you, Alexander would instantly become the king of Protecia by birthright. Then, he would have every right to go across the portal and begin ruling our kingdom as well as this world. It has to be someone else."

David was about to volunteer to be the one end Alexander's reign, but Martin spoke first. "I want to be the one." With a deep sigh, he added, "After the whole involvement of Lenore in this,

I don't think he would suspect me to make a move like that. He probably thinks that I would no longer be part of the group anymore. Surprise is the only element we have to our advantage, and I think we should use it as best as we possibly could." There were nods all around without any hesitation.

One of the farmers from Protecia was the one to burst out speaking. "You say that surprise is our only advantage. What about numbers? We'll most likely have the backing of the other people. What about determination and will power?" There were looks of agreement from some, but the others just looked solemn and concerned. For the most part, the serious faces were worn by those who lived in this world rather than Protecia. This led the farmer to ask, "What exactly are we up against?"

It was Bryan who answered. His words came slowly and were very quiet. He was trying to remember a nightmare from long ago, but this nightmare was real life. "When Protace first came to our world and began to establish a rule, he was accepted quickly and almost universally. After all, he showed us the light of civilization, so to speak. But that only lasted so long. It took less than a month before people began to speak against him. A little bit longer before they began to act against him."

Protace looked out among the people that had gathered to listen to him speak. He was standing just before them now. A crew of workers was chiseling away at the mountainside to make his speaking platform and the immense cage to house the beasts, so now he simply stood in the courtyard with the people he was addressing around him. As if he was an equal to them. It was a setup they had accepted, but things were about to change.

With Soranace and his staff only a few feet away, Protace spoke to the people. Their concentration was split; barely on Protace and his words. Protace only spoke for a few minutes before he suspected that something was going to happen. The people were going to do something to stop him from ruling. There was something in their eyes that he recognized all too well. They would take his gift of civilization and turn it against him.

To end any idea the people may have of rioting, Protace motioned to Soranace for the staff. Slowly, the man dressed in the explosion of colors began to make his way towards their leader carrying the staff in his hand. The people knew that once Protace changed into the monster, there would be little chance of stopping him, so they sprung their plan into action.

First, Soranace had to be stopped. The first few of the group of perhaps fifty that occupied the courtyard grabbed some stones from the ground. They were quickly hurled forward, and Soranace soon fell under a shower of rock. Beside him, the staff fell to the ground. The eyes of the reptile that was wrapped around its head stared idly and powerlessly up at the rioting crowd.

With Soranace lying on the ground in a dazed state, the rioters turned their violent eyes towards Protace. His reaction was nothing they expected. In their minds, the sight of such a riot would send Protace running in fear or perhaps even surrendering right then. He did no such thing, though. His eyes met theirs directly and without wavering in the slightest. For a moment, it seemed as though the rioters may back down, but then their cautious stares became ones of persistence and assertiveness. They were not going to give up, and this was most likely the worst move they could have made.

Hoping that their numbers would be enough, the mob of fifty people began to charge towards their self-proclaimed leader. Brandishing nothing more than rocks and large sticks, or some with only their fists, the group ran forward much as their counterparts would do years later. Each of their faces wore a stone-cold stare that would have been enough to kill an average man in itself. But Protace was by no means average.

Protace began to spin around where he stood. In a single revolution, Protace reached towards the ground to grab his staff from where it had fallen and leapt into the air. He was lost in the swirl of his black cape, and when it stilled around him, the people saw that he had become the monster. With staff in hand, he was levitating in the air about ten feet high.

The people still threw rocks at him knowing that their efforts were wasted. Still, there was no turning back at this point. They had to try to complete what they had started. Quite simply, Protace's reaction to this was to rise higher into the air. Without effort, he began to drift skyward right along the side of the mountain. He ascended straight up into the air past where the workers were constructing his platform, almost to the peak of the mountain. The people in the courtyard below had difficulty seeing him that far into the sky. He was just a black smear against the sun-bathed afternoon.

From that height, Protace looked down at the people that had tried to kill him. They were scared. He could not see their faces, but he knew from their movements. The miniscule black dots that were his would-be assassins were beginning to back away from the mountain. They were contemplating whether or not running would save them at this point. Perhaps if they escaped into the forests, they would be safe. Protace was nearly laughing at this idea. They were so very wrong.

Protace looked at the scurrying dots beneath him and extended the staff at full arm's length. The orb at the head of the staff began to glow as if it was an ember from someone's fireplace. Tiny arms of blue flame reached from the orb, and from below, Protace could already hear their screams.

The rioters and would-be assassins were running frantically throughout the courtyard with their flesh ablaze. Their screams were of absolute and total agony. As the fire began to eat away at them, each of their bodies began to drop to the ground. While the swirling masses of fire diminished, the number of skeletal remains on the ground increased. It only took a minute for all the conspirators to be reduced to nothing more than bones and ash.

Protace eventually descended from the sky and landed next to Soranace. Lying on the ground in a daze of confusion, the man did not realize what had just happened. From the swelling red lump above his right eye, it appeared that one of the rocks thrown at him hit him in the head and caused some kind of disorientation. Protace helped his second in command to his feet, and they walked away together towards the village. They had to tell everyone that the assassination attempted had failed, and as a result, a new set of rules would begin to be enforced.

"He displayed the skeletons in the courtyard for over two months to remind everyone that they lived not only for him but because of him. This method worked all too well. Out of fear, the majority of the people in his kingdom will follow his rule blindly no matter where it may lead. Over the years, the fear has become mistaken for loyalty or respect, or even reverence, but just beneath the surface, terror is the only thing binding his people together." Bryan sat back and took a deep breath after telling his tale to the group. He began to fill a cup with water while everyone else just stared in amazement at him.

So that Bryan could rest for a minute, Martin finished the story. "One of the changes he implemented was mandatory attendance of his public addresses. This was adhered to for a while without enforcement, and when the people began to falter, the daily executions began." Martin chuckled to himself, and added, "That is what we were supposed to be bowing down to. This is the very reason we have to kill him. Some of us just refuse to kneel before a monster anymore."

There was a silence so profound that anyone would have begged for it to stop. Without any conversation or simple noise even, these people were trapped into thinking about the story they had just heard. It was something no one wanted to do, but they were too shocked and scared to find the words that would fill the void.

After a few moments, Bryan shattered the deafening silence. "The best time to do it would be during a public address, the sooner the better." No one spoke for a few seconds. The idea did not seem to make any sense for a moment, but then Bryan began to clarify. "His palace is carved into the mountain. It is heavily guarded and only accessible through a series of cave passages. There's no way we'd ever be able to get to him in there. The only time we could be certain of both Protace and Soranace being out of that heavy protection is during his address. We have to act on this soon, before he thinks of a way to get around it.

"I doubt he would try anything like he did the last time. If he were to kill everyone in the courtyard like the last attempt on his life, he would be left without a following. A king without a court has no power, and he would never give that up. He brought that on himself by requiring that everyone be at the public addresses."

One of the other group members, Michael, now spoke. "One of us could get to the address after it's already started. Soranace would have to escort that person to the platform, and as he's going through the crowd, we could ambush him. Have the person he's taking fight back when they get close enough to us, and that'll slow him down long enough for us to do something." Michael's eyes darted back and forth to the other members of the group. "This'll cause enough confusion so that one of us could get up onto the platform and kill Protace."

"If any of the guards see us bringing weapons into the courtyard, they'd arrest us right away. We'd be imprisoned or fed to the beasts ourselves before the address even begins," Patrick's wife whispered. After a second, she added, "We might be able to get Martin to hide in a crater on the side of the mountain with a sword, but if anyone else is armed, they would be noticed. We'd have to be in the middle of the courtyard, and if we were carrying weapons, we're as good as doomed."

Finally, one of the farmers from Protecia spoke softly. "We don't have to use real weapons." There was a brief silence, but the man soon filled it. "Beforehand, we could bring rocks and branches into the courtyard. Just leave them on the ground until we're ready to use them. Like we did today against Chenrile, and like that other group did years back." After a few seconds, the farmer corrected himself, "Soranace, not Chenrile." He sighed deeply and then continued, "They wouldn't be noticed as out of the ordinary on the ground, and they could do quite a bit of damage if used properly."

What seemed to be the only remaining question was who was going to be the one to lure Soranace into this trap. As before, Angelica was willing and eager to take on the job. After speaking, she began to argue her point immediately, as she did before, and this time, no one could find any fault in her logic. "If I stand in the crowd with the rest of you, there is a good chance I will get noticed there before too long. Just think, everyone in this village has been told that I was the Evil One for years. I will probably be noticed and pointed out before any of you are." A smile developed across Angelica's face, and she added, "Anyway, if someone else happens to show up at the same time as I do, Soranace would not be able to resist choosing me to throw to the beasts, right?"

This time, everyone was in agreement. The plan seemed set. They had quite a bit of time before that afternoon's address, so they would be able to prepare and try for the assassination that very day. With the anxiety in the room growing, the group began to discuss the plan again to make sure everyone knew exactly what they were going to do. Then, they all started on their way towards the outside.

When the run began to rise, Soranace walked towards the platform. The courtyard was already getting crowded by that time, but he did not take notice of anyone. His unmasked face was looking down at the ground in shame. This shame was not because of the scrape going along the side of his cheek or the several bruises he had received. It was from the simple fact that now he was unmasked, and those who had just arrived from Protecia already knew his identity.

Quietly, Soranace got to the platform and climbed the steps to the side of them. Protace was already standing on the platform nervously pacing back and forth. He gave one look at Soranace's unmasked face and then turned away in disgust. He looked at the wall where his staff was mounted and just waited. Soranace was nearly shaking as he approached, ready to give an excuse for what had happened. However, he did not get a chance to speak.

Without turning around, Protace began to talk in a droning, almost lecturing voice. "If there was ever a reason that I do need to access Protecia again, you would have been the one to go. The people there did not know that you were, in fact, my accomplice. According to the situation you set up, they were all led to believe you died in a carriage accident. Now, if any of those people Angelica brought over here go back to Protecia, everyone there will know your identity. You would be arrested or killed immediately. It would appear that a great part of your function as a member of my rule had now dissipated."

Protace placed a palm over the handle of his sword and removed it from his belt. Since his back was still facing Soranace, no one saw this action. After about a second of contemplating, Protace spun around and hacked down at Soranace's ankle with the sword. With the cape engulfing his movement, no one even saw the sword blade move. The smooth surface of the swords width, rather than the edge, swatted at Soranace's leg, and he fell to the stone platform almost immediately.

As if savoring every second of it, Protace slowly began to walk towards Soranace. His sword was still pointed towards the fallen man, but Protace made no attempts to strike again. When he was standing over Soranace's frantically gasping body, he stopped walking and pressed the point of the sword over his accomplice's recently exposed neck.

Trying to remain as still as he possibly could, Soranace was nearly in tremors on the ground. The cold stone beneath him offered no comfort from the sweat that was dripping from him. He was only able to listen and wait as Protace dragged the tip of the sword over the features of his neck and face. "You have failed me many times, and I have forgiven you many times. Because we are friends. Because we are royalty. Because you and I will bring about great things in this land and back home. My patience for your incompetence is now running out. If you fail in your duties one more time," Protace whispered as the sword point ran underneath Soranace's right eye. It pulled the eyelid away from that eye slightly as it drifted down his cheek. "If you fail me one more time, you will not have to worry about the army Angelica is massing in this land. They will not get their chance to kill you." The sword drifted along Soranace's jawbone, and its tip nestled its way behind his ear lobe. "Do you understand me?" Protace whispered as he pulled the sword back.

Soranace let out a brief gasp of pain and his hand slapped against the side of his face. Blood seeped between those fingers as Soranace rolled onto his side and then sat up. Lying on the ground where he had just been was a small puddle of blood. In the center of this puddle, was the tiny lump of flesh that used to be his earlobe. Soranace held his hand against his bleeding ear as best as he could while the stinging pain radiated from that point to the rest of his head. A feeling of heat washed over him as he was trying to understand what had just happened. Protace walked back towards the wall of the platform, replacing his sword as he moved. While holding a hand over the wound that was bleeding much slower now, Soranace stood. He felt he had been let off easily, considering some of the things he had seen Alexander do the guards he disliked in Protecia. Those injuries were much more extensive that the injury to his ear. Much more blood was spilt at Protace's hands for much lesser offenses.

With a sigh, Soranace turned and walked towards the ladder to go down from the platform. He stepped down quickly and turned into the crowd. In a second, he had disappeared into the people that were already waiting for the address to begin. Soranace had his mind so preoccupied with the events of that morning and the relief of finally telling Protace the bad news that he did not even realize he had just walked past Martin.

As still as a statue, Martin was waiting inside one of the deeper depressions in the side of the mountain. There was a shadow cast over him, but it was not much cover at all. Anyone who was slightly inquisitive or observant would have been able to find him without a very extensive search. During the whole time Soranace was walking by, Martin did not breathe once, and he could have sworn that his heart had also stopped beating for those few seconds.

CHAPTER THIRTY

The Attack

The hours between that time and the beginning of the address stretched out like an endless chasm for not only Martin but the ten people who had been entering the courtyard one at a time the entire morning. With their faces low, they each wandered towards the middle of the courtyard where two small tree branches and eight stones slightly larger than a clenched fist had been placed during the very early morning hours. At around this time, Angelica would be hiding in a nearby cave waiting for the moment to come when she should go to the courtyard herself.

The sun shone brightly in the blue sky. It was the sort of day people painted so that it would last in their memories forever. Even the cold, gray stone of the mountains looked perfectly breathtaking in the gleaming light of the sun. Not a cloud occupied the sky, yet everyone could feel a storm in the making. The air had that strange feeling of heaviness and had an almost metallic taste to it. Despite the beauty of the day, there was something in the air that was sinister.

There was a loud cheer as Protace began his public address. This time, he was running it differently, however. Soranace was not appearing from the crowd dragging that day's sacrifice with him, but they were on the platform together. Soranace's mask looked hastily mended, but was still covering the lower half of his face.

After only a moment of Protace's speaking, Soranace removed the staff from its mount on the wall and handed it to Protace. Protace went into a fit of convulsions as he normally did upon first holding the staff, and while he was doing this, Soranace walked away almost as if in disinterest and disappeared into the crowd. Most likely, he was about to grab someone from the back of the crowd to be sacrificed now. There was thunderous applause as Protace began his transformation on the platform and the mountainside beamed with a bright glow. This change in the usual address did not affect how they would attack Soranace, but it drastically changed how Martin was to kill Protace. Suddenly, a difficult job seemed as though it would become nearly impossible.

As Soranace was walking through the crowd, the members of the group tried to divert their faces from him. Bryan then nudged Michael with his shoulder and nodded towards the ledges up on the mountain beside them. These were also filled with people watching the address, as they always were, but right in front of this ledge was Lenore. She was staring fixedly at Protace as he began to still and reveal the monster the staff brought to the surface. From that ledge, she was just as high as he, but still seemed to blend into the crowd like anyone else would.

When Protace began to roar, the screaming in the crowd got even louder. Everyone cheered on their ruler as he transformed into a monster before them as he did every other day since his rule began. Through all the cheering, Soranace saw a young child wandering towards the courtyard. She was covered in a plain cloth smock that hid her entire identity, but as Soranace neared, she tilted her head upward and looked directly at him. Their eyes met, and a quake of shivers filled both their bodies immediately. The instant Soranace saw Angelica's face, he ran towards her. Angelica took a few frantic steps away from him to give the appearance of trying to escape, but before two seconds had passed, Soranace wrapped one strong hand around Angelica's arm and began to escort her through the middle of the crowd towards the platform.

As always, the crowd parted to allow Soranace to get through. The event that such a densely packed group could act that way was almost miraculous. There were the usual sighs of relief from people seeing that no one they knew or cared for was being sacrificed that day. Soranace was walking very slowly, most likely in a combination of pride for have captured Angelica and simply giving the crowd an opportunity to move. He was already imaging how Protace would thank him and take back what he had said earlier about his being a failure. However, in his strutting towards the platform, his grip on Angelica's arm loosened ever so slightly.

With a quick jerk, Angelica pulled free of Soranace and began to run towards the group of people ahead of her. She could hear the gasps from the crowd as well as the sound of Soranace's footsteps bounding against the ground behind her. Without letting her eyes deviate from the cluster of friendly faces ahead, Angelica ran.

Soon, her group was all around her. Angelica pulled off the simple cloth smock as she spun around letting the cloth she just shed fly around her like a cape. Beneath, the queen's gown, purple and red and encrusted with red stones and gold, glistened in the sunlight to the gasps of the people filling the courtyard. Angelica threw the dress she had fashioned from a grain sack towards Soranace. It struck him in the face, and that slowed him enough for everyone in her group, her Angelic Army, to grab the items they had brought here during the night and early in the morning. In an instant, rocks and branches were in hand, and before Soranace even had a chance to remove the cloth from his face, a tree branch whistled through the air and crushed his nose. As the cloth fell, Soranace was under a storm of blows from rocks and branches. It was a position he had, regrettably, been in many times before, but this time, it was relentless.

The guards from the perimeter of the courtyard saw what was happening and began to fight their way through the crowd to get to the location of this squirmish. Martin watched from the shadows as the guards ran by him, and then he silently walked out from the depression in the mountain wall. The ladder to the platform was right before him, and he quickly and quietly began to climb up. Each step seemed more labored than the last, but he knew he had to continue. Still, what he saw at the top was something he had not expected to see and nearly shocked him into falling back down those steps.

Protace was not standing in the middle of the platform as if he was in the middle of his speech. His pure black eyes were glaring out into the crowd, but he was now the monster rather than the man. The staff was in his hand, and it had transformed him from the human into the creature that kept all of them sleepless and terrified after their first experience viewing a public address.

The rest of the group continued to strike down on Soranace with their branches and rocks. Soranace was trying to touch the weapons like he had earlier that day to transform to them into anything that was harmless, but there were just too many of them hitting him too rapidly. He was now lying on the ground, unable to move, with blood flowing from his head and across his costume. They had formed a mob around him, and the guards were still too far away to anything to stop the attack. Angelica was on the outside of this mob now dressed in nothing short of her royal dress gown. Her dagger was drawn, and she was trying to get deep enough into the group to use it on Soranace. Still, she was not able to. It was the first time she had drawn that dagger with the intention of ending a life, and now she was unable to even get close enough to use it.

On the platform, Protace was howling and screaming in fury. He watched as his second in command squirmed on the ground under the constant blows. With his black, infuriated eyes, Protace watched Soranace fail him one last time. Angelica must be down there with that group. Even though he could not see her, Protace knew that to be true. She would be the only one who would organize such an attack against him. Soranace had failed him, but at the cost of his friend's life, Protace will kill Angelica after all of his failed attempts.

While raising his staff into the air, Protace walked to the edge of the platform. His cape was rippling through the wind behind him as he slammed down the shaft of his staff on the small latch at the platform's edge. The latch jolted under this blow, and Protace repeated the action. This time, the latch fell from the platform and tumbled through the air in front of the mountain and cage until it landed on the ground below. This was all that needed to be done. Now, the rest was out of his hands.

The large bars that were holding the beasts in their cage began to shift. They were sliding to the side under the force of dozens of slithering, green, reptilian bodies. With the latch now removed, there was nothing to hold these bars in place, and the beasts were breaking free. Protace had released the beasts to kill Angelica, her fellow conspirators, and anyone else who was in the way. When the bars had slid enough to leave five feet of empty space, the beasts began to pour out of their cage and into the courtyard like water spilling from a ruptured dam.

For an instant, every living thing in the courtyard froze. No one had ever seen that cage opened once it had been constructed. The sight of eminent death spilling away from its opened stockade sent ice through everyone's veins, and that ice froze them where they stood. This did not change until the first of the beasts let out its ear-splitting shriek into the still and peaceful day.

The group that was surrounding Soranace began to break apart, and finally someone yelled, "Get up the walls! They don't know how to climb the rock walls!" While all of the law-abiding citizens ran from the courtyard as quickly as they could possibly move, the group members all ran towards either side of the courtyard.

Soranace, now completely alone on the ground of the courtyard, screamed as five of the beasts covered him. Their massive green bodies lunged upon him and began to tear into his flesh with their jagged teeth. His screams quickly died away, but he was still moving, pushing the beasts off him as long as he could. One bleeding hand reached up into the air through the snapping jaws of the beasts. It looked like Soranace was trying to reach for help that would not come, but there was something wrong with that hand. There were a series of lumps moving just under the skin. As the beasts continued to find new places to bite and claw, one of these lumps exploded through the surface his index finger. A hornet buzzed away from Soranace's hand, soon to be followed by thousands more. Through his outstretched hand, a swarm of hornets began to fly, and Soranace's body seemed to deflate as this happened. Within a second, his body was gone. The beasts continued to squirm and fight one another over the remnants of blood and cloth that were on the ground, but all that was left of Soranace was a black cloud of buzzing hornets that moved as one entity into the sky.

Nervously the people in the courtyard, Angelica and Protace included, looked on as the black cloud of insects took to the air. It blurred out the beams of the sun as it passed overhead. A maddening buzzing sound filled the courtyard making everyone's ears hurt so badly they could feel the vibrations in their teeth. This cloud did not disperse into the air, but instead tightened into a black knot of humming, buzzing bodies. This dark smudge in the sky flew over the platform and hesitated a moment before Protace's eyes. It then proceeded over the mountains where it became invisible to the people in the courtyard.

Angelica replaced the dagger on her calf as she ran. Soon, she reached the wall, but she could hear the rapid footsteps of the beasts coming up from behind her. With a leap, she began to climb up the wall leaving the snarling beasts on the ground below. Angelica climbed upwards, knowing that the ledge was about fifteen feet above her. The side of the mountain offered a great many opportunities for a foothold, so she was able to climb rather quickly. Her scraped and bleeding hands grabbed hold of the rocks along the way and she pulled the rest of herself up along the side of the mountain. All the while, she could hear the beasts screaming below her. Before long, she placed on hand on the ledge above and began to pull herself up onto it. She made it to safety.

With a deep breath, Angelica held her hand still for a second on the corner of the ledge. Before Angelica was able to pull herself onto it, she felt a stinging pain on her hand. Her fingers were being ground into the rock above her, and Angelica could feel them losing their grip on her salvation. She looked up and saw someone standing on the ledge looking down at her. From this angle, it was hard to see who it was, but whoever was standing there was twisting one foot into Angelica's hand. Through clenched teeth, Angelica screamed at the pain filling her body through that hand. There was no place else for her to go, and Angelica knew that it was get on this ledge or die below. With no other options, Angelica grabbed hold of the ledge with her other hand, and the person backed off a step. When she did this, Angelica was able to see Lenore's face staring down at her.

A quake of terror rushed through Angelica when she made eye contact with their group's betrayer. Lenore had a scowl of disgust cut into her face as she stared back at Angelica. From where she stood one step back from the ledge, Lenore now kicked Angelica's hand, and the young girl began to scream in pain. Beneath her, she could hear the beasts leaping into the air and landing again. There were trying to reach her. If her grip on this ledge was to waver in any way, she would most likely be torn apart by the beasts as she fell. She would not even live long enough to die as she hit the ground.

Lenore kicked Angelica's right hand again, and her fingers slipped from the ledge. For an instant, Angelica was swinging in the air, pivoting from her left hand, and Lenore was just standing above her, laughing. Soon, Angelica's body slapped against the mountainside once more. It was as though she was having her stamina drained from her in quick bursts. She was now lying flat along the side of the mountain, but before she got a chance to place her right hand on the ledge again, Lenore was running up to kick Angelica's left hand. Like a wave of needles, pain flowed through Angelica's arm and into the rest of her body. The look in the woman's eyes had changed. It was not one of anger or fury, but rather simple obedience. She did not want to anger Protace, so she was to kill his enemy without question.

However, Lenore's foot froze in midair before it reached Angelica's hand again. Her eyes went blank for a moment, and she uttered a single cry, "Martin!" It was a shocked scream, and Angelica knew immediately what it meant. Lenore saw her husband standing on the platform with Protace. Angelica did not have a chance to look at Martin for herself, but she did have an opportunity to act. While Lenore's attention was diverted, most likely wondering what her husband intended to do, Angelica reached up and noticed that she was able to grab hold of something better than the rocky edge of rock this time. Her hand grabbed hold of Lenore's ankle.

In her state of shock, Lenore did not get a chance to react. Angelica gave one firm tug, and Lenore fell to the surface of the ledge. With her other leg, the woman began to kick wildly. Her leather-clad foot swung back and forth as Angelica began to pull the limb towards the edge. All of Lenore's kicking made it harder for her to hold herself still, and she began to slide towards the end of the platform easily. At one point, the heel of her foot struck Angelica in the cheek, but the queen barely felt it. Her body was covered in a cloak of agony by this point, and her attention was fully on Lenore. There was no room for pain. Angelica continued pulling on Lenore's ankle until the woman was finally far enough over the ledge to fall.

The force of her last kick gave enough momentum for Lenore to fall over the edge. She began to scream as she fell, and as a last resort, one flailing hand grabbed hold of Angelica's shoulder. The young girl slipped from the ledge immediately. With the screaming beasts getting louder, they both fell. Angelica reached out, and the protruding rocks struck her hands, batting them away from any firm purchase. Her sore and swelling hand was knocked away by the protrusions at first, but soon she was able to grab hold of one of them. She stopped with a jerk that sent another wave of pain slamming through her body. Lenore kept falling. Soon, one of the leaping beasts plucked Lenore out of the air, and she was dead before the beast got a chance to land on the ground with its prize.

Angelica sighed deeply, trying to ignore the warm rush of pain filling her entire body and also trying not to listen to the sound of ripping flesh and screaming beasts filling the air. Currently, they were tearing Lenore to pieces below. The queen quickly climbed up the rest of the way to the ledge and pulled herself onto it easily this time. For a moment, she just lied there trying to catch her breath. The air felt good and cool inside a body that was on fire with pain. Finally, she stood. The ledge went on towards the platform for another ten feet before narrowing to about three inches in width. Just beyond that was the platform where Martin slowly advanced closer to Protace.

Carefully considering every motion and every breath, Martin was taking steps towards the monster before him. He had been so involved in his actions that he did not even see his wife plunge to her death, and that was most likely for the best. With Protace howling in fury as most people ran and few others remained to fight the beasts, Martin approached the monster from just behind its right shoulder. As if handling the deadliest of chemicals, Martin removed the sword from his belt, and there was the quiet hiss of metal sliding along leather.

Protace stopped his howling immediately and stared fixedly at the courtyard below him. There were still people and beasts running from one another, but most had managed to get away safely. They either climbed the walls or ran to the village, but either way, the beasts were unable or unwilling to pursue them.

Without even noticing the change in Protace's actions, Martin took a careful step forward. A light wind was gently blowing through the air, and it was just enough to blow Martin's hair into his face. He raised his sword to shoulder height as slowly as he could and then drew it all the way back so it lined up with Protace's neck. After a very slow and deep inhale, Martin swung the sword forward towards its target.

For an instant, Martin saw the kingdom in peace. He saw Protace dying and turning into dust before him. He saw people cheering not only him but the freedom he gave them. He saw happiness and prosperity. He saw a world where there would be no more death, no more pain, and no more monsters masquerading as men. He saw the end of Protace's reign of terror. He saw happiness and peace.

What Martin saw never came to pass. His sword got no more than halfway through its arcing path when it stopped with a loud metallic reverberation. Protace had swung his staff out to the side. It was a casual motion anyone with a staff might do, but this was not. Protace did that knowing it would block Martin's sword. He saw or heard or simply sensed the impending attack, and he knew what needed to be done to stop it. The loud metallic clang hung in the air for a few seconds, echoing off the mountains, and no one in the courtyard was able to move, or breathe, or even think. This was what they had feared since they conceived this plan.

For a moment, Martin was frozen with fear as well. He looked at Protace, who had not moved at all after intercepting his sword's blow. Finally, the monster slowly turned his head to face Martin. Those black eyes were almost hypnotic. Protace looked like a monster from someone's nightmare. His features were distorted slightly from a human's but just enough to give him a sinister and demonic look. When he saw Martin starting back at him, Protace shifted his whole body to face Martin fully.

There was a tense moment where no one attempted to move or make a sound. Martin and Protace remained staring into one another's eyes for a few seconds before Martin finally pulled his sword back from Protace's staff. Martin knew the safest thing to do now would be to run, but how long would that extend his life? Until he was able to set foot in the courtyard? Maybe into the night if he was lucky? This entire plan could not be repeated at this point. Protace would never allow for such an opportunity to exist again. It was either fight knowing there was a chance of defeating Protace or run knowing that his tyranny would never end.

Martin chose to fight. He lashed forward with his sword again, and Protace stopped it with his staff as he had done before. As if it was just another mock duel in the courtyard, Martin continued to strike down with his sword accomplishing nothing but hitting a solid object. No matter how fast he moved, Protace moved twice as fast. His movements were almost lost in the swirl of his black cape, but he kept swinging the staff towards Martin. He blocked every hit with a blow from his staff without seeming to exert himself at all. The black cape swirled in the air as he moved creating a sickening cloud around the monster. Even though Martin could not hear it, Protace had begun to howl again.

From the ledge, Angelica watched frantically. Martin was backing away with every blow, and soon he would be at the edge of the platform. There would be no way to stop him then. If Martin were backed against nothing but the fall behind him, there would be no way to win. He would either fall to his death or be killed by Protace's staff. Angelica was screaming on the inside, but externally, she looked as still and as scared as her stone sculpture by the portal.

Martin continued to get closer to the edge of the platform when Protace slammed the head of his staff down on Martin's knee. The scream was loud enough to make everyone feel the pain that was surging through Martin's body. Those that were close enough even heard the snap. His leg was broken. The limb was twisted beneath in a position that could bring tears to someone's eyes. Trying to keep all of his weight on his right leg, Martin began to limp back away from Protace who was now simply standing still rather than fighting. With one leg bent sideways out in front of him, Martin tried to continue fighting. He raised his sword up into the air above his head, and Protace acted quickly. Using the same maneuver he used in his duel with David back in Protecia, Protace brought his staff around over his head intercepting Martin's sword. The staff continued to arc down and come up again behind its opponent where it slammed into the back of Martin's head. At that instant, his sword fell to the ground, and Protace was pulling his opponent closer with one clawed hand. Martin was overcome by a gray cloud of haze that was filling his head. He just followed Protace's lead without struggling or even knowing what he was doing. As Martin got nearer to Protace, the monster opened his mouth and bit down on Martin's cheek. Blood flowed both into Protace's mouth and Martin's own mouth for a second, and then Protace released him.

Gasping for breath and wreathing in pain, Martin tried to take a few steps back. His one leg complied and the other dragged along uniformly. Protace only took slow steps forward to match the ones Martin was agonizing over. Soon, Martin realized his foot was on the last inch of rock on the ledge. In one panicked moment, Martin looked to Protace as if pleading. There was nothing left for him to do. Protace kept advancing with blood dripping down his mouth and the staff standing menacingly tall in his hand.

Martin's diminishing choices were soon brought out of his hands entirely. The last several inches of the ledge gave way, and a storm of rocks began to fall from the platform. Martin began to fall from the platform as well. He was absolutely silent, knowing this was the easier of two deaths, but he had no idea what horrors were still in store for him.

As Martin began to fall, Protace moved his staff so that the beast's image on its head was staring into Martin's face. The staff's eyes began to glow like bright yellow stars, and suddenly Martin stopped falling. His body was hanging in midair, completely motionless as if frozen in time. Caught partway through a roll into the air and a reflex action of shielding his face, Martin stopped moving. He began to scream, but no one reacted. No one knew how to react to such a sight.

The eyes on the staff began to glow brighter and more intensely. The soon began to pulsate like the light inside the portal. Martin screamed as loudly as he could, whether it was in pain or fear, no one knew for sure, but his screams were loud enough to send echoes off the mountain walls. Everyone that had fled the courtyard that day could hear those screams. Soon, his eyes began to slide shut despite his efforts to keep them open. There was a pained look on his face as he tried to face his attacker, but his efforts failed. Those eyes remained closed for only a second before they slowly opened again without Martin's control. Now, his eyes were glowing in unison with the eyes on the staff.

His screams got louder as the bright yellow light began to sparkle away from his eyes and as it began to grow bright and intense. The light soon began to glow so brightly that it blocked out his body entirely, making it impossible to even see him there anymore. All that existed was a bright yellow, pulsating glow in the sky. Even his screams were drowned out by the high-pitched hum coming from this bright light. It looked as though Martin body had erupted into a new sun.

In Protecia, Beatrice jumped from the floor of the cave where she had been sitting. There was another glowing coming from the wall this time. It was not the bright white light as if someone was coming through the portal. This was a faint, yellow glow, more of an outline, around the sculpture of Martin. It lasted for only a second, and then the light faded. When the light returned to darkness, however, the sculpture began to crumble. While the others remained unharmed, Martin's image fell to the ground in a pile of small stones. His place on the wall had become vacant, something that apparently did not happen even if that person died. Something happened to Martin that was even more final than death.

For a moment, Angelica was just able to stare in disbelief. The bright yellow light was gone, and where it had been, there was nothing but air. Martin had vanished. Protace made him just disappear from existence right before the eyes of everyone there. More than just being dead, there was not even a body remaining to fall to the ground. He just disappeared in a flash of bright, golden light and a sudden, immediately dissipating funnel cloud.

Angelica found the air in her lungs and screamed. Whether it was in fear of what would happen next or just surprise about what she had just watched, not even she knew. The faint breeze wafted by and the sun shone down on the mountains while Angelica's shriek filled the air. Then, she saw Protace turning to look at her. He had not known if she had been killed by the beasts during this whole attack, and he probably would not have known for some time if she had not called out like she did. Upon seeing those pure black eyes, Angelica's scream died on her tongue, and she could only stare in fear.

Without taking her eyes off of her, Protace began to run towards Angelica. He was slammed one foot on the ground in front of the other, but he was not running towards the narrow ledge that connected the platform to the wider ledge where she was standing. The monster that had once been Alexander was running directly towards the edge of the platform and the drop to the courtyard.

Still, he did not stop, even as the edge drew near. When Protace finally reached the edge of the platform, he leapt into the air. Rather than rising for a moment and then plunging back down, Protace continued to rise. Angelica could see that he had not jumped quite as much as he had begun to fly across the air to her.

A shadow stretched over the courtyard almost as if a heavenly body was eclipsing the sun. The rippling of the cape could be seen in that shadow, and so could the image of that horrific staff. It was the staff that turned Alexander into a monster and seemed to have the power to make people vanish from the world as if they never existed before. As the shadow neared the edge of the courtyard, even the beasts began to quiver in fear.

Angelica did not know what to do. With Protace flying towards the ledge with that horrid staff clenched in his hand, Angelica looked frantically around. Finally, she turned to run towards the platform. Protace would have to make a complete turn in the air to catch up with her then, and she did not think he would be able to do such a thing. He was moving too fast. So, Angelica ran towards the platform and managed to get only about ten feet closer by the time Protace landed on the ledge behind her.

His back was facing Angelica, and she took this slight opportunity to run farther towards the platform. There was the extremely narrow ledge between where she was standing and the speaking platform, but traveling that ledge was the only way to get down at this point. Behind her, Protace had turned around and began to run towards Angelica. Dirt propelled from his feet as he bounded to her, raising the staff across his chest into the air. After a second, he got close enough to Angelica to use it.

Protace swung the staff back across his chest sending a crushing blow to Angelica's left side. Only able to get out a brief gasp, she fell against the mountainside to her right and slid to the ledge from there. For a moment, she felt hardly able to stand up. Her lungs were unable to pull in air, and her muscles became completely useless. An incredible pain was reaching into her body on fiery fingers plunging their way through her ribcage. Her entire body was sore. Angelica remained on the ground for a moment, but soon she began to force herself up. She needed to begin moving again. With her body groaning in pain, she grabbed hold of the mountainside and began to pull herself to her feet. It was a very slow process, but soon she managed to stand on her own. As she did place weight on her two feet, she realized how much time she had given Protace to catch up with her.

No sooner did Angelica get to her feet than she turned her head to glance behind her. Terrified to see Protace standing right there ready to crush her under the force of his staff, Angelica received another, more devastating shock. Just at her eye-level, the head of the staff was being held. Protace was holding it right in front of her, and its eyes were gleaming with their bright yellow glow already.

Instantly, her body froze. A high pitched hum began to fill her mind, and it was the only thing that existed in the world for her. Her hands clenched at her sides and her legs froze into tree trunks. Angelica was forced to stare straight ahead at the brightening eyes of the staff before her. "Help me!" she began to scream as loudly as she could, but no one seemed to hear. That horrible whining sound from the staff made it impossible for her even hear her own screams for help. That sound drilled its way into her mind. It was as if a swarm of insects had covered her body, and they were all she could hear or feel. "Somebody, help me! Please!" Angelica continued to scream, but there was still no reaction from the people below.

Ahead of her, all she could see was the bright flashing of the yellow lights. That glow began to fill the world. A constant, pulsing yellow glow. It was almost hypnotic, and for a moment, Angelica forgot what had happened to Martin. She began to scream louder even though her own voice was drowned out by the hum of the light. All attempts to move were met with a pain similar to knives being plunged into her body. Soon, she felt her eyes begin to slip closed. Despite her attempts to keep them open, they closed on their own as if the yellow light was controlling them.

With the world blackened around her, she was only able to feel everything going on. The light gave off waves of tingling heat that now were either filling or consuming Angelica while she stood there with her eyes closed. She screamed for help again, but nothing happened. Finally, her eyelids began to spread apart.

She could not see anything even with her eyes opened. The yellow light was coming from them now, and it was getting more intense with every second. Her screams became more frantic with every passing moment as her body filled with a feeling of almost tingling hot pain. Her body felt almost foreign to her, as if it belonged to someone else. That light had her under its complete control.

Finally, David ran towards her. He was further down the ledge, and did not even see Angelica on this side until a second ago. Now, he was running towards her and Protace. With all of his concentration on his queen and that horrible light, Protace did not even realize someone else was approaching. Soon that light would wipe Angelica out of existence, sending her to some vacant emptiness where she could not interfere with him anymore. David had no idea how to stop whatever the staff was doing to her, so he acted the only way he knew how. Take away whatever was threatening the queen.

David ran towards Protace and grabbed him. The two of them fell towards the side of the mountain immediately, and the staff went dark as soon as Protace was moved. With the connection between Angelica and itself broken, that light had no more purpose and simply died away. However, the queen's reaction to the severing of this connection was much more severe. The light in Angelica's eyes disappeared with audible snap like the breaking of a branch. Angelica gasped loudly, and her body was propelled into the air. She spun as she plunged back down to the ledge further towards the platform than where she was. When she landed, her face was hanging off the side of the ledge and staring down to the vacant courtyard below.

Slowly, Angelica propped herself up on her hands and then to her feet. She was standing right at the edge of the wider ledge with only the very narrow one before her. Even that slight breeze that had been filling the courtyard throughout day would have been enough to send her falling down to her death. Still, she had to get away. With her arms spread out on the mountain as if hugging the rocky wall, Angelica slowly began to make her way across the platform on the narrower ledge. There was hardly enough space for her toes to rest on, but she continued on her way, holding onto the mountain with her hands for support. That seemed to be the only thing keeping her from falling to the ground and the beasts below.

Protace grabbed hold of David as soon as their bodies collided. Without letting go of his staff, he hurled David into the wall of the mountain. There were some muffled cries as the guard struggled to push his face away from the rock. Protace did not budge, though. He just held David against the wall by pressing the staff across his back. With his other hand, he reached up towards David's neck. Protace placed one extended claw over the back of the man's neck, and the guard tried to squirm out of the way. It was of no use, though.

David could not see what was about to happen, but he knew his life depended on his escape. Despite all the guard's efforts, he was unable to move under Protace's strength.

As if savoring every second of David's struggle, Protace slowly pushed one claw into David's neck just below the skull and to the right of the spinal column. Through clenched teeth, David let out a loud moaning scream, but Protace did not stop. He dragged that claw from the right side of the neck to the left, and the screams got louder before stopping in their entirety. The claw cut across his spine, and David died immediately releasing his last breath against the mountain wall. The guard fell to the ledge soundlessly then as if someone had simply shut him off.

With David dead, Protace looked up towards Angelica. She had made her way across by the narrow ledge and was now racing along his speaking platform. Protace ran towards the edge of the ledge he was on and continued to run towards the platform even after his feet left surface of the stone. He rose into the air smoothly and quietly, almost as if he was one of the arrows he had shot at the queens before him. As he drifted effortlessly through the air, Protace brought the staff around behind him ready to swing. Angelica was getting closer now, and he was not going to let her escape this time.

Before she even got halfway across the platform, Angelica looked behind her and saw Protace flying towards her across the courtyard. She knew she could not outrun him, and that if she did not do something right away, he could certainly kill her. As if to seek his help, Angelica ran towards the spot where Martin had died, or more accurately, disappeared. Right at the edge of the platform, there was only a sword and few spots of blood remaining of him. Angelica turned away from the edge and faced her back towards Protace flying towards her with his staff ready to strike. She looked around and saw the sword lying on the ground, almost beckoning her to pick it up.

Protace got closer to the platform as his cape whipped through the air behind him. Below, he could see Bryan remaining in the courtyard fighting off the constant attacks from the beasts with his sword. He appeared nearly unharmed. That did not matter though. Without its leader, his group would be powerless to do anything but continue hiding or simply die. Protace knew that killing Angelica would end this resistance against him. The young queen was right before him now. One hit from the staff would be enough. If it did not kill her instantly, the force would be enough to throw her off the side of the platform for her to die below.

As Protace began to swing his staff towards Angelica, she turned to face him. Martin's sword was clenched tightly in both of her hands, and she swung it at Protace. He did not even react to this. As Angelica hacked Martin's sword at the air, Protace continued swinging his staff towards her. After what could have been an hour, the sword struck Protace in the arm, right at the crook of his elbow.

It nearly imbedded itself an inch into the flesh of his arm when Angelica yanked it free. Blood shot away from the wound, and the staff began to slip from Protace's hand. He was trying to hold onto it. The muscles and tendons of his arm were visibly quivering in this effort, but the gash in his elbow would not allow it. Within a few seconds, his arm went limp. The staff slipped from his hand and landed on the platform.

Immediately, Protace began to fall from the sky. The monster he had become let out a shriek as it fell to the stone platform only a few feet away. He began to change back into a human as soon as he dropped the staff. The blackness in his eyes vanished as if a membrane had ruptured in his corneas. As a few drops of blood wept away from them as though they were tears, his human eyes reappeared. His claws broke off from his fingers and scattered to the ground leaving nothing but his nails behind. The fangs simply retracted back to their normal size. His monstrous shriek began to change as well. Soon, it was nothing more than the cry of a human in pain. Protace began hiding his face with his hands as he fell from the sky and hit his speaking platform, shoulder first.

Angelica did not want to take any chances leaving the staff so near to Protace. With her foot, she pushed it towards the edge of the platform. As soon as its head went over the edge, the staff toppled over and fell down to the ground below. It looked almost beautiful as it drifted down along the mountainside. The staff drifted past a single one of the beasts. This creature was beginning to climb up the side of the mountain. They were always known to be very intelligent, and now that the situation called for it, this particular beast was beginning to learn how to climb the rock walls to get to the waiting meal above.

Protace stood before Angelica with blood dripping from his eyes and nose. "Angelica," he managed to whisper. He was talking to her as casually as he always had back on their world. "Angelica," his voice sounded strained, almost as if he was in great pain. Slowly, he began to take a step towards her.

Without any thought of the new, friendlier disposition Protace was showing, Angelica held her sword up in the air with the tip pointing at him. "Keep away from me, Alexander." He did not listen. Maybe he just did not want to answer to that name, but Angelica made no attempt to please the image he had of himself. He was no great founder of their kingdom. "Alexander, get away from me." Angelica shook the sword toward him for a second, and Protace stopped moving.

Behind her, the beast that was climbing up the wall reached the platform. It stretched its long body towards the sky and far surpassed Angelica's height. The long horns protruding from its neck were closed around its head, but they were slowly opening as it lifted itself higher into the air. Protace saw this creature, but he did not react to it at all. If he was going to run, he would do it after this creature had killed Angelica. With those four horns now fully opened, the creature began to open its mouth. It let out one high-pitched shriek, and Angelica leapt in fear. Terrified of what she might see, Angelica turned to face the beast that was behind her.

There was a moment of absolute horror when she did not know what to do. Just like her sculpture back on the other world, she was staring directly into the eyes of one of those horrible, hideout lizards. Its mouth was opening more fully, and Angelica did not want to wait any longer before doing something.

She swung her sword at this beast, and the creature snapped at it. Its mouth closed around the blade and began to pull it away from Angelica. With all of her fury, she was struggling to keep it in her hands, but the beast was too strong. Soon, it grabbed hold of the sword with its four clawed feet, and for an instant, Angelica was holding the enormous creature over the courtyard. The beast lashed its spiked tail at Angelica, who was struggling to keep the sword in her hand. In doing so, she was getting pulled towards the edge of the platform by this creature's weight, but she did not want to let go. In a second, her efforts failed under the massive weight of the beast. The sword slipped from her hands, and the beast, still holding onto it with its mouth and all its legs, fell with it.

For a moment, Angelica was certain she would fall off as well. She remained perfectly still with her arms extended to her sides to keep her balance. A quick series of gasps was coming from her as the beast and the sword continued to fall to the ground. The balls of her feet were over the edge of the platform, and she knew any slight breeze could push her over the edge. With a squeal, the beast hit the ground and impaled itself on the sword it had fallen with. Slowly, Angelica managed to calm her breathing and began to lean back putting her weight over the platform behind her.

That did not last long at all, though. Before Angelica was able to fully pull herself back onto the platform, she was shoved from behind. Protace had taken advantage of the situation and had pushed Angelica from the platform. She flew into the air over the courtyard screaming and calling for help. From below, the ground began to rush towards her. Protace simply stood in the place Angelica was a moment ago and watched as she began to fall towards the ground. He felt a moment of triumph; he had finally managed to kill the queen.

Her arms and legs were flailing as if she believed she could possibly begin to fly back up to the sky. It did not happen, though.

She continued to fall with Protace watching from above. At that speed, she would have died as soon as she struck the ground. However, she did not hit the ground. Bryan had run to meet her, and although she was going too fast for him to catch her, his arms embraced her enough to slow down her fall. The two of them landed on the ground together, but they were both alive.

Angelica felt unable to stand for a few moments, but Bryan was on his feet immediately. Through hazy eyes, Angelica watched as the endless number of beasts began to approach him. With the sword out in an instant, he was fighting off the lizards, which had diminished in number but were still constantly coming. "Run!" Bryan screamed at her with spittle spraying from his mouth. A beast leapt towards him, and he swung his sword at it. Just as it was opening the horns around its head, it was decapitated. Its head fell to the ground and rolled to look up at the sky. "Get back to your world! We'll meet you there!" Another beast was approaching, and it seemed more vicious that the others. "Go, now!"

Angelica stood and began to run towards the side of the platform where the passage to the portal was. From above, Protace, no longer a monster at all, was watching as Angelica ran by, but he saw something else as well. A single beast raised its head, still enclosed in its cage of four horns, above slithering bodies and few fighting people in the courtyard. It looked at Angelica running away and began to run after her. Bryan slammed his sword down at this beast, only to have the blade ricochet off its encaged head. As the beast's feet slammed against the ground, the horns fanned away from its head, and it let out a squeal.

This was a sound Angelica recognized. She began to run faster. Ahead of her, there was a line of high bushes that led to the portal. There was no time to waste at all. She did not slow down as she ran between them. Branches scratched the skin of her arms and legs, but she still continued. If she could get to the portal, then she would be safe. There was only one beast able to pass through the portal, and that one may have died in the courtyard moments ago.

Angelica emerged from the row of bushes in a cloud of kicked up dust. The sound of the beast pushing its way after her was already filling the air. It was catching up with her. Branches were breaking around its body as it plunged through the bushes towards its target. There was not much left for her to go before she reached the portal, but she did not know how much distance that creature had gained on her. To look behind at this point would almost certainly waste too much time.

She was only halfway to the pool of water when the beast exploded out of the bushes and began to scamper towards her faster than ever before. Its black eyes were gleaming in the light as it watched Angelica climb up the edge of the portal and jump in. She slipped into the water without effort, and began to swim towards the pulsing light ahead of her. With each stroke, Angelica slowed down more and more. It seemed as though she had managed to outrun the beast. Then, everything changed.

There was an enormous splash as the beast fell into the water. Air bubbles drifted up from its mouth and under its scales. Small slits began to open on the sides of its neck exposing a set of gills to the water. Then, it began to kick its legs and swish its tail. The beast was swimming towards her, and it was swimming very fast.

In a scream, Angelica nearly let out half of the air she had been holding in her lungs. The sound drifted away with the distorted quality most noise made underwater. She began to move her arms and legs frantically to get towards that bright light ahead of her, but it seemed so far away. It was pulsing faster and brighter with every passing second, but Angelica did not think she would actually be able to get there before the beast reached her. She could almost feel the water currents given off by its stroking legs.

Swimming as fast as she could, Angelica began to feel cramps developing in her limbs and ribs. She still tried to go just as fast, but she could feel herself beginning to slow down. Her body was not able to keep up. No matter how hard she tried, Angelica could not go any faster, and she could feel the beast gaining from behind. The light was just about at her fingertips and flashing very as if it were about to explode. Angelica could almost touch it with her hand.

With the light only an inch away from her fingertips, the beast reached Angelica. Its claws closed down around her leg, and immediately, blood began to reach out into the water in a cloud. Angelica coughed out the rest of the air she had in her lungs as she was pulled away from the light towards this beast behind her. Her arms still reached out in front of her for the pulsing star, but it was now too far out of her reach. It was the last desperate attempt to get back to Protecia, and it failed.

The beast reached out with the claws of its front legs. It dug these claws into Angelica's flesh as it climbed up her body and bit into her stomach. Angelica brought her hands down and began to pound her fists against the creature's head. This did not stop the beast from biting into her. If there was any air left in her body, she would have begun to scream in pain, but she could not. Her lungs were empty, and her screams only producing throbbing icepicks in her chest.

The sting of the water flowing into this gaping wound filled Angelica's body with agony. A dull ache began in her chest. She needed to breathe, but she would not allow her body to do it. Breathing now would mean drowning in this strange passageway between worlds. Her teeth were clenched, and her lips were pulled back in a snarl. Through eyes that were only barely opened, Angelica looked at the reddening water around her. Bloodstained water began to trickle into her mouth, and she nearly wretched at the salty tang.

Despite Angelica's weak attempts at fighting this creature, its claws reached up again and dug into the queen's back. She could feel the sharp fingers tearing her flesh as it pulled its way further up her throat. Angelica was able to look directly into the black eyes that nearly seemed to gleam as the beast began to dig its claws into the back of Angelica's head. She was able to feel the claws cutting through her scalp and pressing against her skull. There was an incredible aching followed by a series of sharp stabs as the bone began to crush under the beast's grasp. The beast was still looking up at her eyes as it gnawed deeper into Angelica's throat. Angelica's eyes began to slip shut, and she did not know if this would be permanent or not. There was so little energy left in her to resist this attack, but she had to do something to fight back. The beast removed its mouth from her throat, and a new, darker cloud of blood jetted away from her in a crimson cloud. She knew if she was going to have the opportunity to do something, now would have to be now.

With a hand that was reluctant to obey her commands, Angelica reached down to her calf and removed the dagger from its place there. She brought it back up through the blood-red water towards the beast. It was so hard to see the slithering creature anymore. Even though it was right in front of her, the blood in the water nearly enveloped Angelica in an opaque curtain she could not see past. Even the pulsing of that bright light just beyond did not make it any easier.

Finally, the beast leapt forward to strike again. Angelica did not waste any time, though. She slammed the dagger forward and buried it underneath the creature's chin. It let out a howl that sounded somehow fragmented in the water. With all of her fury behind her, Angelica forced the dagger further in the creature. It began lashing its tail at her, but its efforts seemed half-hearted. The growls became more strained and forced, but Angelica did not stop. She forced the blade further still into the creature's head. Her hand was nearly pushing beneath the surface of its skin.

The howl from the creature grew worse. As it got louder, its quality seemed to change to one of suffering. It was in a great deal of pain, which was most likely, something it had never experienced before. The howls grew louder and louder, and the creature began to buck as if in the grips of a seizure. Angelica was thrown away from it, but the knife pulled the beast along with her. Soon, both plunged into the bright, pulsing light, and that flawless white beauty consumed them both.

CHAPTER THIRTY-ONE

The Queen and the Monster

The caves were dark despite the light spilling in from above. Whether it was a cloud or an eclipse that blocked the sunlight, no one in the caves could tell. All they could see was the dark. A stale smell of dankness filled the caverns as the walls dripped with condensation. Aside from Beatrice's nervous footsteps on the ground, there was one other sound. Faint, but undeniable. Coming from deep in the caves where none of them dared to venture. It sounded like screaming.

Beatrice was pacing in the caves as she usually did since Angelica began her trips to the other world. Every few seconds, she stopped and stared at Angelica's likeness in stone, grinning while holding the tip of her dagger under the chin of the snarling beast. Two guards were standing with Beatrice as they always did, whispering amongst themselves about how her pacing would wear a trench in the cave floor. The guards rotated this job among all their number, but there were always at least two in the caves with Beatrice at all times. Just in case Alexander returned or something worse happened. The three of them were looking over the crumbled pieces of Martin's image, now barely recognizable as anyone, wondering what could have happened to him to warrant such a reaction from the wall. Nearly every hour, Beatrice would consider not staying in the caves as she was, but today, she was very grateful she did not heed her own advice.

The wall of sculptures began to glow with its bright white light. Beatrice immediately ran towards it to see who was coming through. This light appeared to be coming from where Angelica's image was located, but something different happened this time. A second after it began to glow, it intensified greatly as if two people were coming through this time. For a moment, Beatrice was overjoyed by the possibility of everyone coming home. It would mean that their battle was over and that they had defeated Alexander. Deep down, though, Beatrice was terrified that was not the case. She then remembered which image was just next to Angelica's, and she knew exactly what was coming through the portal.

No sooner did Beatrice remember the location of the beast's sculpture than the light disappeared. The two of them remained in their places for a moment. In that split second, Beatrice could see Angelica's grin as she knelt on the ground with the dagger extended in her right hand. The tip of the dagger was pressing against the throat of that horrible reptile. This creature simply looked back at Angelica as if humoring her for a second before asserting its authority. It was just like the sculpture, except this time, they were real. It was all really happening now. They remained in this position for what seemed like an eternity, and then they fell as overcome by a wave of exhaustion. Angelica hit the ground without offering any resistance. The dagger slid from her hand and landed on the stone floor beside her. She rolled towards the smooth part of the wall where her sculpture was a few seconds ago. It appeared as if she was trying to shield herself with its stone surface.

As Angelica was lying on the ground with the horrible rasping sound of her breaths surrounding her, the beast hit the ground only to rise to its feet in moments. The guards began to move towards it, and those black marbles of eyes began to dart back and forth. It was trying to figure out where it was or why nothing looked the same anymore. Also it was injured. Quite seriously. There was a jerking motion in its movements that could only be described as convulsing. The beast was scared, and instead of fighting, it fled for safety. Past the guards, it ran into the small, narrow cave right across from the remaining sculptures. This is the cave where Alexander discovered the broken pieces of Protace's staff, and the rock that had sealed off this passage was still lying just next to that cave opening. Without wasting any time thinking, the two guards grabbed hold of that rock and began to slide it into place. It was almost sealing off the cave when the beast realized it had no way out. In an attempt to keep from being trapped, the beast fled back towards the side cavern's one opening into the main chamber. Trying to push its head through the gap between the cave wall and the rock soon proved futile. It was too weak from its injuries to mount a significant defense. The caged head remained anchored between the rocks for a moment, and then guards began to wonder if this creature would ever back down. It eventually turned away into the cave again, and the guards moved the rock completely into the place. The sight of that cave being sealed looked like a crypt being locked away forever.

With the beast's howls echoing off the walls, Beatrice ran over to Angelica. The women fell to her knees beside the young queen, and looked at her quivering body. She did not look that bad. From how the was lying, pressed against the cave wall, Beatrice could easily see the left side of her face and most of that side of her body. There did not seem to be a single cut or scratch on her, and Beatrice had to assume that possibly the water of the portal had done something to heal any injuries she had sustained. Gently, Beatrice placed a hand on the queen's left shoulder, covered in the bright purple robe of royalty, and rolled her so they could face each other.

When Queen Angelica rolled to face away from the cave wall, Beatrice saw how wrong she was. There was nearly nothing remaining of the right side of the queen's face. The cheek had been torn off completely, leaving her jaw and all of her teeth clearly visible. Four claw gouges extended from her nose, across her eye, and ending in her hairline. The eye was intact, but it was rolling aimlessly in its socket as if the slightest shake of the head would send it careening out onto the ground. Fang marks covered the neck and blood was pumping from three of these punctures in bright red spurts that doused the walls and floor of the caves. Her clothes were not torn at all, most likely due to transporting through the portal, but there was blood seeping through the purple fabric in large blossoms. There was no way to tell how extensively she was injured under that gown, but Beatrice knew there was no hope. No miracles for the Protecian kingdom were going to rescue their queen again. Protace's reach could only go so far.

"You're going to be okay, Angelica. Just hang on, and you'll be fine," Beatrice was whispering through the tears that poured from her eyes. They drenched her face in what felt like an acid bath, but she did not notice. She could not take her eyes off of Angelica. "Just wait and see. You'll be fine."

Their hands found each other, and for one horrifying moment, Beatrice saw that Angelica was missing two fingers from that hand. Still, their grasp on each other was firm. The queen's hand felt so cold that Beatrice began to shiver at her very touch. When Beatrice looked into the girl's eyes, she could see the life slipping away from them. It was almost like a golden smoke was drifting from her as her soul left her battered and wrecked body. Blood was dripping across the left side of her face now, standing out against the paleness of her skin. Not knowing what else do, Beatrice kept repeating, "You're going to be okay. You'll get through this," as she rocked back and forth on the cave floor.

Even if there was a royal physician to call for help, Beatrice did not think he would have been able to get there in time. That may have not been an issue at all, however. Judging from the extent of her injuries that Beatrice could see, it did not seem like there would be a doctor in the history of their kingdom that could save her. None of this mattered, though. Their physician had been trying to kill them for some time now and was now somewhere in some other world.

Angelica knew Beatrice was lying to her. There was no way she was going to be okay after her fight with the beast. She could taste the blood filling her mouth and could feel it flowing away from her body.

Surprisingly, she could not feel any pain. For some reason, the only sensation apart from the tightness of Beatrice's hand on hers was an overwhelming numbness. Staring directly into Beatrice's eyes with vision that was unable to focus fully, she began to say, "Please do not let him have the kingdom. Do not let him kill us all." The words were spoken so quietly Beatrice was barely able to hear them, but still she knew exactly what was being said. Angelica's eyes said it all.

In response, Beatrice just nodded. A smile began to touch the one remaining corner of Angelica's lips, and then it faded away again. The queen's body settled on the ground as all her muscles loosened. Beatrice just stared at her for a second, not wanting to believe what she was seeing, but there was no way to deny it. The queen's eyes were staring directly up at the ceiling of the caves, their pupils barely more than pin holes, and they were not moving in the slightest.

Queen Angelica was dead.

Beatrice tried to look away from Angelica's body but was unable to. Even like this, she was beautiful and looking away, for what would be the last time, made her soul ache. Finally, she began to scream in fury and anger. That sound drowned out the howls of the beast contained in the caves behind her. Tears began to pour from Beatrice's eyes even more heavily than before, as her eyes managed to close. Alexander had now killed the last three monarchs before him, essentially clearing the way for his rule. The guards just stood by and watched in disbelief. This would be the hardest sight they would ever have to see in their service to the kingdom. Soon, they began to move as well. Their movements were not in grief or sympathy, however. They were moving to stand at attention.

For an instant, the shadows of three human forms stretched across the floor of the caves, extending from the entrance to this room. The wave of fear and shock elicited by these three could almost be seen as their shadows quaked like the rolling waves of the ocean. One of them, the center shadow, receded and soon disappeared from the other two. It vanished around a corner as the others froze in their place.

At the sound of a voice, a very familiar voice, Beatrice's screams stopped immediately. "If you would have just let me declare her unfit to rule, none of this would have ever happened." Beatrice turned and looked further down the wall of sculptures. Alexander was lying against the stone flames as his image had done the entire time she was pacing these caves. He was now right there. Right after Angelica and beast went through the portal, he had followed. Now, he was here, back in Protecia, standing from his lying position on the wall.

Beatrice just looked up at him for a moment. The dagger was lying on the ground beside her, and she grabbed hold of it immediately. Not really sure if she was actually going to do anything with the blade that was meant to help Angelica through her dark times, Beatrice leapt to her feet and bounded towards Alexander. He just stood there as calm and composed as he had always been. Through clenched teeth, Beatrice let out a high-pitched shriek as she ran towards Alexander with the dagger cutting through the gloom of the caves.

Before she got too close to do any real harm, Alexander reached out and grabbed hold of Beatrice's wrist. She still managed to take another step and the dagger ended up an inch away from Alexander's throat before he stopped her entirely. "That would not be a good idea. She is dead, which makes me the king. Killing me would be a high assassination."

Now, it was said. Beatrice just froze in fear for a moment refusing to believe what Alexander had just whispered to her. Angelica was dead, and Alexander was the next in line to the throne. He was king now. Everything Wilhelmina and Angelica had worked for seemed wasted and demolished in a moment. Alexander was king. His assassinations and attempts that spanned back for almost ten years now bought him the goal he had desired. After all the scheming and the endless plots, vast arrays of disguises and battalions of accomplices, Alexander had finally become the King of Protecia, and there was nothing more that can be done to stop him.

In fury, Beatrice managed to push out some words. The dagger was still clenched tightly in her hand, and now it was shaking with fear as well as fury. Alexander still did not allow that blade to creep any closer to his neck than it already was. "A high assassination? What do you think you just did to her?" It was the only thing Beatrice could think to say. He had accused Beatrice of attempting an assassination when he had just done the same thing to secure his title. Anything she said could not change the fact of his bloodline, but there were guards here. Their hearing this may cause the beginnings of dislike towards King Alexander, and that was a beginning at least. Even a revolt and the end of their way of life would seem desirable to King Alexander's rule.

Still, even under this degree of pressure, Alexander answered in the same calm and composed voice he had always spoken in. "I did no such thing. She took it upon herself to trek through a mysterious portal into an unexplored, uncharted world. She was killed by one of the native creatures to that world. There was nothing I could have done to stop her voyage or her death." A smile began to develop on Alexander's face. He seemed to have impressed even himself with that excuse. "If you insist on saying she was assassinated, the only suspect should be the child, herself."

Just as Alexander spoke these words, he noticed the two people standing at the opening to that chapel-like room of the caves. It was time for the guards to rotate, and the two new guards had just arrived. There were now four in total. Just out of sight from that room, Cassandra was standing. When she saw Alexander passing through the portal, she ducked away from the two guards she had arrived with and now was hiding from her former master. She had her back pressed against the cold wall of the cave inside a small recess in its surface. A shadow was obscuring her from view, but if anyone listened too closely, they would hear her spastic and frightened breathing. Maybe even hear the thudding of her heart. The sight of Alexander standing there in the caves was too much for her to face. After seeing him there, she had to hide herself from him. There was no telling what would be done to her if her involvement in helping Beatrice became known to Alexander, and Cassandra wished to postpone that knowledge as long as she possibly could.

"Guards!" Alexander called out, and the four guards began to walk towards Beatrice and him. As they were walking over, Beatrice seemed to grow faint. The dagger slipped from her hand and landed on the stone of the cave floor. As she stared at Alexander, the tears flowing from her eyes intensified. The guards finally approached her from behind, and Alexander began to give them orders immediately. "I want this woman arrested for crimes against the people of the Protecia Kingdom. She is to be executed upon her arrival at the prison." Two of the guards immediately grabbed Beatrice's arms and began to escort her away from Alexander. Beatrice seemed too shocked to actually fight back in any way. She just obediently let them walk her away. It seemed as though they were already halfway out of the caves before Beatrice even realized that she was moving. The servant was in the numb state of shock after the queen died in her arms, and there seemed to be little that could have rescued her from that state.

Two guards remained. Alexander looked at the first one and said, "I am going to be making a public address to announce my ascension in one hour. Send out the horsemen to tell everyone in the kingdom." The guard began to walk away when Alexander added, "Anyone who fails to be in the courtyard when I begin speaking is to be killed. Understand?" The guard, trying his best to mask the disgust he felt, grunted a response and began to leave the caves.

The last guard just looked at Alexander for a moment. Finally, the guard asked, "What about her?" He nodded towards the dead girl on the floor of the cave. The light from the openings in the cave wall seemed to brighten slightly and began to gleam off of her blood-soaked body making her look more like an angel than ever. For a moment, the guard feared that asking such a question would mean certain death, but he did not see an angered look on Alexander's face. Soon, he realized that the new king was just thinking of an appropriate answer.

Finally, he said, "Burn her." The guard froze in fear. Just the sound of those words was enough to send chills down his spine. Even though he was trying not to, he knew his eyes were bulging in horror at the task ahead. "Burn her and throw whatever's left into the Particion River." The look on the guard's face did not change, but he felt a twisting pain in his stomach. "And I want you to get her mother, and do the same with her. Now, go." The guard turned around and left the caves as calmly as he possibly could. The very idea of what was being asked of him was simply too much to handle. He felt an acidic burn creeping its way up from his stomach, but he managed to hold back the vomit until he was far from Alexander's sight.

An instant later, Alexander walked from the caves with his cape lashing behind him. As soon as he was gone, Cassandra crept out of the small hollow in the wall she had been hiding in. She quietly looked around to see if there was anyone left in the caves. The rocky passageways seemed to be deserted, so she walked out into the room with the portal. First, she saw the rock had been moved in the way of the small side cave. Although she could not be certain, Cassandra thought she heard a faint growling from behind it. Then, she saw Angelica, and tears found their way to her own eyes. For a moment, Cassandra could not even remember that a few short weeks ago, she was conspiring with Alexander to kill this young girl. Cassandra walked over to the body, and then she saw the dagger on the ground.

Slowly, Cassandra lifted the dagger, and it glowed in the light from the openings above. Its gleam was almost blinding, but Cassandra could not look away. Her vision was filled with the sight of the light reflecting off the dagger. After all she had done, this dagger seemed like the way to make up for her crimes. Crimes against morality rather than the kingdom. She had heard all the orders that Alexander had just given, and she knew exactly what he was trying to do. Destroy the bodies of Wilhelmina and Angelica, and it would be impossible to complete this side of the sculpture. Only his side, the sinister side, would be the one that it would be possible to complete after that. Cassandra took the dagger and left the caves already sorting out what she would do in her mind. It was time for her penance.

"She must have gotten back. I told her to, and I saw her running that way." Bryan was looking calmly towards the others that were standing there. With the exception of Martin and David, they had all survived this attack. The beasts had all either found their way back to the woods or the caves or had been killed. None remained to fight them now, so the remnants of their group managed to meet together in the middle of the courtyard. For the first time, this meeting was not in a hidden location but right out in the open.

Michael walked towards Bryan and whispered, "Did you see where Protace went?" It seemed as if the world stopped for a moment. At some time during this whole confrontation, Protace had managed to get away. His staff was lying on the ground near to where the iron bars that held the beasts once stood. "Do you think he got back to his palace?"

There was an uneasy silence for a few moments. As most citizens, none of them knew where Protace's palace was even located. It was carved into the mountain, but aside from that, it could have been anywhere. Michael was finally the one who said, "He always appeared from behind the platform, so the entrance to the palace must be back there. Right?" It did seem to make sense. So the remaining eight of them walked over towards the ladder to the platform and quickly climbed up.

From there, they did not know how to proceed. The wall of mountain behind the platform seemed unflawed and entirely without caves, caverns, or recesses. Still, they felt obligated to look. The eight of them spread out on the platform and began to examine the contours of the stone wall behind it. After only a few minutes, one of the farmers from Protecia found something.

When he called everyone over, it was immediately decided that this must be the entrance to the palace. It was a small opening in the ground of the platform all the way against the wall. From the looks of it, this passage seemed far back enough so it would not lead into the cage filled with the beasts, not that it would matter now since that cage was empty. The sunlight shone part of the way down this opening, and they could not see any ladders or ropes on the way down. Just a drop that looked as if it was at least fifteen feet deep.

Bryan was the first to volunteer to go down. Even though it appeared like a straight and quick drop, Bryan thought it seemed like the best option they had. He slowly positioned himself over the opening and began to slide down. What no one realized was that the passageway was so narrow that friction was enough to slow you on the way down. Bryan landed comfortably on his feet just beneath where the shadows ended.

As the others followed him down, Bryan took a few steps into that first corridor of the palace. Although it was not as ornate as the palace in Protecia, it was more elaborately decorated than any other place in this world. Stone and wooden carvings lined the walls, and the arched doorways seemed as though they led to an endless number of rooms.

It only took a minute for all of the remaining group members to slide down the passage into the palace. Soon, they were spreading out through the corridors of the stone castle, trying to keep from marveling at the beautiful ornamentation that surrounded them. Images of the beasts and the monster Alexander became when he held the staff covered the walls along with sculptures of trees and wildlife. The palace seemed to be deserted, but they searched anyway. Although they could not find its source, the faint crying of several infants could be heard from within the labyrinth of the palace. Protace had a way of hiding when he was being looked for, so they all kept looking through the seemingly endless rooms.

Even though they did not find Protace in the palace, they did find the two children of Martin and Lenore. The older child was too scared to speak to any of them. However, he did not need to say a word for them to understand that his time here was not a pleasant one. There was a large welt under one eye that nearly kept the lid swollen shut. To go with this, he had a split lip and a jaggedly slanted nose that must have been broken. There was a crust of dried blood under his nose and around his lips. The younger child's face was unharmed. There were bloodstains around the waist of the cloth he was wrapped in, however. When they found the two of them, they were embracing each other in the corner of what appeared to be Protace's bedroom. The two children joined the group as they continued to patrol from room to room looking for Protace.

CHAPTER THIRTY-TWO

Living God

Cassandra slowly made her way out of the caves and began to walk the path across the front of the palace towards the prison. Knowing that Beatrice would put up as much of a fight as possible, Cassandra was fairly certain she did not have to run to catch up with them. If she was going to do anything at this point to stop Alexander from destroying their civilization as its king, she was going to need Beatrice's help to do it.

It only took a couple of minutes before Cassandra rounded the corner of the palace and was looking at the two guards escorting Beatrice to the prison. They were getting very close, so Cassandra had to act quickly. She could not be certain, but it seemed as though Beatrice saw or sensed her approaching and was ready for whatever was going to happen. With a deep sigh, Cassandra began to act.

After a moment to mentally ready herself, Cassandra began to charge towards the closer of the two guards with the dagger extended out in front of her. Cassandra did not make a sound as she ran up, and with the commotion that Beatrice was causing, the guards could not hear a thing. They did not even have a chance to react. She plunged the dagger into the throat of the guard on Beatrice's right. He let out a quick yelp that changed to a gurgling sound as he fell to the ground. Immediately, the other guard turned to Cassandra looking ready to fight back. He, however, also did not get that chance. Once she was released from the iron grasps of the guards' hands, Beatrice reached into the black pouch and removed the slingshot. Without having the time to waste loading it with the metal discs, she used the slingshot itself as a weapon. While the guard was turned to face Cassandra and reaching for his sword, Beatrice threw the rope of the slingshot over his head, and it fell around his neck. With a quick pull, the guard fell backwards. Slowly, Beatrice guided him to the ground by the neck, and soon he was lying defenseless before them. Cassandra immediately fell to the ground beside him and plunged the dagger into his chest.

The door to the prison was opening up. Behind it was the same old man that had always been there. He was old and hunched over with a pockmarked face and thinning white hair. He did not look able to fight, but all he needed to do was call attention to them. More guards would get there in a matter of seconds, and the two women were in no condition to withstand that kind of assault. Beatrice ran up to him while drawing back her clenched fist. When she got close enough, she struck him in the side of the head with all her fury towards Alexander behind her. He began to fall from what seemed more like shock than from her blow, and on his way down, he struck his head on the side of the prison wall. The old man seemed alive, but certainly injured and unconscious. That was all they needed.

Still, they did not have much time. Without saying anything, they began to grab hold of the three bodies, one alive and two dead, on the ground. They had to be brought out of plain sight, so they began to drag them through the opened prison door. It only took a minute, and soon all three of them were hidden inside the prison. The old man who had served as the prison's warden began to scream for help while this was being done. The two women ignored the noise and quickly exited the prison. The screaming soon died away. By the time any reinforcements arrived, if they even did arrive, the two women were gone.

Only about twenty feet from the prison door, Cassandra began to tell Beatrice everything she heard in the caves. All of Alexander's plans became known between the two women, and they began to think of ways to undo them. They spoke for a few minutes as people began to walk towards the courtyard. Each wore an aggravated look on their face. Alexander's sudden decision of having an address that everyone was forced to attend required all of them to drop whatever they were doing to show their support for the new king. This was what made Beatrice and Cassandra realize they were running out of time. The address was going to start soon.

Inside the last royal crypt in the row, two guards were standing. There was a single stone square that they were removing from a long series of them. Carved across the front of this one was the name, "WILHELMINA." The stone square was placed on the ground alongside the opening it now left in the wall. The putrid smell of death plumed from the crypt in a hiss as the marker was removed. In the darkness was the body of the late Queen Wilhelmina. It was beginning to decay, and pieces of bone were starting to show through the rotting skin. The stench wafted up into the air and filled the room. It was so strong that the guards had to back off for a few seconds to let the smell dissipate. Then, they finally had to begin the slow process of removing the body from what was supposed to be its final resting place.

They placed the body on a sheet of cloth and began to carry it out towards the immense grill within the basement of the palace. Once that body was there, they would go back into the caves to retrieve Angelica's body and bring it there as well. Then, the mother and daughter would both be cremated together under the orders of the new king. They would be burned and then disposed of in a river so that no one would ever be able to find them again. Then, Alexander would be certain to have his side of the wall completed and along with that the chaos that would ensue.

Terrified looks passed among the people that were walking to the courtyard when they saw the remains of the woman who ruled them over a month ago. They all watched and wondered what was going to happen to her at the same time that they pondered why Alexander had suddenly reappeared. They knew the answers would be too terrifying to search for, so they simply let the questions remained unsettled. In the palace, answers had a way of being found if you were patient enough.

"You've got to stop them from burning those bodies," Beatrice whispered to Cassandra. "If he does that, there won't be any way of stopping him from building his link between the worlds. After all he did, we can't let him rule these people. Do you have any idea what would happen?"

Cassandra had only the slightest of idea about what would happen if he was to rule there. It never occurred to her that someone could be capable of the atrocities that were taking place in the other world. Forcing people to arrive to his addresses hours ahead of time to ensure that they would not be the last ones to show up. Daily executions. People afraid to live in their own homes. Treating their ruler as if he was a god. Cassandra would not have believed that all of this could have been the actions of a single person, but she said she knew anyway. After working for Alexander for all those years, she had only a faint idea of what he was capable of, and that scared her enough.

"I'm going to see if I can get into the courtyard unnoticed." Beatrice looked determined. It was the same look Angelica had on her face when she marched from the platform to the caves after the first attempt on her life had been made. Cassandra knew there was no stopping Beatrice, so she just nodded instead. One of Beatrice's shaking hands touched the surface of the black sack attached to her belt. She whispered in the voice of a maniac, "I'm going to make sure his rule is a short-lived one."

With that, Beatrice stormed away, and Cassandra was left alone. She had to find where the guards were going to burn the remains of the past two rulers of the kingdom. Alexander's projects left a fire burning nearly every hundred feet from the natural gases harvested in the caves. That left a great deal of distance to be covered, and not a lot of time to do it in. Cassandra began to run to try to find the spot these guards had chosen before it was too late.

The decaying body of Wilhelmina was rolled haphazardly from the cloth it had been carried in to a metal grill. This grill stretched back for about ten feet, and currently the coals underneath it stood silent and cold. No one had started the fire yet. The guards turned quickly and left without igniting the flames. They would get Angelica's body first and burn the two of them together. Outwardly, they said it would be more efficient that way, but deep down, it was because they did not want to stay there long enough to watch two bodies burn separately. Letting them burn together would mean less time they would have to stay and watch this nightmare.

"He's not here." Bryan had just reentered the small room by the passage to the platform. The rest of the group was already there, and they all bore the same puzzled expressions on their faces. "We searched the entire palace, and no one is here. Protace must have found some other way out."

They all nodded and murmured agreement, but no one wanted to say anything. Every room they could find in the beautifully ornate palace had been searched. Not one guard or a single servant had been found there. There was absolutely no trace of Protace hiding in any of the rooms either. It seemed as though he had just vanished. They knew the staff had a great deal of power, but no one had ever seen Protace make himself disappear with it. Besides, the staff had been nowhere near him when they last saw Protace on top of the platform. It was down in the courtyard.

Michael finally spoke up. "He didn't enter the palace, and courtyard was filled with beasts. It would have been too much of a risk, even for him, to try getting into the village through that way. Where else could he go?" There was a single moment of terrified realization for all of them. What Michael had said was true. He could not have gotten to the village, and he did not go into the palace. That left only one place for him to retreat. Through the portal and back to the other world.

The members of the group, along with the two children, went back to the passageway they had previously gone down. While searching the palace, they discovered another passageway that was a little ways down from the first one. It had a rope attached to it and appeared to join the other passage at a fork right near the top. As before, Bryan grabbed hold of the rope and began to pull his way up first. After about a minute, he emerged from the passageway back onto the platform. Everyone, including Martin and Lenore's two children, followed behind him quickly.

Cassandra continued running from one bonfire to another seeing that each was burning brightly without a sign of the guards or the kingdom's previous two rulers. She found it ironic that these fires were fueled from the gases harvested from the caves and lit under Alexander's order. It seemed like so much of their kingdom revolved around the caves and the mountains. It was the boundary of their world and lately the passageway to a new world. This made her think of Alexander possibly ruling the two worlds, and that thought horrified her more now than it had in the past months. Now, it seemed as though it may become a reality. She continued to run getting farther and farther from the opening to the caves, and there was no sign of what she was looking for. Soon, Cassandra began to feel faint, but she knew she had to keep going.

Then, an idea occurred to her. The guards would not want to do something like this out in the open. Just carrying the two bodies through the kingdom would be enough to rouse unneeded attention to Alexander's plans, so they would want to find someplace secluded and close to the palace. That only left the grill located in the back room of the palace basement. It was constructed a few years back for the purpose of burning garbage and dead animals found near the palace. To Cassandra's knowledge, no one had ever placed a human body upon it, but she had the idea that with Alexander in charge, there would be a lot more of that in the near future. This was the only place it would make any sense to carry out such a gruesome task. Cassandra began to run towards the palace.

Beatrice began to force her way towards the center of the growing crowd. Staying too far towards the front or back may attract attention. Being off to the sides would be too difficult to get a clear shot at Alexander. She had to remain right in the middle of the crowd and hope that none of Alexander's guards spot her. The kingdom's people were densely packing themselves into the courtyard to hear the words their new king had to give them. Never before had a king required all the citizens to attend an address, and the courtyard was not meant to hold all of the people of Protecia. There had been no time to set out tables or meals or entertainment, but Beatrice also thought that with such a king, no one would bother with such frivolities anyway. People were just crowding in, barely speaking to one another, and looking generally upset. Still, they moved to the side to allow Beatrice to get through towards the middle of the courtyard.

For the time being, Beatrice just waited. She did not want to start preparing the slingshot just yet. If a guard was to see her with it, she would surely be killed on the spot. Alexander was not even on the platform yet, so Beatrice decided to wait. With her eyes on the ground so as to avoid looking at anyone, Beatrice just stood in the center of the courtyard waiting. The servant whose job it was to announce the members of the royal family before an address was now walking up onto the platform. It was about to begin.

The caves lit up with a nearly blinding light that emanated from the entire wall. They were all coming through. A little bit at a time, the light got dimmer and eventually went out entirely. All of the members of the group that had failed in assassinating Protace and Soranace were not here to try again against Alexander.

They all stumbled from the wall and took a few steps away from it. Behind them, the wall was nearly smooth. The only figures still appearing on it were the broken pieces of Protace's staff, David and Chenrile. He was still covered in his costume, sitting on the floor with it swirled around him and a single rose caught in its folds. His eyes still looked content, unlike how they did on the other world a moment before being attacked by the beasts.

After a few seconds, one of the guards that originally was from Protecia and was now just returning through the portal made a horrible discovery. There was a large stain of blood on the ground just by the wall. They all stopped and looked at it for a second already beginning to deny what they knew to be true. Angelica must have been killed. The beast's image was not on the wall behind them either, and that meant it was now here, in this world. From where they stood, the group members could hear the snarling from the nearby cave, and they knew it to be true.

There was no denying that horrible truth now. Angelica must have been killed by one of the beasts as soon as she entered this world. After all she had been through, her battle was finally lost in the middle of a nearly uncharted cavern. It was hard to believe, but that was exactly what happened. Similar to the way Beatrice had come to this knowledge, so did the group members. In a moment of absolute terror, they began to realize that Alexander was in fact the king in this world as well.

In the other world, there was sight that no one was around to witness. That side of the wall was almost completed. Protace stood with his arms outstretched and fire blazing behind him. One of the beasts was curled at his feet like an obedient pet. Everyone else was in pain. Wilhelmina stood in terror holding Angelica to the wall behind her. The other group members were standing in a variety of contorted, twisting positions with looks of utter disgust and agony on their faces. They all just stood there, frozen in time with the exception of David, Soranace, and Protace's staff. There were empty spaces for those items as well, but that may change in within the next day.

Two guards opened the wooden door at the back of the palace and walked in carrying the body of Angelica in a bloodstained sheet. With slightly more care than with Wilhelmina, the guards placed the body on the grill. Mother and daughter were lying side by side as this horrible task was about to begin. One of the guards, the one Alexander had ordered to do so in the caves, walked to the side of the grill and ignited it.

There was a soft popping sound as flames roared from underneath the two bodies. Gas was being pumped directly from the caves to the bottom of this grill allowing for the palace's garbage to be burned. Now, it was the past two rulers that were being burned here. It was horrible, and the guards both kept their eyes focused on the ground at their feet rather than the grill just before them.

The hair and clothes were the first to ignite. They burst into flames in a matter of seconds. The first arms of fire reached high, but did not come near to the high ceiling of this room. Unable to block out the sound, the guards just listened to the roaring of the fire as the two past queens were being burned before them. It only took a minute for the hair and clothes to burn away, and then the flesh began to sear. The smell of roasting meat filled the room, and the guards, despite the fact that they were looking away, both closed their eyes in sorrow.

During the past years, their kingdom had been a glorious one. The citizens were prosperous and content. They were always well fed and well-tended to. Whatever problems they experienced were met by quick resolutions. It was all the work of Queen Wilhelmina, and now, their queen, after being robbed from the people by an assassin's arrow, was burning. It was an insult to the kingdom that could not be paralleled.

"The ruler of the Protecian Kingdom! His royal highness, the King Alexander!" These words died in the air as soon as the servant atop the platform called them out. Alexander, with a sickening grin twisted across his face, began to walk across to the center of the platform. There was no more walking all the way to the end to be ignored for him now. He was the king, the ruler of these people, and he was the only one they were here to listen to.

No one applauded. There were not even the heartless claps that usually accompanied the calling of the Royal Bachelor's name. Nothing. Not a single sound was uttered in the courtyard. Each time Alexander's foot hit the platform it was clearly heard by everyone there. Angered faces stared up at him knowing that the only possible reason for him being here was due to the death of Angelica. Although no one had heard any news of her death, it was the only thing that could have possible happened. Otherwise Alexander would not dare call himself their ruler.

When King Alexander assumed his position between the staring stone images of Protace and Soranace, a great wind began to strengthen around him. His cape lifted into the air and began to blow to his right. This black streak behind him appeared like an indicator of the dark years ahead for these people under his rule.

Cassandra stormed through the main entrance to the palace. There was no one there. Everyone would be in the courtyard, and that included all the servants and guards that normally occupied the palace during the day. Anyone could have walked in to do anything he or she pleased, but this did not concern Cassandra now. She just wanted to get to the back of the palace to stop the incineration of those two bodies.

She ran across the lobby with its mural of Protace building the bridge that made him the ruler and god of the people. Through the hallways built under the order of Soranace's daughter, Queen Alleha, the forth ruler of Protecia. Past the corridors where years ago assassins killed King Jonathan and nearly a third of the royal heirs. Despite the pain in her legs and chest, her shortness of breath, and the dizziness that had begun to set in, Cassandra continued to run through the hallways where Prince Victor and his family were abducted before being exiled from Protecia. Through the lavishly decorated gold and marble, past the jewels and beads that lined the walls, Cassandra continued to run to get to the back of the palace.

The group slowly navigated their way through the caves. None of them had made this trip without Beatrice guiding them before, and they were not exactly sure of the path to take. At every turn, they checked for the scratch left by a sword blade over a month ago. That was how these caves were navigated at that time, and it still served as a good indication of where they were going. However, it took a very long time.

Each turn they encountered was met with a careful examination of the walls around them. The marks had faded considerably in that time, and no one had ever bothered to refresh them. Besides that, they did not have any torches with them, and the light from the room they had come from and the room they were heading for was drastically fading. They moved slowly through the corridors knowing that one wrong turn could very easily mean being trapped down here forever.

After about half an hour, they began to see a light ahead of them. The entrance to the cave must have been nearing, and they began to run. Time was very important in a situation like this one. If they did not get there to stop Alexander in time, there was no telling what atrocities would be awaiting the people of Protecia.

"First, it is my responsibility to inform you of some very sad, very tragic news." Alexander managed to keep the grin from his face for the time being. It would seem in bad taste if he were to show his smile while telling of Angelica's death. "Your Queen Angelica died earlier today. She was the victim of an attack by a wild animal, and due to the absence of the royal physician, there was nothing that could be done to save her. However, her passing was a quick one, and we must be thankful for that."

With a deep sigh, Alexander continued. As he spoke, the smile on his face continuously widened. "That makes me the king." There was another pause that Alexander expected to be filled with applause. As before, the courtyard was plagued with total silence. "I intend to make a great deal of changes to the civilization as you know it. For too long, we have been ruled by people concerned with only their well-being and their ability to bring themselves wealth and good fortune. All under the claim that it was the will of Protace and Soranace. I intend to change that."

Beatrice began to look up at Alexander, the new king. Even though he was on this world without his staff, she did not see a human standing on the platform speaking to the people. Despite his lack of claws, fangs, and black eyes, Beatrice saw this creature for exactly what he was. When she looked up at the speaker on the platform, Beatrice saw a monster. Without her even realizing it, Beatrice began to run her fingers along the bag attached to her belt.

"I intend to change all of that." Everyone looked on anxiously as Alexander spoke. He was openly saying that he planned to alter everything in their kingdom. The people were in shock, and they were scared. "We are going to begin a new order of rule here. The old ways will be removed in favor of the new ways. My ways." With that, the sculptures of Protace and Soranace began to move. The crowd panicked for a moment, and then they realized that this was something Alexander had planned. Those movements were not caused by some supernatural force from the people these statues represented. Guards had attached chains to them and were pulling them back under Alexander's careful direction.

From the small space between the platform and the rest of the mountain range, the guards were continuing to pull on their chains. The statues lurched and shook as they did this, but they did not move. For hundreds of years, they remained in that exact spot, and they refused to give up this foothold. They rumbled and groaned but stood strong. After about a minute, they finally gave way. The series of five guards standing behind the platform ran as the two sculptures fell backwards. As they fell, they hit the mountain range and began to break apart and crumble. By the time there were nearly to the ground, they had already been reduced to about ten pieces each, and as soon as they hit the ground, they crumbled to thousands of pieces of rubble.

Cassandra slammed all of her weight against the door made of wooden planks. It flew opened quickly and she stormed in holding Angelica's dagger ahead of her. "Stop that!" she cried, and the two guards turned to look at her. They did not move or react in any other way. "Get them off that flame, now!" The guards were looking at her desperately. They wanted nothing more than to do what she asked, but they knew the consequences of disobeying Alexander all too well. Finally, Cassandra cried out, "Under the orders of King Alexander, get them off that grill."

This was what the guards needed to hear. As one immediately slid the nearby sheet of metal directly under the grill to smother the fire, the other began to reach for Angelica. She was lying closest to the edge of the grill, and she was the easiest to remove. Within a few seconds, they guard had removed Angelica's dead and charred body from the grill, and he began to reach for Wilhelmina.

Cassandra felt she had to stop and look at Angelica for a moment. Her hair was burned down to the scalp, and her skin was riddled with the dark lines where the fire had burned her. Most of her body seemed intact, though. Still, she looked as if she was in much more pain than she appeared lying dead on the floor of the cave where Cassandra had seen her not too long ago. Now, not even her body was allowed to rest.

"I am the one you should fall to your knees to worship!" Alexander's voice rang out to the people. He was standing with just a mountain off in the distance behind him. The people watched uneasily as a new leader spoke, but for the first time their ruler did not have the critical eyes of Protace and Soranace watching from behind. He was alone one on the platform speaking of how he would change the world as they knew and understood it.

Beatrice did not just stare idly as the others did. Her hand was fully inside of the pouch, and she was removing the slingshot. It fit in her hand naturally as she lifted it towards her eyes. No one saw her doing this. Everyone's eyes were completely fixed on King Alexander.

"I am the one you should give your lives to protect!" He continued yelling his words towards the crowds that had no choice but to listen to him. The wind continued whipping past him pulling his cape along to his side. The pale sky behind him contrasted with the blackness of his cape and his clothes making him look like a black tumor in the pristine and clear sky.

Beatrice was reaching for the first of the metal discs as Alexander called out, "I am your ruler!" The edge of the disc sliced along Beatrice's thumb, but she barely felt it. She just removed the disc from its pouch with her blood dripping across its shining surface. "I am your savior!" She placed the disc into its pouch at the end of the slingshot. "I am your god!" Panicked now that this moment had actually come, Beatrice looked up again. Her eyes scanned the faces of everyone around her. They were not only listening, but they actually believed everything he said. "Fall to your knees!" Whether it was just because he was the last one with Protace's blood or because they truly thought that he was a god, all of these people were simply standing and awaiting his next command. "Fall to your knees and hear me!" The last word resonated off the rocky surfaces of the mountains for what seemed like ten minutes, and Alexander seemed ecstatic at hearing it echo back to him after finally having the opportunity to speak it. It was a speech he had waited for years to call out into the crowd.

Just like well-disciplined animals, everyone in attendance began to fall to the ground on bent knee. In the crowded courtyard, people were bumping into one another, but no one cared in the slightest. They just fell down to their knees to listen to Alexander's next words. All, but Beatrice. She stood perfectly still like a giant surrounding the knee-bound courtyard. She looked directly at King Alexander and hurled the first disc towards him.

It glided easily through the air just as the wind began to die away. The hem of Alexander's cape fell down to his ankles and that disc drifted through the air towards him letting out the tiniest of whistles as it did. Just as Wilhelmina had done, Alexander froze in shock and fear. He did not know what to do. He never expected anything like this to happen to him. The others were understandable casualties, but this was him. How could someone from this world be making as attempt at his life?

Alexander just stood there as if he was made of stone. No one in the crowd knew what to do. Just like the assassination of Wilhelmina and the attempt on Angelica during their addresses, the crowd only stood and gawked in shock, watching this disc glide through the air towards their king. It was glistening in the bright sunlight, and nearly looked like a single star flying across the courtyard towards Alexander. He simply stood still and stared at it approaching.

The disc was slightly off target. It plunged into Alexander's left shoulder and tore right through him, exploding through the back of his shoulder blade. In shock and surprise, he jumped back a step as the disc hit him. Through clenched teeth, Alexander let out a shriek of pain, and his hand went up to cover the new wound. A second later, he brought his hand away from his shoulder clenching a fist as he did. When he dragged his fingers across his palm to loosen that fist, he saw his fingernails scraping a dark patch of blood away from four crisp lines leaving the pale white of his palm exposed. There was no denying it now. Someone had tried to kill him.

As Alexander stared at his own blood on his palm, Beatrice grabbed the next disc out of the bag. She began to load it into the slingshot when she saw eyes falling upon her. These eyes were both shocked and enraged. More so than anything else, they each contained a furious danger within them. The people saw what she was doing, and they were going to do exactly as King Alexander demanded of them. They were going to sacrifice their lives to protect him. Whether it was because Alexander was the last living person with Protace's blood or if they actually believed his claim to be their god, they were going to try to stop her from assassinating their king.

Without any time to waste, Beatrice quickly spun that disc around to build up speed, and then she hurled it towards the platform. It glided as gently as the first one had done. The sun again made it glow in the sky. As it found its way towards King Alexander, people in the crowd, not guards but ordinary citizens, were trying to fight their way towards Beatrice. She was going to have to act quickly if she was to get that last disc into the air before it was too late.

The second disc made it to the platform faster than the first. This one sailed through the side of Alexander's neck without even slowing down. Still, Alexander found himself backing away another step as it hit him. He was now only about five feet from the back edge of the platform. Where he was now standing was where the statue of Protace had been standing moments ago, and where it had stood undisturbed for hundreds of years. Blood began to find its way from his neck wound in great spurts. Despite his efforts to slow the bleeding with his hand, it found its way through his fingertips and splattered across the platform almost far enough to start raining on the crowd.

With the sun beating down on her and the infuriated citizens finding their way towards her, Beatrice loaded the last of the discs into the slingshot. She began to spin it. A man, someone she had known and been friendly with for years, broke through the crowd and began to raise a hand to strike her. Beatrice knew she did not have any time to waste. With one great heave, she thrust the last of the discs into the air just as the man batted her arm down with one of his own.

The disc wobbled through the air for a moment as it began to reach higher into the sky. As it found its way above the heads of the people in the crowd, that last disc straightened its path and began to ride smoothly towards its target. The sun did not shine off of this one. It seemed to consume it entirely. The glare from that disc was so bright that no one in the courtyard could bear to look at it. Even Alexander had to look away knowing that he may very die as a consequence of that.

A crowd of five people formed around Beatrice. The first blow was to her left eye, and it sent bright explosions of color across her field of vision. They began to beat her with their fists and kick her with their feet. The slingshot slipped from her hand and landed quietly on the courtyard ground. Beatrice fell to the ground next. There was blood flowing from her head and nose. Bruises were already beginning to swell up on her face and around her eyes. Still, the fists and feet kept coming almost as if it show what Alexander's rule would have done to these people if given the chance.

The disc gave off its blazing light as it glided easily towards King Alexander seeming to pick up speed as it went. The king screamed at it as if that would stop it from flying towards him. It was the horrible shriek that the monster gave. Finally, the disc struck him.

It imbedded itself about an inch into Alexander's forehead. At a diagonal, it cut through his eyebrow and crushed the right side of his skull. Alexander went flying backwards with the force of that blow. His scream became the shrill howl of the monster he was in the other world. Then, it faded to nothing. Alexander flew backwards through the air off the back of the platform and began to fall. His body limply tumbled down to the crushed statues of Protace and Soranace below. It landed atop the crumbled rock and slid down the gravelly mount until it came to rest about halfway to the ground.

As the crowd began to progress towards a riot, the remnants of the group from other world emerged from the caves. They saw the unoccupied platform and the growing mob in the center of the courtyard. As if planned and practiced, the group began to filter into the people trying to get towards the center where Beatrice was slowly being beaten to death.

Beatrice was lying on the ground now, unable to fight off the continuing blows and no longer willing to even try. Still, the punches and kicks did not slow down. In fact, they became more intense. Blood was flowing down Beatrice's body in a dozen places. She did nothing to stop them. At this point, she felt certain that she would die lying there on the dirt in the middle of the courtyard.

Under the endless blows, Beatrice understood she would be killed by a mob of people she smiled into the faces of for years, not even knowing if she had succeeded in killing King Alexander or if he had survived her attack.

The group closed in around Beatrice appearing as if they were nothing more than angered citizens planning on putting in their own blows to the woman who had attacked their king. This allowed them to get right up close amidst the constant punches and kicks. As soon as they surrounded Beatrice, they all picked her up so that she was standing on her feet, and began to walk away from the crowd with her.

In the confusion of the fight and the assassination, the crowd did not realize what was happening until Beatrice was nearly to the other side of the courtyard, limping along with the help of five others and leaving a trail of blood behind her. The other group members formed a protective shell around Beatrice so that any citizens still desperate to get in their punch would not be able to.

Judging from the density of the crowd, the only way they would be able to get out of the courtyard would be to go farther from the palace. That was the only place where the crowd was thinning out. So the group began to walk Beatrice in that direction when she stopped walking and whispered, "I have to see him." They all stopped walking for a second even though it meant giving up some of their head start. "I have to see that he's dead." They were already to the side of the courtyard, and going the rest of the way to the platform would not be much of a detour at this point. It seemed as if her request was not unwarranted. After everything Alexander had put them through, Beatrice wanted to make sure that it was really over.

With Bryan in the lead, the group progressed slowly towards the small opening behind the platform. They half expected Alexander, or more likely, Protace, to be standing there waiting for them when they arrived. Beatrice expected the same thing, but her fear was much worse than all of the others put together. Finally, they reached the small opening behind the platform and were able to see Alexander.

The dead body of Protecia's last king was lying on a pile of broken rocks that had once been the monumental sculptures of Protace and Soranace. Blood was dripping away from him and forming trails across the pale gray stone. Alexander was just lying there, halfway down the mound of rocks with one dead arm curled around a single image in the stone. Almost as if caressing what he had tried himself to be, Alexander's arm was curled around the stone head of Protace. Blood dripped across the image of their founder's face staining it with the new truths they discovered about his rule and his life.

Aside from a small and rapidly diminishing pocket of people, everyone still looked up to Protace as a great god and the ruler that helped everyone around him shed the chains of barbarism and become civilized people. After all they had researched, it seemed that this was not what really happened. The stories they had read about Protace's staff were true. It made him into a monster, and anyone who tried to stop him from what he wanted so much just vanished into thin air. Now, Alexander, trying to achieve the same viscous goal, was lying dead atop the wrecked ruins of his mentor.

The entire group that surrounded Beatrice turned and began on its way past the angry mob towards the palace. Halfway across, they met Cassandra, and she simply merged to their side. They all walked towards the palace together. Beatrice had wounds that needed to be cared for, and then, they had to see if they could alter Alexander's plan into one that would unite their worlds under kindness and happiness rather than terror and fear.

CHAPTER THIRTY-THREE

Building the Bridge between Worlds

About three hours later, another crowd had formed inside the caves. Beatrice and Cassandra were right there, and aside from them, it was everyone that was able to travel between the worlds. Even the dead bodies of Wilhelmina, Angelica and Alexander were lying on the ground of the caves. They all just stared ahead at the nearly blank wall. Only David, Chenrile, dressed as a court jester, and the broken pieces of Protace's staff were visible on this side. The two people seemed happy in these sculptures even though they were dead in that other world. They probably were happy. As all of them have wanted to do, they died in the service of a great ruler.

First, Bryan went through the portal. He jumped into the water as he had only a few times before. Everyone watched anxiously as if they expected something different to happen this time. However, as they watched, the same rumbling rose up in the caves, and a stone image of Bryan pushed itself through the wall into its place on the relief sculpture. He was lying on the ground looking up above him with a wide smile on his face and eyes that looked perfectly at peace.

It was decided that the hardest parts of the trip would be done first. Some of the guards that were able to pass through the portal approached the large rock just opposite the wall of sculptures. Just as they began to near it, the loud snarling and hissing rose up from behind it. The beast was still locked back there, and since it was part of the wall just as everyone else was, it had to go through to the other side.

The guards pushed the rock back slightly so that one quarter of the opening to the small side-cavern was exposed, and then they stood back to watch. The sound of the growling intensified and then stopped. There was no visible movement from within those shadowy depths. For a few seconds, nothing happened, and one of the guards took an apprehensive step forward. Maybe the creature became frightened and retreated back farther into the cavern or perhaps knew another way out it now planned to use. The guard leaned forward to look closer into the blackness when the beast leapt from the shadows. It only managed to push its snout and neck through the opened space but it was enough to make the guard jump back. This gave the guards enough of an opportunity to grab hold of it and begin dragging it to the portal. Just as Alexander's guards in the other world, they carried the beast, squirming and snapping, to the portal. Then, they simply dropped it in. A few moments passed before its image appeared on the wall.

Everyone else began to go through as well. Some carried the bodies with them. First was Alexander's corpse. The head was misshapen from its fall to the rocks and there were gouges covering the body from where Beatrice had hit him with the slingshot. A cloak of blood was beginning to crust over his face and upper torso as well. Despite the look of disgust on his face as he lifted the corpse, the farmer from the other world did it just the same. After some time had passed, Angelica was carried across. This action also elicited a disgusted look, but it was for a very different reason. Soon, Angelica was back on the other side of the portal, and her sculpture had resurfaced on this one. The last person to go through was Michael, the group member from the other world. Even though he had only the vaguest ideas of who this person was, he carried Wilhelmina's body with him as he climbed into the portal, dove in, and began to swim towards the bright and pulsing light.

There was the same rumbling sound, and soon Michael's sculpture was pushed through to the Protecian World. A moment later, the vacant space in the middle of the sculpture began to crumble. In the puff of dust that followed, Beatrice could see Wilhelmina's body coming through the wall. Her arms were stretched above her head and her palms were turned up towards the sky. The sight of her face was like a visit from a long lost, and long missed, friend. A wide smile was on her face, and Beatrice immediately felt as if all of the problems of the world had just been solved.

For one panicked moment, Beatrice and Cassandra just stared up at the sculpture. It looked beautiful. Aside from the absent image of Martin, who had vanished from wall before, everyone who was able to travel through the portal was now represented on this wall. Everyone looked completely content and happy with what they were doing. Looking at that wall was like a reminder of the way things used to be in that kingdom. The way it was before Alexander began to interfere in the business of Protecia.

Then, the image began to change. A bright glow came from around Wilhelmina's image. The sculpture itself was not glowing, but the area just the right and left began to glow a brilliant white. A moment later, the illumination stopped, and both Beatrice and Cassandra stared in anticipation of what would happen next. There was now an opening in the wall. Extending from the ground to both of Wilhelmina's outstretched arms, there were now two wide openings. They seemed to trail off into the shadows, but the two women suspected they knew exactly where they led to.

It took a few minutes, but soon they heard footsteps coming towards them through that opening. A smile grew across the faces of both Beatrice and Cassandra at the sight of Bryan staring back at them. He was the first to travel between the worlds without having to swim through the portal. He emerged beside the image of Wilhelmina, the sculpture's central figure, and he began to smile as well.

What was once thought to be two different worlds was now discovered to be one of the same world on opposite sides of a mountain range. The mountains were so vast and high that no one who that attempted to climb them had ever survived coming from either side. Now, there was no need to. A new portal was created. One that allowed anyone who wished to walk between the two worlds. Everyone else marched to the Protecia side of the mountains, and they were all happy to see that it was finally over. The portal was completed now, and it was this side, the side that seemed to represent happiness, that had completed it.

As if its job was finished, the pool began to change. The enormous leaves that flanked its sides began to grow. They reached towards the center of the pool and soon closed off that thick, rainbow-streaked water completely. There was only a solid stone structure remaining in the caves as a reminder of what everyone went through in order to combine these lands.

Everyone that was in the caves soon gathered in the palace dining hall. The chef prepared a meal for them, and they all ate heartily. In the courtyard, the angered, and now confused, crowd began to dissipate. Their future, the future of who would lead them, now was an uncertain one, but for the time being, those who had just completed the wall celebrated in the dining hall of the palace, and none of that mattered.

It was not until later on that night when Beatrice and Cassandra walked through the tunnel into the other world they had previously been unable to see. On the other side, they walked through a hole in the cave wall that was completely smooth. They were now in that other world. The world where so much had happened and so many people had died horrible deaths. Ignoring the remains of a matching pool of water on this side, they walked over to the dead bodies that were still lying right by the wall.

They were able to see that the bodies of Angelica and Wilhelmina had been carefully placed on the ground. Most likely there were people waiting right by their statues to catch them as soon as the appeared in this world. Further along the wall, the dead body of the beast and that of Alexander were intertwined with each other. Their statues must have been right next to one another. They were just lying on the stone as if they had been placed on the ground completely without care. When the beast came through, Bryan had been standing right there with his sword poised to kill it as soon as it entered this world. Alexander's body was lying just where it fell after appearing on the wall. No one had even attempted to catch it.

With a sigh, the two women walked away. The sun was setting behind them as they walked away from the wall towards the courtyard. When they arrived, they saw Protace's staff lying on the ground near the edge of the mountains. Closer to the center of the courtyard, they saw the torn and shredded remnants of Chenrile's costume. The bright colors were now dominated by red, but there was no body. Then just above the ledge, they saw David's body. He was laying there, his body completely intact facing the side of the mountain. For a while, the two women just stood and looked at this sight.

Life went on with some change. Without another heir to the throne, the only viable alternative was decided upon. The remaining members of the group that had tried to remove Protace from power on the other world formed a rule over the new unified kingdom, which now extended into both of these worlds. Beatrice and Cassandra remained living in the palace, although their duties there seemed somewhat uncertain. They tried their best to wait on these new leaders, but it did not seem like their help was needed. Beatrice was looked at as being a grieving old woman that should not be bothered with such things. On the other hand, Cassandra was never able to enter a room without distrusting eyes falling upon her and whispers filling the air. Her past was never to be forgotten.

CHAPTER THIRTY-FOUR

Mumblings in the Palace Hallways

Although she did not know it for a fact, Cassandra assumed that word began to spread of how she had helped Alexander for all those years. The diverted glances and whispers when she walked into a room soon progressed into accusations yelled at her when her back was turned. More than a few times, she was called a witch or a monster. Cassandra became an expert in ignoring these calls. She began to wear a cloak that covered her entire body and obscured her face from view. Within the folds of this cloak, although unknown by anyone, was Angelica's dagger. Cassandra knew that she would probably freeze in fear if the situation would ever come where she needed to use it, but she was more comfortable knowing it was there. Still, however, Cassandra would spend more and more time in the isolation of her quarters in the palace, only leaving when it was absolutely necessary.

Still, this was not enough. The morning that she decided to leave the palace for good started off as any other day would. Cassandra awoke when the sun washed over her room. She did not leave her quarters until the ache in her stomach was so great it was all she could think about. Over the weeks, she altered her daily routine down to one meal each day, just to keep from being out in the hallways of the palace. When that time came around on this early afternoon, Cassandra unbolted the door to her quarters and opened it to find a horrific shock on the other side.

Lying on the ground at her doorstep, in a dried puddle of blood, there was the body of a dead rat. It had been skinned, and its eyes had been burned out of their sockets. The head was lying at an unnatural angle, so Cassandra was somewhat relieved that most likely its neck was broken before the removal of its skin commenced. The most disturbing thing about this, however, was the long bone protruding from the corpse's chest. It was a horn from one of the beasts, one that would protrude from its neck to encage its head. Whoever had left this message for Cassandra meant for her to know that he could obtain such an item, and if wrestling the beasts was something he could do, Cassandra did not stand a chance.

Within a few minutes of seeing the gift left on her doorstep, Cassandra had packed whatever few personal items she felt irreplaceable into a knapsack and walked from her quarters and from the palace forever. Almost on a nightly basis for weeks from that day, a slim and sickly woman could be seen wandering the kingdom in an unflattering gray cloak as if in a daze. Her eyes would drift up towards the sky, and she would just stare in wonder. Or in terror. Alexander had a way of getting his revenge of people, and she felt that his death did not mean she was entirely safe. The fear of Alexander's ghost, or followers he still may have, was balanced with the fear of the people who hated him during his life and still saw her as his ally. Cassandra was alone in the kingdom without anyone she could trust.

In desperation, Cassandra began to proposition sexual favors in exchange for anything that she could barter for food or shelter. Regrettably, it made her more known throughout the kingdom within certain circles, but she needed some way to survive. As weeks went by, she was able to hear people speaking about her as some kind of status symbol. It became a rite of passage to the teenagers in the kingdom to have an encounter with King Alexander's old servant. Almost as if taking advantage of her in the lewdest ways imaginable made them feel like royalty for a little while. Still, Cassandra did this and pretended she could not hear the horrible things they whispered or sometimes even yelled as she slouched away into the night.

It was one such night when Cassandra was looking up at the stars with the words, "Demon whore," still fresh in her ears when things became much worse. Shattering the still of the dark and cold night, a small tree branch swung through the sky and hit her on the side of her right eye. Immediately, everything that eye saw went dark, and she began to feel disoriented and weak. Cassandra made a few lopsided steps as a cloud of darkness filled the right side of her field of view. Still, she managed to make it almost twenty feet without being hit again before she turned her head to the left to see if her assailant was still there.

All Cassandra could see behind her, almost exactly where he must have been standing when he swung the branch at her initially, was a silhouette of man against the night sky. A single man still holding the tree branch in one hand, but not pursuing her as he could have easily done. She turned away from him, and began to lurch forward again. As Cassandra walked, her head began to clear a little bit even though her vision was far from adequate. Still, she was able to reach within her cloak as she walked and remove the dagger. With a deep breath that hurt to draw in, Cassandra stopped walking and turned to face her attacker with the dagger extended.

He still had not moved. Cassandra was not sure if she should attack with the dagger in hand or turn and run towards the mountains for safety. Considering her life as of late was not one she considered worth saving, she opted for attack. The sound of her exhale became similar to a growl as she charged towards the shadowy, statuesque figure. She only, however, made it a few lumbering steps before something happened. The dagger began to get hot. So hot that Cassandra was certain her palm would be blistered beneath it. She stopped her disoriented run and looked down at her hand. As her eyes made their way towards the dagger, she could have sworn she felt it move. Then, she saw the blade she had grown so familiar with over the past weeks. The metal surface elongated narrowed under her grasp. It soon developed this odd feeling of movement under the surface as the texture began to change away from the cold feeling of metal something warmer.

With a shriek, Cassandra opened her palm and let its contents drop to the ground. She was no longer holding a dagger. It had become a snake in her hand. Cassandra was gasping in spastic fits as the snake hit the ground and began to slither away with a hiss. Despite the horror of what had just happened, something even more horrifying was underway. She was now defenseless and her attacker was still standing in the darkness watching her.

Cassandra turned and ran towards the mountains. That strange sense of mysticism for the mountains washed over her again, and she again marveled at how much of the kingdom's life was based in these mountains. That did not matter though. Not now. The nearest cave opening was only twenty feet away, or so. She thought she could see it through her distorted and hazy vision. Cassandra stumbled forward managing to stay on her feet despite the pounding pain and weird combination of hot and cold that was filling her head. She was able to count ten steps, then twenty, soon fifty. The mountains were no closer now than they had when she had started running. Cassandra kept running her disorganized strides but the mountains never get closer. She could hear footsteps approaching from behind her and knew that her attacker was moving closer again. With a clenched jaw that seemed to double the pain in her head, Cassandra ran harder.

The only possibility was that her injured eyes were playing a trick on her, because Cassandra could have sworn that she saw the rock wall of the mountain side moving. Almost becoming alive. A piece of the rock wall broke free from the mountain and took to the sky. Once it was far enough in the air, Cassandra could see against the moonlight that this piece of rock had wings. It was bird. She looked towards the closest mountain peak, appearing to be an impossible distance away, and she saw thousands of birds taking to the air from the mountain peak. They were flying in a spiral away from the mountain looking like a massing storm cloud. The mountain actually appeared to be getting smaller as this was happening. Somehow, the mountain was turning into a fleet of birds. It was moving away from her, but that could not be possible.

As Cassandra watched the mountain take to the sky one winged bit at a time, hypnotized by the impossibility of it, the branch came down on the back of her head. Before she even realized that she was hit, she was lying on the ground trying to make the world stop spinning beneath her. While lying there, she felt the repeated blows of that branch on her head and back. The whimpers of pain she let out soon faded and stopped. It was too hard to draw in enough air to make that sound. With the last of her strength, Cassandra managed to roll onto her back and face her attacker. The moonlight illuminated his face, a face she knew well, but never actually feared until this moment. Then, the branch came down again on her own face. It shattered her nose and cheekbones. Her attacker's eyes were the last thing she would ever see.

Blood was flowing down from her nose and mouth, but the man did not stop. Cassandra was too weak to scream and too injured to try to escape. All means of her fighting back were gone. Cassandra had nothing to do but just lie there and wait to die. She hoped that as this man was beating her one of the guards would see this and scare him away. No one came though, and Cassandra felt that it was more than coincidence.

For another five minutes, that felt like they lasted an eternity, Cassandra was lying on the ground wincing in pain as this man continued to slam the branch down on her body. Soon, even her agonized moaning became too much effort, and she was just able to twitch with each blow. Blood was gurgling from her mouth, and she could feel herself lying in a pool of it. Finally, one of the blows hit her forehead with enough force to crush her skull.

Cassandra had finally died. Without speaking a word, the man that had done this dropped the branch and grabbed Cassandra's arms instead. He began to drag her out of sight and towards the mountains. While he did this, the birds flew back down towards the rock they had escaped from. They reassumed their position from before they had taken to the air and reformed the mountain just as it was before. Blood trails stretched out behind her on the lush grass as her cloak drifted off of her shoulders and fell to the ground. That was where it remained until the next morning.

The man did not stop there, however. He dragged Cassandra's body through the darkness of the caves he knew so well towards the portal. It was a path he had travelled many times, once while being chanced by guards in a near cave-in. Then, he simply carried her across the tunnel into the other world in with which he was equally familiar. After that, it did not take very long for him to navigate some other caves, swim through a narrow stream, and eventually come out above a nest of the beasts. He had made it his business in the past several weeks to know the caves thoroughly. It did give him something to do while hiding out and biding his time. This was an area he knew very well. It was his favorite hiding spot after his escape from Angelica's assassination attempt. No one dared disturb the beasts in their nest, so no one bothered him as well. This was the first time, however, that he was here with a dead body in his arms. The extra weight barely slowed him down though.

Once on top of the pit of beasts, he looked down and saw three of the lizards looking back up at him. Their black eyes flashed in fury, but the man was not afraid. These beasts were hardly used to climbing the mountains, and they would not do it now. For years, it was something they did not know how to do, and on the day of the assassination attempt, only one learned how to do it. That single beast then died shortly after, and there was no reason to think that another of these creatures would learn that skill for some time.

It was not until the next day that a guard found the place where Cassandra was killed. All that remained was the cloak everyone had grown accustomed to her wearing. The cloak was soaked in blood, and nestled within its folds, there was a small snake. It looked up at the guard, disinterested, and then retreated deeper in the folds of the cloak. After about an hour of debate, it was concluded that Cassandra was attacked by one of her clients unhappy with her performance or someone that she may had threatened in some way.

There were some trails of blood leading away from the sight of the attack. They faded quickly but were headed in the direction of the mountains. Within inches of a cave opening, the blood trail stopped completely. With this as their only lead, it was decided that Cassandra's dead body was dragged into the caves and either disposed of in a side cavern or in the other world somewhere. For obvious reasons, or reasons not obvious to those who were not involved in the attack, Cassandra's body was never found.

As with every event of some importance around the palace, rumors began almost immediately. Mostly these rumors involved getting around the word about Cassandra's involvement with Alexander and the lifestyle she had placed upon herself in recent weeks. Stories about how she helped in the assassination of King Frederick, how she corroborated his lies about the portal for all those years, and how she even helped in the planning of the assassinations of the two previous queens. This part of the rumor was not disputed at all. In fact, it was the only explanation for Cassandra's increasingly paranoid behavior since Alexander's death.

The rest of the rumor remained unproven and unspoken in public. People believed that all or part of the group that had plotted to kill Alexander, or Protace at that time, in the other world wanted to eliminate Cassandra as well. Maybe they saw her as a possible threat, since she knew so much of Alexander's plans, or maybe it was just simple revenge for what she had done. Their reasoning did not matter, however. What was important was that most people believed this group ambushed Cassandra, beat her to death, and found some way to dispose of the body.

In the past, most rumors that made some degree of sense were examined to see if they contained a kernel of truth, but this one was never explored in the slightest. In fact, the idea of speaking any of those accusing words to someone in authority was considered suicide. After the death of Alexander, and therefore the end of Protace's bloodline, that group became a ruling power in Protecia. It was considered extremely unwise to accuse them of murder, and so the rumor was never explored.

If anyone had bothered to look into this rumor, they would have been very disappointed. Each of the group members had an alibi at that time, several being in the company of Beatrice at the time the attack was estimated to have happened. Someone else was behind this attack, and ironically, not a single rumor of his involvement, even though his name was known by everyone in the kingdom, was ever mentioned.

Cassandra was not alone in experiencing misery in the months after Alexander's brief reign. Nearly every day for weeks, Beatrice found herself wandering through what was still considered the Other World. The dead bodies had been cleared away, but Protace's staff had not been touched. It was almost revered as if it was an evil talisman that should be left alone at all costs. Revered, yes. Feared, of course. But never touched.

For hours, Beatrice would wander this world thinking about one of the last questions Angelica had asked her. As all children were, the young queen was full of questions spanning every topic imaginable, but hers always had a more profound undertone. Her rule may become based upon their answers. If Alexander was a really a monster, was she one as well? When asked, Beatrice immediately answered in the negative, but that was mostly to set the young girl's mind at ease. None of the texts said anything about Soranace being able to control the staff the way that Protace had. In fact, the texts said the exact opposite. It would make sense to assume that Alexander's powers are not the powers of everyone with Protace's blood. Still, there was no way to be sure because the staff had been hidden during the rule of all but a few of the Protecia's monarchs.

There was an amazing amount of similarity between Alexander and Protace, and that may mean that they also had similarities not visible to the human eye. Most likely it was one of those unseen traits that allowed Alexander to control such a massive amount of power. Beatrice considered herself lucky that Alexander did not have any children. Most likely the power to control that staff died about the same time King Alexander's dying body was flung from the speaking platform.

These questions and the internal debate that ensued would have driven Beatrice mad if other events had not intervened. Bryan approached her one day, before Cassandra's disappearance but after Alexander's old servant was no longer within earshot, to ask Beatrice a favor. She was to serve on the council that had become the new ruling body of Protecia. It was a strange request to be made of a servant, who did not even hold those responsibilities anymore, but she knew more of the daily operations of the Protecian Kingdom and palace than anyone left alive at that point. She graciously accepted. The amount of time this appointment occupied strained the friendship between Beatrice and Cassandra. Beatrice had no idea of the torments that her fellow servant was falling victim to. She was puzzled when Cassandra fled the palace for a life of seclusion and prostitution, and she wept when Cassandra's bloody cloak appeared near the mountains. Still, the event of her friend's last few weeks remained a mystery to her.

This council discussed a seemingly endless array of topics, but one that kept resurfacing was Chenrile, also known as Soranace. Being the only one of Alexander's ruling elite to have survived the attacks and still be unaccounted for, there was growing amount of concern that he may come back. This topic was one that spawned hours of debate in the council and created more lively discussion than rationing of food, irrigation systems, population density, and proper training techniques for the guards and soldiers that patrolled the kingdom. It was finally Beatrice who attempted put the topic to rest.

"Chenrile did have royal blood in him, and he should have been in line to the thrown before Alexander or any of the recent rulers going back several decades. Joining Alexander was his last and only attempt to have some authority in the kingdom. If he thought it was possible for him to rule without Alexander, he would have made that attempt years ago." Beatrice scanned the faces of the people in the room, about a dozen in all. They seemed to believe her, but there was always the shred of doubt. "Alexander's goal was to become king. Chenrile would have most likely ruled after him or alongside him. Without Alexander's bloodline, his unquestioned bloodline, it would be nearly impossible for Chenrile to attempt ruling. Too much has changed. And if he is anywhere near this kingdom, he has witnessed these changes. He would not even make that effort."

This seemed to settle the minds of the council for the moment. Still, the soldiers in the kingdom were given instructions to be constantly searching for Chenrile and to bring any possible sightings to the attention of the council immediately. It was with this determination weighing on her mind when Beatrice did something she had not done in weeks. She took one of her walks through the caves towards the Other World.

Beatrice walked through the late afternoon sun in the courtyard that served the Other World. Two women were walking through the sunshine ahead of her gossiping endlessly. That familiar sound of half-true rumors and whispered tall tales made Beatrice miss Cassandra even more. With a tear in her eye, she listened in to their conversation and watched the sun begin to set behind the mountains. "Do you know that back there, they actually called him the Royal Bachelor?" At these words, the two women burst into laughter. It had the strange quality of insanity behind it. A few feet ahead of them, a small child of about five years ran back and forth. "Peter, don't go too far out," one of the women managed to push out between her laughs. The child slowed his run to a fast walk, but he continued going back and forth through the increasingly vacant courtyard.

Watching this sight before her made Beatrice feel conflicted. Part of her thought the sight of such a horrific battle, a battle that ended with the death of the few remaining royal family members and the old way of life in the kingdom, should be somewhat hallowed ground. It should not be a place for children to run rampant while their mother's gossiped about the key players that caused such atrocities to become part of everyday life. Still, part of her was happy to see this. Life was going on for some people, at least. Several were still in shock or mourning, but things were moving forward with hope on the horizon for a good number of people in the kingdom.

As their laughter began to die down, the other women replied, "Well, do you blame him?" A smile was still stretched across her face, but the laughter had subsided by this time. "After the way he screwed around over here, it is surprising he had any strength left for that world!" They both began to laugh again.

Hearing these words made Beatrice stop walking immediately. A wave of fear began to sweep over her. If what those women were saying was true, it may be possible that Alexander did have one or several children in this world. According to the myths, Protace was never seen with a wife, but he still had his son, Soranace, as his successor. The group that had raided Protace's palace, which was only a few feet away built into the mountains, reported that they could hear the sounds of several babies crying in rooms they could not find. As these thoughts swept through Beatrice's mind, sweat began to bead on her forehead.

"Peter, leave that alone!" One of the women stopped laughing long enough to call over to the boy again. He was standing by where the cage of the beasts used to exist. Just next to him was Protace's staff. It was lying on the ground, nearly glistening in the last rays of sunshine before the mountain cut away that light. The women strolled through the courtyard talking back and forth, sprinkling their words with laughter, until they were almost out of Beatrice's earshot. "It's almost dinnertime, Peter. Come over here so we can head back home." Those words rang out loud enough for everyone in the courtyard to hear.

Peter turned to look at his mother for a second. His hair was dark brown as were his near hypnotic eyes. Those eyes were the color of his mother's, but they seemed deeper and somehow more sinister. The skin had a ghostly pale look to it. He was wearing all white, but that somehow looked out of place. It was the only trait that seemed wrong about this child. Still, he looked frighteningly familiar.

Beatrice was frozen in fear as she watched the child, Peter, reach for the staff. She knew she should do something. Run over and take the staff away from the child, or just run from the courtyard. Maybe she should go into the shade just to sit down for a while to calm herself. Just standing there would not accomplish a thing, and even if this was just an average child being mischievous, which most likely he was, Beatrice felt just standing there was wrong. It seemed like a time for action. She knew she had to do something, but her legs would not obey her commands.

Finally, that shrill voice rang out again "Peter! You mind me now! Get over here!" Beatrice looked towards Peter's mother, and she found that calmed her down slightly. Just not looking directly at that boy made the whole thing seem better. Then, she saw the light out of the corner of her eye. It was a bright, glowing yellow light coming from the direction of the platform.

Slowly, Beatrice turned back to the boy. As she turned, she could hear the mother's screams rising up beside her. The screams did not fade in the slightest as Beatrice turned to face the young boy. Beatrice did not scream, though. For now, she just stared in shock. Even though this had been something she had been waiting for and fearing for some time, Beatrice could not help but be scared and surprised that it was finally happening. Her eyes just locked on the small boy and the glowing yellow light around him.

Only the boy's body, which was now turned to face the mountainside, blocked the bright yellow glowing. It was so intense that it was nearly blinding even though it was directed the other way. The boy was shaking so furiously that Beatrice had no idea what to expect. He would tear himself apart if he did not stop shaking soon, and Beatrice was beginning to worry that may very well happen. While they all stood and watched, the boy's body would begin the fly apart in front of them, shedding limbs and organs throughout the courtyard. That did not happen, though.

Just as the image of Peter's body exploding to bits passed through Beatrice's mind, the boy stopped shaking. The glowing faded away to nothing, and for a moment, Beatrice found herself just able to stare at the boy's back. He was standing perfectly still as if catching his breath. There was something different about him, though. The way Peter carried himself, the way he was standing there, was not how a child was supposed to stand. Too tall and sure of himself. Too confident.

Then, he began to turn around. Beatrice stopped breathing in fear. The air became too heavy and sour to pull inside one's body. While that boy was slowly turning to face her, the whole world stopped to wait and see. As he was halfway around, Beatrice was able to see his profile against the mountain, and then she knew that she did not want to see the rest of him. She knew this, but there was nothing she could do now. Her body was petrified in fear, and there was no way she could bring herself to run away or even just look in the other direction now.

Finally, the boy turned and looked directly at Beatrice. It was a horrible sight. His eyes were a pure black as if dark marbles had replaced them. Claws were extending from his fingers in black arcs ending the jagged tips. Then there were the fangs. They grew from his top and bottom jar. When he opened his mouth, it opened past the limits of his jaw, unhinged, like a snake's mouth.

Even those characteristics were not the worst. It was the lack of humanity in that face that frightened Beatrice the most. He did not show any wonder or concern for what was going on to his body or how the people reacted to him. The eyes just stared out around him looking at everything as if it was the first time he was seeing it. He kept the claws outstretched as if he was ready for an attack of some kind.

No one in the courtyard was able to move. Everyone just stared at the small child who had now become this contorted creature. This monster. He looked back and forth, and then into the sky, taking in all of his surroundings. An ear-splitting howl rose in the courtyard. It was loud enough to send a wave of echoes throughout the village and the caves. When the sound stopped, it faded away and its echoes slowly died off. Then, he snarled at everyone there. Those vacant, black eyes looked towards each person in the courtyard. He seemed both furious and exhilarated at what had happened to him.

His mother's screaming stopped suddenly as if it was choked off. Peter was not looking at her with those emotionless eyes. Both women looked like they were in pain. So much pain that they could not even scream. Their faces were twisted into unnatural masks as if their insides were chewed apart by something. Then, with a blink of Peter's black eyes, both women scattered into a cloud of sparkling gold dust. Nothing was left of either of them except for a beautiful cloud drifting through the air that dissipated and vanished into the twilight.

Finally, the boy, or what had once been a boy, spread his arms to his sides. The staff was easily lifted into the air, and the monster seemed overjoyed by what he had just done and was about to do. He slowly began to rise into the sky. At an unfaltering speed, the monster that had once been a boy named Peter was becoming airborne. He rose further into the air, and Beatrice watched in horror.

It was after he was about ten feet into the sky that Beatrice began to scream. The sound was so terrifying it sent everyone else in the courtyard into a panic. Beatrice, who was usually a tough as nails, was screaming. As she stood in the courtyard shrieking, the monster continued to drift father into the air. She screamed until it left her lungs aching and her body quivering in fright. When she could not scream anymore, Beatrice brought in as much air as she could and screamed again. She could not stop screaming no matter how hard she tried. It was the only thing her body was able to do.

Beatrice was still screaming as she sat up in bed. It was the only sound in the otherwise silent room. For a moment, she could still see the boy drifting into the air before her as the remnants of his dead mother drifted through the sky. As soon as she saw the darkness around her, Beatrice stopped screaming, and for a moment, she did not know exactly where she was. Everything looked foreign to her, but slowly her memories began to drift back. She was in her quarters in the palace. There was no boy named Peter that had turned into a monster.

Similar nightmares had become more commonplace in the time since Cassandra's death. Quite a few times, Beatrice would find herself wandering through the Other World and looking at the staff lying on the ground. No one wanted to touch it long enough to hide it again. Only a child would ever be naïve enough to touch that staff and lift it into the air. If such a curious child was actually the illegitimate child of Alexander, then there is a great chance that he may become the monster when he held that staff.

Beatrice was not sure if she had really ever overheard a conversation about Alexander indiscretions in the Other World, but she thought those actions fit his personality. Since Alexander discovered that portal, he had spent every night in that other world. There was no saying how many women he may have impregnated over his years there. Most likely, he was planning on making a long list of heirs so that they could succeed him after his rule as king was over.

Since his rule of Protecia only lasted a few hours, none of those heirs got a chance to claim their birthright, and after the council took over the rule of the kingdom, it would have been very unwise to show any kind of ties to Alexander. This was only proven by what had happened to Cassandra. So Beatrice just assumed that

Alexander did have children in the Other World, and that did mean the possibility of someone else being able to draw the powers from that staff.

Even though it never became common knowledge, Alexander, or Protace as he was called in the Other World, had fathered over ten children in the Other World. Most were with different women than the others, but all of the mothers were glad to receive protection from the guards and support from Protace and Soranace in the years that followed them birthing Protace's offspring. The only adjustment they had to make was going back to normal life after Alexander was killed. Still, just as Beatrice had expected, after they received knowledge of how many people were against Alexander, they thought it best to keep the name of their children's father a secret.

The nightmares plagued Beatrice almost every night for months. She became terribly withdrawn from everyone else in the kingdom, and some people even suspected that was attempting to stay awake for days at a time to keep the nightmares at bay. Her life became one of just getting through the day, and not having to worry about what tomorrow held. As this continued, Beatrice's role on the council became less involved and soon only symbolic. Very often she missed meetings, and they never bothered holding up the proceedings to locate her.

After some time, Beatrice vanished. If you were to believe the mumblings of rumors throughout the kingdom, she had one of her nightmares and, in the scared and deluded state afterwards, just wandered off. The next day, the staff was missing from where it always laid by the edge of the mountains. According to the whispers in the palace, Beatrice hid it in the caves where it remained resting silently for so many years. Then, she left the Protecian Kingdom, most likely to spend the rest of her time living quietly in the Nezzrin Kingdom where no one would recognize or bother her. However, those rumors were far from what really happened to Beatrice.

What actually happened to Beatrice was something that no one would ever know or wish to find out. Her nightmares continued for months, and finally, after one of them, she left her quarters and walked out of the palace. Part of her felt like she was joined by the ghosts of Wilhelmina, Angelica, and Cassandra as she made this journey, but even Beatrice felt that was simply a lie she told herself for comfort. Her cold feet were whispering over the dewy grass, and the night breeze was grabbing hold of her nearly trying to push her back to the palace. Beatrice did not care, though. There was only one thing her mind was set on doing.

It only got colder as she crawled through the openings of the caves and into the darkness below. She had been along this path so many times that, like Alexander, she was able to navigate it rather well even in the absolute darkness. With the cold stone pressing against her naked feet, Beatrice walked until she reached the passage to the Other World that was slowly becoming integrated in her home world.

Once she walked thought the narrow opening to the bare wall on the other side, she quickly knew what she had to do. Beatrice walked to the courtyard underneath the starlight and grabbed Protace's staff from the ground. It felt warm to the touch and almost vibrated under her grasp. There was a brief moment of shock as she lifted it into the air. It was much heavier than it appeared to be. Rock, metal, and some other sort of ornate stone were all mixed together on this staff to create the image of one of the beasts wrapped around a central orb.

Beatrice just held the staff for a few seconds. She was half-certain that it would begin to transform her into a monster as well. Maybe not in body, but possibly only in soul. It seemed as though, with the exception of Protace and Alexander, no one had ever lifted that staff to her knowledge, and there was no way of knowing whether it transformed everyone or just certain people. Legends had a way of being distorted, but now Beatrice knew that this staff's power was only attainable by certain people just as travelling through the portal originally was.

This was still too much of a chance that Beatrice did not want to take. She had suffered from that nightmare too many times to just let the staff rest there where anyone would be able to take hold of it. With the staff in hand, Beatrice backtracked towards the passageway, and from there, through the caves and back into the courtyard of her own world.

Beatrice spared one last look at the palace she had called her home for so many years. There were so many wonderful memories within those walls. Then, there was nothing but years of heartache. It was hard to look away from those richly ornamented walls, but she knew that she had to. There was a great deal to be done, and the time for reminiscing had long since passed.

Through the darkness of the night, she walked quickly and quietly. There were a number of soldiers patrolling the palace during the night, and their seeing anyone carrying Protace's staff may very well be a death warrant. So, Beatrice had to walk as carefully as she could through the kingdom towards its center. The place where the kingdom began was soon at Beatrice's feet. Alexander had spoken of a new kingdom in his short time as king, and Beatrice was going to try to bring that to the people. However, it would not be the sort of kingdom Alexander had in mind when he spoke.

Beatrice stood for a while staring at the Particion River. The old wooden bridge that Protace had built all those hundreds of years ago still stood there, and Beatrice began to walk across it. She stopped at the middle of the bridge and looked down into the water. It was rushing by faster than it normally did, but this sometimes happened when a storm was on its way. Or maybe it was the staff she was holding causing some strange reaction in the pull of the current.

This is where the kingdom began. Protace built this bridge uniting two barbarian hordes under his rule. He created a civilization, and in the years since then, it had thrived. Then, due to greed and bad luck, all of the possible heirs died or became unwilling to come forward. Beatrice was glad that some did not want to claim the throne. After all, it was Alexander who brought about a great deal of the horrors preceding the kingdom's end. If his children did not was to come forward, then so be it.

Beatrice stared at the black water rushing by just as Angelica had done before diving in to learn how to swim. That seemed like such a long time ago. Beatrice looked with both fear and anticipation. In her mind, this was the only way that things could be completed. With her and that staff still in the kingdom, there would always be a reminder of how horrible the last king of Protecia truly was. Most others did not know him as well as Beatrice did, and now that he was gone, there did not seem to be anything left for her. Angelica and Wilhelmina were dead, so Beatrice had no one to care for. Alexander's death meant that any quest for revenge was now satisfied. Her dearest friend, Cassandra, was also dead. The council was ruling the kingdom in a way that she had never thought possible, and soon the old ways would be nothing more than a fading memory. Beatrice felt that her duties had come to an end.

Except for one final task.

With the staff clenched tightly in her hands, Beatrice stepped over the edge of the bridge and fell to the water below. It was very cold, and she could feel the numbing claws digging into her body, but this was what she wanted. She could feel the icy fingers trying to loosen her grip on the staff, but she could not let them win. Beatrice almost expected a guard to come diving in after her and try to pull her to the shore. No one did.

The weight of the staff dragged Beatrice down deeper into the river while the current pulled her farther along the center of the Protecian Kingdom. She was pulled down from the world above staring into the crystal eyes of Protace's staff. After a while she felt her body hit the sandy river floor, and she knew she would not go down any further. There was a great ache in Beatrice's chest. It was time to stop holding her breath.

Beatrice tried to form a mental image of all the loved ones she had lost in her life, especially in the last year. It brought her some comfort as she inhaled deeply and felt the icy water fill her lungs. Her hands flew from the staff immediately almost as if to fight off the water that was filling her body. That only lasted for a few seconds. Beatrice died quickly in the darkness of the water, down so deep that she was invisible from the surface. It was there that she stayed until her body was picked apart by a fleet of crabs. The staff also never left the bottom of the Particion River and soon became buried in the sandy river floor.

CHAPTER THIRTY-FIVE

The Fall

The kingdom continued to exist under the rule of the council members for a few more years. During this time, the citizens of the kingdom became increasingly disconnected with the affairs of their rulers and often felt that they were being kept in the dark about the issues of their homes. Addresses were few and far between, and when they were held, they were not attended with the same numbers, enthusiasm or carnival-like prelude as they had previously been. The lack of emotional unity made it very easy for other events to tear the kingdom apart.

Natural disasters began to take their toll on the kingdom as if a message that its time was over. An earthquake, the first in its history, shook the kingdom so hard that it created an avalanche. Most of the self-proclaimed royalty, those who led the council, managed to escape unharmed, but the palace itself was leveled. The hundreds of years of history were wiped out in a few short hours, and there was virtually nothing that could be done about it.

Martin and Lenore's oldest son was the first to notice something was wrong on the morning of the earthquake. The mountains did not look quite right that day. There was an appearance of frailty to them that could not quite be described. It was like looking at fine ceramic plates when one was used to eating in carved out stone every other day. The sun was about halfway to its highest point in the sky when the rumbling began. The child looked and saw the mountains begin to crumble. He ran away from them as quickly as he could, seeking shelter in the palace. This refuge did extend his life by a few minutes and earned him the sight of watching his fellow citizens die as the mountains crumbled on top of them. When the palace finally fell, his death was quick.

It was not for weeks that the extent of that earthquake's damage was really discovered. The caves had been destroyed, and those passages reclaimed by the mountains. Where the previously endless passages used to expand, rock was now piled high keeping everyone out. The two worlds were separated again, and this time, the people on both sides did not even wonder about what was beyond the mountains. Nor did they care about going there again.

The world that never really considered itself to be part of the kingdom, the Other World as most people called it, was the first to regress to its old ways. Being completely isolated from the rulers of Protecia made them plunge back into barbarism in a few years' time. The people stopped living in their cottages once the elements took their toll and the structures needed repair. They began dwelling in caves and the forest like their ancestors had done years earlier. Order among them was quickly lost. Without the organization being forced upon them, there was nothing left but to revert back to the old ways. The ways before Protace came to them.

As it ended up, the slaughtering of the beasts at Alexander's hands was much more extensive than anyone had anticipated. By the time Alexander was killed and the daily ritual of placing a beast into the portal had stopped, there were only about one hundred of the creatures left in that world. None had migrated through the passageway for the same reason that only one of them learned how to climb rock. There was simply no reason to.

Those few beasts, however, did not survive very long at all. Most that had managed to escape capture at the hands of Alexander's men lived in the caves, and all them died during the earthquake. The avalanche and cave-in that followed buried them alive, and despite their uncanny ability to survive in adverse situations, they were all dead in a matter of a week after being blocked off from the world.

The beasts that lived in the forest lasted a little bit longer. Trophy hunters and people that were simply scared of the sight of those things were mostly responsible for their demise. Whatever of the beasts they did not kill simply became isolated and died on their own. Food shortages and lack of ideal breeding conditions were the main causes. Whatever the case, the beasts were all soon dead.

Another natural disaster swept away the remaining countryside in the Other World. The people that were living there, unable to comprehend or even understand what was happening, watched the sky one day as something strange occurred. The mountains, for some reason, did not seem as high as they had the in the time since the earthquake, and there was a noise. A roaring sound from just beyond those mountains. Those that were articulate enough at that point thought that the mountains had grown angry with them while others thought that they sky was falling. When they began to see the white-capped waves cresting over the mountain peaks, some thought that it was a great monster rising from beyond the mountains. When the wave washed over the peaks, there was nowhere for it to go. Everyone that was remaining alive in the Other World drowned in that massive tidal wave.

On the other side of the mountains, however, the world remained with its customs for a while longer. Even though the palace was leveled and there were no more records of their past, the people managed to live a somewhat civilized life for a few more years. This soon faded as well despite the efforts of everyone involved in keeping it going.

The real reason for the falling of this part of the kingdom was simply the lack of unity that had developed after the end of the rule of Protace's blood. Less people began to attend public addresses, and soon most of the council stopped attending them as well. Rumor has it that several of them died in a drunken fight that began in the civilian house that they had seized to serve as a makeshift palace. There was a day when only two of them showed up for an address, covered in bruises and open cuts. The other council members were never heard from again, and it was assumed that they were now dead and secretly buried.

After those two rulers died of old age, a single man replaced them. At this point, there was no interest left in the matters of the kingdom, and most of the civilians did not even know such a change in leadership had taken place until almost a year had passed. Despite the presence of a ruler, these people also began to revert back to their barbaric ways. That single ruler eventually realized what was happening and killed himself on the platform before an empty court. His body laid there, undiscovered, for nearly six months, and the role of the kingdom's ruler was never filled after his death.

As if in final acknowledgement of the loss of civilization, the bridge across the Particion River was eventually destroyed as well. No one really knew how it happened, and the rumors had stopped going through the kingdom long before the bridge was washed away. There was no attempt to rebuild this symbol of the kingdom, nor was there any grieving for the loss of such a significant icon. How could these people grieve since, by this point, none of them remembered the myth surrounding how the bridge was built in the first place? The broken pieces of wood, obviously done by deliberate action rather than an accident or an act of nature, were just regarded and ignored. Someone eventually threw the pieces into the water, and they were never seen again.

Eventually, the Nezzrin Kingdom overtook these barbarians and civilized them again. These people never bothered to try to rebuild their neighboring kingdom, but soon absorbed its people and its land. Most of the people were turned into slaves and soon the old homes in Protecia were demolished in favor of new ones. No one tried to stop such an action. They did not know any better, and by the time the former civilians of Protecia realized what was going on, there was nothing that could be done that could have stopped it anyway.

And that was the how the legend had always been told. After hundreds of years and almost a hundred kings and queens, the beautiful kingdom was over and every memory of it died as well. Unfounded beliefs of superiority were all that was needed to dismantle what had taken hundreds of years to build and perfect. Wilhelmina had once said to Alexander that as long as he drew breath, these people would be prisoners in their own homes, and that was only partially true. Even after his death, long after he stopped drawing breath, the prison of the uncivilized still held them tightly. It seemed as though the struggle between civilization and barbarism had concluded. So finally, the conflict between the conflicted ended, and neither the queen nor the monster stood tall as the victor.

A Sole Survivor

As the ground shook in the Protecian Kingdom, and its people scattered to the far corners of the land to seek cover, they were being watched. When the waves came and washed away all signs of life in the Other World, there was still someone watching and overseeing everything. When an angry teenager smashed the bridge across the Particion River for no reason other than he felt like doing it, he was also being watched.

Like a marionette holding the strings of the world in his hands, the fall of the Protecian Kingdom was carefully looked upon by someone in the distance. Not the hordes of philosophers that would one day write about the beauty of a land that was destroyed. Not her people that were fleeing for cover or watching with glazed expressions as their world crumbled around them. Through all of the seemingly unrelated events, the fluke disasters and remote chances that came through, someone was watching and keeping the wheels of destruction in motion.

In the blazing daylight with the sun beating through the few whispers of clouds that lingered in the sky, a swarm of hornets took to flight.

The End